A Blackthorn Winter

Peter Webster

'If the weather is cold when the blackthorn first appears, then it will remain so for the whole of the flowering period. The spring will be delayed, and instead, for a while, there will be a blackthorn winter.'

Old country saying

Published by Gyr 2006

FIC
WEBSTER

Table of contents

Preface

The publication of this book has been long delayed. The events described here took place twelve years ago in 1993-94, following my discharge from the British Army and SAS. I was discharged on psychiatric grounds after a court inquest found me largely responsible for the death of a wounded Provisional IRA man after a successful ambush by a SAS unit in Northern Ireland which I commanded at the time. Unfortunately, while on leave I also had an unexpected and unwelcome encounter with a Provisional IRA Active Service Unit in the Kent countryside.

These extraordinary events were not publishable for all these years mainly because of security reasons. Certainly my book would not have been welcomed by the Ministry of Defence, especially MI5, who quite rightly at the time would have strongly objected to the details of their work being made public.

But there were additional quite sinister personal reasons for the delay. Early publication would also have drawn attention of the Provisional IRA to the part which I played in a major anti-terrorist operation near Folkestone in Kent *after* my discharge from the Army.

This, as fully explained in the following account, would have further endangered my life for I was already in trouble with the IRA after the earlier ambush of one of their units in Northern Ireland while in the SAS. Also, from the moment of my discharge from the Army ostensibly on psychiatric grounds, I had been 'on the run' from the Provos, so I was reluctant to reveal my whereabouts in any way.

However, since the destruction of the Twin Towers in New York on 11 September 2001 (9/11), and the London bombings of 7 July 2005, media attention has been focused upon Islamic terrorists. Events in Northern Ireland, apart from the continued activities of splinter groups of the Provisionals, and the antics of politicians, are no longer in the news. And in the near future, further terrorist attacks on mainland Britain are likely to come from Al Qaeda or other Middle Eastern groups, rather than the IRA, so that the revelations in this account no longer pose a threat to anyone.

Also, the danger to me from the Provos, has diminished considerably. Gerry Adams and other prominent Sinn Fein/IRA figures have recently declared that the war against the British is over and that they will now pursue only political means to gain their objective of a United Ireland. Weapons and explosives have been 'decommissioned' and there will no longer be 'an armed wing' of Sinn Fein. This meant that my book should no longer be seen as a threat to security by the MOD.

These are the main reason why this book is now publishable without further endangering my existence, although I would never return to Northern Ireland. So, at last the time seemed ripe for my own account. However, one never knows for certain what the future will bring, so I have been cautious in giving exact locations unless they are already known to the Public. There is also the question of my own privacy, which I wish to preserve as much as possible. I have changed the names of most places and locations so that tracking me down, although not impossible should hopefully prove difficult.

I was brought up in a particular tradition of military service in which ideas of patriotism, duty and honour still played an important part. My father and grandfather had been regular Army officers, so although there was no coercion from my parents, I quite naturally and by choice wished to follow in the family tradition. My main area of active service was in Northern Ireland during the Troubles, so that when I first joined the SAS I had certain assumptions about the Irish War - which today seem quite out of date.

For example, I was formerly quite hostile to the Republican concept of a United Ireland. However, my views have since changed, and I can well understand the desire for reunification. With Scotland and Wales wishing for and pursuing their own independence and perhaps ultimate separation from England, the wish of so many Irish for the reunification of their country, despite the legitimate objections of the Loyalists, 'the faithful tribe' now seems understandable for the tide of history has turned.

When I was discharged from the Army, I still very much believed that the Provos deserved to be eliminated just as they believed that I should be. In the battle for my own survival, especially in South Armagh, kill or be killed were the only options. There was little room for doubt, and in any case, such doubts were bad for morale.

However, I discovered another, quite different civilian identity after my discharge. My initial treatment by the MOD as someone expendable, who had suddenly become a liability, was deeply wounding. As my attitudes began to change, I reflected more deeply upon the Troubles as a whole, especially their origins

Nevertheless, I must add these original attitudes were reinforced for a time after my unexpected encounter with a Provo Active Service Unit on my doorstep in Kent. It was only after the final security operation against the Provos in August 1994, which culminated in my betrayal of a close friend (resulting in their death) that I once again reflected upon the increasingly futile nature of the conflict. By then I realised that this could no longer be resolved by force, but only contained, especially as Sinn Fein/IRA had gained the political initiative both in Britain and perhaps more importantly, at that time, in the United States. I also came to the inescapable conclusion that the British Government no longer had the will to continue this long drawn out war of demoralising attrition.

Thus, the whole situation in Northern Ireland has altered to such an extent that it is difficult to believe I once held some of the views expressed in this book. However, after careful reflection, I decided to be true to myself, the historical veracity of my account, and to write faithfully what I felt at the time without the bias of contemporary changes in attitudes.

The danger is that many of these contemporary views are in any case shaped by fashionable trends and political correctness. There is also the lure of romantic nationalism which seems to be growing in intensity despite the phenomena of globalisation.

Yet, my views on the magic of the dwindling countryside which pervades this book have not changed. Indeed, despite the realities of rapidly increasing urbanisation, they have been reinforced by the stresses and strains of my experiences. My faith in the restorative gift of Nature remains. Of course, Nature can be violent and cruel, but in my case, the healing heart of the countryside and also the love which I was fortunate to find there, helped restore my sanity, and above all gave me a renewed sense of place and identity.

So although this book is about a man on the run and a violent encounter with a Provisional IRA Active Service Unit, it is also about the English countryside, my search for a safe house in an ideal place and ideal time, inspired and driven by an ancient myth of Arcadia.

Mark Wynstanley, December 2005

'The Tibetan experiences the house as a microcosm, as a secure enclosure, in contrast to the space outside, which is the playground and hiding place of countless omnipresent powers continuously threatening to ambush him.'

G. Tucci, *The Religion of Tibet*

Chapter 1

I had been searching for somewhere to live for over a month since my discharge from the Army, sleeping in an old VW van to keep down expenses, and parking like a gypsy wherever I could get away with it. Then, one day in early June 1994, tired from hours of driving through the countryside of Kent, quite suddenly I came across the cottage by chance, late in the afternoon with the sun in my eyes, and everything lit up by a strange reddish glow as if the light had been somehow reflected from a furnace.

About ten minutes earlier I had driven through the village of Highdene, a cluster of red brick cottages. I glimpsed hanging peg tiles, and red tiled roofs with massive chimneys, all about eighteenth century I guessed. I drove past the wooden lychgate leading to a church and then continued slowly along a lane until I came across an old sign scarcely visible amongst a white spatter of tall cow parsley. I stopped the van for a moment with the engine still running while I read, 'Highdene Common - One Mile'. Just the place to camp, I thought.

Half a mile down the road travelling west, the valley narrowed and ended in a steep hill or re-entrant, the gradient about one-in-four I estimated. I drove up in bottom gear, the engine whining like a Saracen armoured personnel carrier back in Northern Ireland.

On top of the hill the road continued across a plateau, and this was the common, a wilderness of long grass, wildflowers, small patches of heather, and bracken. There were clumps of hawthorn, blackthorn, hazel, dogwood, elder, sweet briar, as well as the occasional oak. Above and close by, rose the steep slopes of the North Downs, which suddenly seemed to have closed in and made their presence felt. It was exactly the kind of No Man's Land which had become such a part of my life of late.

On my left, as I slowed down to take in the scene against the glare of the sun, I glimpsed an old cottage through the gap in a tall hedge where there was a wooden gate with a shiny new padlock and chain. As the lane was so narrow everything passed my line of sight very quickly so that I only just noticed the 'For Sale' sign half hidden

1

amongst the dark blue delphiniums in a weedy flower bed near the front door, and I could have missed it if I had been driving faster. The hedge was so tall and thick that the cottage was invisible except through a gap - like a breach in a castle wall. In the second I saw the place, the doorway seemed sunk into the stone slabs below the level of the surrounding ground, so it must be old, I concluded.

I could not turn the van around in such a narrow lane, so I drove on until a convenient patch of long grass on the edge of the common gave me a place to back. I got out and checked the ground in case of a concealed ditch and having turned, realised I would have to leave the van on the common as there was little room to park it directly outside the cottage where it would have attracted the attention of anyone driving past.

Walking up the lane, I saw a heavy farm gate set in the hedge, which I had somehow missed as I drove past. It was obviously a vehicle entrance, perhaps an old cart track into the property, about thirty yards from the front gate. This side gate was padlocked and thickly covered in barbed wire with additional strands on top. When I reached the low front gate, I saw that the 'For Sale' sign gave the address of a land agent in Pelham, a small country town I had driven through some ten miles away, but I was not in the mood to drive back. I might as well get some idea of the place now, I thought, before committing myself in any way.

The easiest way in was over the padlocked, low front gate. I noticed that the hedge was very thick, a mass of hawthorn fully out, blackthorn, dog rose, elder, and a field maple right by the entrance. There was no way of getting through such an impenetrable barrier, and I did not fancy tearing my clothes on the barbed wire of the farm gate. But before I started to trespass, I double checked that no-one was around, and walked past the front gate towards Highdene. The hedge alongside this part of the lane had one or two gaps further down, and I was able to pass through.

However, I discovered that I was in a field and that yet another hedge completely enclosed the cottage. There was even thicker vegetation at the back of the property, and I noticed the tops of what appeared to be apple trees, probably an orchard. At any rate I could see no other houses nearby, although I guessed that most of the cottages in this area could be hidden by hedges and difficult to locate. I was clearly in an ancient landscape, mixed Anglo-Saxon hedges impregnable with quick thorn, and isolated dwellings set on the edge of the common and North Downs.

The isolation of the North Downs with their bare slopes of grass, somehow still untouched by the plough, probably because they were too steep and exposed, gave me the feeling of being on a frontier. I could see the chalky outlines of an old cart track leading up to a saddle between two rounded knolls and then nothing but the sky above. The track suddenly disappeared into the pale blue of the northern horizon as if into the unknown, and this too gave me the feeling of being on the edge of things.

The short sward on the hills, an iridescent green like the shell of a beetle was tinged with a coppery red from the descending June sun, and made me long to be up there tasting the breeze and seeing the countryside unroll beneath my feet. A sentence of Richard Jefferies immediately came to mind, 'Hope seemed as wide as the hills', and I felt a sudden surge of optimism.

When I returned along the lane to the cottage, I saw it could be awkward climbing the gate, so I looked around for something to stand on. An old log black with slime along the hedge seemed to be what I needed so I shifted it to the front of the gate. A piece of folded plastic lay at the bottom of the slight dent in the ground made by the log, and when I opened it shaking off the earwigs from inside the folds, in my hand was the key to the padlock.

I was puzzled. Why leave the keys there? I then pushed the log back to its original place, and unlocked the gate. Once inside, I leaned over and carefully rearranged the chain and closed the padlock, so that no one casually passing by would see that it had been opened. I reassured myself by thinking that I was not actually breaking in, but only entering the garden, and there was after all, the 'FOR SALE' notice. I tried the front door of the cottage which was locked, of course. But I noticed another log at the edge of the flower bed, similar to the one by the gate, and I knew at once that the key to the cottage itself would be underneath. This time the key was not in plastic, and lay on dry brick, part of the path.

When I held the key in my hand, cold and slightly damp, I felt somewhat uneasy at following in the footsteps, entering the mind, in a sense, of someone I had never met. I began to speculate - they can't be at all devious, for their pattern of concealment was so simple. Or could it be a temporary caretaker who was so busy with

3

other things that he didn't want to waste any time in retrieving the keys, or even having the bother of carrying them around for that matter? But in any case, I now had the means of entry to the cottage.

I walked right round the place first before entering. The garden was only partly overgrown with weeds, so someone had evidently been keeping them in check, although in a pretty desultory way. The tiled roof came down in a steep cat-slide at the back, and an extension had been added, a kind of outhouse. One of the side walls seemed new: built of coarse concrete, it was an ugly renovation, although it had clearly strengthened the structure of the building. The back door was locked, and I didn't bother to search for the key, but continued right round the extension.

On the other side, I walked into the dappled shade of an apple orchard with old trees which had not been properly pruned for years, some of them heavily lichened up their trunks. A tight green mass of mistletoe hung from a gnarled fork, and someone had picked branches of it fairly recently I noticed. The grass was long under the trees, and I left a trail as I walked, so I realised the caretaker would know someone had been roaming round the property in his absence.

When I reached the front door, I paused a moment before fitting the key into the lock and listened. I could hear no traffic. The only sound was the murmur of ring doves in the apple trees, so I decided all was clear. The heavy front door creaked dramatically enough as it swung inwards on rusty hinges, and I stepped down immediately into a small hall with a steep staircase on my right.

An open doorway on my left led directly into a sitting room, and a large fireplace of red brick dominated the opposite wall as I entered. I looked at it more closely. The bricks were small, worn and blackened by innumerable fires, which had burned there throughout the centuries. I walked up to the dark wooden mantelpiece stained with cigarette burns and greasy with white patches of candle wax. I ran my hands over the smooth wax covered in dust and grime, and wondered about the candles, as the house was wired for electricity. The charred remains of logs partially filled the grate, and these were covered in a patina of soot which had fallen from the chimney. The fire probably smokes back in certain winds I guessed. On one side of the hearth was a pile of ash logs, similar to those covering the keys.

Apart from an old stained table, a mouldering couch, and two armchairs with a faded floral pattern, the room was empty. The

4

floorboards were bare, once polished perhaps, but now worn and scratched as if by hobnailed boots. They seemed sound enough, although some boards creaked as I walked across the room to the windows overlooking the lawn. As I looked out, the long grass rippled in the breeze, and I winced a moment as a house martin suddenly banked away from the window and up into its nest in one of the eaves.

White bird droppings like crude exclamation marks spattered the outside of the windows. These must come from the martins, I thought, although I noticed that the garden was full of birds as if it was some kind of nature reserve. Then, for a moment, a great tit fluttered at the window pane, and I instinctively shooed it away with my hand. I wondered why it was trying to get inside, probably after insects I guessed. Then I felt a sense of unease, perhaps it could be an ill omen for somebody, but not for me I hoped. Omens, portents, and other superstitions including minor compulsions, had begun to play an unusual and unwelcome part in my life of late, and I recognised these neurotic symptoms with some dismay.

I quickly repressed the thought, but images of T.E. Lawrence and the bird which fluttered at the window pane of his cottage at Clouds Hill, a few days before his death in a motor cycle accident came immediately into my mind. I could see for a moment, reflected in the glass, the bloodied face, and then a scene at the side of a road with the limp body being lifted into the back of a lorry by a small group of men. Then, an inconsequential thought followed: they killed the bird after his death didn't they? Someone went to the cottage and actually killed the bird, or had I got it wrong? It wasn't important anyway, I tried to persuade myself, but kept wondering whether I was experiencing the same sequence. Perhaps the owner of the cottage is dead or about to die, and the tit I had just seen was the bird of ill omen.

These morbid thoughts continued as I opened the door into the kitchen, but the large size of the room and the ancient flagstones held my interest. I examined a pre-World War 2 Aga which seemed to be in working order, and surprisingly free of rust. A long pine table ran almost the length of the room which was at least fifteen feet, I estimated, and there were five battered Windsor chairs which looked antique.

I opened the door into a large larder with wooden shelves covered with rat and mice droppings and was repelled by the sour smell. Another door led into the outhouse, but it was locked and I could not find the key in any obvious hiding place. I had not seen the bedrooms, and walked back into the sitting room, remembering the stairs which led up from the small hallway. Upstairs I found three rooms, the centre one locked. The other two end rooms had double beds with massive spring mattresses, faded and stained with rust from the springs. One of the bedsteads was of fine old brass, clearly Victorian, and the other was of wood and steel, painted black.

Both rooms were surprisingly large, and in the one with the brass bedstead, a pine wardrobe stood against the wall to my right. On another wall hung a narrow mirror about five feet in height. Damp had penetrated the back of the glass and my reflection was faded and slightly distorted. I appeared much older than my twenty eight years and I remembered I had the same tired worn appearance when I first saw myself in a metal shaving mirror after a long Army patrol in South Armagh. I stared at myself intently for almost a minute, full of introspection. The sights, sounds and smells from my Northern Ireland past seemed to fill my head triggered by the sight of my haggard reflection in the mirror. I smelt the mind-alerting, anxiety-provoking stink of fire blackened buildings torn apart by high explosive and heard the cries of people in shock and pain. Then the sudden vision of two British soldiers dragging a wounded comrade along the pavement of a street in Belfast and out of the fire of a sniper seemed so realistic that my immediate and unconscious reaction to give assistance made my heart pound in my ears. I wanted to find out which of my patrol had been hit, but with considerable effort, I cleared my mind of these images of war and turned away from the mirror. I looked out of the dormer windows into the brightness and tranquillity of the orchard and the apples seemed close enough to pick.

Surprisingly, all the rooms were dry despite the musty smell, and apart from the incident of the bird fluttering in the window pane, I didn't have any uneasy feelings about the place itself. It was clearly a genuine country cottage with an ancient rural past. Yet I could get no clues about the owner or previous occupants. There were no paintings, pictures, ornaments or decorations of any kind. I looked around in vain for a book, magazine or anything such as a bill to give me a hint about the people who had once lived there.

Descending the steep stairs, I decided to leave at once before someone arrived and caught me trespassing. Indeed, I had a sudden feeling of urgency to get out as soon as I could. I had relied correctly on these premonitions in the past and realised that I had pushed my luck far enough. I opened the front door cautiously, stepped outside, quickly locked the door and put the key carefully under the ash log, making sure it was replaced exactly as I had found it.

Then I walked the few yards to the front gate, and paused a moment. I could see no one on the road in either direction, so I decided it was safe for me to leave. (I had been trained to make use of all the senses in assessing a potentially dangerous situation, and when one has made up one's mind, to act very quickly. It was too soon to drop the habit even in civilian life.)

Just as I was about to unfasten the padlock, I heard a car climbing the hill. There was no time to get out onto the road, rearrange and lock the chain and padlock together properly, so I stood still behind the hedge. I looked through the gap by the gate from the opposite direction to which the car was travelling, so that I could at least catch a glimpse of the driver or the passengers through the rear window.

The vehicle slowed right down as it approached the gate, and for a moment I thought it was going to stop. My heart beat faster, and I backed away, but then I heard the sudden acceleration, and just glimpsed the back of a small black van. I could see nothing of the driver, and only the arm of someone in the passenger seat.

The black van continued accelerating along the lane, and I heard it slow down about one hundred yards away on the edge of the common and then stop. I realised at once that the occupants must have seen my VW parked there, and had probably halted to investigate. I quickly rearranged the padlock and chain, hid the key under the log, everything as before, and then I sauntered down the lane towards the common. However, the black van moved off before I reached my VW and disappeared around a corner.

I checked to make sure that all the doors of the van were still locked, and then decided to make a cup of tea on the gas cooker. I had just lit the ring and was putting on a small kettle, when I heard the van returning. 'Very busy today!' I muttered to myself. Sure enough the van appeared around the corner, and drew up on the grass facing me about ten yards away. I recognised it as a new Ford Escort 35. Two men were in the front, and they stared at me through the windscreen. I looked straight back at them as casually as I could although I was concentrating very hard. I knew from Northern Ireland that when things happened with strangers like this, it was all quite sudden and over very quickly. The driver got out and walked towards me while the passenger lit a cigarette. Both wore cloth caps, and looked like working class extras from the Midlands in a television play.

Still sitting I leaned forwards and partly opened the side door of the van sliding it slowly along the rails, keeping my right hand still firmly on the inside door handle, ready to yank it back. Then I smiled and said, 'Good evening,' loudly and confidently.

The man stopped about four yards away from my van, and ignored the greeting. He seemed ill at ease, rather than deliberately rude when he spoke after an awkward pause.

'Are you looking for someone?'

'No' I replied. 'I'm just passing through.'

The man looked nonplussed, so I said, 'Were you expecting someone?'

'No - no,' he replied, very unconvincingly I thought. 'We saw the van parked here and thought...'

'I thought I heard a car,' I interrupted, 'when I was out for a walk. I'm sure I heard a car along the road about five minutes ago.' I paused a moment to give him the chance to deny it, but he said nothing so I continued, raising my voice slightly, just as he was about to turn away.

'What about you? Do you live around here?'

'No,' he said, 'I'm from Dover. And my friend is - ah - a visitor. I'm showing him around.'

I looked at the passenger still sitting in the Ford. Clearly he was not getting out for some reason. Suddenly something about him seemed familiar, the way he looked at me, his whole expression, but as he had not spoken I could not be sure. My paranoia persisted so strongly however, that I had to know. I jumped down from the VW and the driver moved away to one side, warily keeping his distance. I walked slowly forward until I was about a yard away from the open side window of the van right opposite the passenger bending my

8

head on level with his and said, 'A lovely stretch of country don't you think?'

My movements seemed to have alarmed them both, but the man nodded civilly enough in assent to my question, although he still said nothing. The driver returned to his seat very quickly, and started the engine. He backed the van off the grass towards the road turning his head away from me out of the window, and then drove off quickly without looking at me again. But all the time he was backing the van, his friend like a hunter facing dangerous game never took his grey stony eyes off me. So intense was the alertness of his gaze that I noticed an eyelid flickered for a moment, as if with the strain. Then as the van backed I could see his face only partly though the windscreen. What I remembered most though about him was the hint of a sardonic smile which blurred as the van reached the road, and the light reflected on the glass. But I was left with a chilling image which persisted like the smile on the face of the Cheshire cat.

No sooner had the sound of the Ford died away down the hill, than I decided to stay the night there on the common. It was already nearly ten o'clock, almost dark, and I had driven far enough for one day. Anyway, I couldn't have found a better place, secluded, quiet and yet close to the road. And an absence of any signs marked 'Private Property' or 'No Camping' made me feel relaxed and secure about the site. Yet, I had to check what was further down the road, round the bend where the men had driven their van. The village lay in the other direction and I decided not to return there until the morning.

I drove slowly along the road and around the bend, hidden from the common by thickets of hawthorn and birch. The road then straightened out, and on the left, to my surprise, was a large Georgian manor house, three storied with a grey slate roof. Passing the front gate very slowly, I could read 'The Grange' written on a metal plate attached to the top bar of unpainted lichen covered wood.

A short gravel drive led to the front door and French windows opened onto the lawn. The curtains had not yet been drawn, and maroon lamp shades gave the interior a warm glow as if of firelight. A television screen emanated that curious lambent blue light which makes it so uniquely recognisable at a distance, I could see the silhouettes of children sitting on the carpet watching a programme, as well as the forms of adults in arm chairs.

All very cosy and secure, I thought approvingly. I imagined the family in the house as my neighbours and in a sudden turn of optimistic fancy I thought that if I bought the cottage, perhaps I would be invited round to 'The Grange' for tea. That was the way my mind worked in sudden swings of pessimism and naive optimism. I drove on and turned the van in the wide open gateway of another drive to the right leading to a squat building in the distance all blacked out with no lights. It might have been a barn, but I could not be sure for by then it was almost dark.

When I drove past the house again on my way back, the engine just ticking over, the front door opened and a golden labrador ran barking towards the gate, but with its tail wagging. Then someone switched on the light above the front door, and simultaneously a floodlight came on at the gate. It was fixed to a tall post and lit up the van as I passed. I could see a man standing in the doorway and beside him, a second more slender figure although this was no more than a brief impression for the glare of the floodlight almost blinded me for a moment. Then I was past the bright pool of light, and heading back to the common, forcing myself to press my foot only lightly on the accelerator. I felt like a jackal on the rim of a campfire.

I switched on the headlights, and had soon returned to my earlier parking place on the common. I drove the van about twenty yards off the road to my right, and exactly parallel to it. The windscreen faced the direction of the village from which I expected any night time traffic might come.

I knew that if an intruder, a 'hostile' in Army parlance, came from that direction, I could switch on my headlights, see them at once and then if necessary dive out of the side door of the van towards the common, and escape into the darkness while they were lit up like a Christmas tree.

I had practised this manoeuvre many times while in the Army, with an M16 under my right arm, and from a moving car too as part of the repertoire. And it had been vitally useful once, indeed I owed my life to it, and one of them had lost theirs. My left knee still ached sometimes from an injury to a ligament when it struck the inside of the right back door as I leaped out. Those days were over of course, but they still remained in my mind and clouded my life.

A tawny owl was calling as I heated up some soup on the gas stove. The weather was mild and partly cloudy, but every now and then the moon appeared and lit up the surrounding common. The white flowers of the hawthorn were so dense they looked like snow. It was pleasant in the van, the blue rings of flame burning cheerfully on the top of the gas stove, the battery lantern on one of the shelves emanating just enough glow to see things, but discreetly dim and scarcely perceived from the outside as I had drawn most of the curtains.

Soon there was the comforting smell of toasting bread from the griller, and I turned on the multi band receiver to hear the BBC world news at midnight. I learned of more and more terrorist attacks, the terror had become global. But now at least I had no more direct involvement in it. Here, on the wild heath, perhaps I might have a chance of opting out.

After finishing my supper, I lay down on the bunk and zipped myself into a light nylon sleeping bag. I remained awake for a while looking at the common in the moonlight through the rear window hoping to catch a glimpse of the tawny owl I had heard hooting. I thought about the family in the Georgian house, all sleeping peacefully in their large manorial rooms, having probably discussed just before going to bed the strange appearance of my van along the road so late in the evening.

For some reason, I immediately regarded them as allies. Perhaps it was because in a sudden optimistic swing of mood, they represented to me at that moment quite irrationally in the circumstance, the ideal of English country life. They seemed to epitomise the remaining few of the upper classes who really lived in the countryside, and not only at weekends. I knew their counterparts in Shropshire and the Welsh Borders as people who despite their faults still retained old fashioned virtues. Once again I imagined myself getting to know them as part of a new beginning in my social life. It was these assumptions which made me face the van towards the village, not the manor house. However, I had been surprised at the immediate reaction to my presence that the people in the house had shown. Although I tried not to make any pessimistic inferences, the man with the dog at the front door watching me as I cruised quietly past, and especially the sudden switching on of the blinding floodlight, did seem to suggest that past experiences had taught them to be wary of strangers, as if like me they feared something.

When I fell asleep at about one in the morning, a slight wind was blowing, the occasional gust rocking the van, but all the doors were well sealed and I felt no draught except through a partially open window. I dreamed the usual set of nightmares, or perhaps 'anxiety dreams' would be a more accurate and clinical description. For these days I did not awake shouting as in the past, choking in an effort to breathe, thinking I was trapped in a burning APC, blown up by a land mine. No, these recent dreams were more subtle and passive, the sight of the odd corpse lying face down in a ditch, burned and lividly scarred faces, faeces, vomit, and the experience of walking through a sticky gelatine of green mucous which at first had seemed to be innocuous long grass. Nowadays I awoke intermittently with no more than a rapid pulse, extra beats of the heart, and an accompanying dry mouth which made it necessary to drink water from an Army water bottle which I always kept beside me when I slept.

As my mind drifted off to sleep I thought deliberately of tranquil scenes, often derived from paintings I had seen. Constable's 'Cornfield', or 'The Haywain', for example. Once I dreamed of Renoir's painting of girls walking down a track through long grass with the scarlet poppies glowing in the sunlight, and the bright light dancing on the wildflowers. I could feel the cool grass like raw silk on my bare legs, and then I looked down and saw that I had no foot, only a bloody stump.

These morbid, ghoulish thoughts lay in wait for me like demons, and I could control their appearance only to a limited extent. I was at my most vulnerable in dreams of course, sleep could become a minefield of nightmares, but even in daylight, the demons could intrude, and suddenly appear grimacing at the window pane. However, during the day I could manoeuvre them out of my mind. I learned to deal with these ideas deliberately, neutralising their potential for havoc by replacement with other more positive images. I understood quite early on that the demons could not be simply forced down into the unconscious without appearing with renewed intensity at other times. I felt most at ease in the countryside away from the potential threat of people in the idealised environment of the most happy days of my childhood. Indeed, it was in the repetition of those halcyon days that I now sought to heal myself.

*

I awoke shortly before dawn to a chorus of birds. Mist obscured the common, but the sky seemed clear, and I expected a fine summer morning. I got out of the van to have a pee, and looked around. I could not see far, but mine were the only footprints in the dew. By the side of the road I noticed a stone marker almost hidden by long grass and bracken with 'Public Bridle Way' written on it and a sign pointing past the van in the direction of the common. When I looked towards the common I could make out quite clearly the signs of a track through the long grass. I stretched and yawned a bit, but after I made tea, I felt quite alert and ready for a stroll along the track towards the common before breakfast.

The sun had not risen, and I took my field glasses in case I saw some interesting birds at that early hour, perhaps a fox or even a fallow deer. The mist gave me a sense of security in its enveloping cover. Soon my light walking boots and trousers were soaked with dew and the wet cloth began to make a noise against the vegetation. I looked around and saw a dry patch of brownish grass under the overhanging shelter of a hawthorn where some animals had been lying, almost certainly sheep judging by the droppings and the smell.

I felt quite warm so I took off my camouflage jacket and laid it out flat in the hollow under the hawthorn, easing myself down carefully onto the ground under the spiny branches so that I was lying flat on my stomach and resting on my elbows. I could hold the field glasses very steady that way and focused them on a magpie which I just made out through the mist about fifty yards away. The breeze was blowing towards me and I lay very quiet, certain that I had the best possible cover in the circumstances to view whatever might appear. Soon, through the field glasses, I picked out three young rabbits feeding in the open where the ground rose sharply above the stunted shrubs.

Quite suddenly, a large sparrowhawk, almost certainly a female, flew from behind me with quick strong wing beats across the open ground in front to make a dash at some blackbirds and starlings in the middle distance. I had my field glasses trained on the hawk at once rejoicing at my luck, but although the mist was thinning in the breeze, she disappeared and I was robbed of witnessing the kill or rather of knowing whether she had killed or not. Then, just as I was about to get up for a better view, there she was coming straight towards me, flying fast and low with a desperate kind of courage like a Kamikaze pilot. 'Bloody hell!' I muttered, ducking instinctively, and that may have saved my life.

The shotgun blast was so close that my ears rang, and I heard the rattle of pellets in the branch just above my head. The hawk swerved and then faltered for a moment as if hit, but flew on and over the bush behind me. It all happened in a second, but I didn't make a sound or move, pressing myself further into the ground.

Chapter 2

I lay there stunned at my escape and the suddenness of it. I realised almost at once that someone had fired at the hawk rather than me, but retained the suspicion that it still might have been a useful excuse to do me in as part of a contrived 'unfortunate' accident. Then, thinking rationally, I knew that neither of us had seen one another because we were both concentrating on the hawk, he on shooting it, and I amazed by its strange behaviour which I now understood.

After lying there on the ground for at least 20 seconds, I heard a man speaking to his dog. By the tone, I thought he was telling it to stand still: the hawk had not gone down. After about a minute or so, I very slowly raised my head, tilting it on one side so that only one eye looked through the feathered tops of the long grass in front of me. I saw the broad back of a man wearing a greenish waxed jacket walking away and the dog following. I was worried about the dog because I didn't want it to pick up my scent. The wind was still blowing towards me however, and there was a strong smell of sheep on the ground where I lay along with plenty of evidence of their past presence.

I also noticed a second figure, much slighter in build than the first, a girl, I thought immediately because of her thick tawny hair, and then surmised it was probably a boy, although I don't know exactly what made me change my mind. There seemed to be some disagreement between them, as the boy appeared to be remonstrating, but as both had their backs turned, it could have been my imagination. In any case it was the dog upon which I was concentrating.

About five minutes later, I heard another shot in the distance, and a dog bark, so it seemed safe enough to get up and return. I was still slightly shaken by the shock of the danger which I had run into when least expecting it. There was quite a bit to think about too. I wondered why I had not got up, confronted the man and complained that I had nearly been shot.

Well, in the first place, I thought, answering my own question, because I was so well hidden it was not the shooter's fault that he had not seen me. Secondly, the hawk had flown back towards me so low, and that was why the shot had come so close. Of course, the whole thing happened very quickly too. But then I realised within a few seconds of the shotgun pellets rattling over my head, and the blast ringing in my ears, that sparrowhawks were a protected bird. The man had no right to shoot them, but the point was that the bird had not gone down, it may not even have been hit, and I was the only other witness to the event.

Furthermore, I was not even sure of my legal rights to be there, although the more I looked around afterwards, the more certain I became that I was on a public footpath and possibly on common land as well. But the underlying reason for my silence was also because I did not wish to draw attention to myself, to come into conflict with locals at this point when I was thinking of buying the cottage down the road. The shooter might own it for all I knew.

At any rate, I got up slowly and put on my camouflage jacket. Only the back was slightly wet from the dew and the lining was still dry. As I walked towards the van I reflected I had been lucky the shooter had turned back for some reason. If the dog had not scented me, the man would have seen my footprints in the dew. The dew can be like snow, it gives things away as any hunter or soldier knows. How many dawns had I searched for such tell tale signs? And always aware that they were on the lookout for my footprints as well.

When I reached the van, the sun was well up, and it was so warm that I was sweating inside my jacket and glad to take it off. I stowed away the sleeping bag and the pillow, and converted the bed back into a seat. I made more tea as I was thirsty, and sat in the van for a breakfast of muesli and milk from a carton. The temperature continued to rise, so I pulled back the sliding door to get the breeze.

Just as I had finished the muesli, and pouring myself some more tea, almost as if all my troubles came at mealtimes, I looked up and was suddenly surprised to see the shooter in the green waxed jacket standing about thirty yards away watching me. People don't usually get that close without my seeing them, I thought, and noticed that he was half bent over holding his dog by the collar. I said nothing; it was up to him to make the first move. Whoever spoke first would be telling the other something.

We stared at each other for a few more seconds, and then the man let go of his dog which remained sitting, and said loudly 'What are you doing here?' He spoke as if he owned the place.

I looked at him for several seconds before replying, taking in everything I could as if by some instinct I already knew this meeting was significant. About fifty years of age, I thought, of medium height, very well built with a barrel of a chest. Bald or balding, I guessed under his flat cloth cap of Lovat green, although the grey silver hair like a badger above his ears outside the cap, was quite thick. His moustache in contrast, was still black. He wore a dark olive green waxed jacket, the white metal zip of which was half open, and I noticed that the inside was a light green tartan check. The collar and wings of the jacket were of a brown corduroy, the cuffs already a bit ragged and torn. Brown eyes looked straight at me, the whites very clear, and his tanned skin unblemished, although he had not shaved that morning.

Then I said civilly enough, 'Why? What's the problem?' as if he was making one.

'The problem is,' he said, coming closer and shifting his shotgun from under his left arm and into his right hand, 'that you could be trespassing.'

'Trespassing?' I said inquiringly, raising my voice and its pitch slightly. 'How come? I'm parked right by the road and doing no harm.'

'But you've been for a bit of a walk haven't you?' he asked, or rather stated, indicating with his left hand my footprints in the dew leading onto the common.

'That's right,' I replied, 'but this is a common, and that's a public footpath - in fact it's a bridleway.'

'How do you know it's a footpath for the likes of you?' he asked, getting a bit nasty I thought.

'Well - there's a public footpath marker in the grass to your right,' I said, 'and the Ordnance Survey marks this as a common, I'm sure.'

'Think you're smart, don't you?' he said, slightly nonplussed for a moment.

'No,' I said, 'I'm just replying to your question. But who are you anyway? What's your objection?'

'I'm Colonel Crundale's keeper, and this is Colonel Crundale's land. We've got young pheasants around. I don't want them disturbed.'

I didn't reply to this. Why should I say anything more? I did not have to justify my presence there, I had done no harm. But for some reason I came to know about later, he could not leave it alone, and had to go on.

'So I'm warning you,' he continued, his voice rising. 'Keep off this land. It's private. The Colonel doesn't like trippers wandering about disturbing the game.'

He said, 'Disturbing the game,' as it was some phrase he knew by heart like a catechism, as if it was part of a creed, the expression of a contemporary philosophy he naturally believed in instead of, as it seemed to me, an archaic expression, bizarrely torn from the nineteenth century.

'Is that why you shoot sparrowhawks?' I asked him. 'Are those Colonel Crundale's orders - to exterminate protected species in case they might disturb the game?'

He realised at once what I was referring to, but he did not ask how I came to know of the incident. He just accepted it from me as if he knew from the start, from the moment he saw me in the van, that I was a dangerous person, someone he was right to have distrusted at once.

The colour rose slowly to his cheeks, and the quivering barrels of his shotgun were pointing at me for a moment. His anger was disturbing to watch, and all the more so as he said nothing, while trying to control himself. Temper! Temper! I thought, indeed a very dangerous temper, and pointing a firearm too.

Then he turned abruptly on his heel, called to his dog, and walked away from the road towards the common along the footpath. I did not regret what I had said, he had treated me with contempt from the start, and no one had the right to do that anymore. But I knew that I had made an enemy and that vaguely disturbed me.

There was no evil in the man's face, I reflected, it was his truculent manner which had caused me to dislike him and answer back about the sparrowhawk. It was as if he had once suffered some kind of an outrage, and that this past hurt had become an affliction, a mental illness. That makes two of us, I surmised wryly.

18

I drank another cup of tea slowly while reflecting over the events of the morning, and decided to drive to Pelham to make enquiries about the cottage at the estate agents, having checked their address on the 'For Sale' notice en route. I thought that I should have a look at Highdene, as this would be where I would be buying most of my stores, certainly all my bread and milk.

When I reached the village, it was about 9am and people were about, although only the postman gave me a curious look. My van was painted an inconspicuous dark green, and when I parked it in the deep shade of a large horse chestnut tree outside the church, with its huge green leaves touching the windscreen, the camouflage was complete.

I went into the church first. After all I was in no hurry, and paused a moment in front of the tall wooden lychgate, an unusually imposing structure rather like an ungainly summer house with wide wooden seats on each side partially protected from the weather. Carved in the wood under the eaves of the steep roof in clear lettering was the thought provoking sentence, 'Ye who would live, be not afraid to die'. A reaffirmation of the resurrection, I supposed, giving stark comfort to mourners passing under the gate, and a constant reminder to the faithful attending Sunday services that in life we are in death.

'But in that sleep of death,' I mused with Shakespeare, 'What dreams may come?' Who could really be so sure of life after death? The true believers, yes, but I was not one of them. At a pinch I might believe in some kind of spiritual after life, but I could not begin to guess what form this would take. Certainly not a material form, rising from the grave on Judgement Day. What a gruesome sight that would be!

However, my philosophy of life and death was not as simple as that, but far more complex if not illogical. I supported the Anglican Church, however imperfect it may be, because it was part of my heritage, going back thousands of years to its Catholic past and Anglo-Saxon beginnings before the Norman invasion. And I knew for many, being without a belief in their Church and at least the hope of an afterlife, that they would suffer unbearable anxieties and grief. That's why, hypocritical as it may sound, I would not openly criticize those beliefs.

19

Then I saw the statement in quite a different light, although the wording of the sentence remained the same. My personal interpretation, which, of course, was markedly influenced by my experiences and attitudes developed in the Army and SAS as well as my lifestyle, went something like this. Respect danger. As Herman Melville wrote, 'The harpooner needs to be afraid of the whale.' But don't develop a morbid fear of death. For if a person's main reason for living is fear of dying, then they will never risk anything in the physical sense. They will never live in an exciting way, and I had in any case chosen a profession which was in the business of killing and dying.

Furthermore, every venture has its own risks whether physical or otherwise. To live life to the full, to experience adventure, to know the very limits of your physical and mental capacities, you have to risk failure or disaster. This, of course, as a soldier, included laying my life on the line for my country. And giving loyalty to my sovereign and the unit in which I had chosen to serve. (I am recording my feelings at the time carefully and in some depth, for they not only partly explain many of my subsequent actions, but also because they were to change quite considerably by the end of this account.)

Once through the lychgate, I saw that the church was built of knapped glossy flint gleaming in the sun. It had a square tower without a steeple, and the steep roof of the rest of the building was of Kent tiles covered in dark moss dried by summer winds and sunlight. Quite an extensive porch roofed with similar tiles jutted out to the south facing the sun. From the south west at least, the church looked neat and solid, almost like a traditional English lifeboat, a sort of spiritual lifeboat perhaps. A scratch dial was just distinguishable in a block of sandstone set in the wall near the entrance, and I paused a moment to have a closer look. A notice above the very heavy black oak door read, 'Push hard to open', and I did so to find myself in a nave and chancel of such charm that it almost took my breath away.

The whole place was filled with light from a variety of stained glass so that at first I was dazzled, and could think of nothing else except the glowing colours in their perpendicular windows set in pale sandstone. I also noticed with some excitement that the floor was covered with brasses, at least a dozen of them that I could find within ten minutes. A side chapel slightly sunken to the south of the chancel had five brasses on the floor, and I noticed that one name kept recurring in several forms. In fact, the chapel was built by a knight of the same familiar name in 1572, Sir William Crunesdale, and I had little doubt that he was an ancestor of Colonel Crundale, whose gamekeeper I had met that very morning. No wonder he thought he owned the whole place! But I knew common land has often a long and turbulent history, and I suspected an ancient still unresolved dispute.

The brasses represented ancestors of the Crundales, including their wives, some of whom I noticed had outlived their husbands and set up memorials of their own. Furthermore, on the wall of the chapel high up near the roof were the iron helms of the Crundale knights, and in one place, a single sword black with rust and part of its hilt missing, was somehow pegged to the whitewash. It was clear that the Crundales were part of a knightly martial tradition which had continued for hundreds of years. They would be formidable people I realised to come up against locally. But it was a background which I could understand quite well, part of my own cultural and social being. Any tensions which arose between us would almost certainly be our own responsibility, and that was an advantage.

I spent about fifteen minutes in the church, and then wandered out into the streets of Highdene. First, I went to a small general store which was also the Post Office. Some newspapers still hung on the racks and I bought one from the woman behind the counter, who eyed me quite closely.

'Anything else?' she asked.

'Yes,' I replied, deciding to be bold and to ask a few casual questions. 'I'm a stranger here, and I've just been in the church. I was admiring the brasses and wondered about the Crundales. Do they still live here - their descendants, I mean?'

'Oh yes,' the woman said smiling. 'There's Colonel Crundale up at the manor and some of his family too, Captain Crundale, he...' She did not complete the sentence, as if for some reason she suddenly thought I was too inquisitive for a stranger, and that the Crundales were none of my business. She seemed embarrassed too by the sudden appearance of a customer who had appeared behind me, a short foxy man in his forties, I guessed. Anyway, he gave me a very searching if not slightly truculent look, and I realised that it had probably been his arrival in the shop which had stopped my attempted conversation about the Crundales.

I walked back to the van with my paper, and drove off in the direction of Pelham, retracing my route of yesterday. Soon, the North Downs were left behind, and the road ran along the banks of a minor river on which Pelham was situated

The main street, fronted by numerous historic houses specially restored and painted for the summer visitors, was full of people and parked cars, including mini buses waiting for tourists to set off for the day after a night at one of the local inns. It was all very tourist Tudor as if the buildings had endured the architectural equivalent of cosmetic surgery to make them look presentably old, not young. I had some difficulty in manoeuvring the van into a park down a side lane. A middle aged woman in the adjacent house pulled back the curtains of her bow window and stared at me as I got out of the car. I waved at her and said 'Good morning,' but she quickly drew the curtain. 'You should be used to strangers by now madam,' I said to myself. However, there was no difficulty in finding the estate agent, as it was on a corner and quite conspicuously mock Georgian with a bow window full of colour photos of local houses for sale with their prices. I paused outside looking in the window for a while to see if I could recognise the cottage among the adverts and get some idea of the price, but I had no luck and decided to go in and enquire at once and waste no more time.

To my surprise the place was empty except for quite a good looking blonde woman of about thirty with pale blue eyes who got up from her computer, and came towards me smiling pleasantly. 'Can I help you?' she asked.

'Yes,' I replied. 'My name is Wynstanley, Mark Wynstanley. I'm enquiring about a cottage near Highdene. It's on the common just before you come to a manor house called "The Grange." I saw a "For Sale" notice up in the front garden with your name - I mean Chapman's on it.'

She looked puzzled for a moment, and I thought I must have made a mistake. Then she said, 'Yes, of course I know the one you mean, it's been empty for some time, but only just come into our hands. I'll look it up for you,' and she moved with short quick steps to a filing cabinet, and started to flip through folders. As she walked I noticed that she was shortish, quite slim and wearing a tight fawn

22

coloured linen skirt which made her look very neat and busy. I noticed too that she that she had very rounded firm calf muscles on lean smooth ankles as if she was athletic.

I walked across the room closer to her and as she stooped over a drawer in the filing cabinet, I could see that her blonde hair was dyed. The roots were light brown, although I noticed that the short hairs at the side of her neck were bleached completely yellow, almost certainly from the sun because the smooth skin of her throat was tanned.

After searching for a minute perhaps, she turned round and faced me with a file in her hand, and I moved away slightly as she spoke as I seemed to be standing very close. 'I'm sorry we haven't got a photo of it yet, but you've seen the place haven't you?' she asked as she handed me a sheet with information about the cottage. There was an address at the top of the sheet, Chalk Hill Cottage, Coppice Lane, Highdene, a blank space for the photo and quite a detailed description.

I read the typescript slowly. Eighteenth century building, one and a half acres of land including orchard, three bedrooms upstairs, downstairs bathroom and lavatory in need of repair, Aga stove in kitchen, but nothing about any kind of central heating, although it mentioned that the hot water cistern needed replacement. Then I came to the price at £73,000 - a bargain it stated for anyone prepared to do some renovation. Given the one and a half acres the price seemed very reasonable, although there were bound to be other snags. I knew that I could manage about £30,000 from my gratuity. A mortgage was going to be difficult, however, as I was out of work.

'Yes, that's the place,' I said, trying her out, '£73,000 - do you think they will come down at all?'

'Well that's what they hope for,' she replied smiling. 'But the old lady died just before Christmas, and they, her eldest son, I mean, has only just put it on the market. It's been under probate you see. Anyway, that's not a bad price for a genuine old cottage in the heart of the Kent countryside - someone from London will snap it up I'm sure.' Then she added after a pause when I said nothing, 'The price will not go down now that summer's here - in fact Mr Chapman thinks the place could fetch £80,000 with some advertising, but the new owner wants to sell as soon as possible.'

'Where does the son live?' I asked. 'Near here?'

'Oh no, he - Mr Strickland, the eldest son - is in Australia and his brother in Canada. But the place is in the hands of solicitors, Carey and Co., here in Pelham.'

I thought for a moment while the woman closed the file drawer, and then asked, 'Well, do you have any other offers so far? I mean I need a day or so to think about it.'

'We haven't had any serious offers so far,' she said. 'But the summer has really only just begun. I'm sure the place will sell. In fact, we did have someone in yesterday now I come to think of it. Two men who said they were interested in buying Chalk Hill, but really I think they wanted to rent a place near there.'

'Two men!' I exclaimed, my mind suddenly very alert. 'I think I met them up at Highdene - on the common. Were they in a black van?'

'Well, only one of them came in - the other stood outside. I could see him through the window. But I didn't notice any black van.'

She looked at me enquiringly, slightly put out, and said, 'How do you know about them? Are they friends of yours?' Her manner had changed from friendliness to suspicion as if we were up to something. Indeed, her face looked quite hard all of a sudden. You are a woman who changes mood very rapidly, I thought.

'Oh no,' I said. 'I first met them at Highdene yesterday. I have never seen them before in my life. They must have been looking at the cottage I suppose, but they didn't tell me that. I thought they were expecting to meet someone at Highdene. That was the impression they gave. But the person they expected was certainly not me.'

She seemed reassured that there was no connection between us, no hidden reason for the sudden successive enquiries about the cottage, although I was still puzzled at her sudden change of mood. Then I asked her my key question casually. 'As a matter of interest, did you by any chance happen to find out where they came from? One of them told me he lived in Dover.'

'Well the man who came into this office gave the address of a hotel in Dover, but he didn't say where he actually lived.'

'Don't you think there was something odd about them?' I asked, determined to pursue my doubts.

'Well, you know,' she replied, 'we get all sorts of enquiries. All types of unlikely people from London want a place in the country for the weekends. We deal with a lot of country cottages, not just the one at Highdene. But those two didn't seem quite certain what they wanted. The one who came in, Mr Bailey, he said his name was, seemed quite keen about buying the cottage at first. He said the finance would be no problem. It was only just as he was leaving he asked about renting a place. It was then I began to wonder what he was up to. And as I said, he didn't leave a proper address, only the name of a hotel in Dover.' She paused a moment, her eyes searching my face while she seemed to muse. 'Mr Bailey didn't want us to take him round the cottage either. He said that they would look at it again from the garden, although I warned him that the front gate was padlocked.'

'What about the other man?' I asked. 'You said he never came in here.'

'Well he never came in,' she agreed. 'But I think he was the one who wanted the cottage in the first place. However, something could have changed his mind. I could hear them talking outside. You see that top part of the window was open,' she explained, pointing to a louvre of clouded glass that opened onto the street at the top of the bow window above the display of photographs, 'and you can hear what people say.'

'And what did you hear?' I asked, raising my voice slightly and no longer able to conceal my interest.

She smiled, quite relaxed again, as if she enjoyed telling the story,' Well, the other man was Irish. He had an Irish accent - that's for sure, and he said, "It's no use anyway - it's too damn close!" That's what he said. I wondered what he meant. I didn't like the sound of it.'

I didn't like the sound of it either, but now that my worst fears were confirmed, I suddenly felt quite calm and asked in an even voice, 'Too close? Who lives in the manor - I mean the Grange?'

'Captain Crundale lives in the Grange now. That's Colonel Crundale's son. He's a local bigwig - a kind of squire for Highdene, I suppose. Captain Crundale has just retired from the Army, early retirement I think, and is taking over the estates.'

'You mean Captain Crundale is still quite young, or what?'

25

'Yes, only about twenty seven I think. He left the Army this year. I know because Mr Chapman went to a party at the Grange.'

'Do you know what regiment he was in?'

'I don't know that,' she said, 'but I do know he was in Northern Ireland for a long time, and then added laughing, 'I should think looking after the estates down here would be preferable to Northern Ireland.'

'Yes, indeed,' I said.

'What about you?' the woman asked, 'You haven't retired yet I hope?' and she laughed again.

'Well, not exactly, I haven't retired to my estates anyway, but I have left the Army too, and recently. So Captain Crundale and I have something in common. But whether he and I will discuss it in the pub is quite another matter,' I added wryly. I did not let out my Army past by accident for I thought I detected a certain sympathy, and decided to enlist her help if at all possible.

'Were you in Northern Ireland too?' the woman asked.

'Yes, I was, and that is something else which Crundale and I have in common, and perhaps it doesn't end there either.'

There was a pause in our conversation, and I realised at once that the moment had come for me to make up my mind about the cottage and get things moving or else I could lose it, so I said briskly, 'Right, let's return to business. Let me say at once you've got a potential customer. I'm very interested in buying Chalk Hill Cottage. And all we have to do now is to fix a time when you or Mr Chapman can show me over the place - this afternoon if you like or tomorrow.'

The woman seemed slightly surprised at the definite way I was going ahead with the purchase, but seemed pleased all the same. Her pale blue eyes had widened a little, and she appeared quite excited perhaps because she was making a deal on her own without Chapman.

Then she sat behind her computer, looked up and said off handedly with another rapid change of mood, 'I'm sure Mr Chapman will want to show you over the place himself, it's not my job, I'm just the receptionist. He is out with a client at the moment, but will be back about midday I think. He'll need to have his lunch and then he will be out again this afternoon with clients. So would you like me to make an appointment for you tomorrow, say two pm?'

I said that this would suit me and agreed that I would phone the following morning at nine and confirm with Mr Chapman. She asked my name and address, and the name and address of my solicitor as well as my bank. I explained that I was without a permanent address at the moment, but gave her my mother's address in Shropshire. Once she had noted everything down, she got up quickly and led me to the door.

'Thank you Mr Wynstanley,' she said with a bright secretarial smile. 'I'm looking forward to hearing from you tomorrow morning, and I will try and arrange the visit to the property at two in the afternoon.'

Although it was now obvious that she wished to end the meeting and get on with her work, which was natural enough, I paused a moment in the open doorway and said, 'I don't want to hold you up, but there's one thing - I don't know your name.'

'Oh, I'm Mary Renfrew.'

'Mrs Mary Renfrew?' I asked at the risk of seeming too forward or curious.

She walked up quite close to me, and held onto the door with one hand. 'Yes, Mrs Renfrew,' she replied, 'but I don't belong to anyone. I live here in Pelham on my own, if that's what you want to know.'

Then as she began to close the door, she looked me straight in the eye and added with an enigmatic smile, 'I also have lots of friends, and all kinds. People are very helpful around here.'

I made my way back towards my van thinking about Mary Renfrew, and what she had just said, wondering if I had just been put in my place, and whether it mattered anyway. I also began to think about how I was going to fill in the rest of the day. Things had been moving so fast for the past twenty four hours, and now for some reason, I felt at a loose end until tomorrow when I could see the cottage again. At least next time I would not be trespassing.

Suddenly, I really wanted to buy the place, and was glad that I did not feel the need of any advice. Because of its small scale I suppose, a cottage and its immediate environs, garden, orchard, field, village or street, is a very personal choice. One either feels right about it fairly quickly or one does not, and somehow I felt that Chalk Hill was for me.

Chapter 3

In fact, it took three more days after my first visit to his office in Pelham before I met Mr Chapman. I phoned Mary Renfrew the following morning as she had suggested, but she seemed slightly embarrassed. When I asked her if everything was all right, she didn't answer my question, but said, 'I'm sorry, but Mr Chapman will be busy all week. Please phone again in a day or so.' I guessed that Chapman was there listening and trying to stall me for some reason.

However, after being put off with some excuse on each occasion, I returned to the office and confronted the man I suspected of causing the delay. I was a bit surprised when I saw him there behind the desk in his tiny room, and realised at once that he was the same foxy little man I had seen waiting behind me in the general store at Highdene. I wasn't sure whether he recognised me, although thinking about it afterwards, I realised he must have.

Anyway, it was not until the following week that he showed me over the cottage, and then it was nearly a month before I took possession. At one stage I thought I was going to lose the place as Mary Renfrew warned me that Chapman was negotiating with someone else, and it needed a phone call from my family lawyer in Ludlow to put that right. I also phoned Strickland in Australia one evening, their time, and said I had the money and what was the problem? Strickland sounded as if he had been drinking, and seemed quite angry. He said that there was no bloody problem, and then a long distance echo followed so that his phrase, 'No bloody problem,' seemed to go round the world twice. It was all very reassuring anyway. He reiterated that if I had the money, the place was mine as far as he was concerned, and added that he did not know what the hell Chapman was up to. He said, 'I'll twist the little runt's arm for you mate!' (I thought that Strickland must have settled down well in Australia.) However, I got Mary Renfrew into trouble for that, as Chapman found out she had given me Strickland's number in Sydney.

I finally moved in on 17 July. But before then, while waiting for the sale to go through, I toured around Kent for another week before I stayed with my mother in Shropshire for about two weeks. I wanted to see her of course, especially as I knew she often felt lonely since my father's sudden death of a heart attack some years ago; but I also had to collect some of my gear which I needed in the cottage. In addition, there was the very serious matter of several threatening phone calls, as well as those from journalists, who never seemed to give up.

The calls had begun months ago while on leave after I had organised and led an SAS ambush of the IRA when they attacked Ballyford police station in Armagh.

Although the ambush in October 1993 was highly successful and we killed a number of IRA, several things had gone wrong. Two civilians, one a 11 year old boy, had been killed as well, and there had been an inquest, followed by a secret court of inquiry. For very good security reasons my name had never been published in the British newspapers, but it soon became clear to me that somehow a few members of the media had been tipped off about my identity, and given my mother's address in Shropshire. At first the calls had come from newspaper reporters who wanted to know whether it was true I had been involved in the Ballyford ambush, and asked for a statement or even a personal interview. They said my name had already been published in America.

However, the calls suddenly became more sinister and I was threatened. One night someone phoned our house and my mother answered. The person on the line said he wanted to speak to Captain Wynstanley. My mother handed me the phone with a slightly puzzled grimace, 'Someone for you Mark. He didn't give his name.'

When I took the receiver from her hand, a man with a London accent who seemed to be speaking from a public phone box said at once, 'Captain Wynstanley, I would like to have a little chat.'

'Really,' I replied. 'Who are you?'

'I can't tell you that, but say I'm connected with the Provisional IRA, and I've been asked to get in touch with you.'

I was surprised as I had expected any Provo contact to have an Irish accent, but I knew I needed to keep cool, calm, and even polite, as this was probably the best way to extract as much information from the caller as I could in the circumstances. There was also the possibility the call was a hoax.

'Come to the point,' I said after a pause.

'I will - I will - because I don't have that much time anyway. My friends think you have some very vital information about the intelligence network you ran in South Armagh. They know you worked with 14th Intelligence Company at Bessbrook, and there's no doubt you employed agents. Anyway, they want the names of your informants in the Ballyford ambush last year - names and contact addresses so there can be no mistakes.'

'You must be joking...' I said.

'No, I'm not joking,' he broke in, his voice suddenly growing harder. 'It seems they know a great deal about you. They know you helped set up the ambush. You weren't just acting on information received through Army intelligence or Special Branch. You *personally* were in direct contact with the informers, and my friends need to know who they are without any one else being the wiser. We can easily check because we already have our suspicions. But if you are not willing to help us, they will have to seek your co-operation in other ways which will not be to your advantage. I am giving you the chance to think about it - so be ready with the information next time someone phones. But it won't be me and the codeword is Ballyford. And remember, my friends want details.

'But there is no way; I can give you any information like that, even if I had it. You must know that,' I replied, having decided to go along with the caller for the moment. 'And anyway, I don't have access any more to Army files or computers.'

'Come on, you don't need access to any computer to give us what we want. You know these people well and where they hide out. We know you were running one of them for years.'

This was all perfectly true, but I was wondering how the hell the caller knew.

'Be sensible,' he added after a pause very calmly as if his request was perfectly reasonable. 'The odds are against you. No one's going to protect you. You've been set up by your own side. How do you think your name and address got out? How do you think we know so much about you? You're discharged and on your own now and nobody gives a damn. Give my friends that information and providing you don't go back to Ireland, there'll be no problems - you'll be left in peace for the rest of your life. But if you don't - you won't have a life because your days will be numbered. The IRA will have their revenge for sure.'

30

I repeated myself, 'But there is no way I can give you any information like that, and you must know it...'

Then before I had a chance to say anything more the caller rang off. My mother realised that something was wrong, and I thought that it would be better for me to tell her at once what the call was about, although I did not say that my life had been threatened. At any rate, there was a Ballyford call about a week later, again from a callbox, almost certainly from a railway station judging from the background noise. This time the man spoke with an educated Irish accent, which I could not place, but I had the impression he had lived some time in Britain. Later, thinking it over, I guessed he was some kind of a teacher, perhaps a lecturer at a university of polytechnic. Anyway, he spoke clearly and incisively as if he was a person of some importance in the Provisional IRA's 'England Department'.

'I want the Ballyford names and addresses, and I want them now. You know what I'm talking about, so don't waste my time.'

'You know I can't give you any names, so stop threatening me.'

'We know for certain you can give us what we want - that's if you want to live. Your life or the touts. But we'll give you one last chance,' the man said, 'because I know it's hard for you. We want that information and intend to get it so play our game and that'll be the end of it. But remember we have ways and means of extracting information from people like you even if it takes us weeks. And then you'll end up like your mate Captain Nairac with no one even knowing where what's left of you is buried. So be reasonable, just give us the names and we'll leave you alone. That's the deal and we'll stick to it.'

'All right,' I said. 'I'll think about it,' playing for time. Time to plan my escape. Time to get away. 'But when will you phone again?'

'When it suits us. But no argument or excuses next time. Be quick. Just the names and locations as fast as you can. Don't warn anyone because the deal includes not making contact with the people you've named. And no funny business tracing our calls which wouldn't help you anyway.'

As my whereabouts was known, I would have to go into hiding for a while, if not for ever. Furthermore, if the threats were carried out, it would almost certainly be in front of my mother, or she would be involved in some way if I remained at home. It would be better to die on my own, I thought, or at least have the chance to fight back without getting her caught up in the violence.

I realised with a great deal of unease that my mother too could be under threat as well as me. The Provos had little compunction in killing innocent women and children if the situation made it inevitable from their point of view. Look at what happened in Enniskillen in 1987. But I also knew it was unlikely that they would murder an old woman on her own. This kind of brutal killing of a mother for her son's actions could raise an outcry even from their own followers and would not suit Sinn Fein, their political wing at all. So the best thing I could do for her safety was to stay away from her. But this decision penalised us both to a life of loneliness, far worse for my mother than for me. I was all she had left since my father's death, and I tried to visit her as frequently as possible.

I also knew that even if I gave the information they demanded, which would be unthinkable, my life would still be in great danger from the Provisional IRA. As well as two civilians killed, including an innocent child, which had been one of the reasons for my discharge, five of the Provos best gunmen and explosive experts had been killed in that ambush, and one of their men wounded and captured. Once they had the information about the informers, I would still be a marked man for revenge killing because it would be so easy for them. But, they were right to try and locate the informers because they would hardly dare plan another major action against a military target without first finding out who had leaked the plan of attack on the RUC station at Ballyford. Furthermore, I was one of the few people in the Army who had a reliable informant in close contact with the IRA in the border areas of South Armagh, and that was why I had been so secretive about it.

However, there was another disturbing aspect of the call, and that was the suggestion I had been shopped by my own side. It was disturbing because there was every likelihood that it could be true. Just as Nairac had enemies within the security forces, so did I, and had encountered some intense hostility from some British Army members of an intelligence unit attached to Special Branch about my independent role in intelligence work in South Armagh. MI5 were not too happy about this independent role either.

The truth was that most of South Armagh, and especially places like Crossmaglen close to the border, were totally Republican, so that informers were almost impossible to come by. The strong army presence at Crossmaglen in their cramped quarters inside the fortress like post shared with the RUC, and their frequent patrolling of the countryside was necessarily politically to demonstrate that the area had not been abandoned. But the post was virtually besieged. The narrow twisting lanes with tall unkempt hedgerows radiating from Crossmaglen like a spider's web in any direction could easily be mined and any military vehicle subject to an IRA ambush.

This meant that the Army post at Crossmaglen or Forkhill for that matter could only be supplied by helicopter, even their rubbish was taken out this way. About 26 soldiers had died in the market square at Crossmaglen just outside the post, and patrolling the local countryside was very much an active service procedure, especially along the border where sniping from the safety of the Republic often took place.

The new border observation posts such as those at Glassdrumman were very dangerous places too, as the IRA were making constant efforts to blow them up. This meant that my visits to the border areas were extremely hazardous as I had no direct backups. My informants, especially the most reliable one, were understandably very nervous despite all the precautions which we had taken for they were surrounded by Republican sympathisers.

Furthermore, without giving too much away, even at this late stage, to make things more difficult, my key informant lived just over the border in the bog lands surrounding Muckno Lough, where he worked as a mechanic in a local garage and petrol station, and his wife, served daily in the local store. The garage was also an IRA explosives factory where bombs were assembled with their timers by a resident expert and carried across the border at night by men on foot, although vehicles were used to shorten the carry. It was from this garage too that the getaway van used in the Ballymore raid had been supplied.

This informant had more or less been coerced into working with the IRA and in order to gain the vital information about the proposed raid, I had made several unauthorised trips into the Republic. These crossings at the border were usually at night, and although one of the observation posts was informed, there was always the risk of being shot by my own side as well as the IRA.

My key informant desperately wanted to immigrate to New Zealand with his family and we were trying to negotiate this escape from his situation as part of the deal for information. But if the IRA had found out about this family's intention to emigrate they would have immediately become suspicious. Furthermore, my informant's secret application to the New Zealand authorities through us generated another set of problems, for I knew it was unlikely that they would be able to fulfil the strict immigration criteria which were rightly demanded. I always feared that they too, like so many others would end up as victims of the 'dirty war'.

My unit commander knew about it of course, but there was nothing on record, and as my CO pointed out, if caught, I was on my own for exceeding orders. This was the main reason why I had kept my informant's identity and location in the Republic largely to myself as well as my fear that he might be given away by some lapse of security or whatever. Our unit at Bessbrook was only a very small specialised temporary one which could be disbanded very quickly at any time and all its records dispersed, so security was very tight. We continued to exist only because we got results and were backed by the general commanding British forces in Northern Ireland who was an ex SAS man.

Naturally, Special Branch and MI5 had insisted on being told something about the source of our information on the proposed raid before they would assist; but although they thought the informants were from South Armagh, we refused to give them any names or addresses which added to the ill feeling between us. Anyway, somehow the IRA had got to know that I was the key person in this particular intelligence operation and that meant I was as good as dead without a deal.

In one of my philosophy courses at the University of Kent at Canterbury (UKC), I remembered that the lecturer had told us about a fascinating philosophical problem known as 'The Prisoner's Dilemma'. This involved two people accused of a crime acting in the best way for both of them when they were interrogated after they were arrested and kept totally apart. I will not go into details, but the choice each one had to make separately whether to confess or not confess was an agonising one, as it affected whether they would be set free or imprisoned for varying lengths of time.

Although my problem was not directly comparable, I was faced with an equally agonising choice dealing with ruthless people I could not trust. 'Confession' and co-operation with the IRA might give me freedom, although this was uncertain, but it would certainly result in the death of those I betrayed. It was thus my life which would be traded against the lives of the couple who had trusted me, and morally, of course, I could not give them away.

I could warn them first as in an emergency they could be contacted by phone. But the IRA would surely have had thought of this so any warning to give them a chance of escape might spring a trap, and be a deliberate ploy on the part of the IRA to make my informants 'run' and give themselves away. This would almost certainly seal my fate as well

I also knew there was nowhere for the informers to go and assume a new identity. Given the situation, especially that they were from the Republic and my illegal methods of contact and subsequent discharge from the Army, I could expect no help either from Special Branch or MI5. They would have been only too pleased to have said it was nothing to with them. And I was out of the Army now anyway with no pull at all.

I was taking a risk, of course, in going back to Ludlow, even for a few days, but it was calculated, and I could find out first hand what had been going on since my absence travelling around England in the van Furthermore, in all decency I simply had to spend some time with my mother at home in her own familiar surroundings where we could have chats and long talks in the evening as we used to in the old days.

When I phoned her from a call box in Pelham to let her know I was coming, she also told me that there had been more phone calls from various journalists about my discharge. In addition, she said that two journalists had suddenly arrived at our house by car one afternoon, and checked out whether I was still living there. One of them, a woman from a major Sunday paper, spent the night at a local bed and breakfast, and came round again early the following morning before driving back to London. She had done a lot of sleuthing too, and even tried to get my other address from the village postmaster. Fortunately, the landlady at the local bed and breakfast knew my mother well, and told her what was going on at once, as we all would expect in a small village community where despite personal differences people tend to stick together.

At any rate, as I had deliberately left my whereabouts a mystery, and was constantly on the move in my van anyway, all the journalists drew a blank. However, far more worrying was the threatening call from the IRA, and it was this which had made me decide to roam the country looking for a safe place to hide. The only danger from the journalists was that they could unwittingly give my location away to the IRA. Furthermore, the journalists, some of whom could well have been sympathetic to my situation at Ballyford, unlike the IRA, were able to perform in the open during their search, which made them all the more dangerous from my point of view. I should add that I had been ordered by the Army not to give information of any kind to the Press, although I had no desire to do so in any case. Although discharged from the Army, I was still legally on sick leave for the next five months, up to the end of the year in fact, subject to military discipline and control.

Another of the reasons for my latest visit was to discuss fully with my mother why I had bought a cottage in Kent as a safe house, rather than somewhere closer to her in Shropshire. We had always got on well together, especially since my father's death, and it was up to me to make her continue to feel she was in my confidence.

Meanwhile, without making too great an issue of it, we both agreed that my new address would have to be kept as secret as possible, even from her at the moment. So I asked her, as in the past, to keep writing and forwarding any mail to my regimental depot in Canterbury, where I had arrangements to pick it up from time to time. However, it was a terrible responsibility for my mother to know that my life could depend upon her secrecy, for she was normally such an open, trusting person, and this new role did not suit her at all. Indeed, something of her essential nature suffered as a result, for she had always been as it were, 'a heart at peace under an English heaven'.

Of course, the weak link in the chain was Chapman's office. They knew my name and new address, but not the significance of it as yet. However, I thought I had an ally in Mary Renfrew, to whom I could explain the situation, although I had my doubts about Chapman. At any rate, people in the immediate locality of Highdene would get to know my name and where I lived in the course of time, and being over secretive or mysterious would have aroused suspicion and further attention.

My joining the SAS after my selection and arduous training course with 22 SAS at Stirling Lines near at Hereford had tended to separate me from the camaraderie of my fellow officers in the Queen's. I had been through University rather than the full course at Sandhurst as they had, and this set me still further apart. When I was posted to Northern Ireland as Captain of an SAS troop I lost touch and felt quite embarrassed whenever I met any old my old regimental acquaintances. Some of them would make remarks suggesting I was elitist or thought myself superior. Banter of course, but I began to feel something of an outsider. After all in the end it's the regiment which counts and it was there I hoped to return after my tours with the SAS.

When news reached the regiment about my discharge, not only from 22 SAS but from the Army, many of my brother officers in the Queen's didn't seem to know quite how to react. On the one hand I was one of them in relation to the Irish and the IRA, but on the other hand I had left the regiment for the glamour of Special Forces. Furthermore, although I am not exactly sure of the reason, that is whether my CO at Canterbury really wanted to keep me in the Queen's, he had not actually recommended me by stating I was particularly suitable for Special Forces in section 3 of my confidential report, and once I had joined the SAS, he never congratulated me.

I stayed with my mother for nearly a week in mid-July. Despite the tensions, it was a pleasant time for us both. One evening I went over all my problems as calmly and objectively as possible, and tried not to alarm her. I explained that I had nothing physically to fear from the journalists, only that they might find out my Chalk Hill address. But I also explained that I was possibly in real danger from the IRA, and that anything the journalists discovered could lead the IRA to me. I said, 'Mother, I simply have to keep you out of this. Things will blow over in time, but for the moment, it's better for me to remain in hiding at Chalk Hill. I'm tired of driving all the time, and I simply can't go one sleeping in the van every night, especially in the winter.'

The evening before I left home for Chalk Hill, I went for a long walk up to High Vinnels, the hills behind us, which had played an important part in my childhood. I had been there for many walks with my parents and then often by myself when I grew older and run over them too when I was training to become a long distance athlete. They were the hills of home, part of our family myths.

An important aspect of this myth was the family habit of coming home after a walk late in the evening during the summer or late afternoon during the winter. Then, approaching the cluster of buildings with the chill closing in, if there was a fire in the sitting room one might see the smoke from the chimney perhaps, or smell it from afar in the wind. Most important of all were the lighted windows for if anyone in the family was still out for a walk at dusk, the main lights were switched on and the kitchen and sitting room curtains were never drawn before they returned.

It was always a poignant moment to make out the dark mass of the old farmhouse, to see the yellow lights through the gloom, to smell the wood smoke, and think of supper. Sometimes I was so late in winter on a fine evening that it was dark, the night had come. Then I could only just discern the pale wood smoke drifting across the stars as I walked in the back door. All this represented home, the hunter's return to the hearth, the attainment of safety, the transition from darkness to light, a model of resurrection.

Returning home at the end of the walk I came down off the hills along a bracken shrouded track alive with nightjars, and crossed several meadows before reaching the lane which lead past the front gate of our drive. I walked along the tarmac in my rubber soled boots hardly making a sound. Then I saw the car parked at the side of the hedge as I turned the corner which brought me within sight of the house with the windows lit up as I had expected.

The car was parked right up against a gate leading to a field in the turn off space just off the road, and I could see someone in the driving seat facing away from me. Another person leant across the gate with his back to me. He was watching our house through field glasses. Although everything was only half seen in the gloom, I took in what I could at once, including the letters CJ on the number plate, and knew instantly that they were looking for me.

The man in the driver's seat must have heard the slight sound of my rubber soled boots on the road a few yards away, or he may have seen me moving out of the corner of his eye. At any rate, he looked at me for an instant in complete surprise, and turned to warn his companion by coughing quite loudly. They both stared as I passed, caught out it seemed by my sudden appearance behind them in the dusk. None of us said anything in this brief encounter.

I did not pause at all, but continued at a fast pace down the lane towards the front gate which lead into a short drive to our front door. Safety seemed so close, that I was strongly tempted to turn in; but I realised that I had keep walking past our front gate, pretending that I had nothing to do with the house, that I was not Mark Wynstanley, but someone from the nearby village out for a walk, or a farm hand perhaps returning home late. I was relieved that the men were not the same as those I had met at Highdene, and that they had a car, not a black van.

I continued walking down the lane towards the village, planning what exactly I was going to do next. I decided to go into the pub and use the phone to warn the police, explaining my situation to the owner, Mike Oldethorpe whom I knew quite well. Or, depending upon the reaction of the police, I could go home in Mike's car perhaps with one or two locals and we could tackle the men if necessary. But I also realised that if the two had really come to get me they would be almost certainly armed, and that was the dilemma. How on earth could I persuade the police or Mike of the danger? And in any case, how could I be sure that I was in danger? I was worried about my mother too, but felt that I had probably done the right thing on the spur of the moment in continuing towards the village which was les than half a mile away.

I heard the car start up and come down the lane behind me. They were driving without lights, and beginning to accelerate. I suddenly realised that I had got myself into a trap, for the lane was narrow and the hedge on each side very thick. It was not as dark as near the house for there were no trees, and I could see vaguely about twenty yards ahead. I cursed myself for not thinking things out properly, for getting myself into this situation where everything had suddenly become in favour of my enemies in the car who were accelerating inexorably towards me.

Then I remembered the footpath which crossed the lane, running from the centre of one field into another and leading finally to the village church, some ancient right of way which had its own historical logic. I saw one of the stiles on the left hand side at the top of some rough clay steps, silhouetted against the sky because of the gap in the hedge. I went up the steps in one bound, and vaulted over the stile into the wheat field beyond within a few seconds. I did not linger on the skyline for even a moment and kept my head down among the cool stalks of the wheat wet with dew. This was just as well for as I ducked down and kept going along the track trampled through the wheat, the car lights came on and lit up the whole lane as the engine revved with sudden furious acceleration.

To the men in the car, it must have seemed that I had inexplicably disappeared like the Scarlet Pimpernel. One moment I was there alone in the lane entirely at their mercy, and the next I was gone.

The car slowed down a bit, perhaps reflecting the puzzlement of the occupants at my disappearance. Then it increased speed heading towards the village and the crossroads leading to a main road. I decided not to go back the way I had come and fall into another trap. In Northern Ireland, we had often dropped off people along a lane at night from a moving car, and I thought maybe that could be another reason why the car had slowed down for a moment. One of them could be waiting for me in the lane below the stile, and I would have presented an easy target on the skyline. So instead of returning to the stile, I continued towards the village through the wheat field. The track was well used, the right-of-way carefully re-established each year by the local footpath society, and I came out of the field through a gate which leads into the churchyard.

From the noise of its engine and the moving glow of lights, I thought the car had headed towards the main road. Although I felt certain the occupants had now gone and would have no idea where the footpath led, I was glad to be out of the dark churchyard with its rows of tombstones which seemed to stand in ambush, and onto the road which led to the pub close by.

Once inside the White Hart, I felt a quite sense of relief to be amongst the cheerful crowd at the bar, and ordered a beer asking Mike Oldethorpe, the owner, if I could use the phone at the same time. He was busy and we did not have time to exchange more than a few words. In any case I had decided to say nothing about the incident for it was pointless discussing it with anyone at this stage.

My mother sounded nervous when she answered the phone and I quickly reassured her. 'It's Mark,' I said, 'I'm at the White Hart having a beer. I got very thirsty after the walk! Is everything all right?'

'Of course,' my mother said. 'But I thought you were coming straight home.' Then her voice sounded anxious. 'Mark, while you were out, someone phoned. He wanted to know where you were, so I said simply that you were away and would not be back for some time. Then he rang off.'

'You did well,' I said. 'Don't worry about it. I'll be back in about half an hour.'

I returned to the main bar, and ordered another half pint, I was still thirsty from the long walk and my recent activities in the lane, vaulting over the stile and doubling through the wheat field half bent over like a poacher fleeing from the gamekeepers. In fact I could scarcely believe what had just happened to me. In the friendly atmosphere of the country pub which had always been a place of relaxation for me, it just did not seem possible that I was in any danger, or that I had just escaped being assaulted, kidnapped, run down or killed by the IRA.

Of course, I had been used to sitting in pubs in Northern Ireland very much on my guard, but never here at the local pub. Indeed, it was because all this was happening to me in England that I felt such a disjunction with reality. Thinking about my experience and my reactions to it, there was a curious psychological paradox. For months I had been imagining what was going to happen, looking at England as if I were still in Northern Ireland, my fears and fantasies reinforced by the threatening phone calls.

Now that in a sense some of my worst fears had been confirmed in that I had just met two of my enemies more or less face to face, and most importantly of all that I had managed to outwit them at least in this initial encounter, made me feel more at ease than I had been for months. I had also been wondering about my own sanity for I was not psychologically naive. On the contrary I knew a great deal about paranoia and its sometimes dangerous consequences.

Although I would have preferred to think all my fears could be rationally explained away by the stresses and isolation I had suffered during the last few months, it would have also demonstrated I was cracking up, that the Army psychiatrists were right to have recommended my discharge. But from this evening at least I knew that there were men out there waiting to kill or torture me, real people who wanted revenge. It was no longer just a question of

41

threatening voices on the phone, self incriminating evidence which could have been used against me in a diagnosis of a psychosis by the same people who recommended my discharge. A very curious sort of comfort I reflected wryly to myself. A Hobson's choice between being mad and safe, or sane and in mortal danger!

As I calmed down, I began to look around the crowded room from my corner seat near the passageway where the phone was located. Then I saw Diana. She was sitting with a group of people at a side table beside the open French door leading to the interior garden which had once been part of an orchard. She was small, dark and quite beautiful in her own way with a smooth olive skin tightly stretched over high cheek bones. For a second my eyes moved away from her and focused on the French door as the curtain, caught for a moment in the breeze, moved inward as if someone was entering and pushing it aside. In a flash all my fears returned, and I think Diana may have caught for a second the hunted look which came into my eyes, because she suddenly appeared concerned and surprised.

At any rate when I regained my self control and smiled, Diana looked at me quite quizzically, an eyebrow raised. Then she seemed relieved and smiled back calling out, 'Mark,' waving her right hand in a friendly reiteration of recognition. I kept smiling and raised my beer mug in a banal expression of rustic goodwill. Then, as she continued to look at me, for some reason, probably because I needed company after the incident in the lane, I got up and moved slowly towards her trying to pick out as I approached whether I was intruding upon an escort. I could see a woman on each side of her and three men, one of them standing directly behind her apparently forming a group. They looked as if they had been drinking for some time, and knew one another well.

'We've just been celebrating Howard's birthday,' Diana said as I reached her, gesturing towards the tall man standing behind her arm chair, who suddenly looked quite belligerent. Howard, who had a lanky build similar build to mine and seemed about the same age, must be her date, I presumed. This became evident at once for he sat down abruptly on the broad padded arm of her chair one leg up against Diana almost as if he was riding side saddle on a horse. He kept looking down at her while we were talking with a proprietary air, as if establishing rights to a piece of property, even if on temporary loan for the evening. But for some reason Diana continued to talk to me, determined it seemed to re-establish our friendship.

I had known Diana for years, even in the biblical sense, but she had always been slightly mocking of my career in the Army especially as I had the privilege of a university education. She could never understand, so she kept repeating, what she termed the military mind.

'I just don't understand what's the attraction Mark,' she used to say. 'I thought you were quite intelligent and sensitive. How could you get mixed up with that Sandhurst crowd after all your years at Kent? And a first class Honours degree too! What a waste!'

At any rate we had drifted apart as I realised that she could never understand my motivation for going into the Army, continuing the family tradition, and of course I owed it to my father. But whenever we met, she could never leave it alone so I usually avoided her if I could. This was why I was really very surprised at myself for responding to her that evening at all.

She hadn't changed though, despite the smile and friendly gesture for the first words she said when I got closer were, 'Still in the Army, Mark?' making it a statement rather than a question, and said loudly so that everyone could hear, and would know at once that I was some kind of oddity.

'I'm on leave,' I said. I was not going to demean myself with a lie, or even get her interested by telling the truth that I had left the Army. She would have known nothing about the Ballyford ambush, or even that I was in the SAS. Her mind would have blacked out that kind of information anyway, even if she had seen the headlines in the papers.

Diana laughed and said, 'I thought you had seen a ghost or something when you first saw me.' She laid her hand on my arm for a moment, watched closely by her boyfriend who seemed put out by the familiarity she was apparently demonstrating. But I knew Diana of old. This was all part of her technique for getting her lovers aroused, to stir up a bit of jealously, I mean.

I was uncertain what the next move could be. On the one hand I wanted to get back to my house and make sure that everything was all right with my mother who sounded slightly anxious on the phone. On the other hand I was happy to remain in the familiar friendly surroundings of the pub and soak up the relaxed atmosphere. I was also curious to find out exactly where Diana's friendly overtures were leading as I felt quite emotionally detached from her.

'What are you doing these days?' I asked, looking at her directly and ignoring the rest of the company for the moment.

'These days,' said Diana mockingly. 'What do you mean, these days? Were there other days then?'

'Don't be contentious,' I said. 'Of course there were other days,' thinking of the passionate affair we had on a ski trip to Austria. 'What I mean is - are you living and working around here at the moment?'

'Good God! No one works here,' she said with a slight grimace. 'The only real work locally is in Hereford or Ludlow - that is if you want to serve in a shop or a hotel. But you wouldn't know about that as one of the privileged officer class.'

Here we go again, I thought. Back to where I walked out years ago, but for some reason, I decided to persevere.

'What's the mystery then?' I asked. 'Where do you work?'

'I work in the Zodiac bookshop in Ludlow - ever been there?' she said laughing. It was some kind of a joke, for everyone laughed with her.

I didn't make the mistake of asking them to explain the joke because I vaguely remembered the place which had opened within the last few years, full of feminist books and magazines in the window as well as literature on magic, witches and she devils. Not the sort of place that a straight male like me would frequent I suppose. But suitable enough for a joke against a soldier of the Queen. After all it was we who had to justify ourselves these days, not witches any more.

'And I live at home,' Diana continued. 'You know the little old house up the lane, and I drive into Ludlow every morning at 8.30.'

She paused a moment, and not to be outdone, I heard myself saying, 'I know the place up Kettle lane. You're right, I haven't been in, but I saw the broomsticks in the window.'

Diana looked slightly taken aback as if she had not been used to repartee, but then quick as a flash she said quite defensively, 'Better broomsticks than bayonets anyway.'

'I didn't know there was such a choice,' I said. 'I thought it was either bayonets or the bombers - in the real world anyway.'

'What is the real world?' One of the women standing behind Diana said, lowering her head and looking at the ground. 'What's real to you may not be real to us, especially if you're in the Army.'

I looked at her a moment before replying. Her reddish brown hair was wild and curly and reminded me of the mistletoe I had seen on one of the apple trees in the orchard at Chalk Hill. It appeared to have a glinting copper coloured tinge too, and she had stuck little ornamental hairpins amongst the curls, some of them representing insects, I thought, including a scarlet ladybird whose colour matched her lipstick. She looked up again during the pause before I replied, her greenish eyes narrowed under long eyelashes, and faced me very boldly like a bantam weight boxer squaring up before a fight.,

'Yes - I'm in the Army and my job is shooting people;' I added aggressively. 'But as for the real world that is indeed a problem. So in one sense I couldn't agree with you more, and especially at the moment,' I said thinking of my own situation. 'But if witches are real to you, I have nothing more to say. Let that be your privilege or conceit. But I haven't any spells against ill fortune,' I concluded, as I felt that it was now my turn to mock them.

Everyone looked somewhat put out that the conversation had taken this turn, and Howard seemed quite nonplussed. It seemed as if the two women were, conversationally at least, much brighter than him. He stared at me blankly quite uncertain how things might develop. For a moment he looked rather like the human equivalent of a St Bernard dog which didn't quite know how to carry out a rescue. Although I knew that any playback would have revealed that Diana had started the verbal skirmishing, I had enough serious enemies at the moment without deliberately courting minor ones so I smiled and said as pleasantly as I could in the awkward pause, 'Can I get anyone a drink?'

'No - thanks Mark,' said Diana. 'I think we've all had enough, and it's nearly closing time anyway.'

The awkwardness seemed to have passed, but it was now difficult for me to start a friendly conversation, Diana had seen to that. However, to my surprise, as everyone finished their drinks and prepared to leave, Diana leaned forward and placed her hand on my arm. 'Sorry we had to spar again. Why don't you look in at the Zodiac next time you're in Ludlow? We can have a cup of coffee or perhaps have lunch somewhere.' She lowered her voice so that no one else could hear, 'We can have an undisturbed chat without Mother and Dad. And Howard often pops in during the evenings at home.'

'Next time,' I said. 'Next time I return on leave. I'm going to Canterbury in a few days. Back to the depot,' I lied.

We all began to drift towards the door, Diana and Howard leading the way. I stopped a moment to talk to Mike Oldethorpe, but the place soon emptied and I didn't hold him up. When I got outside, the village was bathed in moonlight and it was a clear night. I saw a group piling into Diana's little car, including Howard apparently. Diana was the last to get in, and she saw me coming out of the pub and moved a few yards towards me as I was passing.

'It's a bit of a crush,' she said. 'Howard's pranged his Jag. It's nearly a write off so I'm acting as his chauffeur at the moment. Don't forget to call in at the Zodiac next time you're in Ludlow. Why don't you come in tomorrow on your way?' I said nothing, but she blew me a kiss all the same.

I did not linger outside the pub, but headed off towards home while there were still a few cars around to give me a sense of security. I could hear that Diana was having difficulty starting, but that's their problem I thought, I have enough of my own. As I hoped, a few cars passed me in the lane and their headlights lit up the road like searchlights. I took a chance that the men had not come back. After all they could not know whether I had called the police or the Army for that matter. Soon I walked past the stile on the skyline, the escape route which had most probably saved my life less than an hour ago. It all seemed quite unreal. 'Talk about different realities,' I said aloud to myself, thinking about the woman in the pub lecturing me of all people on the nature of different realities. Little did she or Diana know.

It became darker as I came near the front gate of our drive and the trees closed in casting long dark shadows in the moonlight. I had a moment of fear as my feet crunched on the gravel approaching the front door. I suddenly realised once again how vulnerable we both were on our own in the isolated house. I didn't have to ring the front door bell as my mother had heard my footsteps on the drive, and cautiously opened the door with the safety latch still hooked up. We both laughed as we peered at one another through the narrow opening, and I said, 'Boo!' somewhat childishly to ease the tension.

'I was getting quite worried Mark,' she said. 'Did you meet someone you knew?'

'Diana,' I said as I stepped into the hallway, 'and she was still as sarcastic as ever. But it was nice to have a beer in the pub, although I had no chance to talk to anyone else as it was almost closing time.'

'What was her news?' my mother asked. 'I often see Mr and Mrs Mathison shopping at the store, but we don't have much to say. I let Diana drive our old Morris last month, when she couldn't get into Ludlow one morning, and phoned me very apologetically for help. We had a good chat when she returned that evening. Diana said she had a boyfriend.' She paused a moment, and went on, 'He's very county. One of the local gentry from Fernhill Park, I think.'

'Diana's working at a bookshop in Ludlow called the Zodiac,' I said, 'but I saw her only briefly.' I continued talking about Diana, but I did not mention the car or the incident in the lane as there was no point in alarming my mother any further. Neither did I question her about the telephone call for me while I was out on the walk. However, clearly it was indeed time for me to leave.

After some thought, I decided to take one of my father's shotguns with me when I returned to Chalk Hill the next day, and a box of cartridges. I realised that physical defence was absolutely a last resort. I knew far too much about the IRA to imagine that I could escape them if they were really determined to kill me in revenge. Armed with AK-47s, they could kill me through the van windscreen at 100 yards range with only a three second burst of 30 bullets. The shotgun was only of some use if I was in a prepared defensive position myself, and the gunmen were unaware of it. However, my intention was to lie low as long as possible, so that it was not worth their time trying to find me and maybe my case would no longer be a priority in a few years.

I could expect no substantive protection from the police, mainly because they were not normally armed in Britain. And in any case, no one would assign an armed detective for my protection. Again, unless the policeman had an assault rifle, there was little he could do against anyone with an AK-47. Furthermore, what was the life of an ex-SAS officer worth compared with say Salmon Rushdie? All they could do was to hunt the killer after my assassination: not much use to me. And of course the IRA had Semtex. If they could blow up someone like Airey Neave in the Houses of Parliament car park what chance had I?

I was enough of a realist to understand that from now on I was pretty much on my own, as my IRA 'contact' had rightly pointed out on the phone. Of course, thinking back, I realised I had been on my own as far as protection went from the very moment of my discharge. Paradoxically, I was safer with my unit in Northern Ireland than in England once my location was known. I was fairly safe in the barracks at Canterbury as the Army was on the alert and armed inside the perimeter. The guard at the main gate had live rounds inside his SA 80 these days, otherwise he could be just another Charlie standing there, a sitting duck for the IRA, who had brought the war to England years ago since the Horse Guards bombings and the Brighton equivalent of Guy Fawkes. The other consideration was the perhaps cynical thought that I was expendable, no longer of any importance since my discharge. All the authorities wanted of me was to keep quiet, to give nothing away about the special intelligence unit I had set up to assist with SAS ambushes.

It was clearly absolutely essential for me to take all the precautions possible to make sure that I could not be traced to Chalk Hill. Meanwhile, 'they' or whoever the men in the car represented, knew I was here, and might make sure that I would not get very far tomorrow. It seemed that it was going to be quite possibly a dangerous drive if my enemies in the car were still around waiting for me to break out. At any rate, I planned to take a very circuitous route, and to keep checking to see whether I was being followed.

Unexpectedly, travelling in the van had suddenly become a bit of a problem. It was slow and could not manage much more than 60mph even on the motorway flat out. It was not at all manoeuvrable either, I could not turn or back with the same ease as a car. Of course, once recognised, it became bloody conspicuous too because of its height and bulk which made it stand out in traffic. On the other hand, I could halt almost anywhere I liked for a meal, or to have a sleep and this was an undoubted advantage.

I did some final packing and checked the van. I had kept it hidden carefully behind the locked doors of our garage all the time I was at home, and parked my mother's old Morris right up close to the front of the garage. In order to open the door or even to unlock it one had to first move the car, so that there was little chance of anyone, say the milkman, in the early morning, peering through a crack. I had already started the engine of the van one morning while I had the Morris warming up outside, and checked the battery (quite a business with a VW), tyre pressures, oil level with the dipstick and cleaned the plugs. I used the Morris whenever I needed transport the whole time I was at home, and so far as I was aware no one in the village knew I had a van. I had arrived after dark and garaged the van immediately as on a previous visit.

Furthermore, there was a small side door from the garden into the back of the garage, and I always used this for unpacking and packing the van. I carefully stowed away all the gear into cupboards in case I had to stop or turn in a hurry, and filled the water container under the sink. I used a torch and the interior light of the van when I completed my final packing late that night instead of the garage light. This was all very important, for my secrecy over the van would be the key to my successful getaway the following morning. I did not plan to leave very early, but to wait until it was light. Then I could have a preliminary look around, and there would be a bit of normal daytime traffic to confuse things to my advantage.

Before going to bed, I made sure that all the house doors were locked and bolted, the downstairs windows fastened and the curtains fully drawn. As I climbed the steep stairs to my bedroom, I was not sure whether the grandfather clock had struck half past twelve or one until I checked with my watch.

Once inside the bedroom, I did not turn on the light, but leaned across the sill of the open dormer window, and looked out. It was a clear night, and the stars were bright enough to silhouette the dark mass of High Vinnels against the western horizon. A roe deer gave its characteristic bark from woods high on the hill, and a tawny owl hooted from the direction of a clump of oaks in the field across the lane. Standing there, I felt the magic of nature working its ancient calming anodyne, and the splendour of the stars filled the window as I lay down to sleep. But before I finally settled down, seeking reassurance perhaps, my groping fingers touched the cold steel of the loaded shotgun barrels on the thick rug beside my bed, and I clicked the safety catch off and on as if I were telling holy beads on a rosary.

Chapter 4

I awoke shortly after dawn, and looked out of the window to check the weather. A light mist surrounded the house, and the gravel on the drive was wet as if it had rained during the night. A grey and overcast sky stretched like a dirty sheet overhead, and clouds obscured the hills. The dawn chorus of birdsong was intensified by the lack of wind, and rang in my ears until I closed the window. I was aware of an uneasy, queasy feeling at the pit of my stomach, and a sense of uncertainty at the day ahead. Not so much dread as a sense of fear spread out thinly like cyanide on a sandwich. This was my home, I reflected, yet I had to leave: this was England, but it had become for me as dangerous as South Armagh.

As I was having breakfast, I heard some early traffic in the lane, and soon there was a steady noise of cars from the main road in the distance. My mother was plainly ill at ease and anxious at my departure, and I tried to appear cheerful. I kept persuading myself that there could somehow be another, an alternative explanation for what had been happening, and that it would soon be possible for me to live a comparatively normal life once more.

I left after breakfast at about seven-thirty. I felt guilty about deserting my mother, but I knew that her elder sister, my aunt Evelyn, would be coming to stay in a few days, and keep her company for at least a month. I walked down the lane to the gate where I had met the men last night. I could see the tyre marks of their car in the mud and the skid grooves where it had taken off in a hurry. I leaned across the gate in the same way as the man with field glasses who had been watching our house last night. I realised from that position he could have seen just one side of the house, and only the top storey as the lower windows were hidden by a thick hedge. However, I could clearly see the gate leading from the field into the orchard and guessed that they must have spotted this back route into our property.

'I do hope you will be all right,' my mother said. 'Please give me a ring during the day.'

'I'll phone from a call box in Highdene,' I said, 'and even before then if I have a chance. But remember no one knows that I have the van and once I've reached the main road, I should be safely on my way. It's the first bit - leaving the house - which is tricky. That's where they could make the connection.'

Then I paused a moment, before finally making up my mind about wearing a disguise which I felt was really a bit ludicrous. However, I decided it could well be the key to the whole affair, so I said to my mother quite casually, 'There's one thing though, and it may seem a bit unnecessary, but will you lend me one of your coats and an old wool shawl? And have you still got those steel rimmed spectacles from the National Health?'

She was understandably surprised. 'What on earth do you want all this for? I mean you're not going to drive the van in disguise are you?' Then she laughed seeing my embarrassment. 'You can have the coat and shawl of course, but I'll have to look for the spectacles - I think they are still in a drawer in my desk.'

'Thank's,' I said. 'The point is that no one knows about my owning the van, but they only have to recognise me as I leave and the connection is made for the rest of the trip. Once I'm out of the area and really on my way I'll stop and change at one of those parking places along the forest road. You know - Andover Wood - no one should be picnicking in the early morning.'

My mother soon found all the clothes and the spectacles in her writing desk as she had thought. I gave her a final hug and said my farewells before I changed, carefully put on her coat, wrapped the green shawl around my head and adjusted the spectacles so that I could see over them. Then I looked at myself in the hall mirror and we both laughed. The disguise was surprisingly effective and created an instant transformation, although my trousers and shoes looked incongruous below the knee length woman's coat.

'Remember not to get out anywhere looking like that or you'll be arrested,' my mother said with a smile and gave me another hug.

Then I moved the Morris away from the front of the garage doors which I unlocked, and left half open. From the gate at the end of the drive I looked down the lane both ways. There was no one about, despite the earlier traffic, and the only sound of a car was in the middle distance from the direction of the village. I opened the garage doors wide, started the van and drove off dressed like some middle aged local countrywoman, a bit of an eccentric in an old van. In order to avoid going through the village, I turned off to the right taking a slight detour past the gate where the men had parked last night.

In about five minutes, I was driving along a familiar side road, the shortest way to Ludlow from our house, along a route seldom used by other commuters to Shrewsbury, and Birmingham. Just before a T-junction, the local council had made a parking place for holiday makers in the summer with wooden tables, and fixed benches for a picnic.

I saw at once that a car was parked alongside one of the benches and it looked very similar to the one I had briefly glimpsed in the gloom last night close to our house. The car faced the road with only the driver in it. I could see his face quite clearly, and I was almost certain that he was one of the men I had seen yesterday. He was obviously watching the occasional traffic, although a newspaper covered the steering wheel, as if he had stopped to rest and have a read.

I slowed down as I came near the junction and my heart thumped at what I saw. I could only steal a glance out of the corner of my eye, but the CJ on the number plate confirmed my suspicions. So I had been right! That was the number! He looked at me quite sharply over the paper, but I suddenly realised with relief that my disguise had worked because he was obviously far more interested in a car behind me. Then, in a moment I was at the T-junction, and almost halted. In my large right hand driving mirror I could see the watcher still looking at the car behind me. (There were no other vehicles in sight.) The person following me was signalling left to go to Ludlow. In a split second I decided to turn right towards wild Wales and a route through the Black Mountains.

My quick decision was not entirely unpremeditated. I had thought of returning to Kent via the Black Mountains, especially if I knew from the start there was a chance of my being followed. I had trained in that area with the SAS on several exercises. This familiarity with the ground meant that I could drive along certain stretches of road that I knew had concealed turnoffs where I could park the van and observe any of the traffic behind me without being seen myself.

As we had used stretches of the road for ambush exercises, sometimes at night or just before dawn, I could do the same for my pursuers. I still did not know whether my followers were armed with assault rifles, but it might be possible to surprise them at close quarters. In such a situation, a double barrelled shotgun loaded with buckshot was a formidable weapon. In fact, I had no intention of shooting anyone, but if I was able to hold up the men who might be following me, I could at least check whether they were armed, as well as their papers, wallets, and see if they could be identified. I felt that I simply had to know whether I was dealing with the IRA, or possibly some other group, although I felt this was unlikely.

However, in my heart I felt that if my pursuers of the last two days were IRA, then I was going to be in somewhat of a dilemma because I knew that even if I caught them by surprise they might not surrender without a fight. Then it would be either me or them, and I had to prepare myself for that situation in advance. Whatever the outcome there was also an important psychological factor working for me. In staging an ambush I would take the initiative myself for a change. It would be they who could be at a disadvantage and simply responding to events.

All these thoughts were racing through my mind as I lay awake for a while after going to bed the previous night. I was surprised and very uneasy at my thoughts of violence, but the tension had to be relieved somehow. Whichever way I looked at the situation and my possible reactions, I knew that my own survival had to be paramount in my actions. My enemies would be thinking exactly the same thing about their own survival in any confrontation and that was the problem of violence.

Within an hour I was approaching the moors and the high road which led to Abergavenny. Wind tugged at the heather slopes around me, and the occasional buzzard wheeled for a moment against dark rain clouds, and then was swept away to merge with craggy outcrops of granite. The van climbed steadily, the engine sometimes roaring as if in mechanical pain. I stopped occasionally to stretch my legs. No one seemed to be following and I became increasingly relaxed as the day went by.

However, all my past training compelled me to have one final prolonged check of vehicles on the road, and the best time to do this seemed to be when I halted for an early lunch. The road continued climbing the moors, and then reached its highest point before descending the distant valleys to the south. Just before the summit of the range, I saw the turnoff I had been looking for, its entrance partly disguised by a rocky gully sometimes flooded with water often frozen hard to black ice in winter. I gently eased the van off the tarmac road down into the gully, and then very slowly up the other side. I winced as the differential clanged on a rock, and the engine revved loudly for a moment as the wheels spun on clay and slime.

This side road was peculiar in that it was sunk well below the heather on each side, scoured out by heavy rain and melting snow. But the ground was firm underneath with shattered rock carefully laid down by the Forestry Commission just after the War. There were birches, rowans, and conifers which thinned and then gave out higher up. Just above the tree line was a lookout point. This had been bulldozed flat by the Forestry Commission as a turning and loading point, but much of the surrounding vegetation had regrown, so that a low vehicle parked there could not be seen from a distance. The mountain rose much higher behind the lookout with a line of sombre granite crags crenellating the horizon.

I had been there many times before on training with the SAS from Hereford, and one could park a Land Rover and sit in it comfortably, spying out the road and the surrounding moors with little chance of being seen. The ground was too rough and slimy for me to take the old van all the way, so I pulled over slightly to one side with the left hand wheels resting on trimmed conifer branches. I intended to back the vehicle the whole way to the road when I returned from the lookout, as I did not dare risk getting stuck in such a remote place.

Before locking the van, I took out my field glasses from one of the cupboards, and a groundsheet to sit on if necessary, which I carried in a light pack with some sandwiches. Then I started to walk the remaining two hundred yards or so to the lookout. From the tyre marks churning up the track, it was obvious that a Land Rover or some other kind of four wheeled drive vehicle had been up there recently.

Anyway, I was glad that I had not brought the van any further. It was good to be walking and stretching my legs after sitting cramped for so long. My shoulders hurt from the heavy steering, and I let out a loud yawn as I approached the last steep incline just before the ground levelled at the lookout. This had been bulldozed flat many years ago, and there was room enough to turn once up the slope in a four wheel drive.

I was looking down at the slippery clay and peat to see where to put my feet on the steepest part of the slope and fully absorbed by the climb. When I raised my head a moment to check how far I was from the top, I saw a dark green Land Rover full of soldiers watching me. The vehicle was parked tilted towards me facing downhill, less than twenty yards away. Its rear wheels were on level ground and its front wheels slightly down the slope at an angle. The men were all dressed in Army camouflage jackets, and armed. Their faces were grim and none of them looked surprised at my appearance. Indeed, I suddenly realised they had been waiting for me.

As I stared at them in astonishment, caught off my guard for a moment, I also realised they were an SAS unit, and I knew the officer sitting facing me across the lowered windscreen of the Land Rover.

'Hello Tony,' I said, 'Fancy seeing you here.'

Chapter 5

Major Anthony Fairburn looked at me intently for a moment before replying. Then he smiled and said, 'Well, well. If it isn't Mark Wynstanley - back in his old haunts. Are you feeling nostalgic or something?'

'Something,' I said. 'Certainly not nostalgic. But you look as if you were expecting me. What's on?'

'We were not actually expecting *you*,' said Tony, 'but we heard a vehicle turn off from the main road and stop. Then you appeared just as we were about to leave.'

'Well - you certainly gave me a surprise, but I could see from the fresh tracks that a four wheel drive had been up here recently.'

I paused a moment to recover my wits as well as my breath. In order to gain a psychological advantage over the soldiers who were watching me I looked them all straight in the eyes, one by one, as I climbed up alongside the back wheel of the Land Rover which was on level ground. Then I continued speaking to Tony, who slewed round in his seat to face me.

'Are you on exercise? Or has the war started?' I asked somewhat facetiously, determined to keep the conversation nonchalant and not show any embarrassment.

'Well, you should know Mark,' said Tony speaking slowly and portentously, 'the war never stops as far as we're concerned.' This was one of the SAS's maxims drilled unto us while training, and I was not sure whether Tony was joking or trying to keep his end up in front of his men.

Then he continued, 'As a matter of fact we're on a practice amber alert right now. And we take all exercises seriously you know. But what are you doing here? What exactly are you up to Mark ? I thought you'd left us.'

Tony clearly expected a proper answer. The preliminary banter was over. Now he wanted to know. I thought for a moment and decided there would be no harm in telling him and gauging his reaction. After all it was a relief to tell someone, and if these people were not on my side, who would be?

'Well, it's an interesting reason, and if you're not in too much of a hurry, I can tell you. But let's go over there,' I replied, pointing to a slightly higher and more open spot about twenty yards away from the Land Rover where we would not be overheard by the men. 'I have to check the road a moment with my field glasses,' I added.

Tony ordered the driver to reverse the Land Rover up the slope slightly until the front wheels were on level ground. Then he and another soldier in the Land Rover climbed out and came towards me as I surveyed the distant road. They both looked in the same direction as me, and Tony said, 'Are you expecting someone along the road?'

'It's possible,' I said, 'but I hope not.'

I looked at the soldier, a short stocky man of about thirty five years, whom I had met before at Hereford, and then at Tony, who said, 'This is Sergeant Corandale.' We shook hands and Tony explained, 'I'm sure you know Captain Wynstanley.' He paused a moment while Corandale and I took stock of one another. 'Captain Wynstanley has recently retired - he was in Armagh at a very interesting time.'

Sergeant Corandale suddenly seemed to realise who I was, because he said quite warmly and genuinely, 'Oh yes, I heard all about you sir from Nick Rose. That was bad luck. It could have happened to any of us.'

'Well - it happened to me - and it was bad luck all right. Looking back I can see how we might have played it differently, but at the time of course...'

'Well, we have learnt from our mistakes,' Tony said. 'What we have to do now is make sure they aren't repeated.'

These people are trying to be kind in their own way I thought. Tony said 'our' mistakes, not 'your' mistakes, and I was grateful for it. In the enquiry it was all my mistake, of course.

There was a silence, and I realised they were waiting for my explanation so I said, 'Well you wanted to know what I am doing here - it's a long story, but I will make it short. I thought I was being followed. Or rather I wanted to check whether I was being followed, because I think I've given them the slip.'

'Given who the slip?' Tony interrupted.

'Probably some unit of the Provisional IRA. They want revenge for the Ballyford ambush. You know - the raid on the police station, and have been phoning me and my mother at home saying that my number is up. They also want me to tell them where I got the information about the raid! They want to know the names and addresses of my key informants and if I give them that information - in exchange- they'll leave me alone.'

Tony and Corondale suddenly looked strained, and I knew they would be appalled at the thought, so I continued reassuringly. 'Don't worry. Of course, I'm not going to tell them anything. But I have to go along with the idea at the moment and stall for as long as I can. And that's why I may still be alive,' I added with a wry laugh. 'But I'm running out of time because last night there were two men watching our house, near Ludlow, and they - or rather one of them was out on the road in a car looking for me this morning.'

'But how the hell did the Provos find out? Your name never emerged at the inquest. And what on earth are you doing here?'

'I thought you knew. Shortly after the inquiry in Belfast, my name appeared in the *Republican Times*, and a New York newspaper. Somebody wanted to do me harm, and gave them the tip off. They also published my home address - my mother's. She lives near Ludlow. That's where I've been staying and that's where I came from this morning. Now I'm on my way to lie low somewhere else for a while where I can't be traced. I had to have a final check to make sure I wasn't being followed. This was the ideal spot. I remembered you can see the road for miles from this lookout.'

'But you can't just run away,' Tony said. 'Have you informed the police?'

'Not yet, but I will. And I am not running away,' I said with some heat and irritation. 'You forget - I'm not walking around with a squadron like you armed to the teeth with the latest weaponry. I had to get out at once before I got killed. The police are not armed here - you know that. I haven't got a weapon either. The gunman has it made - all the odds are against me now.'

Tony and the Sergeant looked at one another, but their expressions gave away nothing. 'But how do you know the men watching the house were IRA?'

'I don't as a matter of fact', I said, 'I don't know who the hell they are. That's part of the problem. What I do know is that if they are IRA and I find out, that is if I live to find out - it will be too late. Specific revenge killings have become part of the routine these days.

58

You both know that, and you know perfectly well that the UK with the help of the so called 'England Department', is within the target zone now, carrying the struggle to the mainland, as they call it.'

I paused a moment, still irritated by their apparent lack of awareness of what it is like to be an unarmed civilian up against terrorists, what it is like to be on your own without both the moral and physical protection of belonging to a unit. Of course, I had been like that once myself, but recently I had begun to understand really for the first why it was possible to intimidate civilians so easily in Northern Ireland. Then as they remained silent, I looked straight at Tony and said, 'Well, if the men watching me were not IRA - who the hell were they then?'

'I don't know,' Tony said coolly, 'but don't do anything foolish before you are sure. I mean don't do anything on your own anyway.'

I realised with some despair, and a feeling almost of resignation that he had still not understood the point I had been trying to make. 'Well, that's the problem,' I said, 'I've been trying to tell you that I am on my own. Can't you understand that if they are IRA - it's going to be a bit late for me to find out when they decide to do me in? I have to find out before then. Can't you see that? So what I am left with? Surely to act first if I am to stay alive.' And I made that last remark a statement, not a question.

'Well, what exactly did you have in mind then?' Tony asked, so quietly and casually that I knew the answer was very important to him.

I thought a moment, while Tony looked away from me and at Corandale. Their eyes met and I knew what they were both thinking. I had said far too much already and realised if I said more on similar lines it was going to give a bad impression. Indeed, if reported to the psychiatric unit, what I had already said could confirm the view I was still unbalanced.

Clearly, it was no use trying to explain myself any further, although in fact, I could not have had a more sympathetic and understanding audience, and they were basically on my side. They just didn't want me to do anything foolish that's all. And they were understandably concerned about my mental state after the various rumours which had been circulating.

Then Tony and Corandale asked me a few questions about the raid, although they knew pretty well what had happened.

'Well, I was uncertain whether the Provos were going to get unto their old tricks and use a digger, as they had so often done in the past. But they knew this would give the game away once a digger being stolen was reported. It would be slow to move as well and make quite a noise when approaching the target. So this time they were relying on vans which were quieter and much faster. They brought a van from across the border the day before the raid, and garaged this in Cullyhanna. This was the getaway vehicle, but they also needed another van for the raid itself. They intended to hijack this and abandon it afterwards. Then escape in their own van to somewhere close to the border and make the crossing on foot possibly later that night.'

I explained in some detail about the hijacking of the van and the small boy who had been killed. 'You know the bastards bound his hands, gagged him and pushed him down below the dashboard in the front passenger seat where McCormack the leader of the raid was sitting. We couldn't see him of course when we opened fire. The local RUC knew the driver well. He was a builder working on a site about ten miles away and took his son to school each morning on his way to work. In hindsight, this was the obvious vehicle to hijack, and we should have been more prepared for it. If there was a mistake then this was it.'

I paused a moment and then said directly to Tony, 'When the van came along the road below the police station, about 80 yards away, it was travelling from left to right so at first I could see only the driver whom I knew by sight from two previous occasions when I was making my recce. My view was a bit obscured by the high wire mesh fence about twenty yards in front of the station, and also by the entrance gate which was padlocked. Then the van suddenly swung up the slight slope towards us, and I saw the man in the passenger seat. For a moment, I though the driver was giving him a lift to the station, but almost at once I knew from the expression on the driver's face and the speed of the van that something was wrong and this could be the start of the raid.' I paused again and Tony and Corandale were listening intently, totally gripped.

'I was worried about the driver at that point of course because none of my men knew about him, as they were brought in at the very last moment hidden in a lorry. When the van stopped about thirty yards away, and armed men in blue dungarees and black balaclavas pulled down over their faces began jumping out of the back, I shouted at them to stop, followed immediately by the order to fire. There was no time for any extended warning, our lives were in imminent danger so - as you know - legally, we were right to open fire.'

'I don't think there was any doubt about that,' interrupted Tony, 'but the Provos must have had a shock when you opened up!'

'Yes - I guessed at once when the passenger pulled a balaclava over his face and he and the driver remained in their seats that the van would come even closer to detonate the explosive when they had the necessary covering fire from the gunmen. But, first - of course - they had to get through the gate. However, we had SAS men hidden outside the wire fence, waiting for the order, and they opened up instantly. Given the urgency, it was simply not on to warn them about the driver.'

Tony and Corandale were still listening intently. 'The noise was tremendous. For a few seconds some of the IRA even managed to fire back, and bullets ricocheted from the bricks around us. The rest, including McCann - whom we had expected up front at once - hid behind the van or started running when our fire began. Of course, we were very careful about our own lines of fire, and made sure we would not shoot one another. So at first most of the fire was pouring into the van at an angle and out of the sides. It was rocking as the bursts hit and sparks were flying off the metal.'

My mind recreated the whole incident vividly as I spoke. The adrenaline began to flow and my pulse rate increased so that I suddenly started to breathe faster.

'Then our fire was switched to those trying to escape. But the truth is I never really thought about the poor hostage at that point. Only about destroying the attackers and also, of course, saving ourselves from the blast if our fire or they had detonated the bomb.'

'But your main problem was with McCann,' said Tony. 'That's what the inquest court was really on about, if I've got it right. Everything else went according to plan. So there's a lesson to be learned for all of us about his end.'

'Yes,' I replied, 'but what's the lesson? If he had been killed only with bursts from American M16 assault rifles there wouldn't have been a problem. It was one of our troopers using his 9mm Browning pistol which caused the problem, as this suggested a *coup de grâce* although the Trooper denied it. Anyway, it was something he didn't obviously think about at the time in the heat of the moment. Of course he said his M16 jammed and that's why he used his Browning,' I added, not very convincingly, and regrettably perhaps we all laughed as M16s rarely jam - that's why we selected them for SAS use.

I now realise how brutally cynical this conversation would seem to civilians, but that's how we spoke at the time and how I viewed the matter and still do, I suppose because my very survival had so often depended upon understanding I had little choice - either kill or be killed.

Sergeant Corandale made the key point for me, as there was no way I could even suggest it myself. 'Well, McCann was their top explosive expert: he had years of practice, and we know he killed and maimed scores of people. If he'd just got another longer sentence in the Maze - a hundred more bombers would have been taught all the tricks of the trade. His death saved lives in the future sir, I'm sure.'

'Exactly,' I said. 'Thank you Sergeant, but actually it was not planned that way, it was just we knew from our informer that McCann was going to be in the raid. We also knew that his first and vital job was to blow the entrance gate through the wire fence with plastic explosive - almost certainly Semtex. Padlock and hinges if necessary.'

I continued by repeating and emphasising my earlier point. 'McCann had to be stopped at once so the main charges could not be brought any nearer to the building. All my men had seen his photograph. It had been in circulation for months after his escape last year. They knew the importance of stopping him; but it seems the 9mm rounds in his head later at close range were unnecessary because he should have been dead already considering the hundreds of rounds fired.'

'Christ! What a show!' Tony exclaimed, and Corandale nodded emphatically. Both knew that it was only by chance they were not now in my shoes. As SAS, it could very well have been their own experience - not just mine.

Well then,' concluded Tony, 'You had your chance and took it. But that fool of a trooper who used his Hi-power was the loose cannon all right, or the loose pistol to be more accurate!'

'Yes, but the bad news for me was that although the court was critical of the Trooper, I was the officer running the whole operation and had to take the blame. Those men were under my command and I was ultimately responsible for their actions.'

Tony and Corondale remained silent and perhaps unwisely, I added bitterly, 'The politicians and the MOD wanted a scapegoat anyway.'

There was another awkward pause and I realised that enough had been said already so I didn't tell them the details about Rory O'Shea. He was the IRA man who somehow staggered wounded along the road and rolled down a slope deep into long grass and lay hidden for about half an hour in thick vegetation beside an overgrown hedgerow. In fact, the truth is I saved him from being shot again when he was found, and the very man I saved was the one who gave evidence against us that McCann had been finished off with a pistol. There was also the awful moment when we checked the van and found the driver dying and his small son dead beside him below the dashboard.

As there was no point in gaining any more sympathy votes. I decided to end the meeting amicably, and the very fact that they were in the area was greatly reassuring. They were also armed, and could easily deal with anyone they spotted following me. I smiled at the thought that it would also give my followers quite a shock to see two Land Rovers full of SAS. They would probably surmise that I was being protected, and they had fallen into some kind of trap.

'Well, don't worry about me. I'm not going to do anything foolish, and it's good to know you are here sitting on my tail. All I ask is for you to look out for a car, perhaps a Ford, with one or two men in it, and CJ on the number plate, although I can't remember the colour or the make.'

'OK,' said Tony, with a smile, 'We'll stop any car with your description. Politely of course as we don't have any such authority and check out the occupants if that's possible, saying that we had a message to do so - after all we're on amber alert - and take it from there.'

Tony gave me a lift down the hill to my van, and a number of Troopers got out to have a look. Sergeant Corandale was very impressed with all the furnishings and equipment, and greatly admired the cooker. 'We need something like that in the SAS.

Perhaps we could convert an APC!' he said. 'I wish I could join you,' he added, quite wistfully, I thought.

The SAS Land Rovers shot off in the opposite direction to mine and I waved them goodbye with some envy myself. My feelings were not mixed. I just damn well wished I could be back commanding my old squadron again with some comradeship and purpose in life. But no self pity. The SAS knocked all that out of me.

My philosophy which had slowly evolved over the years was that in life, we are dealt certain cards, our genes, or social situation or whatever unexpected and if unwarranted misfortune comes our way - that is fate. But I was not a fatalist because I also believed it was up to us, each individual to make the best of the cards he had been dealt.

There is indeed such a thing as bad luck, every soldier knows that. Nevertheless, if possible, the most important thing was somehow not to become a victim, or to assume the mentality of one. No one really ever really gave a damn about victims. Even at the special service at Westminster Abbey after victory in the Falklands, all the disabled from the war in their wheelchairs were shunted well out of sight. But I had found out too that in one sense it was possible to create one's own good luck. Of course, this requires a certain degree of nerve. And that's why, despite sneering criticism mainly from intellectuals, the motto of the SAS, 'Who Dares Wins,' was such a positive one, which I intended never to forget.

I climbed into the van, and slowly backed onto the road. There was no other traffic as I set off towards the south, Newport and the M4 to London, my mind in some turmoil after the surprise meeting with members of my former regiment, 22 SAS. Now I wanted to reach Chalk Hill Cottage as soon as possible, and clearly I had given my would be followers the slip. I felt suddenly elated at the thought of reaching my new home - the first I had ever owned. Although I still had to pick up the keys from Chapman's, Mary Renfrew assured me there would be no more problems.

The van droned on and reached its maximum cruising speed of about 60 mph along the M4, and M25. Apart from a halt for petrol, I kept going without another stop until I turned off the M20 at junction 11 near Folkestone. Then left at the roundabout for Stone Street and Canterbury, and within two miles, sharp right into a country lane towards Postling. I soon passed 'The Pent' where

Conrad once lived and parked the van opposite the church. I walked a short distance to a phone box at a T-junction at the north end of the village, and took out some coins from my pocket before phoning my mother in Shropshire. I knew she would be anxiously awaiting my call, and had all the coins ready.

Just as I was about to insert the first coin into the slot, I suddenly saw a black Ford Escort van coming towards me from the village, braking hard at the junction. There were the same two men sitting in front I had met at the common several weeks ago and neither saw me as the driver was braking hard and very intent on getting round the corner, while his companion seemed to be shouting something, and looking away from me to the right.

The Ford almost halted and then turned sharp right towards Pelham. I was surprised, but almost certain I had not been seen, although the men may have noticed my van. Immediately my old sense of dread returned and I cursed myself for parking the VW in such an obvious place, although the Ford had been travelling so fast I doubted on reflection whether the two men would have noticed it. However, my sense of elation at my apparent 'escape' from my pursuers in Shrophire suddenly evaporated, and I realised that even in my new hideout at Chalk Hill there were unexpected dangers looming on the horizon.

It was in quite a sombre mood that I phoned my mother, and directly the connection was made and I heard her voice on the phone, I knew that something was wrong.

'Are you all right Mark?' she asked at once, quite fearfully I thought.

'Yes, of course,' I replied. 'I'm almost there. But has anything happened?'

'Yes, something happened to Diana, and Howard too,' my mother said and then continued after a deep breath, 'Shortly after you left, Diana phoned to ask whether you could give her a lift into Ludlow. Howard's car is being repaired and Diana's wouldn't start, so she was desperate to get to work on time. I explained you had already left and offered to lend them the Morris, which she had borrowed once before.'

'That's all right, 'I said. 'Diana's a careful driver, but I wouldn't lend any car to Howard. '

'Diana drove,' my mother replied, 'but when they reached Chase Wood, two men in a car, forced them off the road and down a side track into the trees. They hit Howard I think, and tied them up. But Diana will tell you all about it. Diana said they thought Howard was you. She is very upset.'

'Of course,' I said, thinking hard about my own escape, 'but does Diana know what it's all about?'

'Well, she wouldn't tell me,' my mother said, 'and I didn't tell her anything either. But she wants you to phone her as soon as possible. She went home early from work and I said that she could keep the car until tomorrow. As I said she is very upset, and has already informed the police. But I told her to speak to you first before she gave your name to anyone.'

'Don't worry mother. I'll phone her at once,' and after some more conversation, and reassurances about my own safety, I rang off.

Howard answered the phone, and clearly wanted to say something, but I heard Diana in the background shout angrily, 'If that's him, I'll take it.'

'Diana', I said. 'Are you all right? What happened?'

'What happened!' she shouted. 'You bastard! You should know what the hell it's all about. They thought poor Howard was you. They had guns and wanted to kidnap him!'

Chapter 6

For a moment I was somewhat taken aback at the anger in Diana's voice - it was clear she was absolutely furious with me - and I paused a moment before replying, 'Well, I don't know exactly what happened. Tell me first before I say anything. Mother said just now on the phone that you'd borrowed her car and gone to Ludlow with Howard. Then what happened?'

Diana replied in a more controlled voice, lowering the pitch, 'Your mother had to drive round to our house in the Morris to pick us up, and we gave her a lift back. So by the time we left for Ludlow, it must have been well after nine. It didn't matter as I'd phoned the office and told them I'd be late. Anyway, we drove the usual way into town, down the side road, and by then there was hardly any traffic at all. We saw a car at the turn off with the driver - a man - sitting in front reading a paper propped up on the steering wheel, which seemed odd at that time on a side road. I thought it must be a coincidence when this car began to follow us. Then I really felt something was strange. I could see in my driving mirror that someone else had popped up in the back. I thought he must have been asleep perhaps...' Pips began to sound so I hastily inserted several one pound coins.

Diana continued, 'As we got near the woods of the Chase, the car came closer, and I said to Howard, "I think we're being followed," but he didn't really take it in, although he swivelled round to have a look. Then the car suddenly overtook us on that very narrow road in the Chase, the dark shady section where the branches meet overhead. The man in the passenger seat leaned out of the side window and pointed at our front wheel, and shouted we had a flat or something was wrong with the wheel. I let down the window to try and hear what he was saying. I slowed right down as well. Then the car pulled ahead of us and forced me to stop. The passenger jumped out and within a few seconds was standing by the open window pointing a pistol at my head.'

'Jesus Christ!' I exclaimed.

'He told me to drive down a side track about fifty yards in front of us leading into the wood. It was actually a grassy shooting ride, and when I hesitated he shouted in a strong Irish accent, "Do what I say you bitch at once or I'll blow your fucking brains out."

He was very nervous and excited, and kept looking up and down the road to see whether anyone was coming. He climbed into the back seat with the gun jammed against my head.

As we drove down the ride, he said to Howard, "Don't try anything Captain Wynstanley. Don't even think about it, or you'll both be dead."

It was then I became aware all this had nothing to do with us. It was *you* they were after.' Diana paused a moment, and I heard her take a deep breath. I tried to say something about being sorry, but she ignored me and went on, 'I screamed at him that Howard was not Captain Wynstanley, that we had borrowed your car as ours had broken down, and I was driving into Ludlow to work.

"This is Howard Mathison," I said, "and he doesn't even know Captain Wynstanley – he's nothing to do with him. We don't know who you are or what you want either."

The other man left his car off the road blocking the entrance to the ride, and followed us on foot to where we were parked out of sight of any traffic. He came up to us as I was shouting, and heard what I said.

They both seemed put out for a moment and then the one with the gun said, "A good try lady, but we want Captain Wynstanley to come with us for a little chat. He knows what it's all about even if you don't. We're going to leave you here tied up in the car when we make our getaway. And if your friend is helpful, we might even phone someone and let them know you're here."

Howard had kept silent up to then, but he suddenly lost his temper and started to shout. He looked as if he was going to grab the gun, but the other man pulled out a pistol too and dragged Howard out of the car. I thought he was going to shoot him for a moment because he was quivering with rage. But instead he suddenly kicked him very hard in the groin and then, when he was doubled up, kicked one of his knees so he fell to the ground. We were clearly both in great danger of being murdered, so I kept calm and told them to check Howard's ID by looking in his wallet, which they did at once. Fortunately it was full of IDs, driving license, credit cards, cheque book with his name and account number, as well as various other items which convinced them they'd got the wrong person. Then, they tied our wrists with nylon cord they had in a haversack, and bound our mouths with masking tape. They pushed us into the Morris, me in the front and Howard in the back. Finally, while our feet were sticking out of the side doors, they tied our ankles very tight indeed, jammed us inside, locked the doors, and took the key with them.'

'But how did you escape?' I asked. 'I mean how did you get home so quickly? Someone must have found you or you might still be there in the Chase?'

'That's right,' said Diana. 'We were incredibly lucky. Only about an hour after the men left, a gamekeeper, Rod, saw all the tyre marks at the entrance to the ride. Our wheels must have churned up the mud along the track, so he decided to investigate, as he suspected poachers. The first thing I heard was the sound of his dog barking outside the car, and then Rod's face appeared at the side windows. He was pretty surprised I can tell you. He tried to open a door, but course he couldn't get in as the car was locked. He had to smash a window with a rock.'

'Then what?' I said. 'Did you explain what had happened?'

'No, it was just too complicated. I simply said that the men had stopped us by mistake. They thought we were someone else, and tied us up to make their escape safely. We were both pretty shocked, and I thought the less we said at that point the better. But I told the whole story in some detail to the police at the station in Ludlow after Rod kindly gave us a lift there. I didn't mention your name. Your mother begged me not to for some reason she didn't explain when I phoned her from Ludlow just before we went to the station. I thought she had to know at once, even before telling the police. And of course, you had to know as soon as possible. Don't worry – Howard kept to the same story. The police interviewed us at the same time. We said that when they checked Howard's wallet, they found he was not the man they were trying to kidnap. I explained that they clearly wanted to kidnap someone - the police had to know that.'

'And the Morris?'

'That's all right - it's in Ludlow with the police. They took us back to the Chase, and got it started, and then to Ludlow. It's undergoing forensic tests, fingerprints and whatever, for the next few days. I can't remember exactly, I was too shocked at the time, but I think one of the men was wearing gloves anyway.'

'Well, look Diana - I can't talk any longer as I'm in a phone box and running out of coins, and I can't give you the number to ring back for various reasons which I'll explain some other time. But I'm extremely sorry. I'll get in touch with you again tomorrow.'

'That's all very well, but we must know what it's all about. The police will question us again and next time - Howard thinks - I think - we must give them your name, so you'd better give me a good reason not to.'

'Of course, I understand how you both feel. I'll phone again tomorrow and explain in more detail. But those men were after me all right. I'm lucky to be alive. My only hope now is to give them the slip and lie low for a while. If you give my name to the police, someone else is bound to find out - it will all be in the papers, and I'll soon be located.' The pips began to sound, and I added hastily, 'Good bye Diana...'

It took a little while to collect myself. I stood in the tight enclosed world of the phone box thinking hard about the implications of Diana's story. However, the truth is that I thought only about the implications for me, and once more I was aware of a sense of personal threat. No one was in sight, no passing cars, and I felt enveloped in an air of unreality until I opened the door and the sounds and scents of the countryside returned to reassure me.

The truth was, although I felt embarrassed by what had happened to Diana and Howard, I really didn't feel as much sympathy as I should have done. I had been living for years in a world dominated by the threat of sudden death and terror, which people like Diana thought I had chosen as part of my job as a soldier and it's true that glory cannot be disassociated from death. Although there was certainly comradeship, the pride of being part of an elite group, and the satisfaction of leadership, there was absolutely no glory to be gained in the Northern Ireland situation.

I understood completely the necessity for restraint and the need to bear in mind the instructions on the Yellow Card. But any aggressive action against the IRA became a gamble not only in which one could lose one's life, but also be tried for manslaughter or murder. For example, if some of us, including the RUC, had not been inside the Ballyford police station when it was attacked, it could have been said that we had no right to open fire when it was only property being damaged!

Of course, it was rightly always the task of inquests to ascertain whether any killings had been lawful or not. And in a civilised society in peacetime this clearly had to be the case. But there was no peace in Northern Ireland and in what kind of war did the Army have to submit to inquests on every member of the enemy killed? In the past, soldiers needed to justify why they didn't destroy the enemy if given the opportunity. The situation in Northern Ireland was the opposite to this, and from our point of view quite bizarre.

It was almost certainly because of these considerations that Diana and Howard's ordeal left me so strangely unmoved. In one sense, I was indeed a bastard as Diana had said, because I felt that she (and Howard) bloody well needed to know what was going on in the real world of terrorism. And as I walked slowly towards my van along the peaceful main street of Postling I reflected that this was only part of the beginning. As the Provisionals shifted their efforts to the mainland of Britain, and their pyrotechnics and 'spectaculars' such as the mortaring of the cabinet at Downing Street increased, so people like Diana and Howard, would soon realise just how helpless they were in a situation which they had never encountered on such a scale in their lives.

Very little in our institutions could possibly cope with the dilemmas with which we were being presented, because they had never evolved in situations where an enemy could act with such impunity in our midst. Of course, given the entirely changed circumstances, the judiciary was caught out with tragic miscarriages of justice, while at the same time the real perpetrators somehow escaped. In the ensuing mayhem, the injustice of the deaths and maiming of the victims seemed entirely forgotten.

However, it was necessary to put these thoughts from my mind and to concentrate upon the positive. I had somehow eluded the IRA Active Service Unit (ASU), which had set out to kidnap me in Shropshire, and it was now time to settle into the safe house of Chalk Hill. I drove the remaining few miles to Pelham, which I reached about 4pm. I parked the van in a side street, and walked to Chapman and Co., in the High street.

To my relief Mary was at her desk and Chapman out as usual. She greeted me quite warmly, and said, 'I hope you had a good trip. I wondered when you were going to arrive as we close at 5.30. But you said that you'd be here today.'

I looked at her more closely. She appeared slightly older than I remembered, but more relaxed and still seemed quite friendly.

'Everything's in order,' she said, 'and there's been no problem with the payment. Mr Chapman said you could have the keys.'

'I should hope so,' I said. 'There never was any problem at all - only your boss seemed to want to make one. I'm surprised because I thought you were in the business of selling houses.'

'Well, he has a lot to think about, and we've had problems over payment recently.' Then she paused as if there was something else she was about to tell me, and I made a guess.

'What about those two men in the van?' I asked.' Have they appeared again.'

'Well - that's what I was going to tell you. They came back and wanted to rent the cottage...'

'But it had already been sold,' I said. 'You must have told them that.'

'Well, don't mention this to Mr Chapman, but they offered him a lot of money for two months rent. He wanted Mr Strickland to accept that and delay the sale to you.'

'How much did they offer - I'm interested - and of course I won't say anything to Chapman.'

'£1000 for two months, I think. Anyway, £500 a month for up to six months if they could rent the place longer.'

'So what happened?'

'Well at that rate, Chapman said they could rent a better place, and they've rented Coldharbour farmhouse for six months.'

'Where's that?' I asked. 'And who owns it anyway?'

'It belongs to a Mr and Mrs Gates, who have a retirement bungalow in Barham. The farm is being managed for them by someone who lives in their own farmhouse, and the Gates were happy to earn £3000 clear in six months while they make up their minds about Coldharbour.'

'Yes, but where is Coldharbour farmhouse? I mean is it near here or Chalk Hill?'

'It's up on the edge of the beech woods on the high ground east of Barham. Very isolated indeed. The Gates found it really too much for them after they retired, especially in winter when those narrow lanes were packed with snow and they were cut off for days.'

'But the big question is, "What the hell are they doing there?" What did they say they were doing?'

'Well, they said they were thinking of starting up a business locally, something to do with agriculture and Ireland being in the EEC and all that. I think they mentioned agricultural chemicals, pesticides and weed killers. Anyway, what they want to do at Coldharbour is no concern of ours. Mr Chapman gets 15% from the rent, and charges for the general management as well, including the Short Term Agreement, so we have no complaints.'

'But why didn't they open an office here in Pelham - surely they don't need a farmhouse.'

'Look - I just don't know,' Mary said, beginning to sound irritated. 'But they said they needed outhouses, somewhere to stack the fertilisers, and were very happy with Coldharbour.'

I decided to leave it. There was no point in antagonising Mary Renfrew by criticising Chapman's business deals, and anyway her job depended on such arrangements. But the more I thought about it the more suspicious and uneasy I became. 'Agricultural chemicals' - I bet they needed agricultural chemicals - especially sulphate of ammonia, a prime ingredient for 'home made' high explosives. Of course, I could not be sure, but it seemed to me that by an extraordinarily unlucky chance I had come across yet another IRA Active Service Unit and this time in the process of setting up a safe house, perhaps even a base in Britain. I was surprised they mentioned the need for outhouses for their goods. But perhaps it was better for them to give an explanation to Chapman now, in case someone reported to him or the Gates that they were doing business and storing things, but I just didn't know.

'All right, Mary,' I said. 'I won't ask you about them again.' And then, it suddenly seemed opportune for me to get to know her better.

'Look - what about a drink when you've finished work. Let's find a comfortable pub and have a chat before I drive on to Chalk Hill.'

Mary looked slightly worried, and frowned.

'I don't know what time Mr Chapman will be back. Although we close at 5.30, I'll have to wait a while and discuss any work for tomorrow.' I noted that Mary certainly wasn't going to jump at the opportunity, but decided to persevere. Perhaps she didn't want Chapman to know she was getting familiar with an odd customer like me. But in any case, it was clear that if I was going to get any further socially with Mary, somehow I had to prevail over her boss.

'Well - that's all right. I have to buy some stores. So let's say we meet at your designated pub at 6. Anyway, I'll wait for you there until 6.30.'

Mary nodded, and suggested the Kings Arms, a nearby pub, at just after 6.

I wandered round the High Street for a while, and bought some stores at a grocery as well as milk, which I carried back to the van before I went to meet Mary.

The Kings Arms turned out to be a very pleasant old Kentish pub, tastefully refurbished, and already half full with a very lively crowd. Some of them tourists, staying in the accommodation above the bar and dining room on the ground floor. I arrived slightly early and found some good seats in an alcove next to a small fireplace where we could chat comfortably. Mary arrived shortly after 6, and I bought her a white wine. I had already sampled some local ale before she arrived, and continued with that for the rest of the evening. I told her I was extremely hungry and we both had plates of soup with brown bread. She made it plain she did not want to stay for a meal as I would have liked.

Mary was fidgety and slightly ill at ease when she arrived, but soon began to relax after a couple of glasses of wine. But I knew it was going to be tough going as she seemed embarrassed about being recognised by people she knew locally. I got this impression when a rather red faced middle aged man called out to her quite noisily, 'Mary, how's the job going?' and paused near our table clearly curious to find out who I was and to show his familiarity with Mary.

Mary looked up, very briefly, 'Fine - Mr Redpath,' and continued talking to me. The man moved on towards the bar slightly put out by her brusqueness, and my presence apparently, for he didn't look at us on his way back.

'You're ill at ease,' I said after a while.

'What do you mean?'

'I mean you're not really enjoying our encounter. Is something bothering you?'

'No, not really,' and Mary paused twisting her wine glass slowly in her fingers. 'Yes, I suppose you're right. I've just finished a relationship with someone from Pelham, and we often used to come here after work. I haven't returned. This is the first time. I mean coming here with you is the first time I've been back since Anthony and I parted.'

I thought I should continue with the topic of Anthony as it wasn't quite decent perhaps to dispose of him yet.

'So was he working here?' I asked pretending to be interested.

'Yes, he's the local doctor, the only doctor, and I worked as a receptionist in his surgery. We became close after his wife left him, and returned to London with the two children. But things didn't work out. I never wanted to become the doctor's wife, which would have meant being an unpaid receptionist.'

'And did you part amicably - I mean you're not embarrassed to meet him?'

'No - I often see him, and we remain "good friends" as they say, but everyone expected us to get married after his divorce came through. So it's a bit embarrassing to keep on meeting his friends and patients whom I knew from being his receptionist.'

I decided not to ask about her husband, Mr Renfrew, although I wondered about the background of her marriage rather more than her affair with the doctor.

'So, where do you live exactly? Here in Pelham?'

'Yes, in a terraced cottage higher up the hill overlooking the village. It's very comfortable, and very convenient for working in the High Street. So much easier than the time I lived and worked in London, when sometimes it took me nearly an hour even from Wimbledon to get to the office. I was very lucky indeed to find a job with Mr Chapman because I need the money if I'm to remain here.'

Mary suddenly turned the conversation round to me. 'What about you? Do you intend to live at Chalk Hill for some time? Or will you be moving on in a while?'

'I intend to remain as long as possible,' I said. 'I'll need to earn some money to keep up the mortgage and live a reasonable life. I mean I don't want to give up the van because I can't pay the MOT or the insurance.' We both laughed.

'And how will you earn some money? There are few jobs around Pelham, although you might apply for a Chunnel job. Do you speak French? They want French speakers.'

'Well, I've a reading knowledge of French, although my conversation's a bit rusty. But I'm going to try and work at home writing.'

'Writing what exactly?' asked Mary dubiously.

'Well, basically free-lancing articles, short stories. Perhaps even a book on the countryside, or the destruction of it. And once my leave is over, I might be able to get around the official secrets act, and write something about the situation in Northern Ireland.'

Mary said nothing, so I went on.' It's very difficult to start free lancing. One really needs to get a name first by publishing a book, and work through an agent. But I'll have to send my articles direct to the papers or magazines, and hope for the best. Anyway, there is no harm in trying.'

'And what did you do in the Army? Did you learn any skills there? I mean engineering or whatever. Someone I knew went into engineering after the Army.'

'Yes, he was probably a Sapper, I mean in the Royal Engineers, and his skills would be useful in civvy street. But the only skills I learnt were those to do with killing people in a great number of different ways. I was in the Queen's, you know the old Royal West Kents or the Buffs - their depot is still here in Canterbury.'

There was a pause, and I added, with a laugh, 'That's the problem with the poor bloody infantry, you never learn any skills except plain soldiering.'

Mary made no comment. She didn't even smile, but asked, 'And were you with the Queen's in Northern Ireland?'

'No,' I said, surprised at her getting onto the key question, 'I was with Special Forces. I also worked for Intelligence. So I know a great deal about the situation in Northern Ireland, but I can't write about it - that's the trouble.'

'Yes, but all you know is about the military situation. Do you know anything about how the people feel. What it's like to be a Catholic? Did you ever meet a Catholic family? Stay in their homes? Talk with them as a friend? You see, I'm a Catholic myself... lapsed maybe,' Mary added with a laugh. 'But the picture I get from Irish friends, some of them from the Republic is very different from yours, I'm sure.'

'Of course,' I said, 'the Catholic view, and the Protestant view for that matter, is going to be very different from mine. And you're right, all of us in the Army and especially the Special Forces were almost completely isolated from the Catholic civilian population. But that doesn't mean I've have no idea how Catholics feel. I used to hear how they feel almost every day of my life. If they didn't say it - they certainly looked it.'

'Yes, but you're talking about the negative things. How they felt about the British Army - you always heard all the hate, never about their love of family, friends, the good things about them - their humour, their hospitality, and you must have missed the greatest gift of the Irish, their capacity for friendship.'

'You're right,' I said, quite sincerely, 'but remember, the Army was locked into this situation long before I went to Northern Ireland. When the Queen's first went to Belfast in 1969, before Bloody Sunday, they were openly welcomed by the Catholics, even in the Falls Road for Christ's sake! But that was well before my time.'

We both paused a moment, and I looked around the bar which was rapidly filling up, and it would not be before long that the other seats in our alcove would be occupied. So now was the best time, perhaps even the last time, that I could speak to Mary in comparative privacy, for I still had no idea whether she would go out with me again.

'So you know more about the situation I've come from than I thought. That's good. I need to talk to someone like you. To get another perspective - to hear something positive for a change. But what about you - how come you know the Irish ? You're not Irish surely?'

'Well my name was Mary Farrell, and my father came from Dublin, although my mother was Scottish - a Scots Catholic originally from Glasgow believe it or not. Anyway, I always lived in England although we often went back to Ireland to see my father's relatives. And I went to school in England - a Catholic boarding school - and that's where I lost any traces of an Irish accent which I may have picked up from my father.'

She paused a moment as a couple approached and asked if the seats next to us were unoccupied. Mary indicated they were free, and gave the woman a welcoming smile as she sat down and the man went off to the bar to buy the drinks. Then she leaned slightly closer to me and continued, lowering her voice, 'My father was always a Republican - the longer he stayed in England the more Republican he became. My mother was a Royalist, but loyal to what she called the Catholic succession! She used to go to Catherine of Aragon's tomb in Peterborough cathedral and put flowers on it whenever she had a chance. So there you are - a bit of confusion perhaps!'

'So - have you been back to Ireland recently?'

'No, not since both my parents died the same year in 1988. But I'm at fault for that, because I'm still very welcome in Dublin, despite the fact that I married an Englishman and had no children!'

'Well, as you were divorced, perhaps it was a good thing you didn't start a family,' I said. 'If you had kept the children that would surely have been a big responsibility on your own.'

'Oh no,' Mary answered very forcibly, 'I would liked to have had some kids early, and there is no doubt that I would have kept them. Anthony, my husband, was never interested in having kids until we - he - had made enough money to buy a detached two storey house in a middle class area, somewhere like Sevenoaks. And there's no way now that I am getting married again just to have children.'

A thought occurred to me, in a sense a forbidden one, since I had said the topic would not be raised again, but for some reason I couldn't resist it. 'Well, as you're Irish, perhaps you could make friends with the people who rented Coldharbour. One was called Mr Bailey, wasn't he?'

'Now you mention it, perhaps I might. But I don't see why you should be so suspicious. You'd better watch yourself, you're getting quite paranoid about the Irish. You should really try to snap out of it. You're out of the Army now. Forget the past and enjoy your life at Chalk Hill.'

I thought immediately about my lucky escape from being kidnapped and perhaps killed near Ludlow only that very morning, but I decided to go along with what Mary was saying. 'You're right,' I said, 'but you were also suspicious at first. Remember what you heard one of them say about Chalk Hill? "It's too bloody close!" That's what he said.'

'Yes, but that could mean anything. I mean if they were going to set up some kind of business, perhaps they wanted more privacy. I don't know what the regulations are, that's Mr Chapman's responsibility, but maybe they need planning permission Anyway I saw them in Pelham the other day with a woman, not any one local I think and they were all perfectly relaxed and laughing. In fact, they were looking into the window of that new toyshop, Country Living, the one with all the teddy bears, and other cuddly toys, foxes, badgers and squirrels and all those English country animals which the tourists love.'

'And did they buy anything?' I asked smiling.

'No, but I was amused to see as I passed that they were fascinated by the display in one corner of a very realistic scare crow with brightly coloured clothes.'

'A scarecrow?'

'Yes, in a corner of the window, the display had a painted cardboard background of the countryside, with a scarecrow in front surrounded by sheaves of wheat.'

Our conversation petered out after that, and Mary said it was time she went home and fed her cat. 'I've got a silver tabby called Moonlight and he'll be waiting for me on the doorstep.'

I offered to see her home but she said somewhat curtly that was quite unnecessary. It seemed that our evening had come to an end without any further suggestions of our meeting again on her part, so I said, 'Well - once I've settled in, and organized perhaps you will pay me a visit at Chalk Hill.'

'Well, it would have to be a weekend - I have a lot of things to do in the evenings during the week,' she replied not at all enthusiastically, but she didn't refuse. Perhaps that's her manner, I thought.

We parted outside the Kings Arms amicably enough, and Mary politely said that she'd enjoyed our chat .

Walking back to the van along the High Street, I thought about the evening with Mary, rather than about Diana and Howard and all the other things which had happened on that very eventful day. This was strange because there had been no warmth at all towards me on her part. 'The longest day,' I said aloud to myself with a wry private smile. However, whatever Mary thought about me, I was pleased to find that she was a far more interesting person than I had first thought. Her Irish background meant that I could at least talk to her about Northern Ireland without meeting the usual indifference of the average Englishman.

Now that the bombing had come to Britain there had been a revival of interest, but only in the terms of revenge on the IRA, or the need for the withdrawal of our troops from Northern Ireland, leaving the people there to fight it out on their own, like the warring factions in Lebanon. It was perhaps fortunate that Mary had not explored exactly what I had meant by Special Forces. There was no doubt in my mind she would have been only too aware from her Irish Republican friends what being in the SAS implied, especially since the Gibraltar killings, when her namesake, Mairead Farrell, along with two male members of an ASU had been shot by SAS troopers.

I suddenly found myself opposite the toyshop in the High street which we had just been discussing, and paused to look in the window. The scarecrow was there all right, brightly dressed - red shirt and dark blue coat - with a white *papier maché* face. Below it was the steel tube of a modern birdscarer, one of those filled with gas which make a shotgun like noise regularly every half hour or so. As a joke the eyes of the scarecrow had been painted looking sideways at the metal tube as if alarmed by the modern counterpart.

Quite a clever kind of pun, I thought, and smiled. Perhaps, I was indeed getting paranoid. After all Mary was not the first person to tell me so, and socially at least we had really only just met ! But something began ticking away at the back of my brain like the timing device on a bomb and remained there until one day, fortuitously, I finally made the connection .

When I reached the van it was nearly 8pm, and I realised I had left it a bit late to settle in to Chalk Hill properly, as it would be dark within a couple of hours. I also realised I should have checked with Mary whether the power had been switched on as I had originally arranged with Chapman, but there was nothing I could do about it by then. Anyway, it was not long before the van climbed the steep hill in bottom gear which led to the common.

The hedges were even thicker than I remembered, and I almost drove past the half hidden front gate. One of the sets of keys fitted the padlock on the heavy farm gate at the second entrance to the property, and I drove through this up to a fairly dilapidated looking garage, separate from the main building. It was locked and as I didn't want to waste more time sorting out the key, I left the van outside for the moment, and let myself into the cottage through the front door.

Chapman must have stopped paying the caretaker, for there was no key under the ash log outside the front door, and the grass had grown almost two feet high all round the house. To my relief the power was on, although I had to hunt around for the main switch and fuse box at the back of the kitchen. All the bulbs gave out a dim light, only about 40 watt I guessed. There was no way that evening I was going to try lighting the Aga to check whether it worked. Of course, this was the advantage of having the van close by as a backup. I made tea on the gas cooker, and heated up a tin of baked beans which I ate with buttered toast, sitting at the long dusty kitchen table under the pale glow of a naked bulb covered in cobwebs.

I went upstairs and decided to sleep in the room with the brass bedstead and the view across the orchard with apple laden branches almost touching the windows. I laid a dark green Army groundsheet across the old stained mattress, which was slightly damp, and placed my sleeping bag on top. I also brought up from the van two pillows for the head of the bed. I placed a torch, with a halogen bulb, and a combination radio/alarm clock, on a small table beside the bed. I concealed a razor sharp very long bayonet in its black metal scabbard from a World War 1 Lee-Enfield .303 rifle under the pillows. Then I gently laid my father's shotgun on the floorboards close to the bed, so that while lying on my back I could bend down and pick it up easily with my right hand.

I sat in the kitchen for a while at the long pine table writing up my diary with the additional light of a candle stuck to a chipped blue plate which I found on the mantel piece above the fireplace in the sitting room. There was a lot to record, especially as I wrote down as accurately as possible what people had said to me, as well as the main events of the day. This was sometimes extremely tedious, especially when tired at the end of the day, although I sometimes wrote up the previous day's events the following morning when my mind was alert after a night's sleep. However, although it often seemed a terrible waste of time keeping a detailed diary, it was this which so greatly assisted me in the writing of *A Blackthorn Winter*.

When I finished the last entry, I suddenly felt exhausted, and emotionally drained. I sat with my elbows resting on the table and my hands cupped under my chin for a moment giving away to feelings of despair. I've been discharged, I thought to myself. I'm out of the bloody Army in Northern Ireland and back now in peaceful England. 'But, what the hell's gone wrong?' I asked myself aloud. I remembered Orwell's account of reaching England from the Spanish Civil War and his impressions were part of a myth which I had cherished for many years. I had always thought that his warning at the end of the eulogy could refer only to the threat of German air raids in World War 2, or later after Orwell's death in 1950, to an atomic threat from Russia during the cold war.

Orwell was writing about Southern England in 1936, travelling on the boat train from Dover through Kent, '...it is difficult when you pass that way... to believe that anything is really happening anywhere... Down here it was still the England I had known in my childhood: the railway cuttings smothered in wild flowers, the deep meadows where the shining horses browse and meditate, the slow moving streams bordered by meadows... the pigeons in Trafalgar Square, the red buses, the blue policemen... all sleeping the deep sleep of England, from which I sometimes fear we will never wake until we are jerked out of it by the roar of bombs.'

As Orwell was well aware, that was an idealised picture. And of course the entrance to the Channel Tunnel has destroyed the Kent countryside more than any German bombs during the war. Also, I understood only too well how every landscape has to be seen in the context of events and one's mental perspective at the time of viewing it. Hedgerows in South Armagh, especially around Crossmaglen, evoked for me quite different feelings than hedgerows in Kent! Nevertheless, what Orwell described still very much fitted the landscape around me at Chalk Hill, and his warning about us not being prepared for what was about to happen except by the roar of bombs seemed to be unexpectedly prescient about the IRA campaign in Britain today.

Before going to bed, I went outside the front door. There was no moon, but it was a clear night and the sky burned with stars which silhouetted the roof as I looked back at the house from the front gate. Everything was quiet. No owls hooted, no foxes or deer barked, there was not even the muted roar of traffic from distant roads. The only sound was the faint murmuring of wind in the surrounding trees. It looks like a fine day tomorrow, I thought, and may my fortunes change from now on. While standing motionless with my back against the gate lost in a reverie of exhaustion, a chill mist from the dew gathering on the long grass and dark dank bulk of the surrounding hedges suddenly made me shiver, and decide to go inside. As I walked towards the light from the open front door, I could only hope that somehow I had reached the safe house for which my heart yearned.

Chapter 7

As I awoke I became slowly aware of something strange about the room, not alarming in any way. It was just somehow different from what I had imagined. Of course, I was waking in an unfamiliar bedroom, having just spent the night in the first house I had ever owned, and that partly accounted for my puzzlement. But there was something more. It seemed as if the change was in myself, a change of mood perhaps to a more optimistic frame of mind. Then I realised it was mainly to do with the light. At dawn when I first woke, the whitewashed walls reflected the dull grey of the surrounding mist outside, and then they had begun to glow quite luminously.

Suddenly, I understood the mystery: the room was flooded with light from the rising sun which came in through the open windows and occupied the place by right, as if claiming the cottage as part of its domain. The sun seemed to be asserting that it had been doing this for hundreds of years before I was born, and would be there long after I had gone. A subtle sweet scent of drying grass and ripening fruit from the orchard permeated the bedroom, and I could faintly hear the twittering of swallows in the eaves. A mild summer breeze gently swayed the branches of the apple trees outside the windows and their shadows shivered upon the whitewashed walls.

Looking out, above the trees, a deep blue sky reassured me the day was indeed fine, and the breeze which swayed the trees dispersed the mist. In the long grass and on the slopes behind the orchard, a few poppies blazed, backlit by the sun, and the darker heads of sorrel looked as if they had been steeped in madder. When I went downstairs to light the primus for tea, through the cobwebbed kitchen window the dark blue of the tall delphiniums seemed to be part of the panes like stained glass.

Sitting in an old Windsor chair in the flagstone kitchen with the sun warm on my legs through the wide open back door, I felt a strong and reassuring sense of place. I knew from the title deeds that the cottage had been there from the seventeenth century, and that some kind of rough habitation existed before then. I was also aware that my countrymen had been cultivating these orchard fields beside the common for at least a thousand years, and of course the chalk hill track was even more ancient. This was where the landscape had become England, and now I had my stake in it. I was in the 'Home' counties, in a safe place at last behind the ancient thick hedges, where as Edward Thomas had once written, 'a man can hide because even though the people are not hospitable the land is.'

When I once studied Irish history at university, and the psychology of Irish nationalism as part of my prospective work with Intelligence, I had marvelled at the intensity of their love, and the depth and indelibility of their hate. The Celtic mysticism of the Irish seemed like a disease, but more recently I had begun to understand it. Mary Renfrew was right to warn me about the prejudices which I had inevitably accumulated against the Catholics during my service in Northern Ireland (although she seemed unaware that I had some unease about the Protestants as well), but there was another level, both intellectual as well as emotional at which I admired, indeed envied their cultural homogeneity.

Of course, the Irish were always quarrelling among themselves - and the gunmen murdered one another even though their respective factions were fighting the same enemy, that is, the British Army. Nevertheless, Catholics seemed to stick together, particularly at times of crisis. They were also always united by their grievances. In fact, I often wondered what the Irish would do without their grievances

At any rate those ideas which had once seemed so strange I felt that in studying the Irish I was doing anthropology rather than history or political science, those same ideas were suddenly like storm petrels coming to roost in my brain. Now, like the Irish, I needed to establish boundaries and assert my cultural identity too. We in England seemed to be rapidly losing our identity; but unlike the Irish, the Scots or Welsh, our grievances did not unite us. Rather we were developing into a number of disparate factions, all whingeing on about our demands and rights from the State.

I realised too that in a sense, I was no exception. I also wanted something from the State, the protection of my life from the actions of the Queen's enemies. Yet I knew that the State could not provide that protection. Furthermore, although I was obsessively concerned with ensuring my own survival from the gunmen of the IRA, I was also aware that the violence in Britain was general. The State could no longer even provide protection for key witnesses in drug trials, for example, or for that matter save people from the armed gangs roaming housing estates. So many of our citizens, especially the old and infirm, including those who had fought in Word War 2, now lived out their retirement in varying degrees of anxiety and fear. Not just from terrorist organisations, but rather from their fellow citizens, some of whom were the same age as their grandchildren.

Although these thoughts came into my mind each time I read a newspaper, they were essentially negative, and it was now up to me to live the kind of life I wished to in the circumstances. Not to expect the perfect time and place, but rather to create the right atmosphere in which I could write free from the tensions and anxieties which had been enveloping me since my discharge.

After breakfast in the kitchen at the long table, I decided to explore the environs of the house - my house - I realised with delight. I had been too tired to find the right key and garage the van the previous night, but this was no problem in the morning. While unlocking the padlock, I noticed that someone had recently unscrewed the metal hasp and staple on the doors.

The garage was far bigger than I expected with room for two cars parked one behind the other, and wide enough for me to unload the van under cover. Furthermore, there was a long work bench at the far end with a large black vice firmly screwed into the boards. A grimy Coleman lantern, without a mantle, the metal badly tarnished within the glass, hung above the bench from a hook attached to one of the cross beams below the roof. A cheap metal window overlooking the garden must have been added for additional light for the workbench. I discovered more outhouses at the back of the house, unlocked and in varying states of disrepair. One shed appeared almost full of firewood, mainly ash. An empty chicken house smelt strongly of rats which had been feeding on mouldering grain spilt from rotting sacks.

I felt slightly depressed to see how quickly a place, wooden buildings especially, can become run down once they are left empty. The basis was all there to live the country life, but getting things back into order was going to be a full time job. I thought at once about keeping chickens. Fresh free-range eggs and large fussy clucking hens, as well as a cock crowing in the dawn would fulfil part of the idyll of the rural scene.

I remembered that nineteenth century paintings and watercolours of romanticised rural life often showed a cottage with a duck pond or stream with ducks rather than chickens, although chickens were also popular. Standing nearby in most of these idealised watercolours, especially those by Helen Allingham, would be a young and pretty woman dressed in a long skirt with a white cotton apron in front coming down to a few inches above her ankles to disclose neat quite sexy little leather boots. She was invariably with a child, or holding a baby, standing simply looking at white ducks and hens or feeding them from a folded cloth at her slim waist.

Behind a front hedge, there were often bright splashes of colour, flowers such as hollyhocks and climbing roses. The addition of washing hanging on a line depicted acceptable reality as well as domesticity. A woman at home on her own, the husband obviously at work in the fields, and of course only one or two young children, respectably dressed, and not a ragged brood suggesting poverty. A pond was more romantic than a chicken run and water gave the artist an excuse to paint the ducks.

I let my mind run on with these relaxing thoughts. There was no pond at Chalk Hill, but that was not the problem if I wished to recreate the idyll. It was the Victorian ideal of the cottage woman which had passed into history. No one I knew or had ever met could possibly fulfil that subservient role! For Diana, I knew it would be complete anathema, and rightly so. Continuing this line of thought, I realised that hens needed to be fed regularly, and would tie me down. There was too much general maintenance, tidying, and gardening to think of anything else.

The orchard turned out to be even larger and prettier than I had thought, and the load of ripening apples on the trees was staggering. Some of the yellow cookers were huge. I loved to eat apples in any form, and looked forward to picking them later in the year, although I had no idea where they could be stored. Wood pigeons were nesting high in the crook of gnarled branches, and I saw a pair nuthatches searching for insects in the bark of a tree trunk, sometimes running down head first. No other bird does that, I thought, not even the tree creeper. Ubiquitous collared doves cooed sophorically, and I remembered an afternoon with Diana in the dappled shade of a Shropshire orchard, where after making love in the grass, we both fell asleep to the rhythmic cooing of a pair of turtle doves. 'Comfort me with apples!' I said to her, as I slid my right hand under her blouse when I awoke, but I was not sick of her love, not then anyway.

Thinking about Diana reminded me that I had promised yesterday to phone and explain more about the kidnap attempt to her whenever I had the opportunity. I would need to put her off with more excuses for a while, as her friends at the Zodiac would all inevitably be let into my secret, and that could be very dangerous indeed. Then I had a wild idea of inviting her down to stay with me at Chalk Hill. I did not have to give away the exact location, she could travel by train via London, and meet me at Ashford or Canterbury. I could explain the whole situation and swear her to absolute secrecy. When she returned to Ludlow, any reticence on her part could be put down to the embarrassment of having an affair. But of course this would anger Howard, and then he could be more dangerous than her women friends at the Zodiac.

As I walked through the long grass beneath the trees, a young rabbit bounded away into the hedge, and I realised that deserted Chalk Hill had become something of an unofficial nature reserve. A thick hedge of hawthorn marked the boundary at the top of the orchard with an unlocked barred gate at one end of the hedge, half hidden by the spiky unpruned branches trailing across. It was difficult to open because of the long grass, so I climbed over and found myself on the common. I wandered through the grass towards the downs and soon came across an overgrown bridleway, which became more discernible as the ground steepened at the edge of the downs.

The bridleway turned out to be the same one leading across the common to the road and the spot where I had spent the night in my van over a month ago, and encountered the truculent gamekeeper. Near the foot of the downs as the slope steepened, the path sank beneath the surrounding ground and an unkempt hedge grew on both sides. The mixture of hawthorn, blackthorn, wild plum, and dogwood, provided cover from the wind and sheep droppings and strands of wool were every where. Very old, thick set, gnarled field maples, pollarded perhaps hundreds of years ago interspersed along the hedge, confirmed my view that this was an ancient route. Perhaps one of the pilgrims routes to Canterbury, and before that probably a Neolithic track leading to the high ground of the downs, a ridgeway, I surmised.

Suddenly, the track emerged boldly from the sheltering hedges, and lead steeply to the summit of the downs. The bare chalk showed through the banks of earth and grass on either side, and flints lay everywhere glistening in the sun. The grass was short, cropped by sheep, springy underfoot, and a delight to walk upon. I increased my pace and almost ran, torturing the flesh for a while in a sweet ecstasy of effort.

Before long, the highest point of the route came in sight, and I reached a very weathered milestone set in the sward. The flaking yellow sandstone was partly covered with lichen, which someone had scratched away recently to reveal an illegible inscription. (Later, I was to find this stone marked and labelled as 'Canterbury stone', on the large scale Ordnance Survey map.)

About a hundred yards from the track only about fifty feet higher I could see a concrete trig point, at 700 ft, marking the highest part of the North Downs in this area. As I walked quickly towards it, I nearly fell into a deep slit trench concealed by long grass growing horizontally across its edges. There were more trenches, and tarnished brass rounds of blank 5.62 Army ammunition lying on the grass. A wooden notice confirmed that this was a Ministry of Defence training area, but warned the public to keep out only if an exercise was in progress.

Now, I knew the probable reason why the downland had not been ploughed and remained so well preserved. At last the Army as preserver rather than destroyer, I thought! Unintentionally, of course. But as the Professor of Philosophy at the University of Kent (UKC), used constantly to remind us as students, it is always the unintentional results of our actions, especially if they are harmful, which need to be taken into consideration.

As I strode across the springy turf, I noticed that the grass on the steep southern slope below to my right seemed higher between the sheep tracks, and was intertwined with common purple vetch, the bright yellow spreading heads of birds-foot trefoil and the yellow umbels of horse shoe vetch. I paused a moment to look at the ground more closely, and saw tiny blue speedwells, red clover, the bright yellow of creeping tormentil as well as silverweed. Botanising on chalk was always rewarding, although I never understood how a thin layer of barren soil barely covering the underlying chalk provided such an incredibly wide variety of plants.

I was looking primarily for orchids. Although I knew that the common magenta coloured fragrant orchid would be over by now, I hoped to see a bee orchid, one of the most thrilling botanical finds of my childhood. No such luck today, but a bright blue butterfly flew past and alighted on a blade of coarse grass for a moment. Its wings opened to disclose that it was a male chalk hill blue, slightly paler than the deeper blue of the much rarer adonis. I thought the chalk hill blue was a good omen, a welcoming sign from nature for the new owner of Chalk Hill cottage.

I remembered the master at my preparatory school in Eastbourne, who on long Sunday walks on the South Downs had taught me so much botany and natural history at first hand during a very impressionable age when nothing is forgotten. What pleasure that knowledge had continued to give me in later life! And how so much of it had been deliberately put out of mind while I was in Northern Ireland.

I suddenly recalled one unusually still night in South Armagh, with two SAS troopers in a covert observation post (OP), hidden only a short distance from the border, when I heard a nightingale sing from a nearby copse, and the sudden unexpected joy of it. But it was only a few minutes later that one of our special night sights picked out the three armed figures walking alongside a hedgerow less than 100 yards away. 'Shall I slot them?' one of my troopers whispered eagerly... Again, I jerked my thoughts away from these memories, and continued my walk along the greensward of the downs.

I realised that I was now on part of an ancient ridgeway, and heading towards an isolated ring of trees less than a mile away still on the summit of the ridge, before it dropped steeply for several hundred feet, and then swinging to the south, rose equally steeply to a separate rounded summit which looked so symmetrical I wondered whether it was man made. Occasional hawthorn and bramble provided cover for birds, although I spotted nothing more unusual than a whitethroat. Larks rose in front of me as I walked, and their sweet song rained from the sky almost continuously. What joy to be alive!

Looking up at the larks, hands trying to shield my eyes from the sun, I saw the hunting kestrel hovering. It hung there in the blue, defying gravity, its long wings flickering, swivelling and pivoting to meet the wind. Tail feathers down and spread out like a fan, head absolutely steady and bowed to reveal its blue grey crown, dark eyes with yellow ceres intensely searching the ground far below. After a while, shifting position, the kestrel swung across the sky as if on a wire. Then, to get closer to its prey, the falcon banked and descended with outstretched wings showing its distinctive rufous feathers. It hovered again, much nearer to me than before, suddenly stooping at great speed to catch something in the grass, probably a vole, a hundred feet below.

Most country people love kestrels, and I regarded seeing it as yet another good omen like my glimpsing the chalk hill blue at the beginning of my walk. There is a magic about them which defies common description. Only a poet like Gerard Manley Hopkins can do justice to these sprites who sow and plough the wind.

I walked on as far as the ring of trees, a mixture of wind bent beech, sycamore, and hawthorn. I halted a while before continuing down a steep slope to a field of grazing cattle, and then climbed to the summit of the rounded hill. The view was exhilarating: fields and hedgerows stretched away to the south, the chequered pattern brightened by vivid rectangular patches of bright yellow mustard, and the pale misty blue of linseed flowers.

It was a relief not having to scrutinise every inch of the countryside below through field glasses from a covert OP with all the tensions which such a responsibility entailed. I let my mind wander and thoughts emerge as they came, although I could not lose completely my perspective as a soldier. So as I viewed this landscape, I thought of all those men and women, who in a sense, had risked their lives or died for it in so many wars. Not all of them would have come from the countryside of course, but this ancient landscape still represented some of the ideals for which so many of my countrymen, especially Kentish men and men of Kent, were willing to fight.

For many in the First World War, sailing to France from Dover or Folkestone, stationed perhaps at Shorncliffe, like Edward Thomas, and Wilfred Owen, the landscape of Kent could have been their last memory of England before oblivion in the mud of

Flanders. From these fields, farmhouses, hamlets, and villages below me, on certain days when the wind was right during the First World War, people heard the steady low growl of guns from the distant fronts in France. How many of them must have paused in their work, and looked at one another, reminded by the sound of guns, that battles were being fought at that very moment in which friends and relatives lay maimed or dying. And each day, the dread of bad news from the postman cycling down the leafy lanes, that civic messenger of death in a dark blue uniform, with a telegram from the War Office.

Continuing my reflections, and letting my historical imagination have full rein for a pleasant change, I realised that from this same hill, during the Battle of Britain in the summer of 1940, there would have been a grandstand view of the combat far above. From my reading, and from photographs, I knew that sometimes the only evidence of the battles being fought against the Luftwaffe, were high altitude vapour trails. However, the combat often came closer to the ground, and observers could identify the planes, friend or foe. Suddenly, menacingly loud and close, the roar of aircraft engines, the rapid rattle of machine gun fire from Spitfires and Hurricanes, and the staccato detonations of cannons from German fighters and bombers, both sides out for the kill.

As I left the summit, and prepared to return the way I had come, I realised that the countryside is far more than an area in which one might happen to live and commute. We gain from our knowledge, for its resources are much greater than ours, serving generations. I knew that this morning's walk had given me a great sense of place which would grow as I repeated it throughout the changing seasons. I could see myself as part of a familiar landscape, and increasingly reassured of my rightful place in it. That is why the tiredness at the end of such a walk becomes almost a benediction. Moreover, at last after my years as a soldier in Northern Ireland, and so often exhausted from extensive patrolling, I would now be tired walking English miles and over Kentish earth. What more, I thought, could a man possibly want?

Thinking about the past of the people, the countryside around me, my own emotional and historical relationship with the landscape, helped me to understand why the Catholics in Northern Ireland wanted to re-establish their identity with the State which had been divided for so long by the reality and brutality of history. This was all going on in my mind mainly unconsciously, as I too began to discover my own identity as a civilian rather than as a soldier. This did not mean that my prejudices suddenly disappeared, rather that I began to think more deeply about the nature of the situation in which I had become involved as a soldier in Ulster.

I needed to think imaginatively in the SAS, and just as importantly to think positively, but always the main purpose was the fulfilment of a mission. Killing was my business and survival my hope. Group survival as well as individual survival. Now, I was free to think positively in quite another way, and to work out a different philosophy to suit my changed circumstances.

As I walked back towards Chalk Hill elated by that perfect morning on the North Downs, I tried hard not to think about anything negative which might disturb the positive mood engendered by the walk However, I was more or less forced to consider the reality of my situation because it was this which stood between me and my desire for normal living.

My main problem was that I was being hunted by a Provisional IRA Active Service Unit, and needed to continue lying low. I could only hope that after a while, this particular ASU would be diverted to something else especially as any experienced gunman or explosive expert brought over from Ireland to deal with me would be only for a limited time. So, perhaps my case might be overtaken by other more important events in Ulster or even in England, and my life could return to normal.

Unfortunately, I was still also under the impression that by some extraordinary chance I had encountered yet another ASU here in Kent. Yet, despite these suspicions I now realised I should try and take Mary Renfrew's advice and snap out of these paranoid inferences so I could relax and enjoy my newly found safe house at Chalk Hill. I had found the right place in an ideal environment - now it was time to get in the right frame of mind as well.

Soon I was approaching the back gate of my property and climbing over it into my orchard. As I walked through the long grass towards the cottage, I thought I heard voices, and then saw two figures standing with their backs towards me under the apple trees. One was a quite short and stocky man, and the other a blonde young woman. They were both looking towards my house, and talking.

I paused a moment watching them, and as I did so, the man turned round, saw me and alerted his companion to my presence. I recognised him at once, the truculent gamekeeper I had encountered on the common when I first arrived over a month ago.

They both seemed nonplussed and simply stared at me. I realised that the gamekeeper knew he was a trespassing and appeared quite embarrassed to have been caught out, although he was still not sure that I was the owner of the property.

'Good morning. Or rather good afternoon,' I said looking at my watch. 'What are you people doing here?'

The gamekeeper recovered himself, and said, 'Are you the new owner?'

I walked right up to them, 'Yes - I arrived last night. But who are you?'

'I've been looking after this place for Chapman and Co., for nearly a year now. Mrs Renfrew did tell me the new owner was arriving some time this month, but the place looked empty. So I was just checking to see whether things were all right.'

I decided not to make any more enemies, and extended my hand. 'I'm much obliged for your help. I'm Mark Wynstanley.'

The gamekeeper reluctantly shook my hand. After all I had more or less forced him to, but he did not smile or even pretend to be friendly, or introduce himself. I also formally shook the hand of the young woman with him, and said, 'But you still haven't told me who you are.'

'I'm Tom Oakshott, Colonel Crundale's gamekeeper, and...'

'And I'm Claire Crundale. I live in the Grange just up the road.'

Claire was a knockout. Finely chiselled features, bright blue eyes, very fresh complexion, naturally blonde dense curly hair, and a slim trim figure. Aged about 21 or 22 I guessed. She smiled at me, perfectly friendly, and full of a young woman's curiosity about her new neighbour. I asked whether she was related to Captain Crundale, and she explained that Colonel Crundale was her father and that her eldest brother was Captain Richard Crundale.

'I look forward to meeting your brother sometime. I heard from Mary Renfrew that he was in the Army and in Northern Ireland. I was in the Army too, a Captain in the Queen's, and also in Northern Ireland. I left the Army about six months ago, and now I suppose I'm a cottager!'

Claire laughed, and said, 'My brother's taken early retirement too, but I don't think he's enjoying it much. Richard was in the Green Jackets. Anyway, I'm sure he'll be pleased to meet you. I think he finds us all a bit boring - doesn't he Tom?'

Oakshott did not reply. He was plainly put out when I started up a conversation with Claire. It was partly a class thing, I suppose, my accent and Army officer background, which I had emphasised a bit because the Crundales were obviously a military family and this was part of their frame of reference. Furthermore, here was I apparently claiming social equality with Oakshott's employers, and he knew I was the same man he'd treated like a gypsy when we had met previously on the common. And now I had caught him trespassing, and was being very polite about it which must have all been a bit galling.

'Which way did you come in?' I asked, and Claire said that they had just strolled over from the Grange via the common at the back, and would return the same way. Oakshott was already moving off, when I spoke to Claire again.

'Are you at university or what?'

'Well, I graduated last year at Canterbury - UKC.'

'Really? I was at UKC too! What were you studying?'

'Anthropology. I'm taking a year off. Then I hope to do an MA.'

'That's interesting. I did anthropology too as well as political science, and history. But that would have been well before your time - about ten years ago in fact.'

We chatted on for a while, finding similar interests. Claire spoke in a lively, animated way and seemed very bright indeed with a good sense of humour, which means I suppose that she laughed at my wry jokes. We hit it off at once, to the evident chagrin of Oakshott, who looked quite surly.

'Come on Miss,' he said. 'We have to go. I'm late already.'

'You'd better go, Claire' I said, using her first name, and taking the risk of too early familiarity. 'But we must meet again soon.'

'Yes, we must,' Claire said without hesitation, and a warm smile. 'I'll invite you over to meet Richard.'

Walking down to the cottage through the orchard, I looked back for a moment and saw that Claire and Tom Oakshott had halted a moment. She had her right hand on Oakshott's left shoulder and was speaking to him very earnestly, with a look of concern on her face as if she was reassuring him about something. They are quite close, in some way or other, I thought. It was then I realised that I had seen Claire twice before. She was the slim 'boyish' figure standing beside Oakshott after he had fired at the sparrowhawk and who then appeared to be remonstrating with him. She was also the 'slender figure' standing beside the man at the front door of the Grange when I had driven past that late evening on my first visit to Chalk Hill.

Anyway, it was pleasant to speak to a woman who apparently reciprocated ones friendly feelings and hopefully without any of the sudden changes of mood I associated with Mary Renfrew. And it was a relief not to be sparring about my Army career with Diana, on the defensive the whole time, standing up for the things I believed in while she and her friends sneered at them. Of course, Claire was much younger than me, and less experienced with men than the older women. Perhaps she was more open because she had not been through all the bitterness of divorce and separation of Mary, and coming from a military family, unlike Diana, Claire still thought that soldiering was an honourable profession.

Comparing Diana with Claire reminded me again that I must try and phone her today, and to do this, I would have to go to Pelham. It was now just after 1pm, and I suddenly felt both hungry and thirsty. The whole morning had gone on my walk across the downs, and I still had nothing organised in the kitchen. The Aga would need firewood, the ash logs would have to be split, and I had no idea whether the flues needed cleaning. So once again, I was glad of the 'galley' in the van. Lunch had to consist of tinned vegetable soup, bread, butter, and a mug of strong tea.

By 2pm I was on my way to Pelham, and bought fresh fruit and vegetables, as well as other stores before phoning Diana at the Zodiac in Ludlow, getting the number from enquiries. I told Diana that I didn't really want to explain things on her office phone, and that I would try and get her at home once I found a suitable phone box closer to my cottage. To my surprise, perhaps because she was speaking from the shop, Diana seemed quite calm, and told me not to worry. 'I am going to collect the Morris tomorrow,' she said, 'and drive it back to your mother in the evening when I return from work. The police have got something else on their hands at the moment, I think and don't seem to want to question us further - at the moment anyway. So you can leave all your excuses until later.' She paused and added, 'Anyway, Howard and I have decided we just don't want to become involved any further.'

In a way her sudden change of attitude suited me, but I wondered whether it might be easier for my mother to have someone like Diana, who was genuinely fond of her, to talk to about my - our - present situation quite frankly. If Diana knew more she might be persuaded to keep an eye on my mother, and let me know from time to time how things were going. It might also be to my advantage, for example, for Diana to understand that I was now out of the Army and trying to settle down to free lance writing to earn my living. However, it was mainly because of my mother's situation that I was prepared to take the security risk of giving away where I lived at Chalk Hill. I was getting both isolated and lonely and needed to return to a more normal living style.

'Well, look Diana, I'm very sorry for what happened, and I know how you must feel. But I've got a suggestion, just an idea, so don't take offence...'

'Like what?' Diana cut in, 'That you come back to Shropshire, apologise and explain the whole thing to me and Howard personally as soon as possible?'

Although she was being sarcastic, I knew at once that Diana still had not really understood my situation, and after all - how could she? So, I went ahead, and put my suggestion to her.

'Look, I'm sorry, I simply can't return to Shropshire at the moment. Instead, why don't you come down here to Kent - I am in Kent, and stay with me for a weekend. From London, you can come by train to Canterbury and I'll pick you up. Then I can explain everything and I mean everything.'

'You must be out of your mind! Why on earth should I leave here to stay with you? And how do think Howard's going to react?'

'Well, as I said, it was only a suggestion. But I'll write and give you all the details, although I can't give you my address. But if you come down - the whole mystery will be become clear, so please think about it . Anyway, I'll write.'

'You do that,' Diana replied, and then there was quite a long pause before she continued. 'Howard and his parents are going to

Spain for a holiday in two weeks time, so it will have to be then, or never.'

I don't know why I was so pleasantly surprised at Diana agreeing to stay with me, and thought perhaps it might be to do with the attraction of opposites, something very Freudian perhaps. The sparring, I remember was often very sexually stimulating, but perhaps I was really only concerned about arranging a confidante for my mother, although that too could be an unconscious rationalisation.

I thought about going to see Mary, but decided to return to Chalk Hill, and do some general tidying up, as well as getting the Aga stove going. This was essential as it had a wetback and would heat up hot water for a bath, as well as keeping the large kitchen warm and dry. But before I left, I needed to buy more stores, odds and ends such as 100 watt light bulbs, matches, firelighters, candles, scrubbing brushes, dishcloths and a large container of detergent. Now that my living quarters had suddenly expanded far beyond that of the bunks and galley in the van, I had a lot of extra cleaning and maintenance to do, especially if Diana was coming to stay. At least I could get the kitchen clean and cosy. She would be appalled too if there was no hot water for a bath. Indeed, I would very soon have to make a major shopping trip to Canterbury to buy sheets, pillows, and a powerful vacuum as the cottage was dusty and full of cobwebs.

As I was walking down the High Street on the opposite side of the road to Chapman's, to lessen the chances of my running into Mary, I spotted Mr Bailey coming out of a shop about 30 yards away directly in front of me. Fortunately, he was just about to cross the road, with his head turned away from me keeping a sharp eye out for the stream of holiday traffic travelling south towards Folkestone and the M20.

I was even luckier not to have been recognised by his companion a rather plump woman in her mid-thirties, a lecturer in anthropology at UKC, and a specialist in European anthropology, with considerable personal interest in Ireland. She was Dr Maire Maginnity, an Irish American, whom I knew from my days as a student in the anthropology department at UKC. I remembered that she was totally bound up with the Republican cause, and rumoured to have close links with NORAID. She ran an excellent course on

Spain and Italy, and had a considerable following of students, mainly women.

Dr Maginnity, I recalled, always appeared open and friendly as many Americans seem at first. 'Hya,' or 'Hello there,' she would say when one entered her room, 'What can I do for you?' But if challenged or crossed, she would get angry very quickly. If one persisted in any argument contrary to hers, she would become almost hysterical. She had a full round face, almost Korean in appearance, with very pale blue eyes like a faded watercolour, and a pasty sallow complexion undisguised by any make up. She often dressed in faded blue jeans, and oversize nondescript pullovers. When angry, she would change colour like a chameleon, her face gradually becoming redder, and her eyes would start to protrude, the final certain sign that she was losing control.

I remembered too she was known as 'cuntnip' by some of the more chauvinistic and vulgar male students from the strong mint flavoured gum which she brought back with her after each visit home to New York, and chewed while working on the computer in her room.

I avoided her specialist courses after once experiencing her anger in a seminar when I tried to disagree with her, but she never forgot the incident and remained wary of me. However, I owed her a considerable debt as she unintentionally alerted me early in my studies to the disappointing lack of objectivity in so many academics, and this was invaluable in my subsequent dealings with lecturers and professors who peddled their own theories without any thought of attempting to test them with reality. I did not think that Dr Maginnity knew I had joined the Army, but on the other hand, I would be surprised if she had not read about the ambush at Ballyford, and may well have seen my name in the *Republican News*.

I was quite certain that neither of them had seen me, and as the traffic served as a kind of moving screen for my observations, I followed them, keeping on the opposite side of the road. They walked north along the High Street, where Dr Maginnity had parked her dark blue Ford Fiesta opposite a coffee shop. Bailey was carrying quite a heavy holdall, and heaved this up into the boot, of the Fiesta, before they drove off in the direction of Barham.

'Well, well,' I said aloud. 'The plot thickens!'

A passer by stared at me a moment, and I realised that I was talking to myself and smiling idiotically for some reason, for God knows there was nothing to be amused about. I felt curiously elated too and this must have been because of a sudden rush of adrenalin. Seeing Maginnity with Bailey was like suddenly recognising a 'player' in a crowd from a covert OP in Ulster I felt certain she was up to no good, and as this was the long vac when she usually went back to New York, it simply had to be something important. I remembered that Mary Renfrew had mentioned yesterday that she had seen a woman recently in Pelham with Bailey and his friend, someone she did not recognise as local.

I wandered slowly back to the van, and the more I thought about it, the more I realised that I was onto something big. I felt no desire to discuss my feelings with Mary, or anyone else I knew. Anything I said now would only confirm that I was paranoid. However, I wished that there had been someone I could talk too, a friend I could really trust.

It thus seemed inescapably logical that my theories somehow had to be tested. Otherwise, they would be little better than the ideologically biased opinions which I had encountered in the groves of academe. But where lay reality? Where would I find proof or otherwise of my suspicions?

There were several possibilities, but the key one open to me became increasingly obvious. I simply had to find out what was happening at Coldharbour Farm. Only then could I approach the authorities without risking further adverse reports on my sanity. Although discharged, I was still officially on leave until the end of the year, and subject to Army discipline.

If I informed the police of my suspicions, or even phoned a friend of mine in Army Intelligence, and subsequently Coldharbour proved to be a false alarm, there was a good chance I could end up in the British Army psychiatric unit. Checking out Coldharbour was now my priority. Already, my mind was racing and planning my course of action. This would mean going in at night, starting with the outhouses. Perhaps I should begin with a covert OP like Northern Ireland, and then finally a break in once I had gathered sufficient intelligence through surveillance about the number of people there and their movements. Driving the van back to Chalk Hill, I began to have second thoughts, 'sicklied over with the pale caste of thought.' I recalled that there had recently been offers of peace talks from Gerry Adams, and the papers were full of speculation about secret deals with the British government which had been going on for some time. I personally did not trust Adams or his IRA henchmen an inch, but supposing I was wrong. Supposing that this was the public manifestation of high level negotiations, but now coming out in the open and the beginning of a genuine peace initiative on both sides? I doubted whether there would be a cease fire for some time, the IRA had too much going for them at the moment, but one never knew.

Anyway, when I reached the cottage, the tranquillity of the place enveloped me. Perhaps, I should just ignore the whole thing and live my own life. But I remembered my thoughts on the downs that very morning and my feelings about the men who'd died in order that the tranquillity I enjoyed would continue for future generations. And despite the rumours of peace, at the very moment, the enemy was within, perhaps only a few miles away, and very likely up to no good. If I was to be true to myself and the country I still loved despite all its imperfections, it seemed I had no choice except to do something about it.

Chapter 8

The opportunity to make a 'safe' reconnaissance of Coldharbour Farm came far sooner than I expected. It was essential that I not be recognised while carrying it out. As Bailey and his companion had apparently never seen me since our first meeting on the common, I was hopefully out of mind, and wished to remain so. However, the van posed a problem as I knew if either of them saw it again, they would remember me at once. These were desperate men on a dangerous mission and very alert.

Only one narrow lane went past the farm, so there was some risk of being seen if I wished to have a quick look from the van. The safer alternative was to park somewhere in a Barham side street, but even in Barham I could run the risk of the van being recognised as the village was on the main approach route to the farmhouse. There could also be a long return trip to the farm and back, and a lone walker might arouse curiosity, especially as the driver of a car would have a very close view of a pedestrian while passing either way in such narrow lanes.

I checked very carefully on a large scale survey map, and decided to reach the farm from the more remote wooded countryside to the west and the opposite direction to Barham. I planned to park at the turn off to a side road leading into the woods where, if noticed, it would look as if the driver and anyone else in the van had gone for a walk. From there I intended to approach Coldharbour on foot as there were woods almost all the way, and I could disappear into the undergrowth if I heard a vehicle coming.

Then, to my surprise, Claire appeared at my front door the very afternoon I had decided to make the recce, and just as I was about to leave. In fact, I was already wearing black jeans and a dark green cotton shirt for the trip, inconspicuous, and not too obviously military. I was packing a Canon AE1, SLR camera with a zoom telephoto lens and loaded with 400 ASA Fujicolor film, into an olive green canvas satchel with a broad black nylon carrying strap, when I heard a car stop on the road and then someone knocking on the front door. Claire seemed somewhat shy at first, and said she had just come to pass on a message from her brother, Richard. He was interested in meeting me and suggested I came round to the Grange for a drink early one evening the following week.

I thanked her and accepted the invitation at once. Claire seemed reluctant to enter the cottage, but when we got talking, agreed to park a recent acquisition, her blue Triumph sports car, safely off the narrow road, and inside the side gate. My admiration of the car went down well, and I sat in the driver's seat to get the feel of being in a sports car again, which was so low down and near the road after the height of the van. I said how much I liked the leather upholstery, and the polished wood instrument panel with its rev. counter.

Despite her initial shyness, Claire appeared in no hurry to go so I took my chance and said, 'If you have the time Claire I should love a drive in the Triumph. We don't have to go far. You can take me somewhere just to get the feel of the thing. Don't worry, I'm not asking to drive it myself.'

Claire laughed, and seemed delighted to show off her new car. 'All right. I'm free this afternoon anyway. So where would you like to go?'

'I love walking,' I explained, leaning back in the driver's seat of the Triumph, and stretching my arms, 'and I want to look at a bit of wild country just west of Barham. I was just getting ready to drive over there myself, but it would be much more fun with you.'

Claire looked puzzled, so I continued. 'According to the map, there's a long narrow valley between steep wooded hills with a stream at the bottom called Alderbourne, and there's a bridleway along it which looks interesting. A road runs down to the valley too from Barham, just past a farm called Coldharbour. It's marked as one in four on the map, so I hope your brakes are all right!'

'Yes, I know the place, Claire said, 'Last summer I went there with Tom to see the woodcock. They do that strange flight over the trees at dusk, 'roding' I think it's called. Otherwise you'd never see them.'

I moved out of the driver's seat, and stood in the road, watching for traffic, while Claire drove out through the open gate and after I closed it we set off for Coldharbour. She drove down the steep hill to Highdene, skilfully using low gears I noticed, rather than the brakes, obviously a very good driver, fast and safe. We soon reached Pelham and then onto Barham turning left and west at the northern end of the village.

There was little traffic up the side road, although only a short way from Barham, we negotiated our way past a tractor, with a middle aged farmhand driving it dressed in an old waxed jacket with the hood up for some reason although it was not raining or cold. He hardly turned round, and it was not until I saw his face in the driving mirror when we passed that I realized it was Bailey.

I doubted very much he recognised me, but following us on the tractor meant I had little time to stop opposite Coldharbour. The farmhouse and its cluster of adjacent buildings was not visible from the road because of a hedge, but when we reached the gated entrance to a private drive of about 100 yards planted with beech, which also prevented a clear view of the house, I could still see with a sinking heart that the place looked like a fortified farmhouse in the Dordogne.

The massive flintstone walls of a high barn also partly obscured the farmhouse, and there was a barred gate at the entrance to the outer buildings, possibly old stables, and some kind of an inner yard at the back of the house. The front gate had a new Kent County Council sign on it, 'This public right of way has been diverted by statutory order. Please follow waymarkers.' I then remembered the public footpath I had seen marked on my Ordnance Survey map. So somehow this had been changed.

Anyway as Bailey was still a few minutes behind us on the tractor, and no one else visible, I asked Claire to stop and stood in my seat to look over her head. My camera was already in my hands, and I took 3 quick successive shots of the buildings and drive using the zoom.

Just after I had taken the photos, and while still standing , alert for the sound of the tractor, I thought I saw a spectacled face at the top window of the barn. Perhaps it was paranoia, but I suddenly came to the conclusion that the 'spectacles' were field glasses.

'OK. Let's go,' I said to Claire as I sat down. She looked at me in surprise, and paused as if expecting some kind of immediate explanation for our halt and my photos.

'Go! Go! Go!' I repeated in some urgency as I could hear the sound of the tractor approaching.

Claire shot off in first gear, and we were out of sight before I had time to put on my seat belt.

'What on earth was all that about?' Claire asked as we left the hedgerows and entered the cool green depth of the woods, and drove through dappled shadows, with tall bracken scraping the car.

I did not reply at once, but waited until we reached the side road leading through the beech woods on our left. Around the turnoff, the undergrowth had been cut and the trees thinned. Sunlight lit up a grassy verge near a locked gate about 20 yards into the wood across the side road, clearly used by vehicles for tyres had churned up the mud now caked and dried.

Claire parked facing an old fence line to the left of the gate partly hidden by brambles and bracken. The Triumph was sufficiently far off the road, and into the woodland and undergrowth to be concealed from approaching traffic until it passed opposite the gate. I realised at once that this was an ideal place to park the van when I next approached Coldharbour from the countryside to the west.

I faced Claire who was still sitting with her hands on the wheel, obviously puzzled by my behaviour and waiting for my reply.

'Well, I do owe you an explanation, but it's not going to be that easy. The thing is I suspect the people who have rented Coldharbour are up to no good.'

'Really? What on earth do you mean?'

I took a deep breath, and decided to confide in her. I felt uneasy about doing so, although I did not realise, as things turned out, that I was making such a crucial decision.

'I mean that the people now living at Coldharbour may well be an IRA Active Service Unit!'

Claire stared at me without speaking. Her blue eyes widened in surprise, and then narrowed in suspicion or disbelief. I knew she was thinking that things had suddenly turned sour, that the light heartedness of the summer afternoon had gone for ever, and unexpectedly she was dealing with some kind of a madman.

'I know you must be thinking I'm out of my mind, but all the evidence I have so far suggests we have just passed the hideout of an IRA unit. I can't go into it all now, but the people living at Coldharbour were once thinking of renting Chalk Hill. The man we passed on the tractor is probably their UK liaison officer, and we first met by chance on the common near Chalk Hill just after I arrived.'

'Well then, if all this is true, are you on some special mission? I mean, I thought you were out of the Army now.'

'No, I'm not on any official mission. I've been discharged from the Army. I came across these bastards quite by chance! And luckily, so far, they've not connected me with the Army and my service in Northern Ireland at all.'

'Well - why don't you tell the police? It's up to them to deal with the matter surely?'

'Well - unfortunately it's not quite as easy as that. For various reasons I can't go into now, if I was wrong, it would be held against me by the Army. It might land me in a psychiatric unit.'

'I simply don't understand the background. All this about a psychiatric unit. I realise you haven't the time to explain it properly now. But how have I come into it? Why did you get me to drive you here? I thought we were out for a pleasant ride. I didn't know you had all this in mind!'

I carefully explained as much as I could in the circumstances. I emphasised that it was purely by chance that Claire had called in just as I was about to leave for Coldharbour and why I thought I could have a better initial recce with her rather than in the van. She reluctantly seemed to accept my explanation, for the moment anyway. Then, to my surprise Claire added that she had already been to Coldharbour when she came to see the Woodcocks with Tom, and knew the owners.

She went on, 'I didn't know the Gates had already retired in Barham though. Let's call in to Coldharbour on the way back. I'll pretend I don't know and ask if these people will give me the Gates' new address. We used to get permission from them to walk around the woods. They own about 100 acres of beech I think. Then I can make up my own mind about the tenants of Coldharbour – that's if anyone's there.'

'A brilliant idea! But it's possible they may recognise me,' I said.

'So what? There is surely no reason to suspect you of anything. It's you who suspects them. And if they start running scared when they see us - or acting strangely - then that'll simply back up your story.'

'Fair enough, but do you really want to get involved in this?'

106

'For Christ's sake! It's you who has involved me already. I don't like a mystery. I want to try and clear this matter up at once. So let's see for a start how they react to a casual visit.'

'The Colonel's daughter takes command,' I said facetiously, slightly put out by Claire taking the initiative. 'Coldharbour next stop!'

Claire leaned across me, opened the glove box, and took out a pair of steel rimmed driving glasses with yellow lenses. 'If you're really worried about being recognised - wear these,' she said. 'And look more relaxed - you're just too tense for a joy rider!'

Within a few minutes we were back opposite the drive leading to Coldharbour Farm. Claire stopped a moment, and we both looked towards the farm now about 100 yards away. There was no sign of the tractor or anyone about for that matter.

'This is it then,' said Claire, putting the Triumph into low gear, and slowly cruised along the drive, the flint barn looking more and more like a fortress as we approached. However, to my surprise a barred gate into the yard at the back was open, the huge doors of the barn were open too and I could see the tractor parked inside.

'I'll drive up to the back door of the farmhouse,' said Claire and we stopped right opposite it. As there was still no sign of anyone about, Claire got out of the car, and walked towards the door. I sauntered over to the entrance of the barn and took several wide angle photos of the buildings surreptitiously with the camera pressed against my breast bone while I halted as if looking casually around.

The tractor was only a short distance inside as the black Ford Escort van already took up room behind it. On the right of the van, parked right up against hay bales, I saw two trailers covered in dark green plastic tarpaulins tightly roped down. I went inside, and just as I was about to take a closer look, I heard a noise above me, and realised that someone was about to come down a staircase leading to the loft.

I shot out very quickly and only just in time, for a few seconds later as I was standing by the Triumph, breathing heavily, the back door of the farmhouse opened and a young woman appeared. She stared at Claire who said something to her which I did not hear.

The woman looked across the yard at me before replying, and then shook her head at Claire. She looked up again, this time in the direction of the barn, and held up the palm of her right hand as if signalling to someone to wait a moment. Both Claire and I turned to look at the entrance to the barn where we saw a man in a grey cloth cap standing sideways watching us intently from a position in front of the tractor. His right shoulder was towards us, and his right hand crooked inside his jacket. He said nothing and stood absolutely still. I recognised him at once as the passenger in Bailey's black van when we first met on the common.

I walked slowly to the back door, and as I approached I heard Claire saying, 'Well, my family know the Gates well, and any of us passing usually call in. But if they are not here now, it doesn't matter.'

'What's the story?' I said innocently. 'Where are the Gates?'

'They're living in Barham now,' the woman replied with a broad Irish accent. 'We've rented the place for our business - Agrichemicals.' She paused and then added, 'We must get a notice put up at the entrance.'

The woman seemed relieved at Claire's explanation, relaxed a bit, and smiled at us for the first time. She was unmistakably Irish in appearance, a real 'Ryan's daughter', aged about 28 or 30, very good looking with medium length red hair, her face fresh complexioned and covered with freckles. Dark brown eyes switched their intense gaze from one of us to the other, missing nothing, her brow still slightly ruffled in puzzlement at our presence. She kept darting nervous glances in the direction of the barn, and clearly wanted us out of the way as soon as possible.

I thought it was time to go, but Claire was persistent. 'Have you got the address of the Gates in Barham?' she asked.

For the first time, the woman looked slightly flustered, 'No, I can't help you there I'm afraid. Our boss knows of course, but he's not here at the moment.'

I let her off the hook by smiling while I said, 'Don't worry, we'll find out ourselves in Barham, on our way back. Sorry to disturb you and many thanks for your help.'

We both turned round to walk back to the Triumph, and could see the man in the cloth hat still standing in front of the tractor at the door of the barn in the same position.

'Look at his stance,' I whispered to Claire, very quietly out of the corner of my mouth, and as I did so, he disappeared into the building.

While we were leisurely putting on our seat belts, having one last look around, I could see the woman standing at the door watching us off the property. Claire started the car, and as we swung round in the yard, gave her a wave. The woman, now stony faced, just nodded. Clearly, not only was that the end of our visit, but the end of any further visits without arousing suspicion.

Claire turned right at the end of the drive, and continued westwards past the turnoff into the woods where we had parked earlier in the afternoon. 'We'll return home another way,' she said.

We reached the very steep hill which I had noticed on the map. Claire slowed down, revved into low gear and we nosed our way down the narrow road, hoping not to meet anything coming up. There were crossroads at the bottom, and Claire turned sharp left up the valley through beech woods until we reached a grassy parking place just on the other side of a shallow ford, where she stopped the car.

'Now,' she said. 'Let me give you my opinion, and then you can explain yourself further.'

'OK,' I said. 'Go ahead.'

'First, don't ever do that to me again. If you've got some hidden agenda, don't involve me.'

Then before she could continue, I hurriedly interrupted, 'Look I'm sorry, but I just didn't have time to explain, and I realise now you're far more than just a pretty face.'

'That's my point,' Claire said, looking hard at me, 'if you don't have time to explain, then keep me well out of it. And if you're saying you thought of me as some kind of bimbo before you changed your mind, that's not exactly complimentary either.'

Claire paused a moment and I said nothing, waiting for her to continue.

'Secondly, I have absolutely no idea whether those characters at Coldharbour are IRA as you say or not, but I do think there's something quite strange going on. The woman was basically nervous, and certainly not at ease, and for someone starting a business, she was very reticent indeed. I mean they need to advertise themselves, and although they've only just arrived, there was no notice of any kind at the gate either. And the man outside the barn was really spooky, I must say.'

She paused again, this time slightly longer, and looked straight ahead at the ford. A pied wagtail flew up stream in front of us, and as at Chalk Hill I could hear doves in the distance. If only the circumstances were different, I thought.

Then Claire spoke very slowly and deliberately, 'Really, I suppose you should discuss this with my brother Richard. He would be a far better person to give you advice than me. But he was badly wounded in Northern Ireland, a bullet through his left lung, and had to be invalided out as the lung and exit wound took a long time to heal. Anyway, his Army career is over, and he felt very badly about it. He's settled down to looking after the estate now my father's getting older and I don't want Richard unsettled, especially as we - or rather I - don't have any direct evidence that the people at Coldharbour are in any way involved with the IRA.'

'Well, we'll keep Richard out of it then, and you don't have to be involved any more either.'

'But I am involved because of what happened this afternoon. What I don't fully understand is why you can't go to the police. What's all this about being sent to a psychiatric unit?'

I carefully explained my situation in some detail, going right back to the IRA raid on Ballyford when it all started. Claire listened in silence, but she could understand my situation more than most other women I knew because of her family background: both her father and brother having served in the Army.

I did not attempt in any way to arouse her sympathy or whine about my circumstances, but rather to explain how things had ended up for me in the way they had and the dilemma I now faced. Claire was amazed that I had somehow become involved with possibly two Active Service Units at once. She was astounded to hear about my experiences in Shropshire and the IRA kidnapping of Diana and Howard. It was a relief too that she fully agreed I was in real danger if located by the IRA, and she felt this was all the more reason why I should leave an investigation of the people at Coldharbour to someone else.

'Don't be stupid. Leave them alone. Just phone a police station, and suggest they check out the people at Coldharbour. You don't have to give your name or explain,' Claire said. 'You've done your bit. Anyway - there's strong rumours at the moment of secret peace talks with the IRA, and if they ever come off people like you and

Richard will be quite forgotten. Then the only heroes, Richard says, will be the IRA gunmen.'

However, Claire added that Richard had been treated very sympathetically by the Army medical services after he was wounded. He spent a very long time in hospital, and everyone was splendid. His left lung did not heal properly, and had to be removed surgically, and once this was done, Richard himself realised without any pressure from the authorities, that he could no longer remain in the Army. So as Richard had been treated well, Claire was clearly dubious about my fears of the Army psychiatric services. She still thought that I should go to the police at this point, and that my fears of the psychiatrists were exaggerated.

'Thanks for the support and advice,' I said. 'And I'm really grateful for all your help this afternoon. I'll think about what you've said. But I'm still not sure about informing the police. An anonymous phone call is no good. They wouldn't take it seriously enough. There's no point in a local constable cycling up to Coldharbour by himself, because he will end up being shot, and then I would feel responsible. The next step can't be bungled. If the police are to be informed as you said, I'll have to do it myself with all the details, and tell my own people about it at the same time.'

But even as I spoke, I knew in my heart that I was only buying time so that Claire would tell no one for the next few days at least. This would give me the chance of returning to Coldharbour before the ASU had the time to settle in fully, and improve their security. My next visit would need to be soon and at night.

I had looked around the yard for a sensor light, but one had not yet been installed as far as I could see. After all, the group had not been there very long, and were still settling in to start whatever they were up to locally. However, a security light would surely be a priority I thought, and its installation could be imminent, so now was the time for me to break in.

I realised It would be very difficult to get inside the farmhouse, but I had observed that something seemed to be wrong with the barn doors. The old iron hinges had rusted right through and one door was partly kept upright by several hay bales on the inside, and a thick metal stake hammered between the bricks on the outside. This was all to the good, for the trailers inside the barn with their plastic covers concealing quite a high profile load interested me.

'You're very quiet, all of a sudden,' Claire said. 'A penny for your thoughts.'

When I paused a moment thinking what to say, Claire went on, 'Even though I don't know you at all really, I think you are still up to something.'

I did not reply, as my answer would only be misleading. Instead, I changed the subject. 'Have you any time left for a walk? As I said earlier, according to the map, there should be a bridleway running through the woods, parallel to this road.'

'Yes, let's go for a walk. That's what you said we were going to do. We can leave the car here and follow a track up the stream to the bridleway. Then we'll return along the road from about a mile up the valley.'

'So you've been here before?'

'Yes, once with Tom and another time with Richard. The bridleway used to be an old railway line - a side line - abandoned years ago.'

We walked up the track besides the stream, and soon reached the bridleway talking as we climbed. 'I wonder why they built the old railway up here and not down in the valley,' I said.

'Oh, probably because of the river - the Alderbourne. It meanders about and floods quite a lot in winter. In the valley they would have needed to build a lot of bridges. Even up here there's an impressive brick bridge across a side stream. It's dangerous to cross now and the track skirts around it, and then down into the gully where there's a new wooden footbridge.'

The bridleway ran straight through the woods, which were mainly beech with the occasional clumps of oak and stands of ash and hazel. Every now and then we came across coppiced clearings, full of wildflowers, including great displays of rosebay willow herb, odd patches of tall teasel and carpets of purplish bugle with their dark green leaves. Pheasants were everywhere, and plump cock birds ran across the track in front of us.

'Tell me about Tom,' I said. 'Has he been your father's gamekeeper long?'

'About ten years I think. We can't really afford to keep him, but as dad says, we can't afford not to either. Our shooting is also a business you know, and we're part of a syndicate. But what is it you want to know?'

112

'I'm curious as he seemed somewhat hostile the other day - I mean, he wasn't exactly friendly was he?'

'I don't remember. But he is very loyal to Dad and Richard, and everyone else he tends to classify as outsiders. He's even a bit brusque with the shooting guests, but he's a wonderful keeper, works all hours and very conscientious.'

'Is he married?'

Claire looked slightly ill at case when she replied. 'Yes - Tom's married and has two children. But he and his wife, don't see eye to eye. I think she resents all the time he spends on the estate. Up at 6am every day, and sometimes out at night until after midnight checking on poachers. If we hear a shot from the woods at night, we know Tom will soon be out there in the Land Rover. He's got a mobile phone and can speak directly to Dad or Richard, or contact the police for that matter.'

'Quite a dangerous job in a way,' I said.

'Yes, but Tom's used to danger. He was a sergeant in 45 Commando.'

'Well, perhaps I can ask him about that,' I said.

'No - not or a while anyway. Tom's a very private person, and he never talks about the Army. Not even to Richard, and they get on well.'

We came to another coppiced clearing of ash as well as beech, where I asked Claire to stop while I went ahead to take a photo of the sunlit bridleway with her in the foreground. I had learned to treasure such moments in my life, the tall grey, almost silver smooth trunks of the giant beeches, the rotting smell of leaves, the dappled shade along the track, the shrill call of pheasants, the clap of woodpigeons wings as they took off at our approach, and of course, Claire striding along beside me.

When we stared walking again, I said, 'Did you know Tom and I have met before?'

Claire looked quite startled. 'Met before? No. Where? In the Army?'

'No - on your estate,' I said. 'Or rather on the common actually, in June. And that was the point - I had been out for a walk along a right of way on the common, it couldn't have been more legal, yet Tom objected, saying I was disturbing the game.'

'Why? What did he say? What did *you* say?'

'Well, it was all quite unpleasant. As a matter of fact, I think you must have been with Tom very early that morning. I saw the back of someone who could have been you. Neither of you saw me at the time. It was slightly later after you must have gone home that I met Tom.' Claire looked puzzled, so I said, 'Well, do you remember Tom shooting at a sparrowhawk?'

Claire looked at me intently, but did not reply. 'The point is,' I said, 'I've made an enemy of Tom I think, and I can't afford unnecessary enemies. I hope the incident is forgotten, and that we can get on together. You see, because of the IRA threat, I've been forced more or less to live on my own, to keep away from home and my old circle of friends in Shropshire, and Canterbury for that matter. I'm no longer part of any group, I rarely speak to more than one person at a time. And if I do have a conversation, it's always secondary to the reality of my actual life. That's partly why I've enjoyed talking to you so much today.'

Claire looked across at me and smiled. She still said nothing so I went on, 'I wish it was all somehow different though, that I hadn't involved you with my problems. So, returning to Tom, with real enemies out there looking for me, and potential ones on my doorstep, I don't want to make enemies out of potential friends.'

'I shouldn't worry about that. Tom knows who you are now, and after you've seen Richard and met Dad, I sure you can walk where you like. Claire paused and then added with a smile, 'So long as you don't poach anything!'

I smiled too, glad that the conversation had ended amicably, and changed the topic.

'I look forward to meeting Richard, and anyone else you know around here as a matter of fact. As I said, I'm on my own now, and miss the camaraderie of the Army. I miss being in a group, I miss the banter, I miss discussing things, even what I read in the papers!'

'Well, I can understand that,' and Claire gave me a friendly touch on my arm, 'but this is not the most social time of the year. From October, we have shooting parties. Perhaps, you can help us, even if you join the beaters! But over Christmas there are lots of parties, and you will meet people then. Otherwise you will have to join the Folkestone or Hythe tennis clubs, or whatever. Do you play cricket ? There are lots of local clubs.'

114

'No - I haven't played cricket or tennis since I was a school,' I said. 'I am more of a naturalist in my spare time. That's why I thought I might have something in common with Tom. No one like a gamekeeper for really knowing his local countryside.'

'Look- there's the old railway bridge,' said Claire, and through the shade of the trees, I could see the vague outline of a brick structure about fifty yards ahead.

Most of the brick was covered in moss with tweeds and ferns growing out of various crevices. The entrance to the bridge had been partially blocked with tree trunks, and rusting barbed wire, but people over the years had somehow forced their way through. It was possible to get on top of the structure and look down, although we did not bother to do this. Instead, we walked down a steep bank following the bridleway to the stream below where there was a new wooden bridge strong enough for horses and pedestrians.

While standing on the wooden bridge in the deep shade of the gully, I had a sudden feeling of melancholia, an inexplicable feeling of anxiety and threat, held in check only by the presence of Claire. This dark dell had the scent of death about it, as if something terrible had happened here. An ancient ambush, or perhaps an accident, a train and its front carriage toppling over into the stream. I felt old and tired, all my 28 years, and glad of Claire's bright looks and optimism. She also had that rare quality, of knowing when to speak and when to remain silent.

In this pensive mood, while looking at the decaying brick arch of the old railway bridge above, I noticed a track along the right bank of the stream leading to some sort of recess in the brickwork.

'I'm just going along that track to the arch,' I said and walked along the edge of the water which had receded with the summer draught, so I did not have to wade in the stream

Sure enough, there was indeed a recess in the brickwork under the arch, with a few steep moss covered steps going up to a narrow wooden door still black with railway soot and grease. To my surprise, there was a brand new hasp and large padlock on the door. Disappointed like a small boy that I could not enter the 'secret door', I returned to Claire who was still standing on the wooden bridge contemplating the stream.

'There's a room inside the arch,' I said. 'Probably a storeroom for the linesmen in the old days. But someone is still using it, or

115

making sure that no one can get in, because there a brand new padlock on the door.' Then with a laugh, I added, 'Could be the District Council making sure that it's not a meeting place for the local perverts! Animal sacrifices and all that sort of thing!'

Claire smiled and we started to climb the track up to the alignment of the bridleway along the old railway line, both of us glad to get away from the darkness of the damp dell below the bridge, and up into the dappled shade above.

Then, just as we reached level ground, I heard the tractor. It seemed suddenly quite close, and perhaps we had not heard it earlier because we were down in the shelter of the dell. My heart beat faster and the sense of threat returned because I knew at once that it had to be Bailey!

Chapter 9

I gently pulled Claire well off the track into the undergrowth on the edge of the gully and looked down through thick brambles. She was about to speak, but I pressed a forefinger to my lips.

The tractor stopped on the other side of the bridge, and the engine switched off. About a minute later, I could just make out through the bracken and brambles, someone carrying a canvas holdall walking down the track to the stream. The hood was up on his waxed jacket, but I glimpsed his face a moment and there was no doubt that it was indeed Bailey. He disappeared under the arch, and after a pause, I heard faintly what sounded like the door to the room I had discovered being pushed open.

'I think we'd better get moving,' I whispered. 'That was Bailey. The man with the tractor from Coldharbour. I don't think he'll continue this way, but you never know.' As I whispered softly in Claire's ear, the warmth and sweet scent of her hair, suddenly quite deliciously overcame me and I involuntarily kissed her on the cheek. Claire didn't recoil or say anything, so with both hands, I slowly and deliberately turned her face gently round towards me and kissed her full on the lips. It was not premeditated, and we were both probably equally surprised.

Claire looked at me quite intensely for a moment, but still said nothing, so I took her by the arm and we retraced our steps back to the bridleway. Then without a word we walked hurriedly in the opposite direction to the bridge and kept going at the same fast pace for about 150 yards. When we slowed down Claire said, 'What on earth was he doing?'

'That's what I'd like to know. But I've little doubt that our friend Mr Bailey was going into that room under the old bridge. Fetching something or taking it there, maybe. The padlock was his, and the room must be a store, intentionally well away from the house. But it would still be easy to reach. I didn't know that the track entrance where we parked just after visiting Coldharbour was regularly used by Bailey! In fact, I have only just realised that the bridleway we are on is the same one we saw through the gate.'

'I must say, it's all rather strange. Perhaps I should say something to the Gates,' Claire suggested.

'No, please don't say anything to them at all at the moment. If Bailey and Co are up to no good, the fact that someone has seen them using the room under the bridge will put them on their guard. They might even shift what they are storing there, or give them time to think up some kind of explanation. If we're going to mention this to anyone, it has to be the police.'

There was no sound of the tractor following us, so I presumed it was still parked above the bridge or returning directly to Coldharbour. We slowed our pace, enjoying the walk again, and continued our conversation, although after my kiss, Claire clearly had something more on her mind than Bailey and Coldharbour.

'I can't believe,' she said quietly, 'that you don't have a number of girls in tow. I mean why did you do that? We hardly know one another. I've only met you once before.'

'Do you want me to declare my intentions? I asked with a smile. 'You've been really quite amazing this afternoon. I mean I suddenly pushed you into what could be a quite dangerous situation. If those people at Coldharbour are IRA, then you should have been kept well clear of them. I'm sure Richard would agree with that, and I'm really sorry about involving you. I just suddenly felt very grateful, I suppose. And last but not least, of course, you're a very attractive woman. What more can I say?'

'Perhaps you're just lonely,' Claire said. 'And it could have been anyone, I suppose.'

'No! No! It's not like that, I promise you. I'm lonely all right, but that's not the reason for the kiss. I really liked you and then being so close - it was too much of a temptation. Anyway, I'm sorry if I offended you.'

'You didn't offend me,' Claire said, 'but I was surprised so soon after we first met. So it's better to know now where I stand - where you stand if we continue to meet.'

'Well, I haven't got a proper girl friend, a partner or whatever. I know a number of women, but I have no kind of ongoing relationship, if that's the right expression, with any of them.'

'So you are at a bit of a loose end, woman wise, I mean.

'Don't be so cynical. I've genuinely taken to you. You're a very attractive woman as I've already told you, so don't act so surprised. And that's my point, what about you? Am I treading on someone else's feelings? I mean, don't tell me you haven't got a boyfriend either?'

'I have a number of friends,' said Claire 'including someone who wants to marry me. He's a friend of Richard too, in the same regiment as a matter of fact. But I've absolutely no desire to become an Army wife. And anyway, I don't love him, although I'm very fond of him.'

'Well, that's both of us settled, or unsettled,' I said with a laugh, putting my right arm round Claire for a moment, and pulling her slightly towards me. Then I kissed her again, this time a long lingering kiss, and I could feel the warmth from her slim body pressed tight against my cotton shirt.

As we unclasped, Claire sighed deeply and said, 'This is going to complicate a lot of things, I'm afraid, and just as I thought life was becoming simpler.'

'What's the big sigh for Claire? We'll both slowly sort things out and in the meantime, I have the privilege of your company.'

'Privilege of my company! How formal can you get? Don't be so boring!'

'No, I mean it. You're very companionable. I shouldn't have to explain that to a woman. I enjoyed being with you despite everything else that's happened this afternoon. In fact, really for me, you're the only bright thing on the horizon at the moment. But let's talk about us, about you, not about them.'

Claire told me more about herself, her life at the Grange, and her hopes for the future.

'When I got my degree, I had hopes of getting a grant to do some fieldwork overseas, but there's not much chance of that at the moment. You see, I would like to specialise on an Asian topic. I thought of Nepal. Last year I went to Kathmandu with two friends, women friends and then we went on a trek in the Everest region. Up to Everest base camp actually, and it was fabulous.'

'And you'd like to go back as an anthropologist?'

'Exactly! But research grants to go overseas like that are not easy to obtain. And then I doubt if a degree in anthropology would help me get a job. Anthropology can only really be a hobby for people like me these days.'

'So somehow, in the meantime, you are existing. But not too bad an existence surely, living at the Grange. A lot of people would be envious.'

'So you might think. Of course, it's true I enjoy helping Richard run the estate. But he's getting much better now, and soon he'll be able to do it on his own, especially if he gets married and then I would be in the way. A woman has got to have a purpose these days, thank God! Marrying an Army officer, even someone like Charles, whom I have known for years and would let me have a lot of freedom, is still not my idea of having a purpose. I'd still have to do my proper duty as an Army wife that would only be fair to Charles. But what a waste of my life that would be!'

To my surprise Claire had sounded quite angry, almost resentful, as if someone had tried to force her into marriage. Then I thought she was trying to justify her rejection of Charles, who after all had committed no crime it seemed to me in wanting to marry her. Fortunately, I had never even considered the idea of marriage while I was in the Army, especially the SAS. I would have to admit that this could have been partly because the women I met at university were mostly not the marrying kind: they formed partnerships, and such a liaison would never have survived my joining the Army. Certainly not one of them I knew would ever have later accepted the strictures of being the wife of an Army officer.

Determined to enjoy what I could of the present, I put these thoughts from my mind and continued the conversation with Claire as we wandered slowly along the path. Huge spreading oaks appeared more frequently, and already I could see the fresh green leaves of August replacing the old insect eaten ones. Underneath the oaks, massive clumps of bracken filled the glades, and we heard the alarm shriek of blue jays in the distance as they became aware of our approach.

The summer sun slashed through the leafy canopy onto the track, and backlit Claire's blonde hair as she strode deliberately ahead and then turned suddenly to fall into my arms. We stood pressed against one another for brief moments, precious moments in time, which by repetition gave the impression of continuity like the frames on a cine film. If only these woods continued forever, I thought. We would walk on as the seasons changed, the leaves turned to bronze and gold, and then to bare branches, and snowflakes gently falling from dark clouds in a black winter sky.

'You look sad now. What's the matter?' Claire asked.

'Nothing really. I suppose I was just wishing, daydreaming, that this walk could go on forever. That we would never grow tired, that the summer would turn to autumn and we would still be walking together.'

'Happily ever after,' Claire said, and we both laughed.

'Don't mock me, Claire. I was only being sentimental. Something I did not indulge in during my Army years, I can tell you.'

'No, I'm touched. But be careful. You're very vulnerable at the moment. Even in my short experience, I've found that sort of sentimentality leads to tragedy. And we hardly know one another. Let's see how you feel, how I feel, in a few months time.'

I knew Claire was right, that we hardly knew one another, and our mutual attraction had suddenly emerged almost by chance. Its intensity needed to be controlled, especially on my part. Better now to play things coolly, otherwise I could blow it..

Self absorbed as we were, it did not seem long before we came to a narrow track to our right leading downhill, and Claire said, 'This is it. This is the track to the road, and then it's an easy walk back to the car in about half an hour. I suggest you come home and join us for a beer or even supper if you like. No point in waiting until later this week. During the week, we all have afternoon tea in the kitchen about 4, and they will be wondering where I've disappeared to, although Richard knew I was coming over to see you.'

'I'd love to: better than eating in the kitchen on my own at Chalk Hill, especially as I've not got everything properly organised yet. Are you sure it won't be inconvenient. Who does the cooking at the Grange?'

'Mother and I take it in turns. I'm cooking tonight, and there's plenty of food. Only supper mind you, nothing substantial, although you can fill up on bread and cheese!'

We met no traffic walking back to the car along the road, and I realised that the Alderbourne valley was really quite a wild place, and an ideal backdoor approach and exit to Coldharbour, not only for me, but also for the ASU. Every now and then, through hawthorn, dogwood, willow, bramble, and the dark green leaves of alders growing along its banks, we could see the waters of the Alderbourne river flowing gently towards the south.

'There's still some trout in the river, Claire said. 'Richard comes here to fish occasionally, but there's lots of poachers. Anyway, you can buy fresh trout up at the trout farm further along the valley, and pretend you caught them yourself when you get home!'

We crossed the ford over the stream by a wooden footbridge at one side of the road, and I quickly settled back into the passenger seat, and relaxed while Claire started the engine, which coughed and spluttered before suddenly roaring into life. She turned and smiled. Then we were off across the ford and along the wooded valley, bypassing Barham, and up the steep hill to the common and Chalk Hill.

I asked Claire to stop a moment outside my cottage, while I got a coat, and changed my boots for shoes. I didn't ask her in, or kiss her again in the car, and deliberately kept things as light hearted as possible. I knew that in a few minutes, Claire would have to make quite a transformation in front of her family. Not one of them should be given even the faintest inkling of what had happened between us in the short space of one afternoon, for I was very much aware that I was still a complete stranger to them all. So relations between us would have to seem entirely proper without a hint of familiarity.

We turned into the drive at the Grange, and Claire drove round to some old stables at the back where her family parked their cars. As we walked towards the back door and the kitchen, I saw Tom standing by a Range Rover looking at us. Claire waved at him as she went in the back door, and Tom nodded.

I followed Claire slowly and at a little distance, halting outside the back, so she would have the chance to explain why she was late, and about her invitation for me to stay to supper. I turned my ahead away from the door for a moment, towards the yard, and Tom looked directly at me. I was about to smile or give him a wave when I saw from his expression that something was wrong. There was no mistaking his disapproval of my presence at the Grange. Indeed, he looked so strange, so tortured, I suddenly felt that he might be jealous of my friendship with Claire Just as well, I thought, that you don't know how that friendship developed this afternoon.

122

Then I heard my name being called, and saw Claire in the doorway, gesturing me to come in. A brown labrador ran out with its tail wagging, and I patted it on the head as I climbed the two broad stone steps into a small annexe leading through to the kitchen. Claire first introduced me to her mother, Carol, a grey haired slim woman of about 60, who gave me a pleasant welcoming smile, 'Come on in Captain Wynstanley,' she said, still keeping things formal. 'I hear you've been to Coldharbour, and a walk through Covert Woods.'

'Claire didn't tell me the name, but we came back to the car along the Alderbourne.'

Then, with a smile very much on my best behaviour, I added, 'I'm sorry I didn't bring you back a trout. I hear your son Richard fishes there'

'Yes, you'll meet him in a moment, but here is my husband, Alan.'

I shook hands with Colonel Crundale, standing behind her looking slightly puzzled as if he should have been told of my visit about a week ahead. He was tall, with quite a bulky figure, ruddy faced like a traditional countryman, and such clear intensely blue eyes, that I was instantly reminded of Claire's

'Come on through,' he said. 'We were wondering what had happened to you.' Then turning to Claire he continued. 'Tom went out to look for you. No one at Chalk Hill, so we thought that dammed car of yours might have broken down as usual.'

'Come on dad, it's only broken down once, or rather you've only had to fetch me once.'

'Anyway, no harm done - good that you went for a walk,' Colonel Crundale said as I followed him through a sitting room and out onto a small terrace at the side of the house overlooking the main garden.

The terrace and the small lawn just below, was hidden from the road by a high brick wall. Directly below the wall, a flower bed with a wide variety of flowering plants, including delphiniums, hollyhocks, and clumps of lavender at the edge of the grass was being watered by a man with a sprinkler hose in his hand, who appeared not to notice us as we sat down on hardwood seats covered in large brightly coloured cushions.

'Would you like a beer?' Colonel Crundale asked, and then without waiting for my answer, turned towards the figure on the lawn and shouted, 'Richard - come and meet our guest.'

Richard turned towards us, and waved. 'Thanks - I'll be along in a minute. Just got to finish this, and then I can turn the damn thing off.'

Not actually rude, I thought, but certainly in no hurry to meet me. Why should he be, I reasoned putting myself in his place. After all I was not invited for this particular evening, and Claire who goes missing all afternoon, suddenly turns up with a perfect stranger for a meal. It must all seem very odd of her, and me, I suppose. And of course, Claire's rejected suitor, Charles, is a close friend of Richard and in the same regiment, so it might seem disloyal to be too affable at this point. Another person to be kept totally in the dark about Claire and me I concluded.

Colonel Crundale disappeared a moment to fetch two bottles of beer from the fridge, and placed them down on the Indian brass tray where his own half empty bottle was standing. There was an awkward pause in which I looked around desperately for Claire but she was nowhere to be seen. Probably in the kitchen talking to her mother about me, explaining herself no doubt.

'So you've been for a walk up in Covert woods. Haven't been there for years. But Claire has. Many pheasants around?'

'Yes, a very enjoyable walk, and plenty of pheasants. And woodcock, or so Claire tells me.'

The conversation continued in this vein, the Colonel too polite to start asking personal questions, and I was determined on this occasion to follow the old upper class adage, 'Never explain, never complain.' However, he made a tentative try to find out something about me, at least to locate me spatially. 'So are you visiting or do you live around here?'

Before I could answer, Richard appeared, having apparently finished his hosing and we were introduced. He was tall, with blondish hair, and a frank open countenance, a young version of his father, almost a clone. We shook hands and he looked at me quite hard before he sat down, when he addressed most of his remarks to his father.

Colonel Crundale seemed determined to get an answer to his question and said to Richard, 'I was just asking Captain Wynstanley where he lived.'

'I'm sorry, I should have explained. I've bought Chalk Hill Cottage, and last week I met Claire and Tom in my orchard by chance. Tom has been looking after the place for Chapman, the land agent, and didn't know it was occupied.'

'I had no idea Tom was performing this service for Chapman,' said the Colonel. 'Did you Richard?'

'No I didn't,' replied Richard, who seemed put out by the news. 'But I suppose he could have included it with his rounds on the common.'

I noticed that neither the Colonel nor Richard had any interest in the cottage. After all why should they? In their eyes, as part of the county aristocracy, I was indeed no more than a cottager as I had earlier described myself to Claire, and a cottage indicated subservient status. Their only interest was the connection with their employee, Tom, and his caretaker role for Chapman which he had not told them about. Indeed, I now realised that if they had seen me in passing standing at my gate, I would probably have merited little more than a cursory glance. So much for my naive hopes that we would naturally be friendly neighbours. It was only my chance meeting with Claire which had brought me into the Crundale household this evening.

We chatted away and got onto the subject of the Army and Northern Ireland. I told them that I had been in the Queen's, and asked about the Green Jackets, but Richard was not going to be drawn. He said that he had already heard about me and my Army background from Claire. 'I retired from the Army, as no doubt you have heard from Claire, and now I'm settling down to farming and estate management. '

There was a long awkward pause, and then to my surprise Richard asked directly, 'What do you do?'

'Me? Oh - I don't have any estates to run, so I'm going to try some free lance journalism, perhaps starting with articles on country matters.'

I immediately saw from the expression on the Colonel's and Richard's faces that this was not an approved occupation in their eyes - that some executive post in the city perhaps would have been more acceptable..

'Journalism? What sort of paper would you be working for? Not the tabloids, I hope?' asked the Colonel.

'No, not the tabloids, but beggars can't be choosers. As a free lancer I can work for anybody. I thought I would write for those country magazines for a start, *Country Living*, *The Field* perhaps, and if successful, then perhaps I could try for a regular column in a paper, but who knows, I may have to stick to the magazines.'

Then Carol Crundale appeared to say that supper was ready, and we all filed into the spacious kitchen, and seated ourselves at a long pine table already laid with plates and cutlery. Colonel Crundale sat at the end nearest the door leading into the hall, and his wife at the other end. Richard sat next to his father on his right, and I sat beside him and next to Carol Crundale on her left. Claire was opposite me, but she had work to do handing out the dishes while her mother apportioned the meal of Shepherd's pie. There were no vegetables, but plenty of bread and butter, as well as cheese and jam.

Carol Crundale was a charming woman and did her best to put me at ease. She was curious about my buying Chalk Hill cottage, and wondered how I was going to manage in the winter as the place had no heating except for the fires. She asked me about my parents, and I told her my father had been an Army officer and died of a heart attack some years ago, and that my mother still lived at our old home in Shropshire. Her eyes filled with tears, and she said, 'Your poor mother. I expect she's glad you're out of the Army now.' She paused a moment, and looking at Richard said softly, 'We nearly lost our son too.'

However, I noticed that although I sat next to him neither Richard nor his father spoke to me at all. They both talked at length with one another about estate maters and their friends and then became totally immersed in discussing the pros and cons of a new forestry scheme they were engaged in and the replanting programme Once or twice, I looked attentively at them when they were speaking, trying to catch the Colonel's eye, but my efforts passed unnoticed, and neither even glanced in my direction. Indeed, it was as if I did not exist. I began to feel like an intruder, and Claire looked embarrassed.

To my surprise, towards the end of the meal, Richard suddenly turned round in his chair towards me and said in quite a friendly manner, 'I expect you've got a lot to tell us about Northern Ireland, but the truth is that Ulster has not exactly been a topic of conversation in this house for some time - at my request - I must add and we always try and talk about something else.'

'Fair enough,' I said. 'Of course I understand. And anyway, there's no need to talk to me about Northern Ireland or the Army for that matter. Actually I was very interested in hearing your conversation about the estate and forestry plans. It sounds all go to me. But remember you've been out of the Army much longer than I have. I'm in the early stage of settling down and the Army's still very real to me.'

'Well, I don't know why you left. That's your affair, but my guess is that you've got to go through that,' said Richard, turning round in his chair to look at me directly. 'You've got to talk it out the way I did. I could talk about nothing else for months. But really it's all over for us now, and we have to get on with our lives.'

Richard paused a moment, buttering himself a piece of bread, and reached for the apricot jam. 'Remember that if these rumoured peace talks succeed and we have a cease fire and then some kind of peace, you and I will be the bad guys. The villains in fact, and the IRA gunmen and bombers the heroes. There will be no VE or VJ days for us. It's they - the Queen's enemies - who will hold the victory parades, and the remembrance days for the martyrs who died for the cause.'

I was slightly taken aback and said nothing. Richard munched a few mouthfuls and then continued, his tone growing surprisingly bitter.

'Forget about it all as soon as you can. Our government has lost the will to win. There's no way in a democracy like ours and in this increasingly liberal climate that the Provos can be defeated. The situation can only be contained. Meanwhile they can kill our troops whenever they like or blow up anything they want. Our soldiers are just sitting ducks for their snipers with the long range high tech rifles they've got from America. And if they're caught, all that's going to happen is that they'll be with their mates in the Maze for only a few years, swapping their special terrorist skills with everyone else. Or doing some educational course at the British taxpayers expense until their release.'

Then Richard continued just as vehemently, 'And it seems they'll all be let out quite soon after the so called Ceasefire when it comes. On their terms, of course. So put it all behind you. My father told me the first thing an English speaking German said when they captured any of us in the last war was, "For you the war is over." So that's what I'm telling you. And don't think I'm being defeatist. It's the truth, and soon you'll see sure enough I'm right. So put the whole thing behind you and get on with civilian life.'

Every one was silent for a while after this unexpected outburst from Richard, and his father, looked quite embarrassed as if he didn't agree. There were tears in Carol's eyes, but Claire looked approvingly at Richard having hung on his every word. Then she looked hard at me for a moment, and nodded, as if to say, 'Take note of what my brother has said.'

I realised with a bit of a shock that Richard was probably right. While recovering from his physical wound he had also clearly adopted strategies for coping with the psychological stresses of his enforced retirement. His evident immersion in the affairs of the farm and estate, disengagement from the Army, and realistic appraisal of the Northern Ireland situation, which could have been mistaken for cynicism, were all strategies for engendering a positive attitude to his civilian future. And this was possibly one reason why he had ignored me at dinner. He just didn't want to get engaged in talking about the Army, and as neither he nor his father had the faintest literary pretensions, my proposed career as a free lance writer was almost beyond their comprehension.

The lesson of Richard's adjustment was not lost on me, but my position was quite different. I had quite unbelievably somehow got myself involved with two Provo Active Service Units, and they were on my doorstep, not in Northern Ireland. They were here in England out for murder and mayhem. Innocent people were going to be killed. So how could I put them out of mind?

Indeed, fate seemed to have played me a cruel trick - although unlike Richard, I still had my full physical strength and health. But it was clear that in no way could I involve him in my present situation. Here was a man, who unlike me, had through his own efforts, apparently managed to escape from the legacy of the past, and it would be completely selfish to push him back into it.

These reflections made me feel all the more guilty about involving Claire earlier in the day. But at the same time I became more determined to work on my own again. That very morning I had gone through an intense emotional experience on the downs, and felt I simply could not ignore the enemy within whatever the outcome.

We all chatted on for a while, and when Richard and his father left the room, I insisted on helping Clare and her mother with the washing up. Once I had started on the washing up in the sink, Claire suggested her mother relaxed in the sitting room, so we had a chance to talk together in private.

'I like your brother,' I said. 'I admire the way he's adjusted to civilian life and taken up the estate so enthusiastically. And he gave good advice about settling down and putting the past behind me. But as you now know, it's not that easy.'

'Just phone the police as soon as you can,' Claire said very firmly. 'And get yourself out of any responsibility. But don't involve Richard in any way.'

'Of course not,' I said. And I'm really very sorry for getting you involved today.'

I looked around to check whether anyone was still in the kitchen, and gave her a kiss on the forehead. But Claire was slightly uneasy for some reason, and barely managed to smile.

'So when do we meet again?' she asked to my surprise. 'And next time I want to know what the police had to say about Coldharbour. Otherwise, I'll begin to lose patience. That sort of thing just can't go festering on. You have a duty you know.'

'I hardly dared mentioned our next meeting,' I said. 'Because I know you've had time to think a bit since you got home. I know I'm still very much of a stranger. But I'm glad you introduced me to your family.'

'So what does all that mean? You haven't answered my question.'

'Well, what about a visit to Canterbury some time? We could do a bit of shopping, look at the bookshops and have lunch. Maybe walk up to the University. But whatever you suggest.'

129

'A good idea. But don't go near Canterbury on a Saturday morning or Friday afternoon. You won't find a park for hours, and the crowds are awful.'

'All right. What about the day after tomorrow - Thursday - I can pick you up in the van about 9am or earlier if you like. And on the way back we can have something to eat at my place. Then I added with a smile, 'Afternoon tea if you're on cooking duties at home.'

Claire looked quite pleased, but I knew this was a tricky time in our relationship and I could blow it at any moment with an invitation to come inside Chalk Hill on her own. She seemed independent minded with adventurous ideas, but her family had become very closely knit after Richard's wounding and lucky escape from death, so they were very much her priority at the moment. I would try and fit in somehow, but they were all clearly decent people in an old fashioned Orwellian sense, so there should be no problem. Of course, they were local 'county' with a long history of land ownership in Kent which my parents could not match. But it was Richard who would inherit the Grange, and thus his potential partners, and the nature of their eventual relationship which would come in for the most scrutiny.

'Well, I'd better be going,' I said. 'It was nice of you to invite me, but everyone has lots to do I'm sure, so I'll say goodbye to your parents and be off home. And I'll walk - it's only about 20 minutes if that.'

Richard and his father had disappeared somewhere in the garden, so I thanked Carol Crundale, and kissed Claire goodbye, full on the lips this time, as we stood on the road outside the front gate of the Grange. Then I set off for Chalk Hill in the gathering twilight.

It had been an eventful day and there was plenty to think about as I walked along the darkening lane. First, the start of my unexpected relationship with Claire and then slowly yet inexorably my plans for a close recce of Coldharbour Farm. The moon was rising over the trees and hedges as I reached Chalk Hill, with scudding clouds giving sudden patches of darkness. I decided that tomorrow night if the fine weather held, was the time to put my suspicions and resolve to the test.

Chapter 10

Although the next day dawned cloudy, the evening was fine and clear with no moon. I had a light and early supper as I wanted to be in the best physical condition for my recce, especially if I had to run any distance.

I decided to take the shotgun to be used only as a last resort if I was pursued and in danger, but left it hidden in the van as it was just too cumbersome to carry. Of course, I did not like the idea of going into such a dangerous situation unarmed and without any kind of backup, and I certainly wished that my Army 9mm Browning High-power was safely tucked in its holster under my left armpit.

During the day I made a sketch map of Coldharbour sitting at the kitchen table. I decided upon my route in and where to park the van, so when I set off from Chalk Hill for my recce, I would have little to think about except the actual job in hand. The main thing was to keep a clear head and use the tension to my advantage, for while it can give one a heightened feeling of awareness, anxiety, as I had learned in the Army, can be crippling and maladaptive.

I left the cottage at 9pm, and drove slowly along the back route to Coldharbour, parking the van in the Alderbourne valley at the bottom of the hill right opposite the crossroads. I backed the van off the road and up a slight grassy incline into a neat little parking bay surrounded by trees and undergrowth, ideal as a place for a camper van like mine to spend the night. I already knew the hidden entrance to the bridleway at the top of the hill where I had parked with Claire yesterday, was used by Bailey on his tractor and to be avoided. I also realised that on a still night, the noise of the VW climbing the hill in bottom gear might be heard at Coldharbour.

Soon after I parked, a few cars passed along the road. However, as night fell, there was no traffic at all. I sat in the back of the van drinking strong cups of coffee, waiting for it to get completely dark before I emerged.

When the last light seeped from the sky, I stepped out of the van and started to walk up the very steep and narrow road which leads to Coldharbour. It was a clear night and the stars were out, although obscured by the trees which arched overhead and I felt as if I was in a cave. My rubber soled boots made no sound on the tarmac.

At the top of the hill, just before I reached the bridleway used by Bailey, I heard the sound of the tractor coming through the woods. I hid in the undergrowth before it appeared menacingly with headlights full on and turned right into the lane from the bridleway. I followed at a very fast walk keeping my distance. From the beginning of the diverted right of way (another bridleway), I watched the headlights as the tractor slowed to take the turning into the main drive leading to Coldharbour. It halted there a moment as someone got out to close the gates. Then it continued into the farmyard. Working late tonight -I thought - something must be urgent.

I walked along the track which led to the back of Coldharbour, and then turned off slightly downhill further into the beech wood on my left. I waited nearly an hour sitting on a tree stump until 10 minutes to midnight. Then I walked very slowly, silently and carefully along the bridleway until I could see the farmyard through the wire fence. By now my eyes were totally accustomed to the faint light from the stars, no longer obscured by trees, and I could just make out that the back gate was closed. The fence was quite low at this point, and I got over it surprisingly easily without becoming hooked in the strands of barbed wire which ran along the top.

There were no lights on in the back of the farmhouse or the surrounding barns and old stables. I approached the barred gate with great caution, moving very slowly indeed. Then I climbed over the gate, which shook slightly and the padlock rattled very faintly, but loud enough to have alerted a dog in the yard. Thank God, they don't have a dog yet I thought!

I moved towards the barn which was open, as I expected, and went into the total blackness of the interior, my pulse quickening. I took out my small narrow beam torch and a pencil of light cut through the blackness like a laser, picking out the tractor, and then the two trailers parked close together behind it. The bonnet of the tractor was still warm as I steadied myself against it with my left hand, gently making my way around the front wheels making sure I did not trip over anything on the ground.

The trailers were covered with light green plastic tarpaulins, and tightly secured with quite thick bright yellow nylon ropes which gave them the appearance of huge wasps. (I had seen this cheap nylon rope on sale in Barham, probably the only rope available locally). I moved right up to the nearest trailer, and realised that to look under the tarpaulin required the rope to be undone somehow.

I carefully noted exactly how the rope had been tied and the knots positioned and then firmly began to unloose the knot nearest to me. Once this was undone, the next knot was easier, and I concluded they had been logically and expertly fastened to enable a quick release when the time came.

Once I had a sufficient amount of the yellow nylon rope untied, I was able to pull back part of the nylon tarpaulin covering the load. A row of steel tubes pointing upwards focused my attention and I could see that the large metal base plate to which the rear three had been attached in a row was riveted to the floor of the trailer. I could also make out the bottom sections of another row of tubes in the front of the trailer.

I had not seen the whole picture because only a section of the tarpaulin had been uncovered, but there was no doubt in my mind what I was looking at. The trailer contained six mortars and they appeared about the same size as the British Army 81mm mortar, although slightly larger I guessed. There was no sign of any mortar bombs., but they would hardly have been stored in the trailer. Tension and danger can focus the mind wonderfully, and I suddenly thought that the mortars in the trailer resembled the steel tube of the crow scarer I had seen in the window display of the hardware shop in Barham. Now I knew why Bailey and his companions were staring at the display that day I saw them outside the shop. No wonder they were all laughing.

I now had no doubt that I was dealing with a Provisional IRA Active Service Unit, and knew that I was in very great danger, standing there right next to a trailer full of mortars without a weapon to defend myself or backup of any kind. I was in two minds whether to get out as fast as I could, a natural reaction, or whether, more logically to replace the end of the tarpaulin and retie the knots exactly as I found them so that the ASU would not be alerted and take immediate evasive action. My professional pride overcame my fear, and with my torch between my teeth, I methodically retied the knots and finally made sure the rope was pulled tight.

Once I had refastened the tarpaulin, I had a look at the workbench at the back of the barn beyond the parked trailers. There was strip lighting above a massive bench with several large vices attached, and a lot of tools lying about. But what interested me most was an area clearly used for welding with the protective eyepiece and steel mask hanging from a hook like a medieval helmet above two gas cylinders standing upright on the floor below. It looked as if the metal tubes had been adapted here in the barn to become missile launchers, and the welding equipment must have been used to attach the mortar base plates firmly to the bottom of the trailers. Anyway, this was certainly a nest of vipers which I had uncovered.

It was now clearly time for me to leave, and my immediate inclination was to move quickly. But this natural impulse had to be resisted, as equal care needed to be taken on my exit as on my entrance. However, things did not work out that way. Suddenly, a light went on behind the door at the other side of the barn behind which was a staircase leading to rooms above me.

The door opened and a figure stood framed against the light for a moment. My mind was racing, for I knew that the main light in the barn could be switched on next. But the figure still stood there, and it was then I noticed he was carrying an assault rifle in his right hand, which looked ominously like an AK-47. Not good news.

He had a torch in his left hand and shone this in my direction, but I had ducked behind one of the trailers. Then he switched on the main light. Fortunately, this was only a very low power 40 watts bulb high near the ceiling which dimly it up the interior. I guessed and hoped that the switches to the powerful strip lighting above the bench were somewhere behind me, and not within his immediate reach.

I knew I had made no sound, so I was puzzled at his appearance. Perhaps there was some kind of a warning system of which I was unaware. Anyway, he slowly began walking towards me, the torch lighting up the ground ahead.

I reached back onto the work bench and picked up a couple of tools, a large spanner and a monkey wrench. Then, as the figure approached, and at a distance of about 10 yards, I stood up and threw the spanner followed by the wrench as hard as I could. The spanner missed, but the wrench struck the man in the face with considerable force, and I heard him gasp with pain.

I took off straight towards him for there was no other way out. I managed to twist the apparently uncocked AK-47 in his hand as I went past, and pushed him backwards and over with it pressed against his body. The man was not the gunman I had seen in the van but someone younger, and the dark green balaclava pulled right over my face gave him no opportunity to recognise me if we met again.

I was through the door in a flash, and this time vaulted the gate with a loud metallic crash of hasp and padlock. I then raced for the fence, and got over this fairly quickly tearing my right hand on the strand of barbed wire, so that it bled quite badly.

However, as I crossed the fence, the man with the AK-47 recovered sufficiently to stagger across the yard to the locked gate, and perhaps in shock and panic fire a burst in my direction. The rounds passed very close, and I was lucky in a sense that the gunmen had fired at me erratically on automatic. If he had steadied his aim on the top of the gate and taken a more purposeful single shot I might well have gone down.

I raced along the bridleway only looking back at Coldharbour as I got closer to the lane. Lights were coming on, and I heard someone shouting. I kept running along the lane, and down the steep hill where I had to use my torch, although by this time I was well out of sight of Coldharbour.

I reached the van covered in sweat and breathing heavily. I stood in the darkness with my hands stretched out against the front door bending my knees and moving my feet to keep the blood flowing while I recovered myself.

I was thinking hard about the next step. The question was whether anyone at Coldharbour would come out in the black Ford van to look for me. I had noticed that it was parked in the yard just outside the back door to the kitchen, and knew it was much faster than my VW, so if it came down the hill, instead of going towards Barham, I would not have much time to get away. It thus seemed sensible to make my getaway at once. Luckily the engine started at the first turn of the ignition and I edged my way down the slight grassy slope onto the road without revving at all, heading off for home along the Alderbourne Valley road

Driving carefully along the narrow side road, I also guessed that no one at Coldharbour would have any idea of the direction in which I had fled, and once they thought it over would probably come to the conclusion that the best thing would be to lie low, rather than tear around the countryside at night illegally armed with AK-47s.

As there was no evidence that I knew what was in the trailers, and had been first seen at the back of the barn near the welding gear, they might hopefully assume that I was a burglar on my usual round of farmhouses and second homes in a rural area. Criminal activity of this kind, especially in gangs, was now common in the countryside, so I could only hope that the members of the Coldharbour ASU came to the conclusion that my unauthorised entry was part of this normal pattern in the district and nothing to do with MI5.

Indeed, I suspected that the young man who had fired at me would receive a blasting from Bailey, although the bruising on his face from the wrench would show I was violent, and his panic was understandable. The group would soon grasp that an unknown corpse or badly wounded burglar on their hands at this critical juncture of their plans would have presented all sorts of problems, and it was just as well that I had got away.

This was the optimistic view. On reflection, I knew that I had made a major mistake going into Coldharbour without wearing gloves. Instead of treating the recce as an army intelligence operation, I should have planned it more as a criminal activity. I had now left a perfect set of fingerprints on the greasy bonnet of the tractor, the spanners, and a lot of fresh DNA on the barbed wire.

This meant that the ASU could get rid of all the evidence against them, but still preserve that which could be used against me on a charge of attempted burglary with assault. But I didn't really think they wanted to draw attention to themselves by going to the police; I was just annoyed with myself for making such an elementary error.

I reached Chalk Hill about 2am, and went to bed immediately, although it was some time before I fell asleep as my mind was still racing. It felt as if I was back in South Armagh. It would have been ironic too if I had been killed and then disappeared like Nairac!

But I also kept wondering about the target for which the mortars were intended. Mortars had been used to attack the British cabinet meeting in Downing Street, an amazing coup. They had also been used recently in March with less effect fortunately in three attacks on the runways at Heathrow where the mortars were apparently fired by timing devices. Could the next attack be at Gatwick only about an hour's drive away from Coldharbour?

Or... and my mind leaped. Or... could it be something major and very close by...? The Channel Tunnel! Jesus Christ! That had to be it! Of course, the whole thing fitted. Otherwise why go to all this immense trouble. It had to be a major target, a spectacular in IRA terms. I was on to something really big. And what a responsibility!

Despite my lack of sleep, I awoke quite early the next morning, and thought what I was going to do while I drank a cup of tea in the kitchen. First, it seemed that now was the time to communicate with the authorities and report the definite presence of an IRA Active Service Unit at Coldharbour. But communicate with whom? That was the problem.

The local police would not have the faintest idea who I was, and there could be a lot of time wasted checking with the Army. Someone would have to come round to Chalk Hill, or I would need to go to the station. On the other hand, if I phoned anonymously, and they treated my information as some kind of a lunatic's complaint, they might send a constable up to Coldharbour to investigate routinely, and things could then go completely awry.

The most logical thing to do, I decided would be to phone MI5 in London although I knew this would create problems for me. At the time of the Ballyford ambush, the SAS, as at Gibraltar, had been working in close liaison with MI5 and relations had been good. However, I knew that one of their senior officers had taken exception to my secretly running the key informers for the raid on my own. My refusal to divulge the source of such vital information had apparently caused him or possibly her, considerable annoyance.

Unknown to me at the time, MI5 had been about to take over responsibility for all anti-terrorist operations and put the running of informers on a much more formal footing. It seemed sheer cocky arrogance on my part not to trust them with this key information about my sources so that they could assess it just before a major operation in which the lives of their own people as well as ours could be in considerable danger. They felt that this sort of secrecy from a comparatively junior officer should not be encouraged, and on reflection they were probably right. Anyway, when things had gone wrong for me after the ambush, I did not get the assistance from MI5 which I had received in the past, and it was passed on to me that I was *persona non grata* with one of their very senior officers.

However, as I no longer had any contacts with MI5, I changed my mind and decided to phone the Army Intelligence Corps in Ashford first, and tell them what I had discovered. I had done a special course there, when I first joined the Army. Because of subsequent events, they would have a file on me, and at least know where the information was coming from before almost certainly handing me over to MI5. But I decided not to give them my address, or any clues to it, or any really detailed information until I found out their initial reaction to my warning.

This meant I would have to use a phone box farther away from Chalk Hill than Pelham, for example, because the call would immediately be traced. Canterbury seemed the most suitable place, and I would use a phone in a main centre at a busy time, and quickly disappear into the crowd once the call was made.

I drove to Canterbury about 8 that morning, and shopped. New sheets, a vacuum, and steel cooking pots, for the cottage. Then I made my phone call to Ashford about 11am from a booth near the Cathedral. I eventually got through to a man in the main office, and said, 'This is Captain Wynstanley speaking. I wanted to phone MI5 direct, but I don't have a number. The matter is urgent and important. Please put me through to someone in authority dealing with IRA terrorism in Britain. My name and details will be on your files. Is Major Bain still working for you?'

'We cannot pass on information about staff I'm afraid.'

'Of course, I understand. It was just that he knows me personally.'

The man kept asking for more information, but I persisted and the section head somewhat coldly answered my call. No one gave their names. I introduced myself again and the man said, 'Ah - Captain Wynstanley, just a moment - your file is coming up on the computer. Where are you phoning from?'

'From Canterbury.'

There was a long pause, and he continued, 'Yes, what's the problem?'

After checking with him that the line was secure I said, 'I've discovered an IRA Active Service Unit down here in Kent, and wish to report it.'

138

'Really - that's very interesting. Good work!' the man said. 'But I thought you were on leave or something. Anyway, how exactly did you find out about it?'

'I've been into the area they're using as a base, and seen from close up six mortars in two trailers parked in a barn.'

'And how on earth did you manage that without their knowledge?'

'I didn't. I went in at night and one of them shot at me with an AK-47.'

'Shot at you! Well all this is very interesting, Captain Wynstanley, but not entirely our province any longer as you must surely know, so I'm going to give you a number to ring MI5 in London. I will phone them first, so give me half an hour. Here is the number...'

I walked around Canterbury for a while, had a coffee in a cafe full of tourists, and after making sure I had enough 50p change for the call, returned to the phone box.

A woman answered from the MI5 number. I repeated my introduction, but added that I was calling from Canterbury.

'Hold on a moment will you Captain Wynstanley.'

Another long pause (a feature of dealing with these bastards), and a man said, 'Ah - Captain Wynstanley, I understand you have something to report.'

'That's right. An IRA ASU right here in Kent.'

'Yes, and I hear they have mortars and that someone shot at you with an AK-47. They missed, I hope?'

'Fortunately, yes,' I replied noting the doubt in his tone.

'Well, I have your file and anyway I know very well who you are, and your various problems. Recent medical problems especially.'

'What medical problems exactly are you referring to?'

'Well, I think you know what I mean. I have a copy of the psychiatrist's report here in front of me, and read it several times before. That's why if you don't mind, as you are still officially in the Army on final leave, we would like you to have a little chat with Major Atherton at Dunmore Park before proceeding any further.'

As Atherton was the bastard whose report ended my career, I had no desire at all to speak to him. I had spent nearly two weeks last year in the psychiatric wing of the Army hospital at Dunmore, and Atherton was the psychiatrist in charge of my ward. Atherton's idea of psycho-analysis was to interrogate the patient until he admitted everything that he with his superior knowledge as a psychiatrist had suggested in the first place. That was his definition of therapy. Only then, and under the conditions imposed by Atherton would he let anyone out.

An intelligent and friendly senior nurse had told me that I was almost certainly suffering from post traumatic stress syndrome, probably exacerbated by the investigations after the raid, and the accusations of guilt. She had seen several men with such a condition after the Falklands war, and said that all I really needed was tranquillisers for a time, plenty of sleep and to do whatever I found most relaxing. But this was not Atherton's opinion. He wanted a much more serious diagnosis, and by his own behaviour and negative attitude, made my condition worse.

As an officer I had a room of my own, but this reinforced my isolation so I wandered about as much as possible. I chatted up whoever I could, even the gardeners in the grounds who at least were officially sane. I really needed someone both sympathetic as well as competent, like Siegfried Sassoon's doctor, W.H. Rivers, described so vividly in *Memoirs of an Infantry Officer* when Sassoon was thought to be shell shocked during the First World War. Instead, I had Atherton, who was enough to put anyone out of their mind.

I noticed several men in the psychiatric wing who seemed to have been there a long time and depressingly were clearly insane. However, apart from being disciplined, they were generally ignored by the staff until their discharge from the Army to civilian hospitals. Others under treatment by Atherton who appeared closer to normal were heavily medicated or so dumb that they hadn't got the message. Agreement was the way out. Denial meant indefinite incarceration. So I got out by my initial agreement with Atherton's diagnosis of paranoia, but that cost me my career. Anyway, Atherton was someone I intended to avoid for the rest of my life, and if by chance we did meet on a dark night, and were alone and I had the opportunity of slotting him without any risk of being caught, I would cheerfully do so.

'But why are you taking no notice of what I've told you. Don't you believe me?'

'Well - I'd hardly put it as bluntly as that, but we've already phoned Major Atherton, and mainly on his advice are delaying any further action until he has let us have an opinion.'

There was a long pause as I considered the full horror of what MI5 were suggesting. I had always felt that Atherton and MI5, or a senior officer of MI5, were linked for some reason over my discharge, and now my fears were being confirmed.

'You're in Canterbury you say. Well, as you know Dunmore Park is not far away in Surrey. You can drive there or get a fast train to Guildford from London, and the hospital will send transport to meet you at the station. There will be a bed there for you from next Monday.'

It was now my turn to express doubt with sarcasm. 'Thank you for the suggestion. But I don't want to go back to Dunmore. Anyway, I think I will end this conversation which clearly seems to have been waste of time.'

'Not if you go and see Major Atherton. I know he'll be helpful, so keep in touch. Anyway, what's your contact address in Canterbury so the people at Dunmore can confirm by letter?'

'No contact address at the moment. I'm off to France tomorrow for a month - the Pyrenees,' I lied.

'Well, I'm sure the holiday will be beneficial. But the hospital will get in touch when you return. I see from the file that you have given an address in Shropshire - High Oaks Farm. Is that correct?'

'Yes, they can write there,' I said, and put down the receiver.

Christ! I thought. Now I've really blown it.

Chapter 11

My first reaction was a sudden feeling of complete weariness, drained of energy like a spent battery. The temperature was in the eighties, and I sweated with the heat and stress.

I had pushed my luck too far, through an excess of zeal. I seemed to be getting deeper and deeper into a nightmare world from which there was no escape. I thought I had done something for my country, old fashioned as that may sound; but now I was being treated like a mental patient, and as if I were criminally insane.

I decided that in a few weeks, I would write to Dunmore Park, saying I was in good health, and decline their offer of a bed for the night and a chat with Atherton. Jesus! What a session that would be! And once I was on a cocktail of his drugs, I might never come out. I remembered one of his patients, a depressive from the Royal Engineers, had nearly died of lithium poisoning. So the more I could delay the better, for my leave was drawing to an end, and then I would be out of the Army, and Atherton's clutches for ever.

I decided to collect my mail from the Queen's barracks, just in case there was something important. However, I had been regularly phoning my mother from a call box at Highdene, and I knew she had not forwarded anything. Then I would return to Chalk Hill at once and lie low for a while. No more solo operations against the IRA. Let them mortar the Channel Tunnel entrance, or blow up what they wished. One ASU was already after me. Why take on another?

Before driving to the barracks, I strolled down the High Street among the crowds, recollecting earlier and happier days in Canterbury when I first joined the regiment as a second lieutenant. They were not carefree days, as at university without responsibilities except the handing in of assignments on time, although final exams always loomed ahead.

For in the Queen's, I understood the concept of duty, and learned the practical responsibilities I had for other people, primarily my men. I also absorbed the ancient traditions of the regiment founded in 1572. One of these traditions included the daily ritual of an officer and three men marching down to the Cathedral. They turned a page in each of the two books of remembrance in the Warriors chapel, one book for WW1 and the other for WW2. The Warriors chapel, actually that of St Michael, was the regimental shrine of the Buffs, the Queen's, and since September 1992 the amalgamated Princess of Wales's Royal Regiment. Despite the intellectual and scathing attitude towards military tradition I experienced at the university, because of my family background, I had always listened to the distant beat of a martial drum. The cynicism and the lack of patriotism of most of my teachers tended curiously to reinforce my own patriotism. I began to understand how intellectually corrupt so many of the academics were, not necessarily at the University of Kent, but in general.

I remembered the awe I felt when I first entered the chapel and stood under the laid up colours, the battle flags of the regiment. And in the centre of the chapel, the incredibly lifelike 15th century alabaster figure of the beautiful Lady Margaret Holland lying between the equally lifelike effigies of her two successive soldier husbands never ceased to intrigue me. 'Who would not sleep with the brave?' Lady Margaret, you did just that, I thought, remembering Houseman. I wondered whether the two husbands knew one another and were thus once brothers in arms? Perhaps Lady Margaret survived them both, and loving them equally had the tomb designed before her own death.

However, the strange thing was that unless I visited Canterbury and the barracks, my early days with the regiment seemed so long ago I had difficulty in recalling them. And despite my reaction to the intellectualism of some of my teachers, academic studies, especially in philosophy and history had made me aware of the ideological and emotional forces which lay behind historic events. This meant there was always some distance between me and my brother officers in the regiment who had come straight from school and Sandhurst.

However, my experiences in Northern Ireland were as vivid as if they had happened only yesterday. Nothing I had learned in any way prepared me for the kind of war which was being fought there. For it was a civil war, in which Britain was divided as in the times of Cromwell, and the bitterness was that peculiar kind one finds only in such wars. I also soon came to the conclusion that this was Britain's last colonial war, in the sense that the natives wanted their independence, whereas the 'settlers' preferred to retain their links with Britain.

More important to me was the nature of the war itself. Unlike the North-West frontier of legend, where one of my ancestors had fought and died, this frontier had little glamour to it. Sure, there was excitement and adventure to be had among the hedgerows of South Armagh, and the wild border country which we patrolled both night and day; but we were basically an army which had been emasculated by the politics of democracy and the rule of law. Of course, that was what we were fighting for, so the paradox was inevitable.

However, the truth was that in order to win, or to teach the Provos a lesson every now and then, and curb their audacity, we simply had to subvert democracy and fight a dirty war. Success for us always depended upon good intelligence, information we could rely upon, and then the action which followed had to be highly efficient and ruthless. And it was for this kind of action that we in the SAS had been trained.

In contrast, the 'green' army at Crossmaglen, for example, despite their bravery and occasional lucky encounter with the enemy, were basically sitting ducks for the IRA. Men were being lost month after month, shot by unseen snipers, or blown to pieces by explosives. And after each death, the local inhabitants cheered or celebrated in the pubs, as if they had won a football match. Irish Rangers versus the Brits.

Anyway, my memories of the regiment had begun to fade, and with those memories some of the values in which I had been brought up. There was no doubt that I was a very different person then, full of ideas of honour and incredibly naive about the real nature of the war in which I was to be engaged in Ulster. I concluded too that had I remained in the regiment instead of joining the SAS and 14th Intelligence Company, I would never have taken part in the ambush which we had laid for the IRA at Ballyford or fallen foul of MI5.

It was strange then to be back in Canterbury where so many of my formative years had been spent, yet now in a liminal position, on the margins of society, belonging nowhere. It was if all my past life had been in some previous re-incarnation, from which I experienced periods of unconscious déjà-vu.

For some reason, habit I suppose, in this contemplative mood, I turned down narrow Mercery lane towards the Cathedral, and the Christ Church gate. In the old butter market I thought of having a beer sitting at an outside table among the throng, as I had done many times as a student at the university. The young half naked tourists pressing around me looked sunburned and happy, chattering away in French or some other continental language as if they hadn't a care in the world.

A couple of deeply tanned Scandinavians gave me the glad eye. One of them, a Nordic blond, with bright clear blue eyes, and breasts like ripe peaches bulging out of her blouse, smiled at me. She said something to her companion, and they both giggled. I was tempted, but there were other things on my mind.

However, the blonde was determined to make contact. She clutched a town map, and was obviously looking for somewhere, her gaze now fixed inquiringly on me. I smiled, and encouraged she came forward and asked if I knew of a cycle shop. She pointed at their touring bikes, which were leaning against the back of a public seat. They were heavily laden with gear, panniers crammed to the limit. The rear wheel and right pedal of her cycle had been damaged, she told me in perfect English. 'And I have also hurt my knee.' I could see a large purplish bruise on her right knee, which appeared to be slightly swollen.

'Sorry,' I said. 'I don't know. But I suggest you ask at one of the Tourist Information offices.'

She absorbed this information slowly, but that was not the end of it.

'Do you live here?' she asked.

'Yes,' I said, 'but out in the country.'

'That must be nice. We cycled here from Dover. But on the way, I was knocked down by - what you say - a van. It came from behind us round a corner very fast and must have hit one of my panniers, knocking me off onto the road The van only stopped for a moment, further up the road, and then drove away.'

'Where did that happen?'

'Oh, I don't know. We turned of the main road from Dover, and looked for somewhere to make coffee on our stoves.' She pulled out another map, which I held for her, while she showed me the place, her face very close to mine so that I scented her hair. The

145

index finger of her right hand was on Bishopsbourne and her left hand very gently pressed against my back.

'What colour was the van?' I asked trying a very long shot.

'It was black,' said her companion very definitely. 'And the number was PS 13208. I am good on numbers. A man got out and looked back towards us. Then he drove away very quickly.'

I looked closely at her. Brownish hair, streaked blonde, and strange stony dark brown eyes, very alert, swivelling to look me over, and a body lean as a greyhound. Certainly not just a pretty face. It needed great presence of mind in the circumstances to memorise a number like that and write it down at once.

My heart quickened. Bailey's van was a black Ford and the number was PS13208! This was incredible. I could hardly believe it! What a coincidence! Or was it some kind of malign fate pursuing me like a hound from hell?

'Have you reported this to the police?'

'No, not yet. Of course, if we want the insurance, we must do that. But first we need to repair the cycle.'

'Yes - I understand. Look I will help you. But how did you get to Canterbury then?'

'A lorry driver on the main road gave us a lift.' said the blonde, who first spoke to me.' She paused a moment, 'My name is Anna, from Sweden and this is Brigit, also from Sweden.'

I introduced myself, leaving out the Army rank, and we all moved off slowly towards the tourist office, Anna limping slightly, so I walked slowly. The two young women were definitely in tow, but for how long exactly I had no idea. But as usual there was a purpose in my actions for an idea was forming in my mind connected with Bailey. The tourist office knew of a cycle shop which did repairs, and also directed us to the nearest police station, where Brigit reported the incident. The constable on duty inspected the damaged wheel and took down all the necessary details. He said he would try and see what he could match on his computer with the registration number. Something came up, and he asked the tourists if they wanted him to investigate further.

They were naturally reluctant to get involved and further spoil their holiday. While they were making up their minds, I said quite casually to the constable, 'Can you tell me if the owner of the van is a local? I mean does he come from Kent?'

'Yes,' said the constable, 'but I can't tell you who he is, unless you decide to make an official complaint.'

'Well by a strange chance, I might know. It could be a Mr Bailey, who lives at Coldharbour Farm near Cobham.'

The constable looked back at the computer screen and his expression changed slightly, so I knew I had scored a bull's eye.

'And who are you?' the constable asked, somewhat irritably, thinking I was some kind of Mr Know All.

'Oh - I'm nothing to do with it. I just met these two ladies in the town, and said I would help them out.'

'But what makes you think you know who owns the van?'

'Well, I live locally on Highdene Common. I've seen a black van, a new Ford Escort driving around our lanes at great speed, and traced it to Coldharbour Farm.'

'Do you want to act as an additional witness then?'

'It depends on the girls,' I said. 'What do you want to do Anna?'

'We just wanted to report what happened for the insurance, that's all.'

After some further discussion with the constable, I said as we were leaving, 'I know they haven't made a complaint. But I think it would be worth your while checking out Mr Bailey, if that's his name, because he drives too fast for country lanes and will kill someone sooner or later for sure.'

The constable made no comment, but he had recorded the whole incident. I realised that entirely by a chance meeting with the two women I had drawn the attention of the police to Bailey and Coldharbour without actually getting involved myself. And this was definitely a positive step forward, far more so than I appreciated at the time.

We then moved off to the cycle shop, some distance from the centre of town, and I explained the situation to one of the young mechanics. He promised to do what he could, but said that spoke straightening and wheel re-alignment would take several hours. He might finish in the late afternoon, or perhaps the next day, spurred on perhaps by Anna who flirted with him quite shamelessly.

The women were disappointed, but I suggested that Brigit also left her cycle at the shop and that they came and had some lunch with me at the coolest place in town, the Crypt restaurant below ground in Debenham's.

Brigit seemed reluctant to leave her cycle, but Anna agreed and persuaded her to come and have lunch. The Crypt was not too crowded, and pleasantly cool. We found a side table to ourselves, and the women were delighted with the food, fresh crisp rolls, ham, salad, and surprisingly good coffee. We all ordered ice cold fruit juices as well.

Brigit was slightly off hand. She knew I knew that Anna was using me. But I was using them, so the score was even. Anyway, whatever developed, unknowingly these girls had done me a favour.

Both Anna and Brigit were students, and on vacation. Anna had a part time job while attending a Polytechnic in Copenhagen studying Graphic Art and design. Brigit was not very forthcoming, but I gathered she was an Honours student studying History and Archaeology. Both were bright, and a man could easily underestimate Anna, who played the dumb blonde to her advantage. They had met through a friend of Brigit on a previous cycling holiday, and were now on their way to London, with a few days in Canterbury, and then by train to Scotland.

'So what do you do?' asked Brigit, slightly aggressively it seemed to me, not so much out of interest, but rather because, I had questioned them, and now she felt it was her turn.

'I'm in the Army. I shoot people.'

But it was the wrong kind of joke, and unnecessary too. Both women looked shocked.

'Actually, I'm on leave from the Army,' I added. 'My final leave as a matter of fact. Then I will be looking for a job. I mean I've left the Army.'

'But you were in the Army!' said Brigit, obviously horrified. 'You mean compulsory service?' she asked, trying to put a better complexion on it.

'No, I chose it as a career. My father was in the Amy too.' Anna laid a warm hand on my arm. 'We in Sweden don't have any more wars. We forget that the British do.'

'Well, that may be so, but I believe you make excellent weapons of war and export them overseas at a good profit too.'

Anna looked slightly put out, and I realised that in future it would be better if I told people I met that I was a free lance journalist. Never mention the Army, anyway.

148

I had already paid the bill at the counter, so we went upstairs to the street outside. As we stood there for a moment in the doorway of the store, slightly to my surprise, Anna said. 'We are coming back this way at the end of our trip. We want to look at the Channel Tunnel on our way to Dover. Perhaps we could call on you?' Brigit was looking away down the street, as if not wishing to associate herself with Anna's suggestion.

I hesitated a moment and thought, why not? I have to try and live a normal life.

'By all means,' I said. 'I'll show you on the map where I live.'

While I was marking the approximate location of Highdene Common, Brigit silently took out a small notebook and wrote down my name and address.

'Call in to see me first. You can stay the night if you like. Then I'll drive you up the hill above the whole Tunnel complex in my van. You'll see the full horror of it all from there. My van is a Volkswagen camper. There's plenty of room. We can put your cycles in the back.'

I didn't know why I was doing this. Perhaps it was an unconscious effort to get back to normal.

Then I had another idea, 'It's up to you. But Ana I think you should give your knee a rest tomorrow. It looks very swollen to me. So I will take you both to the Exhibition Centre at the Tunnel entrance and we'll go up to the viewpoint afterwards.'

After a short pause, when Brigit shrugged her shoulders at Anna's questioning glance, we arranged to meet the next day at 10am inside the Watling Street car park which I showed them on a map of Canterbury.

Anna looked back a moment and waved after we said goodbye and they set off down the street in the direction of the cycle shop. I watched them go. Just as they were disappearing into the crowd, Brigit turned her head and looked back. For a moment our eyes met, and she looked at me intently, almost quizzically it seemed. She didn't trust me an inch, I realised.

I was home within an hour, and settled down to an afternoon of gardening. Using an old rusty sickle, which I sharpened on the garage workbench, I began with the long grass around the apple trees nearest the house.

Despite the shade from the overgrown unpruned trees, I was soon drenched with sweat, and paused a moment from the heat, wondering whether I should wait until later in the day. It was then I heard a woman's voice calling my name somewhere at the front of the house. Not the Scandinavians again, I thought.

I walked round the side of the house, and to my astonishment saw Mary Renfrew standing outside my front door.

'Hello,' she said. 'I thought you must be in because your van's here.'

'So what can I do for you?'

'There's something you ought to know,' Mary said. 'I don't want to alarm you but I've just been up to Coldharbour Farm.'

Jesus! I thought. Surely they cannot be onto me that quickly? But I showed no emotion. 'Yes, and what's the problem?'

'Well, they phoned our office this morning to say they had an intruder last night. Someone trying to steal equipment from their barn. I thought you ought to know, because the same person – or it could be a gang - might try and rob you.'

'That's very kind of you. There's nothing much of value here, but I don't want people breaking in. I will have to double lock the front and back door at night or if I'm out.'

'The point is - you're on your own. There's quite a crowd up at Coldharbour. Not just your friend Mr Bailey.'

I would love to have quizzed Mary further, but I did not want her to know I was still very interested in Bailey and his friends.

'Really? So have they reported it to the police?'

'No - and they don't want us to report anything either. You see, nothing was stolen. But they're going to repair the barn doors and install security lights as soon as possible. That's why they phoned. They're getting a dog as well - a Doberman.'

Mary paused a moment before continuing, 'Why don't you get a dog? This is an ideal place for one, although I prefer cats myself.'

'A good idea. I thought of getting a lurcher once I find somewhere I can legally shoot rabbits outside my orchard. But traditionally lurchers should not be encouraged to bark so perhaps, as you say, I'll just get a watchdog. An Alsatian might be ideal.'

She smiled and looked quite friendly, so I said, 'Now you're here. Why not come in a moment ?'

'Well - just a moment. But I've got to get back to the office. I came out for Mr Chapman to look at a house near Highdene at the bottom of the hill. The owner, an old lady, might sell, so I went to have a chat. I thought I would drop in to see you as well But Mr Chapman doesn't know I'm here.'

We walked into the kitchen through the sitting room. Mary appeared quite relaxed. I could see she was older than I first thought, but more sexy too. Difficult to analyse but her figure seemed more rounded, and her movements quite surprisingly sensual. It would be mature sex too - perhaps comforting as well as competently satisfying.

'Well - you've certainly been cleaning the place. And scrubbed the kitchen table! Is the Aga working?'

'Yes,' I said, 'but it makes the kitchen very hot in summer, although I'll be glad of the warmth in the winter.'

The banalities continued for a while, and then Mary said, 'Would you like to come for supper and take pot luck? Next Saturday night if you are free.'

'Thank you,' I said. 'I look forward to another good chat. But I may have a guest coming,' suddenly remembering Diana. 'I'll phone them tomorrow morning from Highdene, or maybe this evening and let you know.'

I said 'them' rather than 'her', which might have put Mary off. I wanted to make friends locally, and one never knew how Diana was going to behave. She might take one look at the cottage and leave at once. Of course, I was calculating. I had to be. That is how I had survived in the Army, and Mary was still really my only source of information on Bailey.

I saw Mary to the front gate, where she paused a moment before getting into the car. I gave her a quick kiss on one cheek, and she responded quite graciously, giving me a light hug in return. I looked her straight in the eye, and saw an expression of angst on her face, just for a moment, and then it was gone.

Reflecting on the events of the day, I realised that quite unexpectedly, and totally unlike the Army, women had suddenly begun to play a part in my life, which I really did not know quite how to handle. The most important woman for me at the moment was Claire Crundale, and I was determined to get to know her better. More than that I wanted to become her lover, but this was going to be tricky mainly because I really had no idea how to win her affection.

151

Furthermore, long term, given her situation, I had very little to offer, no job, no prospects of sufficient wealth to keep up her present standard of living, although I knew that she did not think consciously in these terms. It was our personal chemistry which was going to be the most important factor, and I had no magic formula to attract her. I knew that she was part of a very closely knit family, and this gave her great moral strength. But at the moment her family came first, and our budding romance, second. Her main concern was for her brother, Richard, whom she would protect at all costs, and I admired her loyalty. However, the question in my mind remained whether this loyalty could ever include me. There was also the strange menacing jealousy of Tom, and I wondered about the nature of their relationship. Something seemed to be going on between them, and if so, there was a side to Claire which I knew very little about.

After being in the Army, and especially Special Forces, such as the SAS, where men's relationship with women seemed relatively simple, or we made it simple - the regiment came first, and one's mates were all important - things were now very different.

I had won the respect and approval of my troop by personal example, by leadership, and by a kind of affable courage which was so important in the egalitarian atmosphere of a regiment engaged in very dangerous and secret operations. Furthermore, the SAS had a mystique of their own, which enhanced loyalty. Many of the things we did, especially ambushes, or observation posts as they were euphemistically known, were so marginally just within the law, that secrecy was all important. Until recently at least, personal exploits were rarely publicised, even if we were killed in action because it was the group which counted. This increased our feelings of brotherhood, in which women played absolutely no part. Many men, especially long time serving SAS, went through wives and partners as if they were throwaways like the American anti-tank rocket launchers we used in the Gulf war. Of course that's an exaggeration, because there were real emotions involved on both sides. But the men could always return to the regiment, their mates, and the additional excitement of overseas action, whereas the women were often left in some kind of a grey housing estate perhaps, with the immediate responsibility of children and the problem of finding a fully supporting job.

Fortunately perhaps, I had no serious relationships with women while I was in the Army, and there was no 'carry over' from the relationships which developed at university. Women I had known at university, especially the very bright ones, were dismayed when they discovered my military interests, and the idea of actually joining the Army as a career was complete anathema to them. It seemed so totally foreign to the liberal education which we were supposed to be receiving, almost a betrayal in fact of all the predominantly left wing, politically correct, relativistic, anti-colonial, post modern (po-mo), deconstructionist ideas which we had been discussing in seminars and tutorials.

Furthermore, some courses were almost totally politically motivated, the lecturers used their position of power to influence as much as possible the students who attended. And it was quite openly known that in certain courses all dissenting views would be unfavourably received. One had to toe the lecturer's politically correct line, or be subjected to the ridicule of the class. There was a price to be paid for dissent, a 'B2' rather than an 'A' grade, for example.

Given this atmosphere, during my undergraduate days, I came to realise that apart from their survival skills in everyday life, which were considerable, most of my fellow students lack of knowledge of the hard realities of politics, economics and the complexity of foreign policy was quite breathtaking. The same could be said of my brother officers in the regiment of course, and even more so of the men under their command, but they had not received the supposed benefits of a tertiary education.

There were exceptions of course, students such as Claire, but the sad truth was the small coterie of right wing women who treated the university as a superior kind of finishing school were on the other hand, unbelievably boring and possessed a kind of complacency bordering on stupidity.

Of course in many ways, I was also naive, clinging on to a set of values so much at variance with modern Britain. I was to discover too late perhaps, my ignorance of the nature of the dirty war in Northern Ireland, and the political complexity of that war.

The point was that I now faced an entirely different situation. Almost certainly because I had fallen foul of MI5, my army career was over, and I had to somehow adjust to that reality. But the past was still with me, and this had to be exorcised, if I wanted a normal relationship with a woman.

Anyway, it suddenly struck me that I was wasting time getting myself involved with Diana again, and even the Scandinavians, who were harmless enough. However, my relations with Mary had suddenly become of consequence since her warning this morning about the break in, my break in at Coldharbour. It was vital to know that Bailey and his friends were not informing the police and they were repairing the barn doors, installing security lights and getting a dog. I had been there just in time. If those huge doors had already been repaired, closed and padlocked, I would never have got into the barn so easily.

Of course, I didn't expect Bailey to inform the police. No IRA Active Service Unit would voluntarily draw attention to themselves, and certainly would not want detectives going through the garage! I was surprised that they had bothered to tell Chapman, but I suppose they needed permission for the alterations.

Anyway, Mary was my only source of information about Bailey, and perhaps I could get more out of her when we had dinner together. But that was as far as it would go - I would take no further risks with the IRA or somehow as a result of any meddling find myself back in Atherton' s hands.

I was surprised at myself. This sudden switch was quite unlike me, but I had learned through experience that one had to deal with each problem as it arose, and allocate priorities. Never mind what other people thought: inevitably they had their own interests at stake. My priority was now clearly to continue to lie low, and concentrate my efforts at leading a normal life as a civilian.

My relationship with Claire suddenly seemed of major importance. Obsessed with Colharbour, I put her out of my mind for the last 24 hours; but now seeing her and getting to know her, and the need for her physical presence had become urgent. I needed to feel her body against mine, to scent her hair, to kiss her passionately. All dangerous signs, but the heart has it own reasons, which have to be obeyed.

I decided to walk down the lane and past the common to the Grange, and see whether she was in. I had to declare my interest, the word 'love' might put her off at this stage, but I felt I had to let her know how attracted I felt towards her, and to find out how she felt about me.

So, after a wash, a change of vest and shirt, and cleaning of teeth, I set of along Coppice Lane towards the Grange, and within about 20 minutes was ringing the front door bell. No one answered, so I went round to the back, where I found Carol Crundale working in the garden. No sign of anyone else, so after the initial pleasantries, it made my question less embarrassing.

'I came to see Claire,' I said. 'Is she in?'

'No - she's not. She went out with Tom after lunch in the Land Rover, and I think they're walking though Chesterton Wood down to the lakes. People are picnicking around the lakes in this hot weather - trespassing in fact - and disturbing the ducks - so Tom is going to have to be very fierce with them.'

'That should not be too difficult for him,' I observed, but Carol Crundale defended her gamekeeper vigorously. 'Well - you've obviously no idea how belligerent and rude these trespassers are. They think they have a right to come on to private land with their children and dogs running all over the place. They play those portable radios very loudly too, and leave litter all over the place so Tom has to be strict with them.'

'Of course' I said, trying to mollify her. 'I must ask Claire to show me the lakes sometime.'

'Well, for that matter, you can go there any time you like Captain Wynstanley. I'll tell Richard, but please first give us a ring, first so we can warn Tom.'

'That's very kind of you,' I said. 'But I still hope Claire will take me there first.'

It was clear from the following pause that Carol Crundale wanted to get on with her gardening, so I said, 'Please tell Claire I called. I haven't a phone at the moment which makes things difficult. But I would like to see her about something - although it's not urgent.'

Another pause from Carol Crundale before she said, 'I think she and Richard went round to your house about 9 the night before last on their way to the pub - the Tiger at Highdene - but you weren't in. And your van was not there either, they said.'

'Yes - that's right,' I said thinking quickly. 'I was out for a drive and walk. Please tell Claire and Richard I'm sorry to have missed them.'

I then left and walked back to Chalk Hill. It seemed that everyone locally was keeping a check on my movements! But all with good will in this instance. I was surprised at first that Richard had called in as well as Claire until I realised this may have been because they were both on their way to the pub anyway, and Claire probably suggested inviting me along on their way past Chalk Hill.

When I reached home, it was time to prepare supper, and then for more cleaning and tidying up inside the cottage, when it was really too late to drive to Highdene and phone Diana - something I was no doubt unconsciously putting off. I went to bed thinking of Claire, and perhaps that was a good thing. It showed that somehow my priorities had changed, and perhaps for the better.

*

The following morning I left early for my rendezvous with Anna and Brigit, and took a back route along the old Roman road of Stone Street. It was cloudy and cool, quite welcome after the unusual heat of the past few weeks, with some drops of rain on the windscreen when I reached the high ground around West Wood. The entrance roads to Canterbury were still crammed with cars and lorries, but I was not held up, as I would have been by the early morning traffic, and used the Watling Street car park, although it was already nearly full.

The women appeared about 10 minutes late. Brigit grim faced striding ahead, and Anna limping along several paces behind her.

I smiled at Anna, ignoring Brigit, who made no apologies. 'I hope you're all right Anna. How is the knee? Still swollen?'

Anna was out of breath, poor woman and a little flustered. 'I'm sorry we're late. When I woke up - I thought I could not go out today. But I've bandaged the knee and it feels better. We went to a chemist and they did it for me.'

We slowly walked to the van, and both women approved of it, especially the cooking facilities, and the general snugness of the interior with everything packed away and tidy. Anna sat next to me in the front, and Brigit, who had cheered up a bit since she saw the van, at the back. She asked a number of technical questions, engine capacity, fuel economy, and so on, leaning forward between Anna and me to be heard above the noise of the engine. I explained the difficulties of servicing the engine jammed in such a small space at the back, and she took it all in.

I drove back along Stone Street, where it was still drizzling, and joined the M20 at the roundabout not far from Hythe As the weather suddenly cleared on the motorway, and the sun came out between scudding black storm clouds I suggested we went to the lookout first and the Exhibition Centre later. The women agreed, so I drove off the roundabout at Cheriton, through Newington, and up towards the steep scarp of the North Downs just beyond Peene.

I had to wait for a car to descend Hill Lane, and having engaged first gear, the VW roared its way up to Danton Lane which ran along the lower part of the escarpment, and then climbed steeply again to the top of Cheriton Hill where the lookout was situated.

Driving slowly along the very narrow Danton Lane, suddenly I was astonished to see Bailey and his sinister companion, standing at a gap in the hedge on our right and looking over the burnt grassy slopes below towards the Channel Tunnel complex, less than 400 yards away. They both turned round as the van approached, and I felt they must surely have recognised the VW and me from our first encounter on Highdene Common. They were not surprised, for they must have heard the van long before we appeared. But they looked at us closely, although without a hint of recognition.

I also just glimpsed their black Ford parked up a turnoff sloping uphill sharply to my left, completely hidden until we actually reached it. I had no time to take in anything properly before we passed them and were beginning to climb towards the top of the escarpment and the lookout.

'Those were the men! That was the van!' Brigit exclaimed excitedly, as both women turned round in their seats and looked back, but within a few seconds, the men and the van were out of sight in the twisting narrow lane as we began the final climb to the top of the escarpment.

'You mean the men who knocked you over ?' I said to Anna.

'Yes - that was them, I'm sure of it.'

'Did you see the number of the van?'

157

'No' said Brigit, 'but one of those two was the man who got out before they drove off. I'm almost certain.'

'Well, I can see no point in going back now.' I said rather lamely. 'The lane is too narrow to stop anyway, and they will deny it of course.'

'Yes, let's enjoy the day,' Anna said. 'We don't want to get involved with them anyway.'

In a few minutes we reached the lookout point to the right of us, and I parked the van alongside a number of other cars whose occupants were looking at the scene below us, some with field glasses.

The women got out, Anna helped by me, and she clung to me strongly as I assisted her down.

We looked below at the sprawling mess of roads, concrete and tarmac flyovers, power lines, and hundreds of ugly metal posts which at a distance looked like reinforcing rods at a building site, giving the whole complex a raw unfinished look. Rows of trains stood in the sidings glistening in the sun like long aluminium slugs and convoys of reticulated trucks of every colour slowly drove across a long concrete over bridge towards the trains.

'How horrible!' Brigit said.

'Yes,' I said. 'That's the price of progress. But you can get to Paris and Brussels much quicker now, and who cares how much Kent countryside is destroyed in the process.'

Below us in the fields burnt brown by the long hot summer, sheep grazed, and the dark green remnants of woods and copses reminded the onlooker that this had once been countryside. Overhead larks sang, and in the distance towards Folkestone, a kestrel hovered. Nature somehow continued to exist, and around us in the spring and early summer wild orchids still bloomed. We locals had to live with this excrescence and, no doubt, in time we would grow used to it and accept it like the nuclear power station at Dungeness, and its sinister silhouette which viewed any fine evening from the hills above Hythe had become part of the sunset.

As I was taking in the full horror of the scene vainly looking for any sign of tree planting, Brigit gripped me on my left arm.

'Look!' she hissed. 'They're here.' I turned round and saw that Bailey's black Ford van had stopped about forty yards from us at the end of the parking area. Bailey got out, and nonchalantly went to the edge of the cliff, looking across to the complex, leaving his companion still sitting in the car. He definitely glanced towards us, and saw Anna with her camera taking a photo of the scene below, so presumably assumed we were harmless visitors, and he gave no sign of recognising the women or me. Lulled into a sense of security by the innocuous presence of the tourists, Bailey boldly took out a camera, and casually took several photos of the complex. No one else even glanced at him.

'Stop staring Brigit' I said. 'Leave them alone - it's not worth it.'

'But that's the van! I saw the number!' Brigit said. 'I must speak to them.'

'Leave it,' I repeated more firmly looking her straight in the eye, standing between her and Bailey, as I did not want to attract his attention in any way.

Brigit turned away reluctantly and walked to wards Anna, who was still looking at the view and taking photos. She was obviously disappointed and irritated by my lack of support, and I knew how she felt at my apparent gutlessness, for in any other circumstances I would certainly have tackled Bailey.

However, I also knew at once that what I was witnessing was highly significant. Bailey and his companion were making a recce, the final one most probably, before launching a rocket attack on the Tunnel. By a chance in a million I was here and again by chance almost certainly not under suspicion because of the presence of the two girls, for at this critical moment they would have been especially alert to any surveillance. And if Bailey had recognised Anna as the woman they had knocked off her cycle, then this simply confirmed they were harmless and tourists of some kind.

Bailey and his friend, who never got out of the van, moved away before we did, driving on towards Folkestone, or it even Dover, and their next rendezvous perhaps.

Brigit was silent when we got into the van and drove back down the hill towards Danton Lane, although Anna chatted away pleasantly enough. I was amazed to see what a perfect spot Bailey had found. On our right was a concrete ramp, the beginning of a private side track just wide enough for a car, leading somewhere up the hill. A short way up, the concreted track, was barred by a rough wooden gate which was locked, and beyond this an official looking notice, 'No Entry by Order'.

I parked the VW exactly in the same place as Bailey's van with the bonnet close up against the gate. I could see there was still just enough room off the lane for a trailer as well. But the gate could easily be smashed through if necessary. I got out of the van and said I was going to look at the view, because at that precise spot, was quite a wide gap in the hedge and the road had been widened at that point as well, so that one could stand looking down at the Tunnel complex, yet safely out of the line of traffic.

The women also walked over to where I was standing, Anna still limping, and we looked over a wire farm fence across fields to the train platforms, the nearest only about 400 yards away. I stood there and carefully estimated the range. 440 yards, a quarter of a mile at the most. Nothing for an army 81mm mortar, even a lightweight 51mm could reach the train platforms without difficulty. I felt certain the IRA could manage that too, although homemade mortar tubes and bombs were tricky. I presumed of course that they were still going to use the tubes I had seen inside the barn at Coldharbour. But what a target, and what an ideal spot to launch their missiles! It was as if the place had been specially constructed for them! Surely, the local security must have checked it out since the Heathrow attack? But never assume anything was a hard lesson I had learned in the SAS.

I had often wondered why the IRA had never seemed to concentrate their efforts on getting hold of one of our 81mm mortar, or its Russian or Chinese equivalent. Probably because they had their own homemade Mark 10 'barrackbusters', which were inaccurate but quite lethal if they hit their target. But bringing them across to Britain was getting increasingly difficult, so that was probably why with great ingenuity they had used local material readily available.

'Is something worrying you?' asked Brigit. 'You look puzzled.'

'No- not really,' I lied.

'I think you have some kind of connection with those two men in the van. I think that's why you helped us yesterday, and also why you brought us here today.'

'No- that's not true,' I said. 'I didn't expect to meet them again. But you are right I was wondering what they were doing here.' One cannot conceal everything from this woman, I thought, she is far too intelligent.

'And have you decided?'

'Yes - I know now.' I said enigmatically looking straight at her, but I could see she was not satisfied with being put off, so I added truthfully. 'But it's a very long story, and one day, if we ever meet again, I'll tell you how it began and ended.'

Both women were silent for a moment, and then Anna said, 'Well, I think we must go back now, but I'm sorry you have to take us all the way to Canterbury. Perhaps wc should go by bus.'

'No - I'll take you back,' I said. 'You can't get on a bus Anna with you knee like that.'

I thought for a moment I would detour and show them Chalk Hill, but I put the idea out of mind at once. The tourists had served their purpose, and the Exhibition Centre fortunately forgotten. Anyway, Brigit was getting too curious for me to be at ease.

I dropped them off near the bus station in Canterbury, and they both thanked me profusely. To my surprise, Brigit said with a smile, 'I've got your address. We may see you on the way back.'

It had been an interesting morning, but my previous enthusiasm, a carry over from my past, had somehow gone. Seeing Bailey and his friend like that strongly suggested that action was imminent, and now I almost certainly knew the actual spot from which the mortars would be fired. But really, I no longer wanted to know. I just wished I could somehow get myself out of the dilemma which this additional information had placed me.

I tried to think of something else as I drove off Stone Street and along the twisting narrow lanes to Highdene, and my relationship with Claire immediately came to mind. I simply had to her see again as soon as possible, but I had called once at the Grange and felt embarrassed to do again. Yet, it had to be done, I persuaded myself for I could not be certain that Carol Crundale had passed on the message, so this evening might be the time to return.

On my way through Highdene, when I saw the phone box, I remembered about Diana, and got through to her at work in Ludlow, 'Well - what's the story? Are you coming or not?' I said, no longer caring which way she decided.

'I'm still thinking about it,' Diana replied. 'I can't talk here. The place is full of customers and we're busy. But it would be the weekend after next - so let's leave it at that for the moment.'

'All right Diana. But I'm assuming you're coming and getting the place prepared. New sheets for your bed, and I've got a fridge!'

'Not especially for me - I hope. Christ! What would it be like without one in this weather anyway!'

'Have you seen my mother?'

'Of course - I was with her last night. She's been quite lonely since your aunt left. So when are you coming home you selfish bastard?'

'As soon as I can. But I'll explain all that when we meet.'

'Good - there are lots of thing which need explaining. I've got to go now. But don't count on that weekend. I may remain here after all.'

Not an entirely satisfactory conversation, but I began to worry about my mother. Diana was right, I had been selfish. What the hell had come over me?

Stricken with guilt, I phoned my mother at once. I waited on the ring for about a minute, but there was still no answer. She must be sitting outside somewhere in a shady part of the garden, I thought. Perhaps I should phone her tonight, even if it means driving down to the call box in the dark.

When I reached my front door, there was a note from Claire half sticking out of the tarnished brass letter slit.

Sorry, I missed you yesterday. But suggest you come round this evening, say about 8pm after we have had our meal. Then we can wander off for a talk, and take things from there. Love Claire. PS. I want to know what you have been up to. No good I am sure!.'

Well, that's reassuring, I thought. Claire must care for me. Otherwise she would not have bothered to write a note and deliver it.

I spent the remainder of the afternoon working on the property. It was cloudy with a strong wind and grass cutting in the orchard was pleasant, almost like hay making. Apples had set on the trees, and some were already tinged with red. High in the branches, were several wood pigeon nests, now full of young, and I frightened away a couple of magpies I spotted ominously skulking around. I piled up the grass in a great brown heap just outside the orchard, but dared not risk a bonfire as everything was so dry I could have set the whole place alight in that wind.

Some skill was required in sickling at the right angle, and the judicious use of ones spare hand in gathering the grass. The more I worked away, the more relaxed I felt. When I got my second wind, I became completely absorbed in the rhythm of what I was doing, although I had to stop every now and then to sharpen the blade.

However, it was pretty mindless, but that was exactly what I needed in my present disturbed mood. Also fancifully perhaps, I somehow felt part of an ancient tradition. This orchard must have been sickled for hundreds of years, and indeed sickling linked me to country life all over the world. It was a basic agricultural task, done every day for cattle and goat fodder, and still a way of harvesting in many parts of Asia. Anyway, the hours soon passed, and when I looked at my watch, it was well after six.

My arms were covered in small cuts, and the red weals of insect bites. I used the hot water from the kitchen electric jug for a wash, and I saw in the mirror while combing my matted hair that my eyes were red and inflamed. Hardly a handsome sight to greet Claire!

I had a quick meal of soup and toast and jam, with several full mugs of strong sweet tea, and listened to the news on my radio while sitting in the large kitchen which served as my living room at the moment. The Windsor chairs were very comfortable and after the cramped quarters I had been accustomed to in Northern Ireland, there was nothing to complain about. But I doubted whether Diana would feel the same.

As usual, I walked rather than drove over to the Grange, and I took my waterproof as lightening flickered in the sky and black storm clouds were gathering over the downs. I felt slightly apprehensive, as I walked along the lane and past the common, but since Claire's note, the unease was more to do with meeting Carol, Alan, and Richard. This time I was not appearing as the next door neighbour met by chance and invited through politeness, but rather at their daughter's considered invitation.

Claire appeared at the back door when I knocked, but there was no chance of a kiss as her mother was right behind her in the kitchen where the lights were on. Carol Crundale soon put me at my ease.

'Good evening Captain Wynstanley. I'm sorry I didn't ask you in for a drink when you called, but I had some gardening to finish.' Then slightly accusingly she added, 'Claire came back late anyway.'

'Not so late,' Claire said, with a frown, but she offered no further explanation.

There is something going on between her and Tom and Carol Crundale knows about it, and doesn't approve, I thought. For the first time for years, I felt jealousy, not an edifying emotion, and I suppressed it.

Claire and I walked into the sitting room, but Carol remained in the kitchen still tidying up and there was no sign of Alan or Richard.

Claire said, 'I didn't hear your van. You must have walked. Anyway, would you like a drive in my Triumph! We could have a drink somewhere. But this time, I'll choose where to go!'

'Not Coldharbour anyway!'

'No - certainly not. But I've a strange feeling you've been back.'

'Oh - really. And what makes you think that ?'

'Well, Mr Chapman the estate agent phoned us...' Claire said slowly and deliberately, pausing to look me straight in the eye.

'And what did he have to say?' I asked innocently.

'I thought you might know. He said that someone had tried to break in at Coldharbour the night before last, and warned us to check our security.'

'What about your security?' I said trying to change the subject. 'I notice you have a flood light at the main gate.'

'Yes - we had a break in two years ago, but Grundy, that's our labrador, scared them off by barking before anything was taken. The floodlights were Richard's idea. They are part of an alarm system. Like you he's been very wary since he came back from Northern Ireland. But you're not answering my question.'

'Look Claire, you're very sharp. But let's just enjoy the evening. If I start to confess, it'll be very difficult for you to believe. You won't know what to believe. A lot has happened since I last saw you, but I'm no longer interested in acting the lone ranger. I just want some peace and quiet. And I also want you - that's the truth of the matter.'

We were now out on the patio on the edge of the garden and it was almost dark. Lightning flickered over the downs and we heard the distant drum roll of thunder.

'You mean you want to sleep with me? Is that what you're saying?'

I was taken aback for a moment at Claire's directness, and began to mumble.

'Well, yes. But there's more to it than that. I really like you. I mean I think you're quite exceptional.'

'So you only sleep with exceptional girls - is that it?'

'Don't mock me Claire. Of course I want to make love to you.'

'You want to go to bed with me right now? This evening I mean?'

Again I was taken aback and not sure quite how to reply. I knew I could blow it at any moment, and I had absolutely no idea whether, having lead me on with her questions, Claire was about to give me a broadside - the kind of stinging denunciation which I had become accustomed to from Diana.

I decided to risk it, although there was everything to lose. After all, who dares sometimes dies.

'Well - yes - if you feel like it. But I was only trying to say how much I liked you.'

'All right then. Let's go and have a drink at the Tiger, and then we can go to your place on the way back. But we can't be late. I should be home before midnight.'

I could hardly believe this was happening. Something always spoils such moments, I thought pessimistically. But at least I could act as if it was about to happen, and enjoy the anticipation.

'We're going for a drive and then to the Tiger for a drink,' Claire said to her mother, still in the kitchen, on our way out of the back door.

'Good night Mrs Crundale,' I said as we left.

'Please call me Carol. I expect we'll be seeing a lot of you Mark as we're neighbours and now you've made friends with Claire.'

'Is that the seal of approval, or simple politeness?' I asked Claire once we were outside and on our way to her car.

'A mixture of both probably.' Claire said. 'But she doesn't dislike you, I can say that for sure, so work on it as it will make life so much easier for me.'

We got into the Triumph and Claire leaned across and gave me a kiss on the cheek. 'Cheer up,' she said. 'Smile Captain Wynstanley. Look as if you've heard good news for a change.'

'I certainly have, Miss Crundale. I just hope you're not going to change your mind.'

'No, of course not. I'm not like that, ' Claire replied, adding with a smile, 'unless you behave grossly after a few beers at the pub.'

We didn't stay long at the Tiger or drink much. We found a corner seat to ourselves and I had a whisky as a change from beer while Claire drank a glass of wine. The place was not crowded during the week, and there were no ugly flashing gambling machines. It was a genuine old country pub, quite unpretentious, and had not lost its charm. I felt quite relaxed, and after a brief chat we left for Chalk Hill.

It was a dark night, the sky cloudy and no stars visible, so the black bulk of the old cottage looked slightly sinister in the headlights. I opened the barred wooden gate for Claire and she parked the Triumph in front of my garage. I wished I had left a light on somewhere visible from the front, path, so it was not quite as spooky as we stumbled together arm in arm towards the door in almost total darkness.

I led the way upstairs at once towards the main bedroom already cleaned up with fresh new sheets awaiting Diana's possible visit. I had even polished up the brass bedstead, and placed new clothes hangers on a hook behind the door. And in order to keep things tidy, I had temporarily moved into the other bedroom, where I could spread some of my kit and keep the shotgun and a powerful halogen flashlight handy by the bed at night.

I turned on a new sidelight with a russet coloured shade by the bed and Claire said, 'This all looks as if you were expecting someone, or do you have clean sheets every night!'

Ignoring Claire's remark, I took her in my arms, and we fell towards the bed. I almost smothered Clare with kisses and I could feel her whole body begin to melt into mine. We took off our clothes, and climbed in between the sheets, revelling in our nakedness, both completely turned on by the suddenness and spontaneity of it all, for in sex as with other things, hope deferred sickens the heart.

After an initial period of coupling and uncoupling, my probing right hand gently parted her legs, and reached between her thighs. It was not long before she was gasping for it. 'Now!' Claire said. 'Come on! Now!'

166

Soon, we were panting and groaning until it was over with a gasp and a sigh from Claire. We were still breathing heavily as we fell away from one another and lay close together on our backs. This was a time for silence, and for solace after the intensity of passion had passed. So when we had both recovered a bit, without a word, I leaned across and kissed Claire all over her body, which I had scarcely seen in our haste.

I had rigged up some quite heavy curtains in the window for Diana, who has a thing about privacy, and these were only partly drawn. I got up to pull the curtains back fully to reveal the sheet lightning flickering across the sky so we could lie and watch it from the warm comfort of the bed .

I was about to pull the curtains, when glancing into the orchard, for a brief instant in a lightning flash I saw the dark outline of a man standing quite high up the slope so that he could look into our bedroom window.

'Jesus Christ!' I said involuntarily. 'There's someone out there! Put out the light Claire.'

When the sidelight was out, we stood naked together by the window in the darkness until there was another flicker of lightning, and both of us saw the figure this time, although not at all distinctly. Claire gasped softly in fear and whispered, 'Who the hell is it?'

I quickly got my torch from the side of my bed next door, opened the heavy window with one heave, and shone the powerful beam in the direction of the figure. Now he was lit up like a Christmas tree, and we could see his Barbour jacket, and the shotgun under one arm. His face was partly hidden by a cloth cap and a scarf pulled across the mouth, but there was no doubt in my mind as to his identity.

Then the figure turned around and without another glance in our direction walked swiftly up the slope, and disappeared beyond the torch beam into the blackness of the night.

'You know who that was - don't you Claire. That's your bloody gamekeeper - Tom!'

Chapter 12

Claire was taken aback, and remained silent for a while. We got into bed, and I cuddled close as she was shivering with the cold and shock. Then, I gently turned her around and massaged her back and shoulders to relieve the tension. But the evening had been spoilt: the magic and passion gone.

I sat up, and put on the sidelight. Claire lay there, still silent with her back to me, her face hidden and in shadow. This was our first personal crisis together, and the problem was I did not know her well enough to understand just how upset she might be or how to comfort her.

Our lovemaking seemed so spontaneously magical and I was disappointed things had turned out this way. I felt really angry with Tom, and wished now I had shouted at him from the window to show what I thought of his behaviour.

Fortunately, I held myself in check, for I knew that Claire somehow felt responsible for what had happened. I leaned over towards her, put my hands on her bare shoulders, and said softly in her ear, 'Look - Claire- I'm sorry. I didn't mean to swear at you. It's not your fault that Tom is some kind of a nutter. Or perhaps a peeping Tom would be closer to the truth!' I added with a feeble pun, quite inappropriate in the circumstances.

'No, Tom's not a nutter as you put it,' Claire said very definitely, and on the defensive, sitting up in bed, and folding her arms across her breasts. 'But I'll have to speak to him. I've known Tom for a long time. Since I was a little girl in fact. He's always treated me with respect, as if I were an adult. And we had such good times together. Otherwise it would have been very lonely during the holidays from school. Richard was in the Army and the Grange is very isolated you know.'

'Yes, I understand,' I said. 'But Tom seems very jealous He's always been hostile towards me, and must have been watching us more closely than I realised. Anyway there's no doubt he followed us here, and I don't like being followed. And as for spying through the window, that's really spooky!'

168

'Well, I can hardly speak about it to Dad, and I don't know how Richard would react. He thinks I've been too close to Tom these last few years.'

'Well - as you mentioned it - how close exactly have you been? I mean why is he so jealous?'

Claire surprised me by replying with some anger, 'That's none of your business. My relations with Tom are my affair.'

'For Christ's sake!' I said, 'Don't let's quarrel over Tom, he's done enough damage already. I didn't mean to pry, but naturally I'm puzzled. It's just that things were going so well for us, and we mustn't allow this to spoil it. Tom to spoil it, I mean.'

'Of course not,' Claire said with a smile, leaning over to give me a kiss. 'But it's strange when I'm with you how something always seems to happen. I mean look at our first drive in the Triumph, and ending up at Coldharbour! And then seeing Bailey in Chesterfield Wood.'

'Don't blame me Claire for Tom's behaviour. What happened is not my fault this time.'

However, I thought she was probably right. Certainly in Northern Ireland things tended to happen on my patrols more than others, and the men noticed this. Ballyford I suppose was a prime example. Success - and Ballyford was a major success for us and a disaster for the Provos - always seemed to be at a price.

But I made light of it. 'Well - never mind Claire. We always have an interesting time together so at least you're not bored!'

Claire got out of bed and began putting on her clothes, so I knew the evening, the romantic part of it anyway was over, and except for the kitchen, the cottage was hardly the place for cosy chats.

'I'll take you home now,' I said. 'So you won't be too late.'

'Oh - that doesn't really matter. It's just that I don't feel like explaining myself to the family.' Claire paused a moment, adjusting her bra, 'Not until they've got used to you anyway.'

Then wearing only a dark blue nylon slip, she moved the one chair in the room from her side of the bed and sat down on it in front of the long faded mirror on the bedroom wall. I remembered that this was the mirror in which I had seen my haggard reflection and experienced the flashback to Belfast on the day I first entered the cottage. Tossing her head Claire began to comb her bright blonde hair, perfectly composed and at ease again.

I pulled on my trousers and stood behind her. Perhaps because the bed light gave only a soft glow it seemed from my reflection as if I was suddenly years younger. I bent over, put my arms around her and kissed the back of her head and neck. The sweet scent of her hair made me aware with a pang that in a few minutes she would be gone, and I would sleep alone.

'Well, I now think you should tell no one about Tom. And I wouldn't say anything to him either. Let Tom bring it up if he wants to. But I'll make sure he not around next time.'

Claire remained silent, so I continued, 'There will be a next time Claire - won't there? Or are you so spooked you won't come back?'

'It's not a question of whether I'll come back. Of course I will.' Claire turned round and looked at me directly, before continuing. She had recovered her normal composure, and as usual I had underestimated her. She was a determined woman, and took our friendship seriously.

'You live here, and anyway we can hardly make love over at the Grange. My parents are much too old fashioned, and they don't know you anyway. It's Tom's behaviour that worries me. He's not a nutter, but he's certainly jealous as you say, and I'm not sure what he will do now he knows we saw him watching us.'

'Well if it's any consolation - from where he was standing I doubt whether he could really see right into the bedroom. Anyway, I'll check on that tomorrow. But I still wouldn't say anything to him at the moment. Let him calm down - get a grip on himself - and behave as if nothing happened.'

'Well you might be right. I'll think about it, but my experience has been that's usually it's better to have things out with Tom. Otherwise he tends to brood.'

'All right, let's leave it at that. But I'm angry mainly because his behaviour has spoilt our evening. Of course I wanted to make love to you, but I thought we were going to have a relaxed chat as well, and now we're both too tense.'

'Well, no pillow talk tonight I agree. But I still want to know what you've been up to since we last met. I have a strong feeling you've been back to Coldharbour.'

170

'Look - let's forget all that. Things have become so complex they're almost unbelievable. I certainly wasn't going to discuss those bastards at Coldharbour tonight of all nights. What I want to talk about is us. First, your plans for the future because mine are quite simple. I must tell you now - I want to remain here at Chalk Hill. But I don't know whether you're going to stay on at the Grange. And I'm beginning to get very fond of you - I mean I could easily fall in love.'

'We can't have that!' said Claire laughing, not committing herself in any way. 'But of course we must have a good talk. I can tell you my plans such as they are.'

Then Claire stood up and put her hand on my arm, looking straight into my eyes. 'The truth is Mark I simply can't believe for a moment you've given up on Coldharbour if you really think they're IRA. Something has happened. Perhaps you've reported your suspicions to the police and they're investigating as I always thought they should. But I can't believe you're no longer interested. I mean it's not like you as far as I can judge.'

'Yes - something has happened all right, but as I said it's just too complicated for me to explain at the moment. And I want to try and live a normal life, so in that sense I've cut my mind off from what's happening at Coldharbour.'

Claire looked dubious, clearly not satisfied with my answer, and she changed the subject by saying, 'Anyway, let's go for another walk some time, maybe during the weekend and talk things over. Or during the week if you like, although it depends on the weather I suppose. I'm helping Richard on the farm most mornings mainly in the office I'm afraid. But I'm free after 3.30 when everyone has afternoon tea and a break, and we could go for a walk and then have a drink and something to eat at the Tiger. Richard might join us later in the evening, but we'll see.'

'Well, we don't have to go for a walk to have a chat. I could meet you any evening at the Tiger, or another pub for that matter.'

'Yes, of course, but I like to really relax in the evening, and I have a particular walk in mind.'

'Do you now,' I said. 'Some sort of magical mystery tour perhaps,' and left it at that.

We went downstairs, and into the kitchen. Claire looked around and said, 'You'll have to get this and the sitting room more comfortable before the winter. I can't imagine what it's going to be like without central heating. But the Aga should keep the place warm - that is if you can keep it going.'

'Don't worry - there's plenty of firewood. I found some huge pine logs up near the boundary at the back behind the orchard, and I can burn those in the sitting room. And in case you didn't notice - there's a small coal fireplace in the main bedroom.'

'How convenient for us,' Claire said with a laugh. 'But you know the sitting room fireplace smokes in a north wind.'

'Really - and how do you know that?'

'Tom was caretaker here - don't you remember he told you that when we first met in the orchard. The cottage has been empty nearly a year. He lit the fires to keep the place aired.'

'So you must have been inside the cottage before?'

Claire knew at once she had inadvertently let slip information which she could have kept to herself, and went on the defensive.

'Yes, I've been here with Tom if that's what you really want to know. I helped him clean up the place a bit and light the fires. I mean there was a lot of rubbish and junk about, old newspapers, even old boots and moth eaten rotting clothes in one of the cupboards.'

'Well - I'm grateful. I remember there was nothing in the cottage to give any clue about the people who lived here. And I'm still curious. Who did live here? Did you meet them?'

'Yes. Well - I saw them around. They rented the place for years. An old retired couple in their eighties. The Stodmans. He was a farm labourer somewhere near Canterbury, even before the War I think, and she'd once been a teacher in a small country school. But we never had anything to do with them. Stodman worked as a gardener locally to earn a bit of money, mainly around Highdene. But he was quite uneducated, and thick as two planks. My mother employed him once to help her in the garden, but he did so much damage we never had him back!'

'Did they die here?'

'Well -I'm not sure happened exactly, but I don't think so. He had a stroke, and was taken to the William Harvey hospital at Ashford and died there. Mrs Stodman is still alive, as far as I know, in a home or whatever in Canterbury. Anyway, as you're aware, the place fell into total disrepair, and no one wanted to buy it.'

'The last of Hodge,' I said.

'What do you mean by that ?'

'Well - "Hodge" is an old term for a rustic, a sort of country bumpkin I suppose, and Stodman seems to have been just that from your description. Anyway, I must be grateful, for they somehow preserved Chalk Hill for me. I expect the landlord couldn't get them out on a long term lease. But perhaps I should go and see Mrs Stodman in Canterbury if she's still alive.'

I opened the front door as wide as possible, leaving on the hall light, so Claire could see her way out, and then locked up behind us. We went towards Claire's car, my torch illuminating the brick path. The lightning had stopped and the sky was covered in dense cloud, so that we were enveloped in total darkness.

Claire drove back to the Grange, and I insisted on accompanying her. In the car, I suddenly remembered my invitation to dinner on Saturday night with Mary Renfrew, and the possibility that Diana might come to stay a weekend with me at Chalk Hill. I wished now that I had never asked Diana. Mary Renfrew I could explain away with a good conscience, but Diana was different, and I would have to tread delicately.

'Oh. - by the way,' I said. 'Mary Renfrew - you know Chapman's secretary - asked me out to supper at her cottage in Pelham. Probably this Saturday, and I thought it would be rude for me to refuse. '

'You don't have to detail your social life to me,' Claire said. 'If you've got something going with Mary Renfrew though good luck to you as I think she's pretty strange.'

'Really. What makes you think that? She seemed pretty normal to me.'

'Well you would know,' Claire said sarcastically, 'but she's had a long affair with the local GP, and it became almost a fatal attraction. I mean she was quite obsessive. But don't let me put you off. I'm sure she will cook you a good meal. And it will be interesting to see what develops.'

'Nothing will develop. It's just a question, as I said of not causing offence. Mary was very helpful to me over the selling of Chalk Hill, and it would have been rude of me to refuse.'

'Of course,' said Claire. 'I was only warning you. But that woman does not do things casually. She has a purpose.'

173

I said no more, and realised that the question of Diana coming to stay had suddenly become far trickier than I expected.

The floodlight came on as I got out of the Triumph and opened the main gate. I stood beside the driver's window dazzled by the light and leaned down to say goodnight. We kissed, and I murmured, 'See you soon.' Then as she drove towards the backyard, I closed the gate and walked to Chalk Hill using my torch most of the way, forcing myself not to think of Tom.

Nevertheless, I kept my wits about me and remained alert for subconsciously I half expected Tom to be still lurking around. My torch cut a swathe of light through the blackness of the night, and I felt the loneliness of the single for the first time for years. But there was a lot to think about on my way home.

First, my evening with Claire, and what this meant in terms of my future. I was in a romantic mood full of longing for Claire, and still angry that the evening had ended so bizarrely. Nevertheless, I forced myself to think realistically. Men and women had indefinite relationships these days: sometimes the attachments were short, just a few months, but more often several years as far as I knew.

Marriage and long term commitments were out, and in the Army this suited most of us early in our careers. But I was now 28 years old, and it seemed middle age loomed in the not too distant future.

Claire, on the other hand was still young, about 21 or 22, I guessed, and might well look upon me as too old for her. This was food for thought for it meant that if I wanted to marry anyone in her age group, there was not much time. Quite rightly, few younger women wished to be tied down at that stage of their lives, and certainly not with anyone much older than themselves.

However, with Claire as my nearest neighbour, a relaxed 'modern' relationship could be very convenient for both of us. In fact, I suspected that for the moment, while Claire worked things out, such an arrangement would suit her very well. And most importantly it would give us time to get to know one another well, both mentally and sexually.

I understood that with this kind of relationship, and no thought of children of course, (Claire would have to avoid pregnancy like a sexual disease), the pull of her family would come between us in the end. She might well come and live with me at some embarrassment

174

to her parents, but surely Chalk Hill would be a poor exchange for the Grange.

I would have to do my best to earn a living by writing and this would mean solitude for most of the day, and Claire could not be expected to work like a domestic cleaning up the cottage while I sat at a word processor. She would feel lonely too and probably spend part of the day over at the Grange, chatting with her mother, or working for Richard on the farm and estate.

Living in the country alone as a writer still seemed ideal for me, but once I thought in terms of settling down with a partner, the situation became more complex. In a city, partners shared a rented flat, both had jobs ideally at least, and maintenance of the accommodation was easy.

Chalk Hill, on the other hand was not self sustaining like a farm or estate, where sufficient income could be generated to keep a couple going. And it had become run down in the last few years, so there was a lot of work which needed to be done urgently.

I also understood only too well that in order to make sure the property, including all the various outhouses as well as the cottage did not deteriorate any further, the place required an investment of capital, at least £25,000, but I did not possess that kind of money.

Thinking realistically rather than romantically, any partner of mine would need to be committed to running the place for no financial return, as well as having a job. Of course, I could look round locally, and see if I could find a much younger version of Mr Stodman to employ several days a week comparatively cheaply, but I doubted it. Anyway, I could try, and perhaps Mary Renfrew might know of someone in Pelham.

Then, if Claire still wanted to continue her academic career by studying for an MA, something she had not mentioned recently, she could commute each day of the term to the University of Canterbury by car, while I wrote in the mornings and cleaned up the place during the afternoons with outside help. But why should she leave her comfortable and convenient set up at the Grange, especially if she returned to the university, for the rigours and drudgery of Chalk Hill?

All these thoughts were running through my mind as I walked past the common and along the lanes towards my cottage, my eyes focused mesmerically only on the bright patch of light from the torch.

I had never thought like this before, and the long term reality of our romance was sobering. A very different picture of the country cottage was emerging from those painted by Helen Allingham! Of course, I knew this already, but I had never understood the changing nature of partnership or marriage as an extension of this concept. The Army despite its modernisations, and comparative egalitarianism of the SAS, was still essentially a hierarchy.

Thinking philosophically, morality in the old fashioned sense, the ideal of the family, for example, was thus partly dependent upon exigency. Today, with a radically different economic system, there were also new sets of values, which in themselves, like the idea of partnership rather than marriage, also had strong moral imperatives.

My musings left me in a daze, and slightly confused. I seemed to have lost the certainties I had cultivated in the Army. Nevertheless, it was a pleasant change from working out how to kill people, or to stop them killing me.

However, when I reached Chalk Hill, I decided to concentrate on my security for the rest of the evening. Before I went to sleep, I checked that all the doors were locked and bolted, and shone my powerful torch from my bedroom window out into the orchard, weaving it from side to side like a searchlight. A pair of eyes shone at me, as a fox stared into the beam for a moment and then trotted away into the night. 'No chickens for you here!' I said aloud. But the very presence of the fox indicated better than my torch beam that no one was around.

Chapter 13

The following morning I woke early after a deep sleep full of vivid anxiety dreams, something which I had not experienced lately. I did not know what had triggered them off. Perhaps the shock of seeing the muffled figure of Tom in the orchard late last night and the embarrassment we were being watched, unconsciously brought back all the old fears which had been plaguing me for months.

Slowly and wearily I went down into to the kitchen. I had replaced the primus stove with a new electric kettle, and made myself a strong mug of tea which I carried back to my bedroom. It was a dull grey morning. Although the thunderstorms had passed, and the wind dropped, I felt strangely lethargic, and reluctant to get going so I sat up in bed and drank the tea slowly savouring every drop. In a reflective mood, slightly melancholic, I mulled over the past and what I had to do next.

Despite my decision not to have anything more to do with what was going on at Coldharbour after the phone call with MI5, I still could not get the whole thing out of my mind. Indeed, my obsession with the IRA at Coldharbour seemed part of a pattern which stretched for ever: right back to Northern Ireland and all the wasted years of my youth.

I appeared to have been playing my part in the latest of a series of dramas whose scripts were written by prisoners of its mournful history. Some of the 'players', as we aptly called members of the IRA, I knew by sight or from Intelligence reports. Others I knew quite well, once they had turned and become informers or potential ones. Then there were the shadowy masked figures seen by starlight in an image intensifier, or most dramatically in a gun sight with that curious focused concentration which a sudden flow of adrenalin provides.

Each scene and every act of these plays, created by unwilling stepchildren of a wicked mother England, were basically a repetition of Ireland's colonial past. A reiteration of Ireland's wrongs and a cry that men and women should be prepared to die to right the wrongs.

It was as if injustice always required a sacrifice, and could be righted in no other way. Furthermore, the many years of my youth had gone in that conflict of wills in Northern Ireland and could never be regained. The Protestants of Ulster were prepared to die to celebrate their victories, while Republicans were dying to avenge them.

I could understand clearly now that both sides involved me in the kind of madness which affected anyone connected with the Troubles. The dirty war we fought was simply a reflection of the wider insanity. Anyway, the past had claimed me in the same way it claimed the Irish.

What appeared as an eternity at the moment, was in reality quite short. Tension affected my judgement of the passing of time, so that the last few weeks were some of the longest of my life. It was now well into August, yet my arrival at Chalk Hill in mid July seemed like last year. The threats which emerged after my discharge from the Army and events surrounding Coldharbour prevented my return to normalcy until after I met Claire. Scarcely a day had gone by in which the past had not intruded.

Obviously, my obsession with survival, and the pull of patriotism and tradition had affected my judgement. Furthermore, the confirmation I had enemies on my own side, who were prepared to consign me to an Army psychiatric unit when I informed them of my startling discoveries at Coldharbour, were deeply wounding, and fuelled my feelings of persecution,

However, once I began to think about my relationship with Claire, it seemed as if I had a future, and the past began to fade. Of course, I always retained my love of nature, and this had been my salvation helping me retain my sanity in the times of great stress. But my love for Claire forced me to think of someone else besides myself, and to think of our futures, rather than my just my own.

I finished my tea, and decided to end my somewhat melancholy philosophical reflections, and turn my mind to more mundane practical matters. I had breakfast in the kitchen as usual, and as usual I was running short of food. Today, would have to be a sorting out one. Shopping in Pelham, and phone calls to Diana and to my mother. Diana was going to be a problem. What on earth had made me invite her here? I must have been out of my mind to have even thought of her finding out where I actually lived at this critical juncture of my life when my personal security was vital. However, the invitation was given on the spur of the moment before I had got to know Claire, and grown to love her.

I now realised that Diana *had* to be told the invitation was off. This was made easier for me because she had been so irritatingly indefinite in the first place and her last words, her parting shot on the phone, had been that I was not to bank on her coming anyway.

I hoped it was therefore quite possible that she had decided not to come of her own accord. After all she had nothing to gain, and if Howard found out it would be the end of their engagement or partnership. It could be awkward for me too with Claire. How could I invite another woman to stay with me at Chalk Hill, clearly an old girl friend when I had told Claire I loved her. It was not on, and I had to get myself off the hook as soon as possible.

I phoned my mother from Highdene just before 9am, and she told me that she was all right, and looking forward to my next visit. But now she admitted there had been more phone calls from the IRA, something she had not mentioned before today. One of the callers had indirectly threatened her, by saying, 'Well we think you know where your son is hiding, and it's about time you helped us.'

However, strangely there had been no such calls recently, and she hoped they had given up.

'I hope so,' I said, and added reassuringly, 'You may have read in the papers or seen on TV that there are so called secret negotiations going on at the moment between the British Government and the IRA, and if so - maybe my case is on hold.'

'Oh - I almost forgot, but here I've written it down. A Major Tony Fairburn phoned yesterday. He said he was a friend of yours in the Regiment - you had met recently too. Anyway, he wanted you to contact him as soon as possible at Hereford, Stirling lines. He said it was urgent,, and that Colonel Nick Rose sent his regards.'

'Thanks mother. Yes - I know Tony Fairburn. We met again by chance on my way here in the van just after I'd been to stay with you at the end of June. And of course, Nick Rose is an old friend. He was with me in South Armagh.'

I was surprised and puzzled, but pleased that old friends in the Regiment - 22 SAS - had taken the trouble to try and contact me again. Perhaps there was going to be a reunion of some kind, I guessed.

Then I told my mother that I was about to phone Diana, and asked whether she had spoken to her recently.

'Yes, indeed I have. Diana has been very friendly and very attentive too. She's been very confiding. I think she still has a soft spot for you. Anyway, that's my impression.'

'Well, she seems pretty tied up with Howard. I wouldn't be surprised if they got married.'

'Well, perhaps. The Mathisons talk about Howard's engagement, and I think that's the way it will stay for a long time. And I'm not sure that Hilda Mathison approves of Diana anyway. Howard's earning a lot of money in Birmingham, and Hilda's quite ambitious socially for him.'

There was a pause and my mother continued, 'I must tell you that Diana has suggested we come down and see you together some weekend - next weekend I think and she wants to drive us in her car.'

I was horrified. The last thing I wanted was Diana coming down to Chalk Hill with my mother, selfish as this may seem.

'That's very kind of Diana,' I said, 'but the truth is I was just about to try and get myself out of a very unwise invitation I gave her recently to come here next weekend. It was unwise because she's virtually engaged to Howard, and intended staying here without telling him.'

'Perhaps you still really like Diana after all. I mean why would you have invited her?'

'Well, I suppose she's an old friend. And I wanted to explain about that unfortunate incident when Howard was nearly kidnapped by mistake. But there's something else mother, which I have to tell you.'

'And what's that?'

'Well - I've met a woman called Claire, daughter of a local landowner, living next to me with her parents here in Kent, and we've been getting on well - certainly better than I get on with Diana these days, I'm afraid. Anyway, Claire would hardly have appreciated my having Diana to stay, so I was going to get out of it if possible.'

'All right - I understand. But why don't you bring Claire along with you to see me here at High Oaks. I would love to meet her here in our old home, where I'll be more at ease. And it will be less trouble for you than putting us up in the cottage. And as Diana is already engaged to Howard, she's not going to be put out I'm sure.'

I agreed this was an excellent idea, and said I would find out from Claire if she could spare the time away from the farm and estate.

'Well, if Claire's a real country girl she'll love this part of the world.'

My mother also said she would explain the situation to Diana first, before I phoned her myself, so she would know directly that my mother would prefer me to come home again for a while.

Anyway, I had got myself off the hook, and really looked forward to driving Claire to Shropshire. It would be a great way to go home again, remembering the tensions of my last trip from High Oaks to Chalk Hill.

My next phone call was to Mary Renfrew at her office confirming I was very pleased to accept her invitation to a meal tonight night. She sounded off hand, and very formal, but I knew Chapman might be listening in, and anyway she was a woman of moods.

'I didn't think there was any doubt, ' she said. 'I assumed as I had heard nothing from you to the contrary that you were coming, and have made arrangements for you to meet someone.'

'Who exactly may I ask?'

'Well - it will be a surprise. But they won't be staying for supper, so come along early at about 6 as we arranged.

For some reason, I just could not face phoning Tony at that moment. I decided to leave it until I drove onto Pelham and cleared my mind a bit. Anyway, I left the phone box in Highdene thinking about the various calls I had made, and glad in a way that I seemed to have rectified my mistake in inviting Diana to Chalk Hill. It was really nice of her to offer to drive my mother down, and I felt guilty at putting off their visit.

Yes, my mother was right I did indeed still have a soft spot for Diana, and she was up to something herself - the attraction of opposites I suppose. We always made love most fiercely and passionately after one of our innumerable arguments.

It was good news too that the IRA phone calls had stopped. But, despite what I'd said to my mother, I didn't think for a minute they had willingly given up on me. I knew them too well for that.

181

Giving up was not in their vocabulary. Something else was now their priority - the kidnapping was delayed simply because they wanted to lie low for something more important. It would not be off the agenda because it was good intelligence on our part which would always threaten them in the long run, even their next operation, so someone had made a difficult decision. Perhaps they had understood that with MI5 running the whole intelligence effort, Special Branch sidelined and people like me outlawed they should concentrate their own limited counter intelligence elsewhere.

Then the full implications of my own hypothesis hit me like a missile. The attack on the Channel Tunnel might be more than just a mortaring - something really big - a two or even three pronged attack. By that I mean that 'homemade' mortars are always tricky, especially their accuracy, so for maximum effect there could be a back up of a vehicle full of explosives to be driven into the Tunnel area. The bomb would probably be mainly made up of a mixture of fertilisers, primed with the more useful but difficult to come by, Semtex. This was possibly stored at Coldharbour, although I had seen no sign of it during my brief visit and hurried exit.

If so, nothing else, no other ASU operation, like the kidnapping of an ex SAS officer, for example, should sound any kind of alert - all efforts would be concentrated on the Tunnel. Of course, this was all guesswork. But my mind was running wild with a sudden brainstorm of ideas, and some of them might be right. Then I had another thought. Perhaps there could be a clue in the locked room under the disused railway bridge over the gully in the woods near Coldharbour. An arms cache which could be left there indefinitely.

My mind still racing, I drove into Pelham to buy stores. I tried my best to quell my excitement for during the last few days I had achieved some degree of peace. My pursuit of Claire, unlike the pursuits of Northern Ireland, had led me to feelings of love and faith in a tranquil future, rather than hate and violent death.

When I finished the shopping, I decided to try and contact Tony. Probably some kind of a regimental reunion was my first thought when my mother told me of his call. But I simply had to know, for I felt I was in the grip of fate. A phone box was handy, just off the main street, and I knew the number of Stirling Lines by heart. Once I was through, I gave my rank and name and asked for

Major Tony Fairburn. He was not immediately available, but I phoned back in 10 minutes, and was put through at once.

'Your timing is excellent,' Tony said. 'I've been trying to contact you at home.' He paused a moment, and I waited, determined to say nothing until I knew what this was all about.

'There are some things we need to discuss urgently, but not on the phone. I mean could we meet soon? Where are you at the moment?'

'At a phone box in Kent. But give me some idea at least what this is all about.'

'OK - It's about the film we were all involved in making recently. Some of the actors, the players - have been showing signs of taking up jobs in your locality, and I heard through the agency that you might know their whereabouts. We want to continue the series you see, and keep in touch.'

'Of course I know their whereabouts,' I said very definitely and slightly aggressively, catching on at once, 'but some members of the agency have not exactly been very receptive recently when approached.'

'Yes. Don't worry. That's come to my attention. By chance as a matter of fact. But we have reason to believe you. And we want to use your knowledge of the industry to help us out. And Nick is totally behind you of course, so there are a lot of people on your side.'

'That's a change,' I said. 'I could do with some help. But not of the psychiatric kind - thanks very much. The point is that I can contact the people you want for the next series any time, but they'll need persuasion. So you'd better be prepared to make them a good offer.'

'Right - I understand. So where do we meet and when? Here or there?'

I suggest Canterbury. Outside the Cathedral first and then we can wander in and check the set. But you have to pay these days remember. All the players live nearby and we can audition them together if you like. Bring some camera men along too - as a back up'

'OK. But when exactly?'

'Can you get here by next Monday I mean this Monday, at 11am sharp? The day after tomorrow. Does that suit you?

'The sooner the better. Monday would be all right with me, but 1pm rather than 11am - if that's all right - we're on. And welcome back!'

Tony rang off, and I was left in the phone box with the same feelings of unreality which I experienced whenever I dealt with the activities of the IRA in England. People walking past on the pavement carrying shopping in a sleepy English country town, the summer sky darkened with rain clouds and flocks of pigeons turning and wheeling above the red tiled roofs. Yet the enemy within so close, and planning death and destruction only a few miles from this peaceful scene.

My reaction to Tony's call was mixed. I was glad at last I had friends from the Regiment clearly on my side. They must have got wind of my phone call to MI5 or more probably to Ashford. On the other hand, I was just beginning to settle down into civilian life, and the effects of the past were beginning to fade.

Yet, my conscience was troubling me all the same. Deep down, the old loyalties still remained, despite my feelings about Atherton and the backing he appeared to have been receiving from MI5. So in a sense, the call from Tony, gave me the chance to play my part again in the drama, which on my own had the potential to destroy me. The phone call indicated I was no longer alone and more importantly my own people were taking my report seriously.

I wondered about the sudden apparent change in my status from a psychiatric case with hallucinations about the IRA to someone with valuable information. I began to feel that something was on and the SAS had been called in. My information about a likely attempt to mortar or to bomb the Channel Tunnel must have been found to have substance.

Anyway, I knew that no one but the SAS would be able to take out Coldharbour. The place was like a bloody fortress by now, and Christ knows how many AK-47s they had there. And of course there were the mortars which I suppose could be used to defend the place too.

The trick would be to catch them all out in the open, on the way to the job. This was no longer my responsibility, but my past training forced me to think of the options. If the ASU were allowed to move the mortars, they would be out in the open all right; but once the mortars were in place, it would be a close run thing. They

184

would almost certainly use a timer, but in an emergency the mortars could be fired at once.

However, Danton Lane could be the ideal killing ground I reflected. Unlike the open very public area of Winston Churchill Avenue in Gibraltar, where Danny McCann and Mairead Farrell were shot by SAS, the lane was totally shut in, a tunnel of dense green hedges completely hidden from prying eyes or photographs by chance onlookers. A secluded death trap for anyone caught there. And with the mortars in place and ready to be fired, the public around the Tunnel entrance would be in imminent danger, so none of the ASU would survive.

I stepped out of the phone box, my heart pounding, and forced myself to think of something else. Dinner with Mary Renfrew tonight for example. My next meeting with Claire and how much I should tell her. Professionally nothing, I knew that, but I had other priorities now.

The rest of the morning passed uneventfully, I bought cartons of milk, bread, the *Times* and *Telegraph* at the local store in Highdene, which I always tried to support as much as possible. It was sad to see these local country stores succumbing to the lure of the big supermarkets, and the Highdene one only just managed to keep going, mainly because it still served as a post office.

Rather than play the mysterious stranger, I introduced myself to the owners, a middle aged couple, the Martons, who had been there since just after the War. To my surprise they already knew my name and address, although I received very little mail. They seemed completely reliable, pleasant yet unimaginative people, who in time might be enlisted on my side as part an early warning system for suspicious strangers. As I had found out in Northern Ireland, local stores were founts of information. They often had links to the paramilitary of both sides, on whom they were often dependent for protection, especially the Catholics. When I returned to Chalk Hill, I found a scribbled note from Claire on my doorstep.

'Came round this morning, but obviously you are out. I wanted to let you know that friends of Richard and the family are coming on Sunday for lunch, and I have to be here and they won't leave until late. But instead I have Tuesday or Wednesday free, so let's go for our walk either afternoon, or all day if you like

depending on the weather. Lots to talk about I'm sure! Have a good evening with Mrs Renfrew!

Love, Claire.'

I was disappointed about Sunday, because I really wanted to see Claire as often as possible. I wanted to have a good talk about our future, and I needed her physical presence. But now I could wait until after I had seen Tony on Monday before making up my mind whether to discuss what was happening with Claire. Action was in the offing and the possible elimination of an ASU. If I told Clair, the full story and its implications, such knowledge would place an awful lot of responsibility upon her, perhaps far too much. The more I thought about it, the more I realised that it would go against all my training to give an outsider any hint of such an impending action. Anyway, it was better to preserve her innocence of these things, although she might take my silence badly.

*

I worked away on the property all afternoon and after a bath, and change into clean clothes and a light wool jacket drove to Pelham about 6pm. Mary's cottage was one of many all close together along a lane above the main street, semi-detached, with an old track leading up the hill behind it on one side. I was intrigued by the track and paused a moment to look. It must have once given access to the fields for agricultural labour and had now become a public footpath and signposted as such. Red bricks and very old flint walls protected and demarcated the long and narrow cottage gardens which ran up the hill on each side of the footpath.

Mary's cottage had no front garden, just a narrow strip of earth from which grew climbing roses reaching high to the top windows directly overlooking the lane. The lower part of the cottage was built of red brick, and the upper section protected with hanging peg tiles. Her number, a white seventeen, stood out on the black front door, and below it was a large brass lion knocker which I used by mistake instead of the doorbell.

A moment later Mary opened the door, smiled welcomingly, and ushered me in. She seems in a good mood, I thought, wondering how long it would last.

'I always know when a stranger arrives because they knock,' she said. 'You see I've also got a bell,' pointing to a small button which I had failed to notice.

'Well - next time, I won't be considered a stranger then - will I?'

'No - of course not,' she said, putting her hand firmly on my left arm to steady me while she pointed out the step down into the tiny hallway, before we moved into the sitting room.

'This must be an old house,' I said, referring to the sunken floor at the front door, and looked admiringly at the blackened oak beams which ran across the low ceiling.

'Yes, one of the oldest in Pelham. Or so I'm told. 1750, or thereabouts. Anyway, as you can see it's very comfortable.'

'It certainly is,' I said, as I walked slowly across the room towards the windows overlooking the back garden.

'These gardens seem to run a long way up the hill. I had a look along the footpath when I arrived.'

'About sixty yards. Plenty of room for planting vegetables. I think that was the idea. People still do, of course. Grow vegetables - I mean. But they're so cheap at the supermarket.'

Mary offered me a wine, and I sat down on a large sofa facing the brick fireplace, while she fetched it. The room was full of ornaments, and flowers everywhere in vases and containers of all shapes. There were several huge armchairs with brightly coloured cushions, and the polished wooden floor was strewn with white Indian rugs. A number of medium sized watercolours of country scenes hung on the walls, small white cottages, rough stone walls and dark brooding hills. All a little faded, but originals I guessed.

'Who painted the watercolours?' I asked.

'My grandmother,' Mary replied.' They're of Ireland. Donegal - as a matter of fact. My father was Irish - remember I told you in the pub? His mother was an artist.'

'Of course,' I said standing up and moving closer to one of the paintings over the mantle piece .

It was of a narrow pass between the rock strewn slopes of a mountain in Ireland. A small Catholic shrine nestled into the hillside, the statue of the Virgin Mary lit up ethereally by the slanting rays from the sun half hidden between black clouds. In the foreground, patches of purple heather still retained much of their original colours, although blue sky in the distance was almost white. I looked more closely. On the wooden frame at the bottom centre was a small green label and written on it in black Indian ink to identify the scene, 'Croaghcarragh, Mamores, Donegal, July 1953'. The artist's illegible signature was in the bottom right hand corner of the watercolour.

'I suppose you never went across the border into Donegal,' said Mary almost in my ear, for she had walked up softly behind me while I was absorbed in the painting, and when I turned was standing so close I could scent her hair.

For a moment I was taken aback at her closeness, for subconsciously perhaps I had half expected that her feelings would emerge slowly and equivocally as the evening progressed. I saw that she was breathing quite fast which suddenly aroused me for I realised that her excitement was sexual, and her warm presence overwhelming.

Then I held her gently in my arms looking closely into her eyes to assess the reaction, and when she closed them, I leaned forward and kissed her on the forehead. We stood there clasping one another, our grips tightening as our bodies swayed, and I kissed her again this time fully on the lips, and then on the neck, and back again to her lips.

At that moment the doorbell chimed, and Mary disengaged herself quickly, looking briefly into a small ornamental mirror on the mantle piece to tidy her hair, although the flush on her face remained.

'Friend not foe!' I said jokingly. 'Only strangers like me knock.'

'That'll be Tara. A surprise for you I'm sure, but she won't be staying long.'

Mary went to the door and opened it to welcome someone very warmly in the hall.

I heard a woman's voice with an Irish accent and intonation. Then Mary and her guest came through the door, and standing slightly awkwardly before me, embarrassed rather than shy, was the young woman Claire and I had met at Coldharbour Farm.

'Tara - this is Mark - a friend of mine, who lives near Highdene.'

I walked towards her and shook hands, which she did somewhat reluctantly. Tara looked at me sharply, not with any personal interest, but quizzically, judging perhaps whether I was friend or foe.

I tested her out. 'I think we may have met before. Your face seems familiar.' But there was no response.

'Tara is helping to run a business up at Coldharbour Farm,' said Mary as there was an awkward pause. 'She's been working in London for some years, and wanted a change in the country.'

'How long were you in London?' I asked politely trying for a positive response.

'Oh – Nearly three years. But I was glad to get out.'

'I lent her my car for the day,' Mary said, and then turning to Tara asked, 'Well - How did you get on? No problems I hope.'

'It was fine.' said Tara, 'No problems at all and I've filled up with petrol just now on my way back.'

'And how do you like it up at Coldharbour?' I asked as Tara sat down and Mary gave her a large glass of wine, which she gulped thirstily as if it was beer.

'Its fine,' Tara said and I knew that everything was going to be fine - all answers to my questions would be similar non-committal one liners.

Then Tara shifted the attention from herself by asking, 'Do you work here or up in London ?'

'Oh - I'm a local now. I work from home - from a cottage on the common near Highdene. I'm a free lance writer. Very free at the moment - as I'm just starting. I'm trying for the natural history, countryside market - without much success. But it'll need time to break in.'

'You don't work for a newspaper then?'

'No such luck. I've been an academic until recently,' I lied. 'But I got tired of teaching and want to do something more creative.'

Tara seemed more at ease once I had explained myself, so I was determined to try again to get her to talk. I went up to the watercolour of Donegal above the mantle piece and said, 'I've just been admiring Mary's watercolours of Ireland. Her mother was an artist , and these are her watercolours. This one's of Donegal. Have you been there? I mean which part of Ireland are you from?'

Tara ignored my first question, but brightened up at the mention of Donegal. She got up, then hesitated a moment before standing beside me, and looked more closely at the picture.

'Yes, I admired this one the last time I was here. I know the place. We used to go from Buncrana to Tullagh Bay the other way through Clonmany when I was a kid. And one day we came back over Croaghcarragh, and it was so steep and narrow, my mother prayed to the virgin for our safety on the way down,' Tara said, pointing to the shrine and she laughed for the first time. Her face lit up a moment and I glimpsed the Irish spontaneity in conversation, the warmth of family, the essential humanity.

'And you've never been back?'

But it was the wrong question. I had gone too far. Tara immediately looked suspicious, slightly alarmed in fact., and rightly so. Parts of Donegal had been used as bases for murderous IRA raids over the border for years. It was also a comparatively safe IRA training area, although a watch had to be kept out for the Gardai.

'Why? Do you know Ireland? Have you been there?'

'Yes,' I said. 'I was at Queen's university for a year when I was a student.' I had lied again, and Mary, who was listening to the conversation knew I was lying, but her expression did not change.

'And did you go to the Republic?' Tara asked.

'Down to Dublin once,' I said.

'And what were you studying at Belfast?'

I noticed that Tara had said 'Belfast' rather than Queen's which made me think she was not familiar with the academic scene, and the way she spoke suggested it was enemy territory.

'Irish history and politics,' I said, realising at once that I was the one being interrogated now.

'Well - you should know how we all feel then.'

'Indeed,' I said. 'Only too well. And my opinion is that the Brits should get out of Northern Ireland as soon as possible,' and this time I was not lying.

'Well - why don't you?' Tara said quite aggressively draining her large glass of wine, and putting it down quite hard on the side table.

These are very large glasses, I thought, more like goblets than normal wine glasses. Tara's been driving all day without much to eat probably and the alcohol has gone to her head.

'Because as you well know a large number of Protestants in Northern Ireland still regard themselves as British, and the British Government feels that they cannot be abandoned without guarantees.'

'But the Brits put them there in the first place and drove us out into the bogs. We're only reclaiming what's rightfully our own.'

'Yes, I know and agree, but we can't make matters worse by leaving you all to fight it out - that would be irresponsible.'

'Once you Brits leave, once there's no army of occupation, things will sort themselves out - I'm sure of that,' Tara said very firmly concluding the conversation, which she must have realized had probably gone too far.

Bailey, or whoever was in command of the ASU would have told them all specifically not to become engaged in any political arguments while in England for fear of drawing attention to themselves. Tara had become involved in a frank argument with me only because of my evident friendship with Mary whom she trusted. This made her relax her guard and the wine loosened her tongue.

Mary seemed slightly put out that Tara and I became locked in argument within a few minutes of meeting, but it was certainly not my fault. Indeed, considering the background of both of us, we had got on rather well! Conversation faltered for a moment, while we switched to non-controversial topics, but certainly the air had been cleared a bit. Tara chatted away quite normally with Mary, until I asked her where she had been for the day.

There was a pause, and Tara became quite tense again, although she did her best to conceal it by taking a deep breath. She replied in a slightly rising tone as if unsure of herself.

'I had to go to Dover. A consignment was due from Holland, and it was held up for some reason by Customs.'

Then by way of further explanation, Mary added, 'All the Company cars were being used and Tara's has clutch problems so I lent her mine for the day.'

Tara may have grown tired of the questioning because she suddenly said to Mary, 'I wonder what's happened to Sean? He should be here by now. I asked him to pick me up at 7 in the Land Rover. '

'Mark - would you mind having a quick look outside down the lane, while I discuss a few things with Tara? Sean hasn't been here before. He drives an old green Land Rover.'

'Certainly Mary,' I said, although I could see that Tara was not too pleased with the idea of me looking out for Sean.

I went into the hall, closing the sitting room door behind me. As I did so I noticed a long khaki holdall stained with oil placed away from the front door against the opposite wall. It must belong to Tara, I thought, as it was not there when I arrived.

I was going to quietly unzip it and look inside when it saw it was neatly padlocked. I picked it up and was surprised at the weight - at least 15kg or thirty pounds I guessed. I felt through the canvas, and although the bag had been tightly packed with thick towelling, I could feel at one end, the hard wooden butts of rifles of some kind. Assault rifles, AK-47s from Eastern Europe, I guessed, purchased probably with NORAID funds.

I opened the front door, and went outside, and as I did so, Tara appeared and joined me. She had just missed seeing me checking the holdall, and the consequences could have been disastrous!

'Sean's a bit shy of strangers,' Tara said.

'Really? Has he been in England long?'

'About a year, I think.

'In London?'

'Yes - he's in the building trade.'

It was clear I was not going to get much more out of Tara, but she had told me enough to surmise that she and Sean were 'sleepers', that is IRA recruits with no previous records, whose names would not come up on the MI5 or Special Branch computers when they arrived in Britain.

'Where's Mary's car?' I asked.

'She didn't want it parked here, so it's further down, where there's more room,' Tara said, pointing along the lane. 'Sean will have to pull in close to let anyone pass,' she added.

I looked at Tara closely as she spoke. Her features were more sharply delineated outside in the evening light than inside the cool gloom of the sitting room. A remarkably handsome woman, I thought, about 5ft 9ins tall, very slim, and with smooth skinned arms and legs, no freckles, more Italian than Celtic. Quite a narrow face with high slightly jutting cheek bones, a long nose balanced by very full sensual lips and strong chin. Her shoulder length hair was black, but with a slight reddish tinge, like the gleam of sunlight on copper, possibly created by a touch of red henna, as I knew from Diana. Black darting eyes gave her an alert almost hunted look, and she had very little make up apart from lipstick so her fresh complexion was immediately evident.

Tara was wearing what I presumed to be a modern business woman's outfit, a smart black jacket with brass buttons like a reefer, and a black skirt which came just below her knees. Around her neck was a gold chain with a gold heart shaped locket resting between her breasts slightly exposed by the undone top button of her white blouse. She must have adopted these fashions while working in London, I thought, and the outward presentation of self fitted in exactly with the image of a top secretary or middle rank business executive. Conformity with style, combined with youth, enough to make male colleagues fearful for their jobs, while at the same time be sexually attracted. A dangerous combination for any rival, but a long way from the popular image of an IRA terrorist.

However, the most striking thing about her was the impression of restless energy, a tensile peasant strength and endurance. Tara also appeared to have a stubborn self willed determination, which only ideology could conquer, and this could be her weakness as well as her strength, I calculated.

'There he is !' Tara exclaimed as an old dark green Land Rover appeared at the end of the lane. She waved at the driver, who stopped outside the cottage with a squeal of brakes.

Mary had by now come to the door, and I went back inside with her, leaving Tara to greet Sean on her own. However, I knew that there was no way I could tell Mary the truth about Tara, or what I had guessed was in the holdall. She had almost certainly used Mary's car as a cover, being extra cautious while picking up the assault rifles, just in case her own vehicle has somehow already been spotted and its number placed on an MI5 or Special Branch computer.

So I carried on the charade. I felt bad about it because Mary had been so trusting, so keen for me to meet Tara and to confirm there was nothing strange or suspicious about the people up at Coldharbour

'Tara's a very handsome woman. Quite a character,' I said softly, lowering my voice so that it would not carry into the hall. 'But I'm sorry I didn't have a more relaxed conversation with her.' Then I laughed and added, 'However, in the circumstances, with your connivance, we didn't do too badly, I suppose!'

We'll talk about that later,' Mary said. 'Tara's under great strain in her new job. I think the men are taking advantage of her. I mean she's always running errands like today for instance.'

Tara came into the sitting room followed reluctantly by Sean. He had ginger hair cut short, and a fresh shiny freckled face, like a young lad at a secondary school. I also noticed the long cut with congealed blood, and the purplish bruising above his right eye. Sean stood there in the doorway, grinning, but silent, clearly ill at ease, and obviously wanting to leave at once with Tara.

I recognised Sean at once as the man who had shot at me with the AK-47 outside the barn that night at Coldharbour, and for a moment forgot that I had been masked with a balaclava.

Now I could see him properly, I reckoned he was only about 19 or maybe 20 years old perhaps. Almost certainly chosen by the IRA because of his clean record, not for his experience or specialised knowledge. That's probably why he fired on automatic instead of steady single shots and why I'm alive today, I thought.

The AK-47 was uncocked too and the cocking lever placed awkwardly on the right hand side, so he would have needed to reach over with his left hand, if he wanted to keep his finger near the trigger. Also, the safety catch on AK-47s slid down first to automatic rather than single shot, so all these technical details helped to save my life as well. And of course I was lucky too. One burst into my back at that close range would have exited through my chest and blown bits of flesh out in front of my face. I would have been dead before I hit the ground.

Anyway, it was hard to imagine this shy fresh faced lad had tried to kill me only about a week ago, and that I had thrown the spanner which gave him such a nasty wound. But even harder to comprehend was what he and Tara were up to now.

'We'll have to be going,' Tara said to Mary. 'I'm much obliged for the loan of your car.'

Turning to me she said formally, 'Pleased to meet you. I hope the writing goes well.' Then, with a faint smile she continued, 'But there's more to life than the countryside.'

'Of course,' I said. 'But sometimes it depends upon whose countryside, doesn't it? Especially whether it's, "mine own - my native land", quoting Browning. 'Then there's few things more precious in life to write about, indeed, worth dying in defence of, and I'm sure you'd agree with that.'

Tara looked at me for a moment, but in quite a different way than before as if now for the first time she took me seriously. 'Yes, I

194

would,' she said softly, and quickly climbed into the front passenger seat of the Land Rover.

Tara waved to Mary as they drove off, and then her eyes met mine although her face was expressionless.

I knew what she was involved in, and could never condone it. Yet despite the reality of terrorism, I'd understood the reasons for her commitment to the Republican and IRA cause. And perhaps because I had met her face to face and experienced the force of her character, I felt illogically ambivalent about her being the enemy. Indeed, to my surprise, I felt a strange sense of sadness that this could be the last time I saw her alive.

Chapter 14

Mary and I went back into the sitting room, and there was an awkward pause now that we were both on our own again.

Mary spoke first. 'I'm not sure what it was all about, but there was something going on between you and Tara. I mean I was surprised at her frankness. I haven't heard her get political before. Perhaps it was because you are so obviously English and upper class to her.'

'I like a good discussion,' I said. 'The Irish have genuine grievances, and she was only expressing them. I had no quarrel with her, except perhaps her Republicanism. After all, I'm still a soldier of the Queen - remember !'

'That's what's so infuriating about the English. You're so bloody patronising.'

'What can I say? If I disagree, I'm arrogant and unfeeling. And if I agree, I'm patronising. Tara's a very attractive woman, and patronising or not, I admired way she spoke from the heart. Anyway, I'm grateful for the introduction, and for not mentioning I was in the Army, especially in Northern Ireland. That would have caused a freeze!'

'Yes - you lied very easily, I noticed. I was surprised.'

'Well, it wasn't that easy. I'm not ashamed of being in the Army - so don't think that. No - I wanted to save you any embarrassment. After all I'm a guest in your house. And as I said, it was a kind thought to introduce me. And now perhaps some day we can call on them all at Coldharbour.'

'Yes, why not?' Mary said. 'As a matter of fact I've been up there several times about the lease and the rent. Mr Chapman though it better for us to deal with the tenants direct rather than the Gates, who own Coldharbour, and live in Barham.'

'Yes. Claire's parents know the Gates. We called in one day to see them by mistake when we were out for a drive. Claire had forgotten they'd retired. As a matter of fact, I spoke to Tara then, and she didn't seem too pleased to see us, so I never mentioned our first meeting.'

'So you've got to know Claire Crundale have you? That's aiming high. They're our local landowning squires.'

'Well, it's not Claire who's going to inherit the estate - it's her brother Richard. Claire will have to find a career somewhere else, I think.'

'How disappointing for you,' said Mary quite sarcastically, as if she was somehow jealous.

'No - not really,' I said, deciding to humour Mary, and not start anything unpleasant. I continued with a laugh, 'If Claire was the only child and going to inherit the Crundale estates, I wouldn't be allowed within a mile of her! That's for sure.'

'Well I don't know about that. She's got a mind of her own I can tell you and selects her own friends. She wouldn't be pushed around by her parents.'

'Do you know anything about their gamekeeper Tom? He seems a strange sort of chap. I don't seem to be able to get on with him.'

'You mean anybody you can't get on with must be strange?'

'No - of course not. He seems to dislike me for some reason, and I wondered if you knew anything of his background that's all.'

'You mean you're going out with Claire and you don't know why Tom isn't friendly!'

'No - Why should I?'

Mary looked at me without speaking and tried to change the subject, but I needed to have this one out with her. After all, she would have picked up a great deal about people in the whole district when she was the local doctor's partner, and also in Chapman's office I was sure.

'Go on,' I said. Tell me about Claire and Tom. You can't leave me up in the air like that.'

'All right. But - I'm not giving away any secrets by saying the rumour is they're very close. That's all. I've heard no more, but it might explain why you found Tom unfriendly. I expect he's jealous.'

'Yes - you may be right. But perhaps "possessive" would be the right word. Anyway we were talking about Coldharbour before I started asking about Tom. How did you meet Tara?'

'She's always being sent on errands by Bob Bailey, and she came into the office several times about various things connected with the lease. The Gates, for example. I mean the Gates wanted to be

197

friendly, but Bob Bailey, while being polite, needed warning if they called. Mr Chapman had to deal very tactfully with the whole matter. Tara even called on the Gates to make sure they wouldn't take offence. Anyway, I liked her from our first meeting. And she trusts me.'

'That's because you're Irish,' I said.

'Of course. Why not? But we got on well together before she found out I was Irish. After all I've an English accent. But she wouldn't trust a Brit if that's what you mean.'

I decided to change the subject. After all I had not come here to quarrel, I thought, and it soon became clear that Mary was determined to make it a pleasant evening. She offered me more wine, and then disappeared into the kitchen, after checking that I was quite happy to eat salmon steaks with a caper sauce, as well as spinach and new potatoes.

We had our meal formally on a table covered with a white damask cloth set tastefully with elegant cutlery and three silver candle sticks. The table was at one end of the long sitting room under low oak beams, and Mary asked me to light the candles as the room darkened.

We chatted on very amicably, and I tried to find our more about her life as the doctor's partner as well as his receptionist before they split up about a year ago. I decided to ask no questions about her first husband, Anthony, and Mary never mentioned him the whole evening.

The doctor's name was Michael Groombridge, upper middle class and public school. He had studied medicine at Cambridge and then became an assistant registrar at Guy's hospital, before ending up as a GP in Pelham, where he settled down and become very popular, especially with his middle class patients who saw him as a social equal.

Groombridge married a local estate owner's daughter, Pamela, ex Roedean, who played tennis in Hythe during the summer, and hunted with the Pelham hounds in winter. They had two boys, boarded out at a Prep school in Eastbourne most of the year, from where, having taken the entrance exam, they were going on to a public school. All very conventional I suppose until Mary came along. Then the rumours began, and finally his wife left him when he continued the affair.

After living with him for several years in Pelham, Groombridge abandoned Mary for a job in London, and another partner, this time a much younger colleague in a thriving practice in Hampstead. Although Mary herself had broken up a family, when her own turn came, it was clear that the split with Groombridge affected her deeply and she felt betrayed. She had evidently come up against a section of the locals for having been the doctor's mistress. 'They always treated me as an outsider,' she said.

Mary developed a grievance against some of the locals, mainly friends of Groombridge's first wife, and this focused, it seemed, upon the particular class of English people to which Groombridge belonged.

To my surprise, Mary seemed to want to talk about her personal affairs, and unburdened herself with a rush of information as if the subject had been bottled up inside her for years.

'I wouldn't trust that class of English people an inch,' she concluded and I noticed that she had become more specific by saying English instead of Brit. 'They're all so gentlemanly and courteous, although always in a patronising kind of way. But cross them, scratch the surface, and you find they're far worse bastards than the people they despise!'

'So why are you being so nice to me?' I said with a smile. 'Is it because, despite being English, I'm an outsider too?'

'Well you are an outsider, and pretty isolated too, living out there at Chalk Hill. You're not linked up with any of the people here in Pelham, and don't seem to be the kind of person interested in gossip. And...'

Mary paused a moment, and I waited expectantly as she began to smile in quite a beguiling way.

'And the truth is - I fancy you! Since Michael left I've not felt like that about anyone, so now you know my secret.'

I was taken aback, and must have shown it because Mary laughed and said, 'Come on, don't look so surprised. Lots of women must have found you attractive.'

'Well - I'm not going to die wondering . But I'm very flattered.'

There was a pause and Mary was obviously waiting for me to continue.

'I think you're very attractive too.' I said meeting her intense gaze. 'And very sexy as a matter of fact,' I added unwisely.

'Well - we'll see about that later. But I hope you're not already enmeshed with the Crundales.'

I said nothing. I was not going to get into an argument about Claire and her parents and spoil the evening. But although I felt morally uneasy about not being straight about my relations with Claire, I also had another reason which was professional. Mary had access to Coldharbour, and was my only source of intelligence about the place. I was not going to say anything which might offend her and risk jeopardising that vital link. Coldly calculating, but true, for things had reached a critical point and every advantage had to be gained.

I helped Mary clear away the table, and then we had coffee both sitting on the large cushioned sofa in front of the fireplace. Moonlight, Mary's silver fur Tabby cat, appeared from the garden, and after having his meal in the kitchen, came into the sitting room and sat staring at me from in front of the fireplace. I called him over, but he was very wary, and keeping well clear of me, jumped up onto Mary's lap.

'It's really too warm to have a proper fire at the moment don't you think?'

I nodded, and Mary sat back against the cushions, very relaxed, with Moonlight on her lap, still staring at me.

After a while, Mary slipped off her shoes, and drew up her legs onto the sofa.

'The dining room was separate from this sitting room when I came,' she said, 'and dark and freezing in cold weather. But I had the wall knocked down before I moved in. So although it's quite a long room really, the fire heats all of it in winter.'

The room was now almost dark except for the guttering candles in their holders on the dining room table. I could just see Mary's face, and the smooth whiteness of her bare legs and thigh where her skirt was drawn up.

'Well, you've certainly made yourself very comfortable here. A far cry from my set up at Chalk Hill. I mean this is great - it's wonderful to relax.'

'Very few men seem to be able to make themselves really comfortable - they depend upon women to do that. But I'm glad you feel at ease. You always seem to be so tense - on your guard.'

'Yes, that's true, but perhaps I have my reasons. Don't worry I won't bore you with them,' I replied, realising there was no way I could confide in Mary.

'Well - I'm a good listener,' Mary said. 'And if I can help in any way - let me know.'

'You're very kind,' I said, genuinely touched. After dealing with men like Atherton, Mary seemed unbelievably sympathetic, yet in professional matters such as combat with the IRA, no one outside the Regiment was to be trusted. We were even expected to keep any details of our work from our wives, in case they unwittingly gave something away.

'Turn around Mark a moment, and rest your head up against my knees. I'll give you a relaxing neck and shoulder massage,' Mary said with a smile.'

When I seemed to hesitate, she went on 'Come on now - I won't bite! But first let me get rid of Moonlight because he is someone who'll get jealous!'

Mary put Moonlight on the floor, and got up a moment to turn on a low double barred electric heater in front of the fire. The bars soon glowed red, and cast a warm orange light around the front of the sofa. I obediently turned round and rested my head against Mary's knees as asked, not that I needed any further encouragement.

Mary tugged at my shirt, and I undid the buttons, pulling it off in some haste. Her warm hands were soon massaging my neck, and her strong thumbs pushed up inside my loose cotton vest kneading at the muscles as if she was a professional masseuse. Of course, I wondered where this was all going to lead, but I was so relaxed, I really did not care.

We chatted on, and Mary kept saying, 'Relax, relax - let all your body go loose.' And soon I had totally relaxed, and there followed a great feeling of peace and well being. This is far better, I thought, than any of Atherton's diazepam tranquilisers with their risk of addiction.

While I was in this state of calm euphoria Mary said, 'And if there's anything you want to tell me, anything you need to get off your chest, now's the time while you're so relaxed. Trust me. I'll keep it to myself.'

Immediately a warning bell sounded in my head. There was a great deal I would have liked to get off my chest, as she put it, but in no way, I realised, could this be unburdened onto Mary. Apart from the encompassing professional reasons already mentioned, if I had really opened up and told her the truth about Coldharbour, Mary probably wouldn't believe it. And if she did, then her loyalties would be quite unfairly tested, for she would know the significance of it all for Tara.

The connection between mind and body immediately gave my reaction away to Mary for my muscles must have unconsciously tautened, and she said, 'Now you've tensed up again! What's wrong? No one's forcing you to say anything. I'm only trying to help. After Michael and I split up, I desperately needed someone to talk to about it - but there was no one locally whom I could trust.'

'I'm sorry,' I said. 'You're being very kind, and of course I don't distrust you. It's just that I'm still recovering from stress in the past. It's really something I need to forget rather than discuss at the moment.

I half turned my head and kissed the inner side of her left knee. I felt greatly touched by Mary's interest and concern, and the last thing I wanted to do was to offend her by any hint of a brush-off.

Then I began stroking her leg, and reached up beyond her knee towards the inside of her thigh. The skin was smooth as silk and my thumb dug softly into the warm flesh as my hand moved up and down.

Mary said nothing but her fingers grasped my head with both hands and soon her finger nails dug into my scalp as I turned on my left side and moved my probing right hand further up her thigh. By then we were both sexually excited, and I turned round completely as her legs separated and straightened out on either side of me.

We began to kiss gently at first and then increasingly fiercely, so that I had to hold her head in my hands against the cushion to steady ourselves. Our bodies strained against one another, and I felt down between her legs pushing under the elastic of her panties to the soft moist lips of her vagina.

Then, as if obeying a signal we both began to undress as quickly as possible, pulling off our few clothes, so that within a minute or so we were both lying naked on the couch our bodies warmed by the electric heater and our own internal mounting passions.

'It's all right,' Mary said. 'I mean it's quite safe. I'm back on the pill. But if you're worried there's plenty of rubbers in the bathroom cupboard Michael left behind.'

I was worried, so taking the double precautions suggested by Mary after a quick trip to the bathroom, I returned to our lovemaking. In the interval Mary had found a very light wool blanket, which she half pulled over us.

This time it was Mary who really took the initiative and made me lie on my back while she got on top. The couch was wide enough for her to squat astride resting her weight partly on her knees which sank into the upholstery as she eased herself down gently guiding me in with her right hand.

Bending forward slightly, she moved up and down, at first in a slow rocking motion and then gradually increased the tempo until we were both almost at the point of coming when she slowed and then halted, prolonging the exquisite delight as long as possible. She rotated herself slightly as well as moving up and down like an accomplished horsewoman in the saddle showing off her skills at a series of show jumps, using her knees and legs to grip my flanks and retain her balance as well as supporting her weight on the sofa.

At first, my hands clutched her back, nails digging in slightly, and then I grasped her buttocks as she contracted the gluteal muscles heightening the sensation of penetration for us both. I also held her firm breasts kissing the erect nipples when she paused half upright to prolong the pleasure.

Nearing orgasm, Mary's eyes became fixed in a kind of unfocussed stare. Her dilated pupils glinted in the glow from the heater and her body gleamed, slippery with sexual sweat. Her mouth was half open and her moist lips kept pressing against mine as she moved up and down. Just before attaining our joint climax, Mary bent right over to give me a prolonged kiss and the muscles of her vagina began to contract spasmodically as if she was giving birth.

Then in a series of high pitched gasps she reached a crescendo, and with deep throated cries and exclamations from me, we both came together in an unforgettable moment which obliterated time and space, and left me feeling as if I had suddenly just gone through re-entry back to our own small planet.

'Jesus Christ!' I exclaimed. 'That was mythical sex!'

Mary laughed, shaking the hair out of her eyes, 'Mythical sex! What do you mean?' 'You know perfectly well what I mean Mary. That was wonderful! Beyond belief! To remember with tears throughout the long years', I said quoting a poet whose name I had forgotten for the moment.

I reached for the light blanket, pulling it over us, and Mary lay flat against me her warm breasts against my chest while we cuddled close in a moment of special intimacy. She was covered in sweat, and the scent of her hair and breath infused my being like some magical feminine elixir, restoring my desire. No *post coitus triste* here tonight, I thought, although perhaps that will come later when I have to leave.

'You were wonderful Mark!' Mary said.

'You mean I lasted the course! Well it was worthwhile to both enjoy it like that.'

Mary kissed me passionately all over my face and chest, and we clung together under the blanket while she murmured endearment's in my ear, her hair covering my face. I relished the salty taste of sweat on her body as well as delighting in scenting her tangled hair, and I felt utterly fulfilled by this woman whom I really scarcely knew.

We slowly recovered ourselves, and got dressed. Mary went into the kitchen to make coffee and I remained sitting on the sofa still slightly stunned by the intensity of the experience. There was no sign of Moonlight either, so he must have taken off somewhere frightened by the primal scene and sound effects!

We chatted away happily for about an hour, and I got to know more about Mary's past and her hopes for the future. At first her job with Chapman was only temporary, but gradually as she became more experienced at dealing with clients as well as proficient in her secretarial duties, she became indispensable. This was only grudgingly acknowledged by Chapman when he offered her a permanent job, but her relationship with him was always tricky as he wanted full control and a fairly subservient deference from his secretary.

However, after a while Chapman became quite proprietary, and inquisitive about her private life, almost as if he were jealous, but he seldom revealed anything about his own, or socialised with her at all, even with a drink at the pub after work. At times he seemed resentful of her former relationship with someone of higher status than himself in Pelham, and referred to her job as Michael's receptionist in derogatory terms. Chapman was also obsessed with money, and preferred wealthy clients to people like me, for example.

Despite the unease of her personal relationship with him, Chapman gave her increasing responsibility, although he only grudgingly raised her salary. But Mary now earned enough to support herself at the cottage with a very simple lifestyle. (I did not enquire about any financial settlement she may have reached with Michael having been his partner for several years, but I presume she must have received something.)

Mary felt she had been humiliated by Michael in the sense that he had suddenly left her, and friends of his first wife openly showed that they were pleased that Mary too had been rejected and got her deserts. However, she was determined to retain her moral right to live in Pelham.

Although Michael's first wife had moved out of the area, Mary felt that she was not going to follow suit. On the contrary, she was determined to consolidate her own position. She was convinced that slowly but surely as she established herself as an independent working woman her former close association with Michael would recede into the background, and she would make her own circle of friends. But things had not been as easy as she hoped, and clearly her friendship with Tara had partly developed out of her sense of local rejection. They were both outsiders, and Irish as well, so there was a common link.

It was almost midnight, when I realised that it was time for me to leave, and we lingered over our farewell in the hall way before Mary opened the front door to let me out.

'Next time you must stay the night,' Mary said., as we clasped and kissed one another. 'But remember if you do a lot of people here in Pelham, including Mr Chapman, will get to know about it.'

'Fuck Mr Chapman!'

'That's his problem.' Mary said with a laugh. 'No one wants to.'

'Well, I must be lucky! But seriously - I understand - he's your boss and you don't want him getting jealous or whatever, with only the two of you working in the office. All the same I'm sure we can be very circumspect. And we can start right now by switching off the hall light before opening the front door and leave the outside light off too.'

Mary smiled as she followed my suggestions.

'Clever boy!'

'My van is some distance away under a light in the main street,' I added, 'so that will keep them guessing.'

'Can you see all right?' Mary whispered, as the door opened and we looked out into the darkness of the lane.

'No problem,' I whispered back, and was out of the door very quickly, and walking down the lane in a couple of seconds, a perfect rapid exit. Actually I didn't personally give a damn about any local gossip. My discrete exit was mainly on Mary's behalf, just in case she did have prying neighbours who might peer through their curtains if they heard someone leaving her cottage at that hour. It was now a clear night and the stars were out so I could see my way,

I soon reached the main street, and my van was parked under a light, still lit even at that late hour as this was the main road along the valley with a fair amount of traffic. However, although unworried by the thought of local gossip, when dealing with the IRA, even indirectly through Mary, I took my security very seriously. So, when I reached the van, I got out my torch from the glove, box and checked underneath the vehicle for any sign of an extraneous object, in other words, a bomb. Paranoia or not, my past training and experience could not be ignored.

Then I climbed into the van and drove towards Chalk Hill, slightly dazed and elated by the whole evening. I passed through sleeping Highdene and put the van in low gear to climb the steep hill up to the common, still wrapped in thought about Mary.

*

It was not until I drew up outside Chalk Hill that I came to my senses, and realised fully the extent to which I had betrayed Claire. The truth was that I had scarcely given her a thought the whole evening. Yet, when I set out to have dinner with Mary, I felt deeply in love with Claire, and was no more than curious about how the dinner with Mary would develop. I was hoping for more information about Coldharbour and certainly meeting Tara like that as well as being given the opportunity to check the holdall went far beyond my expectations. After all, I had met the enemy face to face. And there was Sean as well. Both he and Tara were absolutely classic IRA 'sleepers', and Dublin's 'England Department's' dream of recruitment to a mainland ASU.

Thinking about it, I realised that despite the apparently innocuous conversation with Tara, we had both been verbally fencing with one another. Knowing as I did, more about her than she knew of me, and recognising Sean, had made the adrenalin surge. This 'high' perhaps had also made me less circumspect with Mary. Indeed I had given no thought to the consequences of becoming sexually involved, except to take precautions against her possible pregnancy. But whatever excuses I could think of, I was absolutely possessed by her and willingly so. There was no getting away from it, sex with Mary had been like a cosmic event.

However, although Claire and I were not engaged or partners, I loved her and simply could not understand how easily I had been unfaithful. Certainly Claire would not understand either. Indeed, if she found out, that would be the end of our friendship, the end of our relationship. I felt terribly guilty, but there was nothing I could do about it now except perhaps to confess all to Claire and beg forgiveness, but that was to risk too much.

It was thus in a sombre mood I arrived at Chalk Hill that night. I could not bear to enter the main bedroom where Claire and I had made love only such a short time ago. After a cup of tea in the kitchen, and checking with my flashlight that no one was back in the orchard I retired to my bed in the spare room and fell into an uneasy sleep.

Chapter 15

The following morning I spent at Chalk Hill, tidying up the house and working on the property. I kept myself as busy as possible for despite my pleasure at the time I remained very uneasy about what happened the previous evening. There was no one to blame but myself, so the sense of guilt persisted. I should have got in touch with Mary by phoning her at home that morning from Highdene as it was a Sunday, but I could not bring myself to do it until I had collected my thoughts later in the day.

In the afternoon, I felt like a walk away from Highdene, away I realised from any association with Claire, and drove to Saltwood to do a circuit of the castle, leaving my van parked in Castle Road. I passed the small cottage or lodge at the entrance and through the side gate with all the hostile warning notices about private property and dogs being shot or whatever.

I stood for a moment enjoying the fine view of Saltwood castle, with its high main bastion shining light grey in the afternoon sun. Doves cooed from niches in the surrounding walls and I could hear the strange 'chock-chock' of jackdaws flying around the towers. A peacock let out its unearthly call from somewhere inside the walls and I felt the magic of the place.

Then I crossed the old railway line with its rows of high trees on either side, and through a gate into a field leading north-east to Bargrove wood. The public right of way ran along the edge of the wheat which was a rich golden brown, and about to be harvested. Swallows skimmed the surface of the wheat, and wild pigeons rose from feeding at my approach with a loud clatter of wings.

The right of way led over a stream in a side valley at the bottom of the escarpment, and through a boggy area of sedge and wild mint before the track climbed alongside a dark wood edged with ancient oaks and high bracken. The sandy track went straight up the open hillside, which to the right was covered in gorse and bracken with bright purple patches of rosebay willow herb. This was the 'Gossie bank' of the Alan Clark diaries, and like him I tortured the flesh by climbing it as fast as possible.

By the time I reached the top of the escarpment I was gasping with the effort and flung myself down upon the dry brown grass close cropped by innumerable rabbits. Then sitting up, I looked down the way I had come over the valleys, the bright gold of the wheat directly below. The tall towers of the caste rose above the trees along the old railway line, and to the left or east of a long line of cottages cresting another skyline, the darker blue of the sea met the sky.

This was a time and place for reflection, and despite the beauty of the landscape, and the cheerful vision of blue sea in the distance, I still felt deeply uneasy at my betrayal of Claire. The point was that Mary had no idea how far my relationship with Claire had gone, and I should have made that clear to her last night. In the circumstances, Mary would have seen me as an unattached stranger, an outsider like herself.

Of course, I was still an unattached stranger in the sense that my relationship with Claire was known only to the two of us. Furthermore, making excuses for myself, I really had no definite idea how Claire felt about me, so this had made me reluctant to tell Mary. And there was no way I was going to push Claire into any declarations of love at this point for being so independent, nothing would be more likely to turn her off. However, this still left the problem of my future relationship with Mary, although this was not something I could make up my mind about at that moment, so I decided to continue the walk, and concentrate upon the landscape.

The track led along the crest of the escarpment. It was overgrown with gorse and brambles so in places I had to push my way through. I was glad to be wearing long trousers rather than shorts. The slope below was a mass of warrens, and there must have been thousands of rabbits for everywhere one looked, they were sitting in the warm afternoon sun, or fleeing underfoot, white tails bobbing.

The scrub, mostly hawthorn, elder, dogwood, and great tangles of bramble was full of birds, including a chattering group of blackbirds and thrushes mobbing a little owl, which I watched at leisure through my field glasses. A large green woodpecker sat on the ground, almost certainly feeding on an ants nest. Why no sparrowhawks? I wondered. What a larder awaiting them!

I began to traverse the slope below finding a route through the gorse until I reached open ground and made my way across fields of sheep towards the castle. I crossed a sparkling stream over a small stone bridge and up a hill to a brick arch under the old railway line, where a bridle path led me back towards my van in Castle Road.

However, as I came within about 100 yards of the gate with the warning notices, to my surprise I saw Tara and Sean with someone else obviously out for a Sunday walk and a view of the castle. They had halted on the bridle path and to my dismay, I recognised the person with them. It was Dr Maire Maginnity and she was taking a photo of Tara and Sean with the castle in the background. Nothing sinister about that, and an interesting memento if they ever returned to Ireland, I thought. A meeting was now unavoidable, so I put on a friendly expression as I got closer to the group and waved. Tara immediately recognised me, but Sean was more slow witted, and he still seemed to have difficulty looking me in the eye. Dr Maginnity was obviously surprised that Tara knew anyone locally outside the ASU, and stared at me quite hard as I got closer. Fortunately, it had been too warm for me to wear my camo jacket, and my army pullover was in my day pack. But Maginnity noticed the field glasses round my neck, and perhaps instinctively recognised the military bearing, for she suddenly looked quite hostile.

'Hello there!' I said to Tara. 'So we meet again!'

Tara smiled, but said nothing to me, although she murmured something to Dr Maginnity, which I didn't quite catch, but it was about our meeting yesterday at Mary's.

'Haven't we met before?' Maginnity asked.

An awkward question, as it was only about 8 years since I had done one of her courses at the University of Kent in Canterbury, and we had many contentious arguments.

'I don't think so,' I said.

But Maginnity had her wits about her, and recognition began to dawn.

'I know you!' she exclaimed. 'You were at UKC. And in one of my courses too!'

There was no way out, so I went with it.

'I believe you're right. You're Dr Maginnity aren't you? Now I remember. I did your course on Hermeneutic History.'

Maginnity nodded, struggling to recollect more about me. 'And you're...'

'Mark Wynstanley,' I replied, remembering just in time that Tara already knew my name.

'Are you still at UKC?' I asked trying to break her line of recollection, but Maginnity was not to be deflected.

'You did something strange, I remember when you graduated. Like going into the Army or something?'

Before I could reply, I saw the look on Tara's face as she blurted out in disgust, 'You were in the British Army?'

'No - of course not.' I lied. 'I went teaching for a while - then back to University – Queen's in Belfast,' corroborating my story to Tara last night. 'And now I'm a free lance nature writer.'

Maginnity remained puzzled, but she did not pursue her accusation any further. However, by a piece of bad luck, I had alerted her to my presence and my past. I knew it would not be long before she found out from enquiries at UKC that I was lying, and become suspicious. Furthermore any information about me would be passed on to Bailey and Tara. Time was running out for us all.

Tara had nothing more to say. I knew that she was going to wait until I had left and then pursue her enquiries with Maginnity. Certainly I was going to be the topic of their conversation for a while anyway.

I strolled towards the gate, adopting a casual air, as if I was in no hurry to get away. None of them knew about my van which was parked around the corner in Castle Road, and once out of sight, I doubled along the road and quickly drove off.

Then I had a disturbing thought as I was musing on the unfortunate and surprising coincidence of meeting Maginnity and Tara outside the main entrance to Saltwood Castle of all places. Could they, I wondered, have been carrying out a preliminary reconnaissance of the place for a future operation against Alan Clark who lived there? He was certainly a likely (and easy) target having once been Minister of Defence in Thatcher's government. But I put the thought aside as I had enough on my hands at the moment without adding to my problems and decided to keep my suspicions to myself.

I stopped in Highdene about 5pm to phone Mary, and she answered at once.

'Hello Mary,' I said. 'Look I'm sorry. I meant to ring you sooner - this morning I mean, and this afternoon I've been for a walk around Saltwood Castle.'

There was a pause and Mary said nothing, so I continued. 'I wanted to thank you for everything. The dinner last night, and especially the delicious dessert afterwards! It seems like a dream! Mythical as I told you at the time.'

'I was hoping you would phone. Yes - I enjoyed myself too. Where are you now ?'

'At Highdene,' I said. 'By the way, on my walk around the castle I met Tara and Sean out for an afternoon stroll with someone I knew at university - a Dr Maire Maginnity. And the problem is that she knew I had joined the Army after graduating and asked me about it in front of Tara.'

'So what happened then?'

'Well Tara was obviously shocked as I would expect, so I had to deny it.'

'That was unwise. She's bound to find out sometime. And continuously lying only makes things worse.'

'I know - I know. But I wasn't going to be put on the spot like that by Maginnity. Anyway - that's how I reacted and I thought you should know.'

'So you're not dropping in to see me?' Mary asked changing the subject.

'I would have loved to but I thought you would want time on your own. Sunday is your only full day off.'

'I've had plenty of time on my own,' Mary replied with a sigh. 'Anyway Mark, you're always welcome - not just on the weekend - any evening of the week. But bring some wine next time!'

'Of course,' I said, not committing myself any further, but mentioned my visit to Canterbury the next day. I said I was going to see an old Army friend. Then after hearing how Mary had occupied herself for the day, sleeping in late for a start, we ended the conversation by my promising to get in touch with her again later in the week.

When I reached Chalk Hill, I found another note from Claire on the front door.

Hope you had a pleasant time last night. No word from you about our walk, but Tuesday is the best day for me, not Wednesday. Suggest we take a picnic lunch. I'll pick you up about 9am, and we can have a full day out. Love Claire.

I was flooded with guilt. I should have phoned Claire from Highdene as well as Mary, but somehow just couldn't bring myself to switch immediately from one to the other like that.

I wrote up my journal the whole evening, and mentally prepared myself for my meeting with Tony the following day. I also made a list, a coded agenda of things to do and discuss before going to bed early as I felt unusually tired.

The following morning I continued writing up my journal and put together some nature notes which I had started about the same time as the journal. It was time I realised to take my professed occupation as free lance writer seriously. I now had sufficient material to send off to a country magazine as a sample for a monthly column, 'Nature Notes', which would include a description of the changing seasons whenever this was relevant. I knew this would have to be lively, and 'different' if I was to be successful, so I intended to incorporate environmental issues, both local and national.

I left early for Canterbury, and eventually found a park. I walked to the Butter Market directly outside the Christchurch gate of the cathedral and arrived there shortly before 1pm as arranged with Tony.

I soon spotted him among the crowd, in civilian clothes of course, and our greeting was deliberately low key. However, as neither of us had eaten, we changed our plans about going into the cathedral and I suggested the Crypt where last week I had lunch with Brigit and Anna. Tony was then joined by a man who had been sitting at one of the tables in the Market enjoying a beer, whom he introduced simply as Simon.

'Member of the firm,' Tony said, meaning I presumed that Simon belonged to MI5, although he did not make this clear. Naturally, I felt uneasy as the link with MI5 and Atherton was not exactly working in my favour, but I had to trust Tony in this. Anyway the reality was that MI5 were in charge of anti-terrorist operations in England and Tony would be working under their aegis.

213

'Change of plan,' Tony said to Simon 'We're going to have some lunch. I expect you're hungry anyway.'

Then turning to me, Tony said, 'We only just got here, so there was no time to eat.'

Over lunch, which we ate at a table against a wall in the Crypt and well away from anyone else so our conversation would not be heard, Tony gave me in Army parlance, a situation report. This was added to by Simon, who spoke to me with respect, so I guessed that there had been some change in MI5's assessment of my reliability.

This was confirmed when Tony explained he had heard I was having delusions, and told to report to Major Atherton at Dunmore Park psychiatric wing as soon as possible. When it was confirmed by MI5 that I had been reluctant to receive further treatment, 22 SAS had been informed and asked to bring pressure on me to go to Dunmore Park. MI5 also wanted find out whether the Regiment would have any idea as to my whereabouts, as they had written to my Shropshire address and got no reply.

Tony had seen the report about my latest so called 'delusion', and stood up for me against MI5 and Atherton. He told them we'd met by chance while he was on an exercise in Wales, and taking my recent experiences into account I seemed perfectly rational. He added I believed the IRA were following me, but considered this possible as a revenge killing was quite likely after the publicity of Ballyford and the disgraceful release of my name and address to the Press.

Summing up, Tony said, 'Anyway, I insisted that MI5 took you seriously and drop all this psychological crap. So after some investigation at my instigation, mainly done by Simon here, we now know that you were absolutely right about an ASU in Kent, and that they are well armed and dangerous.'

'Thank God for that!' I said. 'But Tony do you know exactly where they're operating?'

Tony turned to Simon, who took his cue, and leaning towards me said, in a voice just above a whisper, 'Well, we know the approximate area, somewhere along the Pelham Valley. But the trouble is we've always lost contact with a van of theirs from Pelham onwards, although we've had a police report about the van in Bishopsbourne. However, several of the group have been seen entering a Land Agent's office in Pelham. The woman working there had an Irish name before she married, although she has an English accent. Anyway, I don't know whether she is part of the ASU or just a sympathiser. I went into the office on a pretext and got her name, but we haven't tried questioning her yet, just in case she's connected with the ASU. So we're putting more people into the field, and should be able to trace their base soon once we've done that.'

'So what was the difficulty in following them from Pelham?' I asked determined to find out exactly how much MI5 knew, and anyway it was about time that I started asking them questions .

Simon looked slightly put out. 'Well, I was the only person who could be spared for surveillance in that area, and I had to return to London each evening. We were already busy watching an import business in Dover, who were bringing in arms from across the Channel, and all our efforts were concentrated there, so I was not given much assistance. But I do know the ASU in the Pelham area has been collecting arms from Dover, and possibly Semtex as well. Mainly AK-47s, but although we've tried making some of them traceable, it's not been possible. '

'Any recent shipments?'

'We think so, but the vehicle we've logged in the Pelham area has not been seen in Dover recently, although it's actually registered in Dover at a fictitious address. That's all I can tell you.'

'So what do you think the Pelham ASU is up to?'

'Well you're the best judge of that. I mean you've seen the mortars, and must have some ideas.'

'Of course,' I said. 'But I wanted to hear it from you first. I mean MI5 have not exactly been receptive to my ideas have they? As far as they're concerned I'm some kind of a nutter!'

'Forget it Mark,' Tony interrupted peremptorily, 'and that's a bloody order! We're on your side and Simon had done his best for you. So get that chip off your shoulder and be positive. Help us all you can. There's no time to waste and you must know that.'

'OK,' I replied. 'Well the ASU is located at a remote farmhouse about 10 miles from Pelham. The place is called Coldharbour Farm, and it's like a bloody fortress now. I was lucky to get in when I did and even luckier to get out alive. As far as I know the unit consists of four people. A Mr Bailey who is O/C, a woman called Tara, a youth by the name of Sean, and last but not least, a man of about thirty five to forty who looks like a long serving regular IRA. He's a real professional, most probably not clean like the others and keeps well out of the public eye. The woman you met in the land agent's office, Mary Renfrew is not part of the ASU or connected with it in any way. They rented Coldharbour through the company she works for – Chapman's - and so they've been contacting her about various problems related to the tenancy.'

I paused a moment, and sipped my coffee which was growing cold. 'And by the way, I was masked by a balaclava when I did the break in and escaped unrecognised, leaving no evidence that I had uncovered the mortars. Fortunately, they think I was a local burglar, so they are continuing as planned.'

'But what exactly are they doing?' Tony asked.

'Well I'm sure you must know. An attack on the Channel Tunnel. It's going to be a mortar attack, and I have even found out exactly where the mortars are going to be fired from.'

'Bloody good!' Tony exclaimed, and it was pleasant to have some praise for a change.

'I have to admit I found it by chance. But there's an ideal launching site along Danton Lane which runs along the high ground above the Tunnel complex. It's very well hidden by dense hedgerows and the range is only about 400 yards, quarter of a mile at the most to the trains and sidings. The mortars are in two trailers now parked in the big barn at Coldharbour. The tubes are securely welded onto a base plate at the bottom of the trailers and these will be taken to the launching site on the day of the attack, covered by tarpaulins. But they can't be concealed for long, and will be fired very soon after the trailers are in place. Remote control or a timer I don't really know. But my guess is that there'll be someone in the area monitoring everything.'

'Jesus Christ!' said Tony. 'We couldn't have better intelligence than that.'

Then turning to Simon he said, 'So that's something to tell Madame Rimington!'

'Congratulations Mark,' Simon said softly. 'Once I heard your report on the mortars, I immediately considered the possibility of an attack on the outside of the Tunnel complex. But in the past we've always thought of a bomb actually inside the Tunnel which would do far more damage.'

'Well that could still be part of their plan,' I replied. 'Indeed - my guess is that the mortaring is only one part of it. This is the big one for them, probably unrepeatable, and they'll surely let off a bomb as well. Imagine a bomb going off inside the Tunnel, and a mortar attack on the outside at the same time. What a coup!'

Simon looked uncomfortable, but Tony was clearly elated, partly because a friend, a brother officer had been vindicated, and secondly because there was the prospect of action, real action in the SAS sense against a bitter enemy - the IRA.

Then Simon asked the key question which was on all our minds.

'Well - when do you think this all planned for? Have you any idea of a likely date? Because that's what they'll want to know in London tonight when I get back.'

'Very soon,' I said definitely. 'Any day now. Sometime this week I should think. So any counter action will need to be planned urgently. And remember - as I said earlier - Coldharbour is like a fortress - taking it out would be very difficult if they were trapped or panicked. You've got to catch them out in the open, en route, or maybe actually with the mortars set up in Danton Lane.'

'Maybe we should take a look at Danton Lane now,' Tony said. 'Simon's got a car, and you can direct us there Mark.'

'I think its urgent we get back to London at once, and get clearance for a counter terrorist operation before proceeding any further,' Simon said very firmly. 'There's a lot of work to be done, and the attack could be tomorrow, if Mark is right. The special police protection unit guarding the Tunnel will have to be informed as well as Special Branch just in case the attack is imminent. But how much we tell them at this point is a tricky one and not for me to decide.'

'Put them on alert, but I would tell them bugger all,' said Tony. 'A leak, any kind of leak will make the ASU wary, and we want them as overconfident as possible. As Mark says, we want them all happily out of their base on D day, and expecting things to go right.'

'Well if you have to return to London now, I have with me here in my bag a large brown envelope containing Ordnance Survey Pathfinder maps - large scale - 1:25000. They're marked in red ink by me and show the location of Coldharbour Farm as well as the probable mortar launching site in Danton Lane. I have also marked a possible site for an arms cache in a wood near Coldharbour, but I haven't been able to check it. I don't want to open out the maps here, its too public I think, but I'll give you the package after we leave, and you can put it in your briefcase,' I said looking at Simon.

'Great work!' Simon said.' 'That's most helpful.'

'Praise indeed!' I replied, adding with a grin, 'Especially from you lot. But put things right for me with your boss - and get me off the hook with Atherton - that's all I ask.'

There was a pause in our conversation, and I drank the dregs of the coffee which was by then cold, and slightly bitter.

Then Simon spoke, 'The site of a possible arms cache...?'

'Yes - is that important?'

'Not a priority,' Simon replied. 'But they may be storing weapons for the future, and perhaps some Semtex as well. I mean after this Channel Tunnel attack is over, and Coldharbour abandoned, they will still have something there for another attack in this area. Anyway, at some stage it's worth checking out. Also, perhaps we could 'jark' the stuff, maybe with transmitters.'

'Well - is that all. Anything else you want to pass on?' Tony asked.

'Yes - there is one bit of bad news - although I'm not sure whether it should be classified as that. By chance yesterday, while on a walk around Saltwood castle, I ran into Tara and Sean who were out for a Sunday stroll and a bit of sight seeing. The problem is they were accompanied by a Dr Maire Maginnity from UKC - that's Canterbury University - and she recognised me from my student days. You see Maginnity, unlike Mary Renfrew, is definitely connected with the ASU. She's an American totally committed to the Irish Republican cause, and a leading light in NORAID. Anyway, she remembered I'd joined the Army, and quizzed me about this in front of Tara and Sean. I denied it of course, but it's only a matter of time before she checks at UKC and finds out I was lying. And that may put them on the alert.'

'Why should it?' Simon asked.' I mean why should she even bother to check?'

'Because I had several run ins with her during a course of hers I attended, and when she found out I'd joined the Army she was horrified. Angry too. I mean she actually told me what she thought about it one night in the college bar. My joining the British Army, a symbol of oppression and all that.'

'But you're out of her way now...' Simon said.

'Yes, but suppose we were on our way to recce Coldharbour, and we ran into Tara or her there or en route. Both of you and Tony especially, has Army or MI5 written all over you...'

'I hope not!' Simon interjected.

'Think about it. After the accusation by Maginnity yesterday, if we were seen together, Tara would almost certainly jump to the right conclusion, and alert the ASU. Furthermore, they now know my name, and IRA intelligence would make the connection with Ballyford and of course, the SAS.'

'Point taken,' Simon said. 'All the more reason why we should get back to London as soon as possible and get the ball rolling before these bastards know we're onto them. Otherwise, as you say, if there's the slightest hint of a trap, they'll abort the op, scatter at once, and we'll lose the lot.'

What this possible scenario would mean for me, did not bear thinking about. Tony and Simon would be disappointed, but at least they would have foiled an attempt to mortar the Channel Tunnel. But most importantly and here was the difference - their lives would not be in danger afterwards because their anonymity would still be preserved.

However, if there was another connection made by the Coldharbour ASU and IRA intelligence between me and the Army or MI5, my cover could be blown. Furthermore, I had hoped that the England Department might have given up on me as they were short of operatives and all their efforts would be on this major efforts to attack the Channel Tunnel. But if the Provos realised that once again Captain Wynstanley was proving to be a thorn in their flesh they would redouble their efforts at getting rid of me. Then, all my seemingly successful efforts at finding a safe house at Chalk Hill and a new life would be in jeopardy.

'Just before we leave,' I said. 'There's one more thing. My cottage is marked on the map, but for God's sake don't go near the place at the moment. I'll contact you so give me a phone number where I can report in every day, say 9am and an emergency number where I can get hold of you in a hurry if necessary. However, if there was a real need to speak to me urgently, I suggest you phone Claire Crundale - her number is in the note with the maps inside the package, and she lives with her parents, Col and Mrs Crundale, next door to me.'

'That's fine Tony said.' I was just about to ask how we could contact you, although I know it's a sore point since you've gone into hiding!'

We left the restaurant, and I passed over the envelope containing the marked maps by suddenly turning off one of the crowded lanes and entering a bookshop with Simon, while Tony stood outside to watch whether anyone followed us in. Actually, I doubted very much whether the IRA's England department had the extra manpower for the kind of surveillance I was guarding against, but I was taking no chances. Simon wrote the phone numbers into my notebook, and agreed I should call him every morning at 9am.

Then Tony also came into the bookshop and we stood at the back behind the stacks and said goodbye. We shook hands formally and I thanked Tony for believing in me and for all his help.

'Forget it Mark' Tony said, keeping his voice low, 'You deserved a break. And helping us out like this will put things right with you know who, especially if Simon has anything to do with it. Anyway, keep in touch, and make your calls as arranged so we can keep you posted. Otherwise we'll have to come looking for you!'

They left the shop, and after browsing a while among the closely stacked shelves, I too left the bookshop and walked to my van which I had left as usual in the Watling Street car park.

On my way home, I stopped at Highdene and made a call to Claire. She was out, but I spoke to Mrs Crundale, and left a message that I looked forward to seeing her the next morning at 11. 'Claire is going to pick me up at Chalk Hill,' I added to make certain there was no misunderstanding.

Then I drove on up the steep hill to Chalk Hill. It had been an eventful afternoon, and I had a growing sense of professional achievement. On my own, anxiety and unease had been all pervasive, especially as at times it seemed as if my own side was just as hostile as the enemy. But now I had a heady feeling of pure excitement about being once more where the action was about to take place. And at last I was able to share the increasing burden of the disturbing information I had obtained.

I spent the evening writing up my journal. So many things had happened recently that my 'Nature Notes' took second place. I thought about Claire, and decided to play things by ear the next day. Something had to be sorted out - I needed to know how Claire really felt about me - to see whether she could be committed in any way. I mean she had never said she loved me. Rather I had been left to infer this was at least possible, but no more that.

At about 9.30pm at last light, I went for a walk along Coppice lane towards the Common and as far as the Grange. The lights were on as I came near the front gate, where I stood a moment wondering whether I should go in and speak to Claire. I thought of her standing somewhere in the kitchen or sitting out on the terrace as it was a warm night

Suddenly, I desperately wanted to see her, to hear her voice, to feel her within my arms. I knew that despite what had happened last night, I was still very much in love. I needed to open my heart and tell her everything. To admit I had been back to Coldharbour and had certain proof that it housed a dangerous IRA Active Service Unit preparing to mortar the Channel Tunnel. Also to explain that from today, I was now officially engaged in assisting MI5 and the SAS to stop them. I was also prepared to confess what had happened with Mary last night.

But my professional training and loyalty to the Regiment prevailed over my personal feelings after all. I decided to still keep Claire in the dark about Coldharbour, and to say nothing about my meeting with Tony and Simon this afternoon. In any case I was in far too emotional a mood and unbalanced by guilt to appear unannounced at that late hour, and unburden myself unjustifiably to a woman much younger than myself.

So instead, I turned away before the Crundale's labrador scented me, and made my way back to Chalk Hill. Clearly tomorrow was going to be an important day. Just how important I was not to know, but at that moment one of the future's many doors had swung open silently on a hinge of fate.

Chapter 16

It took me a while to get to sleep that night. It had been an exciting and significant day, for I was now back in the fold of comradeship which I had been missing since my discharge from the SAS and the Army. Most importantly I felt no longer on my own. I was relieved to be considered normal by my friends, after the hostile disbelief and threats of psychiatric treatment when I had reported the existence of the Coldharbour ASU to MI5. It was also reassuring to have met Simon and to have someone within MI5 on my side, So that although I was kept awake by excitement until midnight, when I drifted off, I slept soundly and awoke refreshed, looking forward to the day with Claire.

While having breakfast in the kitchen, I realized that I had quite selfishly neglected my mother, and drove down to Highdene to phone her at home before she went out shopping in Ludlow on a Monday morning as was her habit.

I spoke cheerfully and told her that there was now every chance things would be back to normal very soon. I also said that I fully intended to bring Claire with me to Ludlow within the next few weeks. My mother was delighted about Claire, and of course my return to High Oaks, but sounded reproachful when she said that Diana was disappointed about not coming to Chalk Hill. She wondered why I had not phoned and spoken to Diana myself, which was fair comment I suppose.

The day had been cloudy and humid when I awoke, but the sun was fully out and quite hot by the time Claire drove the short distance to Chalk Hill to pick me up in her Triumph sports car. She arrived as arranged at 9am, and leaped out of the car to give me a warm hug and kiss. Claire seemed in high spirits and I was dazzled by her freshness, beauty, and vibrant youth.

'Have a look in the boot, Mark,' she said, and I opened it to see that Claire had packed a small picnic hamper for us.

'Chicken sandwiches. The remainder of the chooks we eat on Sunday, which I put in the fridge. And there's a large thermos of coffee as well as a bottle of white wine if you're in the mood - a good mood that is!'

We got into the car, and Claire drove off along Coppice lane, and soon we were descending the steep hill into Highdene.

'You're very silent today Mark. What's the problem?'

'Nothing,' I said. 'I was just wondering where we're heading.'

'Oh - is that all,' Claire said. 'I thought there might be another reason. Anyway, I've got a surprise and I hope you approve. I had a very long chat with Tom on Saturday, and sorted a few things out. I won't go into all that now - as it was a personal matter. But I mentioned the hidden room under the old disused railway bridge in Chesterfield Wood, and he knows how to get in!'

I felt a twinge of alarm, and said, 'Well I hope he's not going near the place at the moment. But what's the story? I mean how is the door opened?'

'Tom once kept an eye on Chesterfield Wood for the Gates when their gamekeeper was sick, and knows the whole area very well. He discovered the old door years ago when it opened easily. Recently, he found it had somehow been closed. At first, he was just as puzzled as we were about how it opened. Then, probing around, he found that more bricks, an extra row, had been added at one end of the door when the railway was closed after the War.'

Claire paused a moment and I interrupted, 'Actually that idea also occurred to me. But I wasn't there long enough to have a closer look at the bricks. Just as well, for if I'd lingered, Bailey would have caught me red handed.'

Claire went on, 'Anyway, Tom chipped these bricks out with the steel sharpener for his hunting knife - the mortar was quite soft - and discovered a padlocked bolt which had been completely concealed by the bricks. Later, he went back with keys which unlocked the padlock, although it needed a good spray of lubricant first. Even the hinges were rusted up, but Tom heaved away and the door swung open. The place was like a dungeon, and had obviously been used for storing tools by workmen maintaining the line. There were even some old rusting shovels hanging on one of the walls. Anyway, he carefully replaced the bricks in front of the padlock and jammed back some of the mortar so nobody would realize what had happened.'

'Very enterprising of him,' I said. 'Must have been his Commando training! But what about the padlock? I expect Bailey has replaced the old one.'

'Look in the glove box!' Claire said with a laugh.

I opened it and inside was a very large bunch of keys of every shape and size.

'Jesus Christ!' I exclaimed. 'Where did you get that lot from?'

'Tom - of course. He was very helpful - wanted to come with us as a matter of fact.'

'I hope not,' I said.

'No - of course not. But he's really very contrite - about the other night I mean. Anyway, Tom's been puzzled by the new Agrochemical Co. notice at the entrance to Coldharbour and thinks that's all bullshit. No one locally has bought anything from them. Tom feels they are up to no good. In fact, he suggested they could be planning some major kind of robbery in Dover or Folkestone perhaps. He's just as suspicious as you are!'

'Well - my own feeling is that we should give anything to do with Coldharbour a rest for a while. I mean why spoil the day by running the risk of being caught by Bailey?'

Claire glanced back at me. She looked disappointed and spoke with some heat.

'God! I thought I was doing you a favour. Solving the mystery of Coldharbour. Having a bit of an adventure.'

I felt a bit of a wimp. Not successful SAS selection material at all. Claire was obviously very disappointed, and I understood why. I had not told her about my break in at Coldharbour, the trailers full of mortars, and being fired at by Sean with an AK-47 so she had no idea of the risk we could be running.

'Well go on - tell me your plan. What exactly do you propose?'

Claire paused a moment, pursing her lips and probably making up her mind whether to drop the whole suggestion or continue with it despite my initial lack of enthusiasm.

'I suggest we park at the usual place most people do during the weekend when they go for a walk in Chesterfield Wood. Act innocent I mean. And if no one's around, continue along the main track - the bridleway - to the bridge. You can have a close look at the bricks, and see whether they're easily removed. If so, we can at least try some of these keys on the padlock. Assuming there is a padlock

224

of course. Then we should know Mr Bailey's secret whatever it may be. I can't imagine what he might be concealing, but I think we should find out anyway.'

I said nothing for a moment, thinking it over. The possibility of some kind of a booby trap crossed my mind, but I decided it was unlikely in the circumstance so kept this thought to myself Anyway, Claire was so enthusiastic I didn't want to put her down.

Claire speeded up her driving slightly, and said impatiently. 'Actually - Tom suggested he and I went and had a look ourselves - the two of us I mean. But I told him that was not on - this was your discovery - or rather your affair and up to you to decide what to do.'

'All right,' I said. 'If there's no one around we can at least check on the bricks, and see whether we can find the padlock. And if you stand up on the main bridleway, you'll hear the tractor miles away.'

We approached Coldharbour from the Pelham valley turning off just beyond Cobham and then up a steep hill towards the high ground. Claire drove down the lane opposite the farmhouse quite slowly, which I glimpsed through gaps in the hedge. Sheep were grazing the field in front. Claire skilfully kept down the revs, but the Doberman which Mary had told me about, heard our engine all the same, and started to bark as we passed the main gate. Otherwise there was no sigh of life.

'Shit!' I said. 'They've got a dog.'

Claire parked the Triumph in the shade on one side of the gate and the bridleway into Chesterfield Wood, and we left the hamper on the back seat with both side windows slightly open to let the heat escape, intending to have a picnic after the walk. Anyway, at that moment, I felt uneasy and not in a picnic mood at all.

The gate was unlocked to let horse riders through, and we walked slowly down the ride or bridleway between the tall beeches and sweet chestnut, both of us saying nothing for a while.

It was a bad start to our meeting, and I could sense the tension between us. Claire was obviously slightly put out by my unenthusiastic response to her suggestion about checking out the room below the old railway arch, and I felt a bit of a spoil sport. But there was not much I could do about it now except to get the whole thing over as soon as possible.

'So how did the Sunday lunch party go?'

'Oh - all right,' said Claire. 'The guests were two Army friends of Richard, both now married, and an aunt whom I had not seen for years. Anyway, what about your dinner party? I mean how was Mary Renfrew? Up to your expectations?'

By Claire's tone of voice and the way she phrased the questions, I knew I was on very thin ice, and decided to tread delicately. This was not the time to raise the issue of my sudden and unexpected relationship with Mary Renfrew or to confess my sins as it were, but rather to get myself back on an even keel with Claire.

'We got on well,' I said. 'And she told me a little about her last partner, Michael, the doctor. It must have been quite a shock for her when he left.'

Claire made no comment, so I continued, 'to my surprise Mary introduced me to that Irish woman we met outside Coldharbour the day we visited the place. You know the red haired colleen who came out of the back door and gave us the bum's rush.'

'You mean you had dinner with her as well?'

'Oh no - she dropped in after borrowing Mary's car for the day. I suppose she stayed for about half an hour.'

'So Mary's made friends with the people at Coldharbour has she?'

'Not exactly. Her boss, Chapman, is their renting agent, and that's how she got to know them.'

To my relief, Claire did not pursue the topic of Mary any further and after we had chatted away for a while, I said how much I had missed her the last few days.

'Really?' Claire said in mock surprise. 'I wouldn't have guessed it from your behaviour. I left two notes for you and got nothing in return.'

'Well - I was going to write you a love letter. But I decided to tell you instead. I really love you Claire. But how do you feel about me?'

'You mean you want to know right now?'

Claire stopped on the side of the path, and looked at me with a half smile. I had no idea what she was going to say, and suddenly began to fear her answer.

We stared at one another for a moment, and then Claire linked arms and said, 'Come on Mark. Let's get this over. Can't you see? We've nearly reached the old bridge.'

Claire was right. Ahead the path dipped to the gully, and we both halted at the top, and listened for the tractor, before walking down the incline to the side track which lead to the old railway bridge.

I had a very careful look at the bricks, and it became obvious which ones were loose, as the mortar was of a slightly different colour. Indeed, it turned out to be a kind of buff coloured plasticine, the sort of thing one might buy in a toyshop. A large packet would probably contain enough to fill all the spaces quite neatly on the outside.

Claire was carrying a small game bag and from it produced a triangular putty knife, a short steel crowbar, a torch, and the heavy bunch of keys, all lent to her by Tom.

'Well done,' I said. 'Now we must remove the bricks very carefully, because they've got to be replaced exactly as before - remember.'

I prised out the strips of plasticine like material from between the bricks, and the old loose mortar jammed behind it. The bricks came out easily, three of them, which I placed carefully on the ground. A bolt and a large new padlock were at once revealed, and I tried almost half the bunch of keys before one fitted.

I knew there was a risk of a booby trap, so I asked Claire to go to the top of the gully and listen for the sound of the tractor as well as checking whether anyone was around. She was reluctant to leave at that exciting moment, so I promised to stay outside until she came back.

Once she was gone, I took a deep breath and pushed hard against the heavy wooden door, and to my surprise it swung inward and open quite easily as the hinges must have been oiled. Then I waited a few minutes for Claire until she returned quite out of breath with the excitement and running up and down. We peered inside, and as our eyes became accustomed to the gloom, we could see that the room was surprisingly large.

Disappointingly it was empty, but we went inside, and I switched on the torch and checked the floor. This was partially covered with an old oil stained piece of carpeting which I easily lifted from one end, and saw brand new black plastic below.

Claire helped me pull up the plastic, and expose loose wooden floorboards, several of which I lifted, and placed carefully aside. I shone the torch into the space beneath, and saw at once a large number of khaki holdalls similar to the one containing the assault rifles that Tara had been carrying, and dumped in Mary's hall until Sean came to pick her up.

With Claire's help I lifted enough floorboards to have sufficient room to open one of the holdalls, and as I suspected it was crammed with greasy AK-47's. There were also several military style ammunition boxes and clear plastic packets of Semtex obviously straight from the factory with the instruction booklets visible inside.

I kept silent as we uncovered the arms, ammunition and explosives, just pointing at the various items that appeared while Claire nodded. Then I stood upright and said,' Well - that's enough. As you can see, this is an IRA arms dump and we better get out as soon as possible. But first we've got to replace all this as we found it, and it may take some time so I'm going to need your help I'm afraid although we're in great danger.'

But it was too late. Claire was kneeling on the floorboards with her back to the doorway, and I was completely bent over the gaping cavity until I stood up and saw the masked figure standing only a few feet away from us, framed against the light with an AK-47 pointing straight at me.

Despite the black balaclava covering most of his face, and the black plastic cape around his shoulders which would have concealed his carrying the AK-47, I knew at once from the eyes and the posture that it was Sean, although it would have been certain death to have said so. Rather Sean than the older man, the hard professional I thought at once.

'What the fuck are you doing here?' the masked man demanded, in a strong Irish accent.

Neither of us said anything. What was there to say? We had been caught red handed and there was no way we could bluff it out. But I decided at least to play for time - anything to stop Sean from making a panic decision to kill us at once, and to divert his attention from coming to the conclusion that we knew he was IRA, and connected to Coldharbour.

'Are you bank robbers or something?' I asked.

'Fuck off!' he said. 'How did you get in?'

'Good question,' I said with a smile. 'We saw this place the other day when we were out for a walk and thought there might be something inside from the old railway days You know old equipment and stuff like that. So we brought along a bunch of keys which might open the padlock.'

I was keeping it simple, too simple perhaps - for Sean - it had to be him - pushed the barrel of the rifle closer to my face, and shouted angrily, 'Fucking rubbish!'

'If you say so, but that's the truth,' I said, thinking at the same time that if Sean brought that rifle just a little bit closer, I had to make my move and yank the barrel over my left shoulder and out of his hands while kicking him in the balls.

But Sean backed away towards the door and said, 'You both come with me. Move out slowly with your hands up.'

We did exactly as he asked, moving slowly with our hands held high, until we were out of the door and standing facing Sean on the narrow track leading to the bridleway. He stepped off the track and made us pass him with our hands up, facing away from him, shouting and swearing at us not to turn round, while he closed the door, and locked it again. I could hear him fiddling with the bricks, putting them in position, but I guessed he was in too much of a hurry and awkward situation with us to replace the mortar and outer putty properly.

Sean then made us walk ahead of him along the track towards the bridleway, prodding me in the back with the barrel of the AK-47. When we reached the wide bridleway, Sean told us to turn left and up the incline towards Coldharbour, as I expected.

Claire went first leading the way, and as she started up the slope Sean prodded me again with the rifle and asked, 'Who's she?'

'My girlfriend,' I said.' It's not her fault. I was the one who suggested we had a look inside.'

'Stupid fucker!'

'Well it looks like it doesn't it'

Anything to keep the tension down, I thought, so I tried to engage Sean in conversation.

'Can you tell us where we're going?'

'No I can't. Just shut up. You'll find out soon enough. But shut up.'

'OK - OK,' I said, and followed Claire up the incline until we reached the level ground.

'Put your hands by your side and walk normal. If we meet anyone - just keep going - I'll be right behind you. Don't try any tricks or you'll all be dead,' Sean said.. 'And move quickly. Now speed it up!'

It was just a few minutes later I heard a sudden gasp from Sean, and turned round to see him half stunned on his knees, and the AK-47 on the ground directly in front of him. Tom was standing behind Sean with the double barrels of a shotgun jammed against the back of his head.

'Don't move,' Tom said.' Or I'll blow your brains out.'

Claire had turned round too and when she saw Tom, she pushed past me and ran towards him in relief and gratitude. It was this which gave Sean his chance. Dim witted as he may have seemed, half stunned by the blow from the shotgun butt on the back of his head, and crippled by Tom's simultaneous heavy kick behind his right knee which had pitched him forward onto the ground, yet Sean still knew that he was fighting for his life and had the sheer guts to make break for it.

He staggered into the undergrowth, and Tom very nearly fired at him in the excitement, but checked himself just in time. I picked up the AK-47 and could have probably put him down with a long burst, but I knew the rules of engagement. In no way could we be said to be in the imminent danger which would justify my killing him.

Claire was hugging Tom, and shouting, 'My God! How did you do it? You've saved our lives. He was IRA!'

'IRA? I don't understand. I thought he was a common crim. I was creeping up close behind him for a while, but had to wait until the gun wasn't pointing at you. Just in case he had his finger on the trigger and it went off when I slugged him,' Tom explained.

Once again Tom had been following us like some kind of pervert, but as he had just saved our lives, and Claire was in such raptures over him in gratitude, there was no point in my raising the issue now.

'So when did you arrive here Tom?' I asked.

'I saw the back of him at a distance from the gate where I parked the Range Rover.' Tom said. 'We just missed each other by a few minutes, but he never heard my engine - not like your car Miss! Something made me think he was up to no good, but I had to keep a long way behind in case he saw me. When he reached the old bridge, at the top of the gully, he took out the rifle from under his rain cape, and once he went down into the gully, I ran all the way. I just had time to hide behind a tree when you all came out.'

He paused a moment, and checked the safety catch on his shotgun.

'I thought you might need some help with the door Miss. I knew you were here because your car was parked at the gate. My Range Rover - Captain Crundale's, is there too, so we had better get back at once in case the bugger tries to start them. No sign of another car, so he's walked from somewhere.'

I pushed the safety catch of the AK-47 from automatic to safe. We had been lucky because even if the assault rifle had not been pointing directly at us Sean could quite easily have accidentally shot us with an unaimed burst as he went down if his finger had been on the trigger. But there was no point in criticising Tom. He had to make a decision over the risks involved, and it was the right one in the circumstances. The lesser of two evils. I knew of course, that we were both headed for certain death after reaching Coldharbour.

'Look Tom - I've got to get to a phone as soon as possible. I can't explain everything at the moment, but there's an IRA unit, what's called an Active Service Unit, at Coldharbour. That room under the railway bridge was full of assault rifles, ammo and Semtex, and the gunman must have been doing a security check when he came across us. We haven't got the time to go back there and show it to you because the bastard will be heading back to base right now. So I've got to inform the police before he reaches Coldharbour, and warns them all. That's absolutely vital. So where's the nearest phone?'

'There's a phone box in Cobham, but I know the people just below us in Stone Cross farmhouse, and we can go there now. They have young children so I think the woman will be at home.'

We hurried back to the gate and Claire and I followed Tom to Stone Cross about two miles along the Alderbourne Valley. I gave Claire a hug and a kiss, just before she started the car to follow Tom, and she gave me a weak smile in return. We had very little to say to one another, and I certainly wasn't going to tell her I had known for certain about the ASU at Coldharbour, or that I had even guessed the identity of the gunman.

There was a certain tenseness between us, and I was not sure why exactly. But I guessed that Claire was in a state of shock, and this was not the time to become inquisitorial. .

Luckily, I was able to use the phone at Stone Cross, and although I could not get through to Tony at once, I spoke to Simon at MI5.

I explained very briefly what had happened, and reminded Simon that the arms cache was already marked with a question mark on the map I had given him. I stressed that Sean was on his way to Coldharbour, indeed may have reached it, and already warned the ASU. It was to Simon's credit that he left out the recriminations and realised at once that we had a crisis on our hands.

'All right. I'll get the details from you later, but right now I'll get things moving. Don't worry about Tony, I'll inform him myself. Meanwhile where will you be? We'll need to contact you again in the next hour or so.'

I'll be at home for the rest of the day, but I'll phone you again at say 3pm,' I said, looking at my watch. 'You know where my place is from the map so if you need a base - there's plenty of room at Chalk Hill and its isolated.'

After the phone calls, I paid the farmer's wife, and I thanked Tom again for saving us. I told him to keep well clear of Coldharbour and Chesterfield Wood for quite a while. I also asked him not to say anything about this morning's events to anyone until the police made their arrests, meaning of course that he should not mention it to Colonel Crundale or Richard.

Tom looked at Claire rather than me when he replied that this was up to her. He said he had plenty of work on the estate and would continue with this for the rest of the day. I shook him by the hand, and said how grateful I was for what he had just done, and he got into the Range Rover without saying a word, and drove off along the Alderbourne valley in the opposite direction to Coldharbour.

Then I suggested to Claire that we had our deferred picnic at Chalk Hill, and she somewhat reluctantly agreed. When we reached Highdene, still in complete silence, I told her without further explanation, that I had to make a short phone call, and dialled Mary's office . However, to my surprise Chapman replied.

'This is Mark Wynstanley speaking. Is Mrs Renfrew there?'

'No - she's out at the moment.'

'Well - it's very urgent, so please tell me where I can contact her?'

'She's just had a call from our clients at Coldharbour Farm. They needed to see her urgently too and she's driving there now. Is there anything wrong?'

'Yes - there is as a matter of fact. I was hoping to catch Mary before she left. Has she got a mobile phone?'

'No - I would have told you if she had. But if it's that urgent you could phone her yourself at Coldharbour, and she can ring you back.'

Like hell she can, I thought, but I let him give me the number, and ended the conversation.

I returned to the car deep in thought, and from my expression Claire knew I was worried.

'What's wrong now?'

'I phoned Mary Renfrew at her office, and Chapman told me that she'd just left for Coldharbour! They phoned her a short time ago, and said there was something urgent they wished to discuss with her about the farmhouse and tenancy. A problem which had suddenly cropped up and could be understood only if she went there to have a look herself.'

'Well she may be on their side for all we know. I wouldn't trust that woman an inch. Michael Groombridge was our doctor, you know, and we knew him and Pamela quite well. From what I heard, I don't blame him for leaving her and going to London, Anyway, she got a grievance against us too, always has, and this could be her revenge.'

'She's got a grievance all right. But I don't think she's deliberately linked with the IRA. I'm pretty certain of that. Anyway, I'm hungry, and looking forward to those chicken sandwiches. What about you?'

'No - I'm not hungry as a matter of fact. You don't seem to understand what a shock this has been. I thought we were going to have some fun for a change. I knew there was something fishy about the people at Coldharbour. I mean I thought they could be in some kind of racket, but I had no idea really what we would find in that room. I wondered whether there would be drugs, but basically I didn't take what we were doing this morning seriously. I certainly didn't think we would be in such danger.'

There was no point in my continuing this conversation because it would only lead to more lying on my part, but Claire had another question.

'Who exactly were you phoning from Stone Cross? You seemed to know what you were doing - I mean whom to get hold of in such an emergency.'

'I was phoning a contact in MI5. They're in charge of all anti-terrorist operations in Britain now, and are going to be very busy at the moment! All hell is about to break loose, so keep well clear of Coldharbour and Chesterfield Wood!'

'So Mary's in great danger. I mean if she's anything to do with the IRA at Coldharbour, then she's in trouble, and if not - then she's in trouble too probably.'

'Too bloody right!' I said.' You've got it exactly.'

Claire started the Triumph and drove off towards Chalk Hill. As we were climbing the hill to the common she said, 'Well - what are you going to do about Mary?'

I wondered about Claire's sudden concern for Mary, but I answered her question. 'There's nothing I can do at the moment, but when I phone my friend in MI5 later this afternoon, I'll explain the situation to him. They're getting hold of Mary and her car, I guess, for a definite purpose. I mean they will use her in some way I'm sure.'

'Well - you don't have to go back to Highdene. You can use our phone if you like. It will be quite private because I've got an extension in my room.'

'You know I've never been in your room!'

Claire laughed. 'Well now is the time to satisfy your curiosity!'

I got out of the car and opened the gate at Chalk Hill so Claire could park off the road as usual. I removed the hamper from the back seat and we went inside, through the kitchen and out into the dappled shade of the orchard where I put down the hamper in a patch of sun. Then I fetched a rug, spread it out and we were cushioned by the grass, hot and dry from the sun, when we sat down. The warmth came through the wool and Claire lay back with a long sigh, her hands shading her eyes from the bright light.

As I got out the thermos, and sandwiches, Claire said reflectively, 'Something always seems to go wrong for us - doesn't it?'

'Not really. It depends how you look at it. Actually we've been bloody lucky this afternoon. Even Tom's nasty habit of following us worked in our favour. I mean that saved our lives. They would have given us no quarter up at Coldharbour. Just a shot in the back of the head. And here we are alive, and I can say how much I love you Claire.'

'Do you Mark? I mean I'm not so sure of that.'

'Well - how do you feel about me? You're not sure about me, but you've said nothing about your feelings.'

'Well - I think I'm in love with you Mark, but really we hardly know one another. We both need time for our relationship to develop normally. And I don't know what you have in mind. But I do know if you were still in the Army, that would have come first, and my career, and my future second. I'm not blaming you - all I'm saying is that you must settle down into your writing, and be certain that's really what you want to do. You're still restless - I can see that - and living in the past. I've got to think of my own career too - what I want to do. And then we can decide whether our futures can be shared.'

'I'm restless because I'm still on the run from the IRA. They forced me to live like this, and I found a refuge in Chalk Hill. But my dreams of a new life ended when I got involved with Coldharbour.'

'I know - I know. But you accepted the responsibility of Coldharbour yourself. For some reason, you couldn't hand it over to anyone else. It took over your life. And look how that's spoilt everything for us.'

'I'm sorry Claire. But soon, I'll be able to tell you the whole story. I promise you that. And then you'll understand better why I had to take on these people alone. But everything has changed now, and it's all out of my hands.'

I leaned over and soon we were wrapped in each others arms. It was an idyllic moment for me, especially after the events of the morning. From our first visit that dark dell in the woods and the old bridge had the smell of death about it, and events had confirmed my foreboding. So lying there together in the orchard, doves cooing in the distance, the scent of long grass around us, and the feel of the sun on our bodies, seemed like heaven. A gift of the gods, a perfect time and place, a myth of summer.

As with our first walk in Chesterfield wood, I wished this afternoon could go on for ever. But time plays such strange tricks. In retrospect, moments of happiness, halcyon days, often seem so brief, like the blue flash of a kingfisher darting across a stream: they fire the mind, yet are such minute fractions of our lives.

Then as the afternoon wore on, and our passion grew and was fulfilled, I suddenly remembered it was time to phone Simon again, to break the spell, and return to reality.

'I'm sorry Claire, but I've got to make that phone call to London,' I said .'Things will be moving by now, and I want to know what's going on.'

'I thought you said it was no longer anything to do with you.'

'Yes. I mean the next move, and the anti-terrorist operation is their responsibility, but I'm still the only person with some detailed information vital to their plans. So I've got to keep in touch, and anyway, they must know about Mary as soon as possible.'

'Well - I'll take you back to the Grange. You can phone at once in private from my room, or anywhere in the house or outside for that matter if you want to.'

I took the hamper back to Claire's car, and went with her to the Grange. The place was empty, Col Crundale and Richard out on the estate, and Carol in the garden, so I phoned Simon from Claire's bedroom.

'I've been waiting for your call,' he said. 'I didn't mention it earlier, but we've had people watching the farmhouse since early morning, and I diverted some of them into securing your find. Well done! What a haul! But things happened just a bit too early, and I'm organising the other business right now. The people on site have been alerted, and they will be concentrating all their efforts there. So Tony's on his way preparing the outside reception. We all agree that's best left to him. And I must add, he's not exactly pleased with you, springing this so soon, but said your maps were vital.'

'I'm sorry,' I said. 'But I'll try and explain later. However, there's a slight complication which you need to know now,' and I told him about Mary and that in my opinion she was quite innocent.

'Well - hold on a minute - I have to inform you - she's just arrived at the farm, and despite what you say we are treating her as a suspect. I can say no more, and I'll be moving out myself quite soon anyway. But we may need your help at the farmhouse. If that's all

236

right - one of Tony's chaps will pick you up at your place in about 2 hours, say 6 pm at the latest. So look out on the road for a dark green Ford Estate and be prepared for a night out. Tony's blokes will bring the gear.'

There was nothing more to say. I just had to wait for things to develop. Clearly, my blundering this morning had sprung things just too soon. Another 24 hours and there would have been sufficient time for a proper ambush in Danton Lane, or the whole ASU could have been picked up at Coldharbour by a surprise dawn raid perhaps.

Unfortunately, they had been warned: the ball was in their court, and we had lost the initiative. There was no longer any chance of complete surprise, and Coldharbour was like a fortress. Nevertheless, the ASU were not aware that their plans for mortaring the Channel Tunnel were known to MI5, or that I had already connected Sean with Coldharbour before the encounter this morning.

It was likely, given the logic of the situation, from their point of view, the IRA still might decide to make a mortar attack at once, or within the next few hours. That is, before they reckoned the police would start investigating the arms cache and make a link with Coldharbour, the nearest habitation apart from Stone Cross.

There was also the possibility that the Coldharbour ASU would decide to cut their losses and make a run for it, although their masters in Dublin would not be pleased. But my guess was that they would still try and see the whole thing through despite the increased risk.

In fact, I expected them to leave Coldharbour with the mortars at any moment now and wondered whether the men watching the place would try to stop them, or deliberately leave them to the reception being prepared by Tony in Danton Lane. I suspected the latter, and thanked God I was no longer involved in such decisions.

It was all beginning to get very complicated mainly because of my stupid action this morning. I also began to wonder whether I should have shot Sean when he ran for it, and so prevented any information getting back to the rest of the ASU. However, after further reflection, I realised that my decision at the time was indeed almost certainly the right one for killing Sean would have resulted in my arrest and another court of enquiry - not worth even thinking about.

Finally, there was also the question of Mary. What on earth did they want with her? To be used as a hostage perhaps, or part of an escape plan. Her car registration number was clean, and therefore very useful to the ASU, as Tara had shown when she collected the holdall of rifles from Dover. But now, unknown to the ASU, Mary had been seen driving into Coldharbour, her number plate noted, and all her subsequent movements would be closely watched.

I was sitting in a chair near the window of Claire's room deep in thought and still holding the phone, when there was a knock on the door and Claire came in.

'Did you get through all right?'

'Yes - thanks a lot. I am being picked up at 6pm from Chalk Hill, and probably being taken to Coldharbour, although for what reason I'm not sure. I've told them about Mary and she's just been seen driving into Coldharbour. I said that it was a trick to get her there, although I don't know why, but I stressed that she was innocent.'

'Well - you can't be sure of that Mark. She's a very strange intense sort of woman, and as I told you before, has a grievance which could have tipped the balance, and of course, she's Irish'.

'I know that,' I said. 'But it doesn't mean she's working for the IRA, and willing to bomb innocent people. She may be sympathetic towards the Republican cause. A lot of people are. But most of them would never even vote for Gerry Adams and Sinn Fein.'

'Well - you may now be better acquainted with her than I thought, but I'm just warning you to be careful that's all. You're not in the Army any longer remembering, so don't risk you life up there at Coldharbour.'

'Thanks Claire. You're right. But I know more about the layout of the place than my friends do, especially the approach from the back to the farmyard, and this may be useful. It depends what the situation is and whose there. Anyway, I won't be taking any risks myself so don't worry.'

I looked around the room for the first time, as I had been concentrating so hard on the phone call to Simon. One side was lined with bookshelves, filled mostly with university texts, and Claire also had a computer and printer sitting neatly on a special trolley with a chair on castors in front of it.

'You seem to have set yourself up very well here. Is this where you work?'

'I used to during the vacations, but it was always easier in college. Too many other things to do on the estate and in the house I'm afraid.'

'Well - we must have a chat about your plans when all this is over. When I get back from Coldharbour. I mean - whether you're returning to UKC or not next year.'

'Yes – we must Mark. I'd like to do that. When you find the time that is.'

'Oh Claire! Don't be cross with me. I love you. Can't you understand? Of course I'll find time. All the time in the world,' and I stepped close and put my arms around her. We kissed, and I kept hugging and holding her until I realised it was time to go back to Chalk Hill and get myself ready to be picked up at 6pm.

As time was running short, Claire drove me the short distance to Chalk Hill, and turned the Triumph round outside my garage.

'I wish now I was coming with you. But take care,' Claire said as she waved goodbye from the car and drove out of the gate towards the Grange.

*

I left the gate open for the Ford Estate and went into the cottage to get ready for the evening. I changed into warmer clothes, and decided to wear my camo jacket, and carry my army pack containing my torch, a scarf, a balaclava, and a thermos full of hot coffee, which I prepared in the kitchen. I also made myself some toast and jam, and drank a large mug of tea. It was like going out on night patrol at dusk in South Armagh and I was following the routine of some food and drink beforehand.

I stood on the road by my side gate at 5.45pm, and it was just as well, for within a few minutes a Ford Estate appeared travelling far too fast along the lane, and could easily have passed the cottage without noticing it. The driver braked hard, and stopped just beyond the gate and then backed up alongside me.

There were four men inside, all in camo gear, but with no weapons visible, and the one in the front seat beside the driver said, 'Hello Sir. We meet again!'

'Good God!' I exclaimed. 'It's Sergeant Corandale! Where's Tony ?'

'Get in the back Sir. We're in a hurry. I'll explain on the way. But can you first direct the driver to Coldharbour? We have map, but you can save us time.'

I squeezed in between the troopers in the back, sitting in the middle, with my pack on my knees and leant forward to speak to the driver. There were no introductions of course, for the identity of everyone had to be protected, but the good will was clearly evident. I was back among friends again, and it was a great feeling.

I had shut the gate, before I got in the car and asked the driver to turn round by backing onto the common, and then we were on our way.

'Slow down!' I said as we approached the steep hill down to Highdene. 'It's very steep and narrow, with no room to pass so watch out.'

The driver braked and reluctantly reduced speed, and we were soon passing through Highdene. We still seemed to be going too fast, but perhaps I was getting old.

'What's the hurry Sergeant?' I asked Corandale, who was looking tense and quite worried.

'Sorry Sir. I'll fill you in. I've just heard that contact has been made with the mortar group at the Tunnel, but no details. There's still some of the bastards left behind at Coldharbour, our next objective. They may try and break out. MI5 are there, but no SAS, and we've got to secure the lot, alive if possible.'

'But Coldharbour is like a bloody fortress!' I said.

I know that,' said Corandale. 'But we should be able to stop them breaking out. I've got a couple of 203s (the American M16 assault rifle with a grenade launcher attached), two M16s, two HP5s (sub-machine guns), and a Minimi (5.62 light support belt fed machine gun), in the boot, as well as four 66 rockets, so they're not going to get away!'

'We've also got G60 stun grenades as well as several L2A2 hand grenades, Lexfoam canisters and PE4 (a plastic explosive) to blow in doors or whatever, so that should be enough to go on with,' added one of the troopers with a wry smile. I could see that everyone was excited and primed for action, but somehow I began to feel slightly distant.

'The MI5 boys have only got Browning High Powers, so we've got to get there as quickly as possible. I'm in radio communication with them and there's no sign of life at Coldharbour at the moment. But they say a woman drove in with a car about an hour ago I think, and there's another vehicle in the yard at the back.'

'That woman is probably a hostage,' I said. 'She works at the estate agency which let out Coldharbour. I rang her office a short while ago. She's been lured there with a telephone message about some phoney problem they needed to see her about urgently.'

'Well we'll deal with that when we get there,' said Corandale, obviously with other things on his mind.

I directed the driver to Coldharbour via the Alderbourne valley, and soon we were climbing the steep hill which lead to the farmhouse. We drove cautiously looking out for the MI5 people. Then, we saw a blue van with several aerials in exactly the same place opposite the gate where Claire had parked her Triumph before we went for our walk this morning.

'That's their communications van,' Sergeant Corandale said, and we stopped beside it. He got out of the car and spoke to someone sitting in the driver's seat. There followed a great nodding of heads, and information exchange. Then Corandale got back into our car, swivelled round in his seat and brought us all up to date about what had been going on.

'The ambush at the Tunnel has been successful. But there's definitely some of them still here at the farmhouse. One of them is a woman speaking with an Irish accent. MI5 have been listening to her telephone conversations all morning. She now knows that something has gone wrong with the mortar attack, although there's been a news flash on TV and radio that some of the mortar bombs were fired.'

Corandale paused a moment, and we waited on his words. 'Now our job is to go into the farmhouse and secure the occupants. They will be armed and in possession of explosives. According to Captain Wynstanley, one of them may be a hostage, another woman seen driving in this morning, so watch out for her, and don't confuse the two. The other one definitely belongs to the ASU. We will ask them to surrender, and no one is to fire unless I give the order. Is that understood?'

The troopers nodded in agreement and Corandale continued, 'We will now proceed to the entrance of the property, where there are several MI5, waiting near the main gate. We will contact them and then check our final approach to Coldharbour with Captain Wynstanley here before deciding on any plan of action. Any questions?'

'Yes Sarge,' one of the men said. 'Is it possible that there are only two people in the house. One the woman from the ASU, and the other one the hostage? I mean - all we've got is two women!'

The other men laughed, but Corandale was not amused, and said, 'we don't know how many fucking IRA are in the house! All I'm saying is we do know there's two women, one of them possibly a hostage.'

That trooper's a bright boy, I thought and he may well be right, so I decided to throw in a word without offending Sergeant Corandale.

'If I may say a word Sergeant. We don't know how many IRA are in the house, but the ASU is quite small and they've been surprised, so our friend here may be right. It's possible there could be only two women in the house. But don't underestimate the IRA one. I've met her. Her name is Tara, and I can tell you she'll fight as hard as any man. And she'll die hard too, so expect some fireworks!'

Then we parked the car slightly off the road about 100 yards from the main gate of the drive leading to the farmhouse. Everyone got out and began removing the weapons and gear from the boot.

We could see another car closer to the drive gate, with the driver sitting in it, presumably MI5. As we were checking the weapons, two MI5 men gave the call sign to Corandale on his radio telephone, and approached us out of the beeches opposite the gate. They were dressed in civilian clothes, unshaven, tired and very relieved to see us.

'Wow!' one of them said sarcastically, when he saw the weaponry. 'The US cavalry arrives just in time!'

'Piss off!' said Corandale. 'If you've got nothing more useful to say than that. Where's the boss? Neither of you wankers - I hope.'

'He's right by the gate watching the house,' said the jester, looking slightly crestfallen. 'But there's no sign of life.'

'Maybe,' said Corandale. 'But someone's been talking on the phone. Your boys in the van have been listening in for hours.'

We moved towards the main gate, where we met the O/C of the MI5 group, and Sergeant Corandale introduced himself and explained his orders.

'That's OK by me,' the O/C said, introducing himself as Max. 'Just tell me what you intend to do.'

Sergeant Corandale turned to me, 'You know the whole area sir. How can we get close without being seen?'

'Round the back,' I said, pointing to the woods on the left of the bridleway along which I had approached the Coldharbour the night Sean had shot at me. 'We'll have to move a bit into the wood, because there's not that much cover, but we can get within 50 yards of their backyard, and even closer perhaps.'

Then I remembered the dog. 'Trouble is they've got a Doberman. Have you seen or heard it?' I asked Max.

'Not since the cars and trailers went out a few hours ago. I think it must have been taken inside.'

'One more thing,' I said to Max. 'Do they know you're here?'

'They might by now, but we were all well hidden when the mortars went out, and they hadn't a clue. I'm absolutely sure of that.'

He paused a moment, and added with a grim smile, 'And now they'll never know.'

'Was it like that?' I said.

'It was like that,' Max replied.

'SAS, I suppose.'

'Probably', Max replied cautiously. 'I know all the police and the anti-terrorist squad were guarding the Tunnel complex in case someone tried to get through with a bomb, so any ambush outside would have been left to your mob.'

Sergeant Corandale placed one of his men in a ditch with the light machine gun facing right down the drive and the other one with a rocket launcher and two spares back in the edge of the wood so its line of fire covered both possible escape routes along the tar sealed road.

That left only three of us to approach Coldharbour, but as I thought this was just an initial recce, and we were not yet planning an assault, I was not especially worried. Anyway, the SAS men were both well armed, although I felt somewhat useless. Sergeant

Corandale and his Trooper were both carrying MP5 submachine guns, and Corandale also had a small battery powered loud hailer slung over one arm.

'We can't have you just as a passenger sir.' Sergeant Corandale said. 'You've got to be able to look after yourself. So take this - it's loaded - there's a full magazine - 13 rounds - a spare one to go into your side pocket,' and he handed me a 9mm Browning High Power.

Without a word, I checked the safety catch and pushed the pistol into a deep breast pocket of my camo jacket.

'OK. Let's go,' Corandale said, and we silently moved into the darkening beech wood on that fateful August evening of 1994.

Chapter 17

The farmhouse, outbuildings, and surrounding fields were still lit up by the fast sinking sun, but the lengthening shadows of the wood helped conceal our movements providing we kept back from the sunlit edge adjoining the bridleway. I checked my watch: the time was 7.30. Over an hour of daylight left, I thought, and then another two hours of summer twilight if the sky remained clear.

Just before we moved off, I asked Corandale to tell me his first name, as well as the soldier's.

'This identity security's gone too far,' I said. 'I'm not going to call him "soldier" all the time.'

'Sorry sir. This is Chris, and I'm Bob.'

I led the way, followed by Bob and Chris several yards behind him keeping an eye on our rear. I followed much the same route as on my last visit to Coldharbour, although I kept further away from the bridleway. The edge of the wood was about fifty yards to our right, and curved round towards the rear of the house so we could get very close to the fence line without being seen. Soon, we reached a position right opposite the back of the farm house. I turned round, and indicated to Bob that we were now as close as we could get without alerting the dog.

Bob and Chris, checked their weapons, and we moved forward slowly towards the edge of the wood, some brambles giving cover almost until we were about to emerge onto the bridleway. Bob signalled Chris and me to remain behind trees, while he moved forward and came out of cover onto the bridleway in full view of the rear and one side of the farmhouse which was then only about fifty yards away. He boldly went up to the fence, and stood there a moment, surveying the scene before suddenly crouching down, and doubling back into the trees.

'I was trying to draw any fire,' he whispered. 'There's two cars parked in the yard, both facing the exit. But no sign of life. And the dog's disappeared.'

'Don't try that again Bob. These people have got AK-47s. It not worth risking your life getting over the fence in full view either, so I should use that loudhailer now. Tell them they're surrounded and should come out with their hands up.'

'Everything depends upon how many of them are there,' Chris said.

'And also whether they know through mobile phones the fate of the rest of the ASU,' I replied. 'And if they know - or have guessed - morale is going to be low, and they might prefer survival to joining them in some kind of death pact. But don't forget the hostage, Mary Renfrew. She must be there for some purpose, and my guess is they wanted her car - one of those in the yard.'

'Well, I'll go closer and use the loudhailer from behind a tree. We've got to make contact before dark. Otherwise they may slip away on foot. Watch out for any movement once I use the loudhailer.'

Bob moved forward again, and using a beech tree as cover, shouted through the loud hailer.

'Hello there! Hello there! Security Forces speaking. You are surrounded. You are surrounded. Come out through the back door slowly one by one and with your hands up.'

He repeated the orders several times, but still no sign of life. Coldharbour could have been empty.

I moved behind another beech close to Bob. 'Keep going. Otherwise we may have to get MI5 to try the main farmhouse phone and see whether they answer that, although I doubt it.'

Then with mounting excitement, I saw the back door of the farmhouse slowly opening. Bob quickly put down the loudhailer, and gripped his sub-machine gun at the ready.

A woman appeared through the half open door. I recognised her at once as Mary looking absolutely terrified. She was being forcibly pushed out in full view of us by someone else inside the doorway. I was surprised to see she was carrying a khaki canvas holdall similar to the ones used by the Coldharbour ASU to store assault rifles and Semtex.

'Don't shoot!' she cried. 'Don't shoot! I'm a hostage.'

Then Tara came out and stood behind Mary. She was carrying an AK-47 with the barrel jammed firmly in Mary's back. I could see her face quite clearly, but her head kept bobbing about on either side of Mary's as she looked in our direction.

As she was threatening a hostage, I knew that Tara would have been well aware she was a potential target. With a first class sniper's rifle, the 7.62mm, L96A1, or better still the new Accuracy International PM with its steadying bipod, it would have been possible to go for a head shot: the 7.62 round would kill Tara instantly. However, we could do nothing in that particular situation with our sub-machine guns. Tara thus held the initiative, but we still had not realised just to what extent.

Tara pushed Mary with the barrel of the gun down the few steps from the back door into the farmyard, and directed her towards the car nearest the gate - Mary's Vauxhall.

Bob picked up the loud hailer and shouted, 'Halt!. Do not get into the car. I repeat - do not get into the car.'

Tara gave us the 'Up You' V signal with her left hand, and shouted at one of us to come out and speak to her.

'I've got something to tell you,' she shouted. 'Something important. I want to make a deal. I've got 15kg of Semtex in the bag,' pointing at the holdall Mary was carrying.

'It's connected to me by this wire, which I've taped to my wrist. So don't try anything or I'll blow us all to bits!'

'What the fuck do we do now?' Bob whispered.

'I'll go forward and speak to them. Keep me covered, but remember she won't be bluffing.'

'Too risky sir. She might take you hostage as well.'

'We have to take that risk. I know them both. The woman's name is Tara. I'll try to talk her out of it. But she's got the upper hand at the moment.'

I did not give Bob the time to reply. There was no reason to make him take all the responsibility, so I stepped out into the open from behind the beech tree, and shouted.

'All right. You can speak to me.'

'OK. Drop your weapon and walk over here slowly.'

'I haven't got a weapon,' I lied, and moved towards the low wire fence, which I climbed before walking the few yards up to the open farmyard gate.

'Right. Stop there,' Tara said when I reached the gateway. 'We're getting into the car. Don't come closer until I tell you.'

The two women got into the Vauxhall with some difficulty as Tara had to rearrange the wires from the holdall which was placed in one of the rear seats. Mary got into the driver's seat behind the wheel, still looking petrified, and Tara sat beside her. Tara then beckoned me to come closer, and with the AK-47 in her right hand awkwardly pointing at Mary with the butt tucked under her arm. Then she got Mary to lower her side window, and the barrel of the AK-47 was now behind Mary's head and pointing in my direction.

I bent down so that I could speak to Tara.

'So what's the deal Tara?'

'So it's *you* is it? I thought as much. Not in the Army and all that crap. You lying bastard.'

'It's all lies in this game Tara,' I said. 'Your whole life in England is a lie and you got Mary here with lies to,' and I touched her on the shoulder.

'Keep your hands away from her,' Tara said with some anger. 'Now listen to me. I'm going to drive out of this place and onto the road, and I don't want to be stopped or followed. Otherwise I'll detonate the Semtex, and you know what 15kg will do.'

'Look Tara. You haven't got a show even if we let you drive out of this gate. You know what's happened to your friends don't you?'

Tara looked grim, but did not reply so I continued. 'Pack it in now. 'You're not directly involved so there's a good chance you'll go free within a few years. You can save your life - you're young - there's years ahead of you. But drive out of here - and you'll be as good as dead.'

'We'll see about that,' Tara said. 'Now tell your people to let us out of that gate and not to follow us either.'

'All right,' I said. 'But you'll have to wait until I get permission to let you out. Don't move until I give you the signal. If you try and drive out of the gate right now, you'll be shot. That's the truth. I'll explain the situation first. So wait until I get my orders.'

'Get moving then - I'll give you five minutes that's all.'

I moved away from the car and climbed over the fence to speak to Bob.

'Did you hear what she said?' I asked.

'Not all of it. But I got the gist. She wants us to let her drive out with the hostage and the car's full of Semtex.'

'Well she's got 15kg in the holdall on the back seat wired to her wrist. All she needs to do is to make the connection, and anyone within fifty yards will be blown to pieces. We must confer with MI5 and I suggest you get onto Tony if you can as well.'

'I'll do that once I've spoken to MI5, so we had better get up to the main gate and see their O/C.'

'She's given us five minutes - so get a move on.'

'OK,' said Bob. 'But I'm not leaving Chris here on his own with that mad bitch - so he's coming back with us. She's quite likely to have her own goal if we're delayed, and she gets excited.'

We doubled all the way back to the gate and Bob immediately explained the situation to the O/C MI5 He introduced himself for the first time simply as Max, so I said I was Mark, although somehow I had the impression he already knew.

'You know the hostage business could quite easily be a con - don't you?'

'What the hell do you mean Max?' I asked.

'Well - what's the threat exactly? We don't give a bugger what happens to her. It's the hostage we're concerned about. So the hostage could be a clever con. I mean that woman could be one of the ASU and posing as a hostage. Just a ruse to help them both escape. Otherwise, you could start shooting at them from here once their car appears at the far end of the drive. At that distance if she wants to blow them both to pieces she's at liberty to do so. We'll all be flat on the ground or in that ditch,' Max said indicating the depression in the ground where the soldier with the machine gun was lying.

'I'm certain it's not a con. I know the woman - her name's Mary - and she's terrified.'

'All right Mark - I'll get back to the communications van and have a chat with HQ. It's up to them to make up their minds. But if you're so sure about the hostage, I'll suggest letting them through. I'm not willing to be held responsible for killing an innocent woman. They won't get far anyway. We'll call in police assistance plus a helicopter if necessary.'

Sergeant Corandale looked relieved, and I knew why. He would be directly responsible for any firing at the car, and the likely subsequent explosion with two women blown all over the countryside, one of them a hostage known personally to me.

Max walked over to the van, and returned quite quickly.

'Let them through,' he said. 'But there's only one thing. I was also speaking to Tony. He's got a hunch that the IRA woman may be heading for the Channel Tunnel and intends to blow up the car somewhere in the assembly area, where it will cause the maximum damage and havoc. The ASU had mobile phones and the failure of the mortar attack has already been reported on radio. So Tony thinks that she may try and save the day with something heroic. Anyway, Tony's setting up road blocks with police assistance on the M20 to halt all traffic near the Tunnel. It all depends on which way they go once they leave Coldharbour. He's taking a chance over the woman going for the Tunnel and wants your opinion. After all Mark, you have met her haven't you? Or seem to know something about her.'

I thought very quickly indeed, and realised Tony could well be right. Tara had the will and determination for such an action, and was prepared to die for Ireland, if the need arose, and she thought it could save the day for the IRA.

So I said, 'Yes, I think he could be right. But for God's sake tell him to think of the hostage too!'

'All right. I'll pass on your opinion to Tony Now try and get them to leave at once before its dark. Otherwise we'll have difficulty in keeping track of them. I'll stay just in case there someone left behind in the farmhouse. But we won't be checking out the place until tomorrow - it may be booby trapped and I want the bomb squad here in daylight.'

Then turning to Bob, he said, 'Get your men in the car ready for close pursuit, and once they're out of the gate - away you go after them. You must let us know the direction in which they're heading on your radio - here's the frequency - but you should have it already. Then you'll have all the assistance we can get. Keep in touch with Tony on your radio all the time. It depends which way they go out of the gate. If they turn left, they'll probably go to the Tunnel via Pelham and if they turn right, it'll be across country or straight down the B2068 to the M20. Anyway, you've got to let us know.'

'OK,' I said to Bob 'I'll walk straight down the road and give them the message now, but don't you dare leave without me. I'll be running right behind their car up the drive.'

'You won't have to sir. Here they are!'

I quickly turned round and saw the Vauxhall approaching the closed gate. It was moving quite slowly, and halted within about twenty yards of us.

'I'll deal with this,' I said firmly.

Everyone took cover, and I half opened the barred gate and walked right up to the car on Mary's side, and leaned down to speak to Tara through the open side window. Mary's face was only a few inches away from mine, and I wanted to pull open the door and yank her out to safety. But Tara was shaking with anger and frustration, and I thought she was about to shoot me. The barrel of the cocked AK-47 was only a few inches from my face, and Tara's finger was wrapped around the trigger.

'I said five minutes. What the hell are you playing at? Now let us through.'

'OK. OK,' I said. 'But first, I have to say to goodbye to Mary,' and before Tara could say anything to stop me, I moved my face close and kissed Mary full on the lips, holding her head in my hands. 'Don't worry love,' I whispered. 'You'll be all right. She'll come to her senses.'

Mary rook her right hand off the steering wheel for a moment and pressed it against mine still resting at the bottom of the open window.

'Don't go anywhere near the farmhouse Mark,' she warned

'Move away!' Tara shouted, and the cold barrel of the gun pressed hard against the left carotid artery of my neck. She was shaking with tension, and I had come very close to being shot.

But still I made one last effort. 'Don't try it Tara,' I said,' don't even think about it any more. It's not worth it. You don't stand a chance - believe me.'

'Open the gate! Tara shouted. 'Or I'll blow your brains out'!

I pulled the heavy gate wide open and the car shot forward turning sharp right down the steep hill and away from Cobham.

Bob shouted at his men, and they all began piling into the car as Max came up and spoke to me.

'Brave effort Mark! You've certainly got guts. Now don't take any more risks. Keep well behind them and by the time they reach any main road, I'll have every available police car in the district on their tail.'

Bob was already shouting at me to come on, and I was pulled in the back of the car, as it was moving

'Go! Go! Go!' Bob was yelling at the driver, and without a glance back, he accelerated along the narrow lane, noisily grazing a hedge on the right as we took off in pursuit.

Then just as the driver re-gained control of the Ford, there was a thunderous explosion from the direction of Coldharbour, followed almost immediately by a second one, and the sky lit up with a vivid flash.

Unknown to us in the car at the time, the barn had exploded in a sheet of flame and as the entire MI5 group dived for cover, there was a secondary explosion in the farmhouse itself. No wonder Tara was getting impatient, for she must have set quite a short timer.

'We've got to keep going,' Bob said. 'Otherwise we'll lose them.'

I thought what a brilliant bloody diversion this had been on Tara's part, and could not but help admire her professionalism. Someone had selected her well.

Within a few minutes we had reached the top of the steep hill, and the driver plunged down it dangerously fast. No sign of the Vauxhall at the crossroads, so I took a chance and told him to turn left towards the south. The road twisted like a grass snake across the landscape, and the driver was only just in control, tyres screaming at every corner.

An astonished and frightened looking middle aged driver of a car drawn up in one of the few passing places indicated the Vauxhall had just gone past. His expression suggested there had nearly been an accident, but he probably never understood the full extent of his good luck. This can't go on much longer, I thought, without one of us piling up, but the risk had to be taken if we were to make contact.

Suddenly, to my relief, we saw the Vauxhall only about 70 yards ahead, and our driver slowed down slightly.

'Don't get too close now Andy,' Bob said, and was on the radio to Max at once giving him our location and the direction in which the Vauxhall was heading. Max said he would relay the message to Tony, but stressed that we should make a direct radio link to Tony, which of course was always Bob's intention.

Max deliberately said nothing to us about the explosion at Coldharbour as he did not wish to divert our attention from the vital pursuit in hand.

Tony's frequency was in full use, and we had to cut in several times to make the urgency of our message understood. By the time Bob spoke to Tony, we had reached Stelling Minnis, and it seemed that the Vauxhall was heading for Stone Street, or the B2608 which being an ancient Roman road ran almost in a straight line across country along the high ground from Canterbury to the sea.

We kept losing sight of the Vauxhall, and I had to make guesses or intuitive decisions at several road junctions. Almost all the lanes were extremely narrow, and ran between dense overgrown hedges on either side or within the green gloom of woodlands. If there had been two cars ahead and the rear one abandoned and locked, while the escapers quickly transferred to the other, the lane would have been completely blocked, forcing us to reverse a considerable distance before turning around.

As it was, partly by luck, I made the right decisions, but without my local knowledge, we would have lost the Vauxhall completely, which I presume was what Tara was banking upon.

At my request, Bob handed over the mike and earphones and I spoke to Tony directly. I knew that we had almost reached Stone Street and this would be the critical point in the whole chase. If Tara turned left and south, she would almost definitely be heading in the direction of the M20, and the Tunnel, but if she turned right towards Canterbury, I really did not have a clue as to her ultimate destination.

For Mary's sake, I hoped Tara would turn right for then there could just be a chance she might abandon the Vauxhall in the streets of Canterbury, and escape on foot among the crowds to some IRA safe house perhaps, hopefully leaving Mary free. But this was all wishful thinking on my part. The Vauxhall slowed at the T-junction leading to the main road, forcing our driver to brake hard and not get too close, but it then turned left and south along it accelerating rapidly.

We had to slow down too, and then set off in pursuit. I was shouting our call sign to Tony and following up immediately with the vital information that the Vauxhall was heading south along the B 2068.

'They're heading south Tony! It's got to be the Tunnel as you thought. They're really accelerating on the straight - we're doing over 80 mph.'

Tony greatly benefited from the advice of special police familiar with the Tunnel area, and it was this which helped him form a last minute plan.

OK,' Tony said. 'Good work. But Mark, they've got to make a choice in a few minutes. Whether to get straight on to the motorway at the first main roundabout at junction 11, or continue to the second roundabout and head towards the Tunnel along the A20. My guess is that they will go straight down the M20, and I'm now taking a chance on that.'

There was a pause, a crackle of interference, and I heard Tony continuing, 'I'm putting marksmen to blow out their rear tyres on a pedestrian bridge across the motorway. Luckily, we can also watch the A20 from almost the same place because that's as far as they can be allowed to go.'

'Tony, you keep saying "they." It's the IRA woman – Tara – who's making all the decisions. The other one's a bloody hostage.'

'I heard you,' said Tony. 'And I understand the situation perfectly well. But the car has to be stopped from getting any closer to the Tunnel, and that's now our priority.'

The Vauxhall suddenly disappeared from view as it reached the edge of the escarpment and plunged into a steep curving gully. We nearly came unstuck here, and skidded just avoiding an ascending car on one of the corners. We then saw the Vauxhall about 100 yards ahead accelerating away from us towards the first roundabout. God knows how Mary managed to keep her car on the road, at that speed, and in one way I was hoping she might crash.

As we got closer to the roundabout, the police helicopter, appeared and I heard the crackle of voices on the radio. The police had spotted the Vauxhall and the helicopter turned and flew low following it to the roundabout. We were now just behind and the whole roundabout had been cleared of traffic with police cars blocking the northern entrance from the M20.

'Tara's turning left onto the M20!' I shouted to Tony, and a police car which had slipped in front of us a moment let us pass. Then a whole line of them with screaming sirens followed. We were all in hot pursuit, and Tara knew it. But Mary was probably tiring as the Vauxhall slowed and began veering from side to side almost out of control. It was as if a struggle between Mary and Tara was going, and for a moment I was full of hope. However, the Vauxhall picked up speed again and the erratic veering stopped, although it was no longer travelling as fast as before.

We were now driving the last few miles to the Tunnel with no one else on the motorway right up to the next roundabout opposite the terminal. There, as the consequence of a police roadblock, the traffic was piled up in complete chaos and given the threat posed by the 15kg of Semtex, Tony had no option except to stop the Vauxhall somewhere along this final deserted stretch of motorway. He came on air very briefly at this point and ordered us to slow down and keep our distance.

'Slow down at once and remain at least one hundred yards from the Vauxhall. I repeat do not get closer than at least one hundred yards from the vehicle in front.'

The helicopter swept down directly over the motorway several hundred feet above the Vauxhall, and our car still led the pursuit followed by an increasing number of police. The noise was deafening, the unmistakable clatter of the helicopter rotors, overhead, the roar of car engines behind us and the wailing sirens made rational decisions increasingly difficult, and I was glad it was now really all up to Tony.

Several hundred yards ahead, only about half a mile from the Tunnel, the motorway entered a cutting spanned by a concrete pedestrian bridge and we could see the Vauxhall hurtling towards it. Then everything happened very quickly in tenths of a second.

We were about the required distance behind, and as the Vauxhall passed underneath the bridge, a figure leapt up above the railings and signalled frantically for us to slow down. I yelled at the driver to brake, and he fortunately did so at once so that the following police cars almost ran into us.

Tony ordered his men to open fire when the Vauxhall was well clear of the bridge, and they aimed at the rear tyres at first with assault rifles. The Vauxhall slewed across the road to the right where there was a grassy strip and low metal barriers separating one highway from the other. It struck the first barrier in a shower of sparks and veered back onto the motorway again, both rear tyres punctured, but still continued heading south, smoke pouring from the rims.

'Stop the car!' I shouted.

Fortunately our driver had already applied the brakes and we skidded to a halt almost under the bridge. Then a General Purpose Machine Gun opened up from the bridge above us, putting burst after burst of 7.62 rounds into the careering Vauxhall.

The petrol tank exploded with a sheet of flame and smoke, and I just had time to crouch down behind the front seats, as the Semtex detonated.

The shock wave hit our car, smashing the front windows and showering us with glass. It was like being struck with a giant sledge hammer. Both Andy's and Bob's faces were bleeding as the slivers of safety glass had been blown in with considerable force, although they had protected their eyes with their upraised arms, anticipating the blast from past experience Luckily both of us in the back had escaped injury by crouching low behind the front seats.

When I looked up shortly after the sound of the explosion and the shock wave which rocked the car, I saw a pall of smoke above the twisted and almost unrecognisable remains of the Vauxhall, which was burning fiercely.

Obviously, neither Tara nor Mary had survived the explosion, although there was no sign of their bodies which must have been blown to bits.

'Christ!' Bob exclaimed, wiping the blood from around his eyes with a handkerchief, 'I wonder if they're all right up on the bridge.'

'Well - let's have a look at you two first,' I said. But at that moment a paramedic arrived at the double from one of the two ambulances following us well in the rear of the police cars He immediately attended to Bob and Andy. Although their eyes had escaped injury, their faces were reddened and sore from the heat of the blast.

I staggered out of the car and looked down the road under the bridge. The yellow lights along the strip dividing the motorway were on, and it was now almost dark. The off white concrete of the road surface reflected the lights making it easier to see the wreckage about 100 yards ahead.

I got out of the car, and joined some of the police and paramedics walking past us under the bridge. I felt quite stunned, and veered off towards the median strip on the right of the motorway, where to my surprise I saw a woman's small dark green handbag under one of the lights resting up against the base of the steel pole.

I picked it up, and had a look inside. I found the usual things: makeup, a dark green matching leather wallet, house keys and a slightly scented lace edged handkerchief. Opening the wallet, I saw that the bag belonged to Mary, for inside were her credit cards and driving license with her date of birth - 1978 - so she was 36 years old. But to my amazement, there was also a sealed envelope without a stamp addressed to me, which I immediately pocketed.

Mary must have thrown her handbag out of the right front window of the Vauxhall as they went under the bridge. Perhaps she had left it in the car when she first arrived at Coldharbour, and then kept it concealed between her seat and the door on her right when she was taken hostage. She must have understood she was about to die, and thrown it out at the last moment. For what reason I could not guess, but felt it had to be something to do with her letter to me.

I concealed the handbag in a large and additional poacher's pocket inside my camo jacket, and followed the crowd towards the explosion site. No one appeared to have seen me pick up the bag: they were all far too intent on the smoking wreckage, Most of the blast had gone upwards and sideways down the cutting, but there was a smoking crater in the road as well. Hardly anything was left of the Vauxhall, just twisted metal, all the paintwork evaporated with the heat. The wheels had been blown off, one of them later found intact in a field above the cutting.

Then I smelt burnt flesh, and was almost sick. Charred flesh was everywhere, all over the blackened concrete surface of the road. I began to shake slightly, and my heart hammered in my chest, so I breathed in deeply determined to keep myself under control. It was as if all my recent nightmares had somehow been prescient leading to this. I felt totally responsible for Mary's death. So many of my actions it seemed, especially my secrecy and silence over the real nature of the people at Coldharbour, had led her towards a futile and unnecessary end. I knew I was not thinking rationally, but I was overwhelmed with guilt.

However, I just could not take out the letter and read it at once. This had to be done elsewhere. Away from the motorway lights, and the smouldering wreckage. Far from the howl of sirens, and the smell of death. I would read it later at Chalk Hill I decided, or up on the downs, somewhere as remote as possible from this utter madness.

I felt a hand on my right shoulder. It was Tony.

'Well - we got them just in time. A close run thing. Only half a mile to the Tunnel, and this was the only stretch of motorway the police could block off the traffic. I'm sorry about the other woman - the hostage - I mean - but I had no choice.'

There was no point in my sounding off at Tony. He was still under great stress, and I knew that all he had in mind was the successful outcome. Furthermore, he had no idea of my relationship with Mary or the way in which I had deceived her over Coldharbour in the interests of security.

'Tony! Are you all right? How did you escape the blast up on the bridge? It must have been bloody exposed.'

'We each sheltered behind a row of steel posts supporting the safety barrier on the south side of the bridge. I had my two machine gunners lying behind the posts and the other two were in a ditch at the top of the cutting overlooking the motorway.'

'Jesus!' I exclaimed. 'The posts wouldn't have given much protection.'

'Better than one would think thank God! The posts are steel and quite thick. There's also a low concrete strip at the base of the barrier, only about three or four inches high, but useful all the same. We wore our helmets of course, and plastic visors as well. But really there wasn't much time. And of course, I was hoping we could kill the IRA woman at once - the machine guns were trained on the passenger seat, and the rounds were going through the rear window all right. But somehow one must have hit the petrol tank, a ricochet perhaps.'

Did Tara detonate the Semtex then?'

'Possibly - probably. But as I said we were aiming at her, and she should have been dead on the first burst Of course, once the petrol tank exploded - the Semtex would have gone too. But that's all for the explosive experts to work out. My guess is we'll never know.'

'How did you find out about the bridge?'

'The local security police at the Tunnel told me. They've been most helpful.'

Then I came to my senses although I was still dazed by the explosion, and my grief and shock over Mary. My mind had been numbed by the events of the past few hours. Anyway, I suddenly remembered I had omitted to ask Tony what had happened about the main point of the exercise - the prevention of a mortar bombing of the Tunnel terminus.

'Tony! I'm sorry. I must still be in shock. What happened about the IRA mortar attack on the Tunnel?'

'Well - I'll tell you the full story one day no doubt - but the less said the better at the moment as you will be well aware. However, thanks to your information we were waiting for them in Danton lane. Only just in time, I must add. Another close run thing in fact.'

Tony paused a moment and then gently turned me round, facing back the way I had come. It was now dark, and we both temporarily blinded by the police car headlights ahead of us.

'Anyway this is no place to talk. I've got to get out of here with my men as fast as possible. MI5 will deal with all this. The Press - the whole bloody media in fact - will arrive any minute now and start taking photos.'

'All right,' I said as we walked back along the motorway, 'But I must have some idea of what happened.'

'The truth is that you sprang the whole thing just too soon .We needed another 24 hours, and they certainly wanted a bit more time. I was very angry with you at first. What the bloody hell were you doing checking out that arms dump this morning? No one asked you to.'

'I'm sorry, but...'

'I don't want to hear your excuses now. Some other time. Anyway, the point is you probably did us all a favour because they had to move at once - and before they were ready. MI5 think there was another ASU from London coming down to assist them, but they never got here.'

'Yes - but what happened in the lane?'

'We - a dozen of the troop - were there waiting for them, well hidden behind the hedgerows. It was ideal cover. They backed the trailers up the side track, and drove their two vehicles further up the lane where there was room to park. Then they came back and dismantled the canvas covers without making any kind of a security check. Some cars were actually going past up and down the lane, but they still carried on. I mean in normal circumstances I'm sure they would have searched the whole area thoroughly, and probably located us. But they knew the game was up and time running short. Once the covers were off, and the trailers steady and at the right angle pointing towards the train platforms, they moved up the lane a bit, and were about to fire them by remote control when we opened up with everything we had. Two gympis (GMPGs) and five assault rifles. Very effective at short range as you can imagine.'

We reached the black Ford station wagon with its shattered windscreen and broken headlights. There was no sign of Sergeant Corandale and his three troopers, but Tony stopped by the car and continued with his account.

'Of course we gave the customary warning. But the public were in imminent danger as the mortars were in place and about to be fired. I mean we waited until the covers were off, but really we did not know for certain what the trailers contained - did we?'

I got the message, and replied accordingly, 'No - you did not. I mean I understand what you're saying, and I presume you're going to leave me out of all this.

'Too bloody right we are! There's none of them left alive to tell any tales either. And there were no fucking stray photographers around as at Gib. The only photos will be those taken by MI5.'

Tony had done well in his own professional terms, but it stuck in my guts to congratulate him for killing Mary.

'Where's Corandale and his men?' I asked.

'They're back with the rest of the troop up near the over bridge,' Tony said, looking at his watch. 'Now it's very late - 10.30 - so we'll climb back up the slope. I'm going to leave you with MI5 or someone from Special Branch. Don't worry – they'll drive you home. As you know, my troop have now got to do the disappearing trick pronto, and hope for the best at the inquest. Meanwhile everything is up to MI5 and Special Branch. But it's already been agreed to keep you out of it so say nothing to anyone, otherwise you'll be in trouble again.'

We climbed up the steep grassy slope of the cutting, and over a fence to reach the side road which lead to the bridge. The whole troop was there waiting for Tony to appear, and somewhat impatiently it seemed, as they were rightly anxious to leave as soon as possible.

Tony introduced me to a couple of MI5 men with a car, and they nodded without a word. Then I had a brief chat with Bob, whose face was covered in strips of plaster.

'Not much glory for us in all this was there,' he commented disappointedly.

'Well - there's no glory for anyone in killing an innocent woman,' I replied.

'None of us,' killed her,' Bob said quite heatedly. 'That bloody IRA bitch blew them both up.'

There was an awkward pause, and to change the subjects slightly Bob said, 'Have you heard the latest news about Coldharbour sir?'

'No - what's happened now ? I mean what more could happen?'

'Max called to say the whole bloody place is still on fire. Fire engines there from Folkestone and Canterbury. Lots of lookers on apparently, although the media haven't yet connected it with the IRA.'

Then Tony came up and shook me by the hand. 'Many thanks for all your help. That was first class intelligence we received, and you'll get your due - all unofficially of course.'

'Well - I hope it will result in Atherton leaving me alone in future. That's all I ask.'

Tony laughed. 'I'm sure it will. Now go home and relax. But give me a ring in about a week's time.'

Then he climbed into the front passenger seat of one of the three SAS Land Rovers and they disappeared into the night to join the M20 and the long drive back to Hereford and Stirling Lines.

As soon as Tony left, one of the MI5 men came up, and to my surprise said with a smile, 'Right - now we can take you home, Captain Wynstanley. Please get in the car and direct the driver.'

The MI5 men did not introduce themselves, and we drove off in silence. Police were already blocking the side road leading off the A20 to the bridge, and I could see a TV team arguing with them for access to film as we passed. It was then I fully realised what a news event the whole episode was going to be. I got in beside the driver, and soon we were back at the M20 junction and number 11 roundabout, heading for Chalk Hill.

I broke the silence first by asking, 'How did you know my name?'

'Major Fairburn - Tony Fairburn - told us about you. And we also just heard about all your good work from Max on the radio.'

'And I expect you've also read my file no doubt. I've not been exactly the flavour of the month at MI5 have I?'

'Well as a matter of fact - you might be now Captain Wynstanley. Things have changed. That's why Max asked us to pass on the message to keep in touch.'

'What on earth for?'

'That's up to Max to tell you. But your experience could be very useful to us here in London.'

'Jesus Christ!' I said, 'You mean I might work for you.'

'I think you'd better contact Max. But as you can see the IRA campaign in England is hotting up - and Max was very impressed with your efforts this afternoon.'

I could hardly restrain myself from making an offensive remark, but I was not going to put myself off side with MI5 again, so I kept quiet.

I was quite overwhelmed by Mary's death, and could think of nothing else as the car sped through the night under my directions back to Chalk Hill, so any further attempts at conversation became increasingly difficult.

However, I suddenly realised that someone would need to inform Mary's employer Chapman, and were I to do so, it would place me in a difficult position as I was not supposed to know such details about the explosion. So I explained the position to the two MI5 men and asked them to let Chapman know as soon as possible. He would have to inform Mary's next of kin, and of course Mary's now empty house would need to be made secure. There was also the question of Moonlight, her cat, but any local friends or neighbours could to attend to this.

I did not tell them that I had picked up Mary's handbag or about the letter. This was something I intended to keep to myself perhaps for the rest of my life. Anyway, the MI5 men agreed to phone Chapman as soon as they reached London even if they awoke him at home in the early hours of the morning.

It was not long before we reached Chalk Hill, and I opened the side gate to allow the driver to turn without going further up the narrow lane as far as the common.

'So this is where you live?' the driver asked. It was the first time he had spoken.

'Yes, but I'm not on the phone yet. If you want to contact me urgently, you can phone my nearest neighbour, Colonel Crundale. Ask for Claire Crundale and she will pass on any message,' and I gave them her number.

There was no point, I realised only too well, in acting hostile or difficult with MI5. All I wanted was Atherton off my back, and the best way to do this was to play along with the apparent good will at the present.

We said good bye, amicably enough, and the car sped off towards Highdene.

I was just about to unlock my front door, when I heard the sound of Claire's Triumph approaching. The time was then about midnight.

I re-opened the front gate and Claire drove straight in and jumped out of the car, and ran towards me. I caught her in my arms.

'Mark! Are you all right? We've been watching the news on TV all evening. The whole family. Dad, mother, Richard and me. They are all appalled. I explained as much as I could, but I couldn't tell them everything. About the arms cache as well I mean as that would have got Tom into trouble.'

We hugged one another for a while, and I said, 'Look - the first thing you should know is the very sad news that Mary Renfrew is dead. Tara took her as a hostage from Coldharbour and made her drive a car full of Semtex towards the Tunnel and it blew up on the M20.'

I did not go into much further detail, except to explain that I had been following them in an Army vehicle when Mary's Vauxhall blew up ahead of us.

Claire had very little to say about Mary's death. She expressed her regret of course, but perhaps because I was slightly overwrought I thought she sounded callous when she then commented that she could not understand how Mary got herself involved.

'Well - I can understand,' I said. 'She thought Tara was a friend. Another Irish woman she could talk to. Mary felt pretty isolated here, I can assure you.'

'So you got to know her better than I thought,' Claire said quietly.

I heard the cock crow at once, so I told the truth in my fashion.

'I suppose you could say that. I'm certainly very upset at her death. And I can assure you she had nothing to do with the IRA.'

'Well obviously you would know,' Claire replied.

I was not sure whether she was being sarcastic or not, but I had enough problems without starting a row with Claire, so I kept quiet.

Claire then dropped the subject of Mary and told me that the Gates had phoned very distressed several hours ago to say that Coldharbour was on fire, and they were driving up there at once.

'Yes. I know as a matter of fact. Tara blew the place up when she left with Mary. She set a timer.'

I didn't tell her of the circumstances in which Mary had warned me of the danger, or how close run a thing it had been. That could wait until later.

'Look - have you eaten anything?' Claire asked. 'Because if not - I suggest you come home and I'll get you a light meal. There's plenty left over from supper. Everyone's awake and wanting to see you so come and join us. There's going to be another more detailed TV news report very soon.'

I was tired, but grateful for the offer of a meal and really needed to talk as I was too hyped up for sleep. So I was only too pleased to get in the Triumph and join the family at the Grange.

As we drove down the lane, Claire told me that she had explained my involvement with the IRA at Coldharbour and the SAS ambush on the motorway to her parents and her brother Richard as best she could in the circumstances. She had not told them about the arms cache and our capture by Sean and Tom's role in our release because that would have confused matters even further. But they were still completely puzzled by the whole affair and could not understand I was involved mainly by chance. Claire suggested I told them about Coldharbour being an IRA base, and also about Tara and Mary, but no more. Of course, even Claire did not know the full story, and that I had a lot more explaining to do as our relationship developed.

Slightly to my surprise the Crundales were quite friendly, and wanted to know all the details I could give them about Coldharbour, especially as they were friends of the Gates and knew the place quite well. They were absolutely appalled by the news that the farmhouse had been blown up, and wondered whether the Gates would be able to put in an insurance claim as it was a terrorist act.

They had both met Mary Renfrew, several years ago, but her death as an innocent victim did not seem to have made as much impression as the loss of the farmhouse, and as with Claire, I sensed a certain degree of hostility. Anyway, Richard shook hands and we had a long chat, while I had a beer with him in the kitchen as Claire heated up some soup. He felt that this was probably a last attempt by the IRA to force the hand of the British Government before the rumoured so called Peace Initiative started any day now.

'So you think there will be peace?' I asked, as Claire placed a bowl of steaming soup and a plate of toast on the table in front of me.

'I've no idea. Too out of touch with events in Northern Ireland to know really. But I hope so. God knows how they will sort out the political process. But I suppose it's just possible. What do you think?'

'Well - I haven't got access to Intelligence reports these days, but from my past experience I'm certain the IRA will never surrender. By that I mean they'll never give up their arms. Why should they? That would be political suicide for them. And if we Brits don't understand that - there is no hope at all for any progress - whatever that may really mean given the circumstances. So there's still going to be the potential for violence if the IRA don't get exactly what they want. And what they want is a United Ireland with themselves and Dublin in control. So I can't imagine how the Protestants will react to that. But I suppose it's just possible there will be some kind of a peace. I hope so anyway.'

Mrs Crundale came in and suggested I took my soup over to the TV in the sitting room to watch the latest special newsflash.

The TV teams had not been allowed into Danton Lane, but they had somehow got onto the footbridge across the M20 and with special lights and a powerful zoom lens had filmed the remainder of the Vauxhall in which Mary and Tara had died.

'It is understood,' said the announcer, 'that the vehicle was being driven in the direction of the Tunnel with an explosive device on board as well as a hostage. It is believed to have been fired upon from this footbridge by the SAS, and the car caught fire from a bullet in the petrol tank and then exploded. Both occupants were killed. According to Special Branch, a full enquiry is to be held.'

The camera zoomed onto the charred remains of the Vauxhall, and at once I recalled the smell of burnt flesh. I felt slightly sick, and overcome with grief at Mary's death.

A piece of toast stuck in my throat , which had suddenly gone dry, and I carried the remainder of the soup back into the kitchen, followed by Claire.

'Sorry,' she said. 'I didn't think it was like that. Stupid of me I know. Just relax here and I'll make you a cup of tea.'

'It's all right Claire,' I said. 'It's not your fault. I'm a bit overwrought at the moment. So I think I'll just go home and get some sleep. It's been a very long day for both of us.'

We had a brief hug, and then Claire offered to drive me back to Chalk Hill, but I thought it would be good to walk. After thanking the Crundales, who were all now longing to get some sleep themselves, I walked the short distance home and by the time I reached the cottage, I had managed to get a better grip on myself. I soon drifted off into an uneasy sleep full of anxiety dreams, waking throughout the remainder of the night with the shakes and sweating as if I had fever. My pulse was racing and each time I awoke I struggled to remember where I was and what had gone wrong.

*

The following morning after breakfast, I decided to walk through the orchard and up onto the summit of the North Downs. It was a fine August day, already heating up by the time I left the cottage at 9am. The grass was burnt a bright orange and the ground dry and parched as if the landscape was that of Tuscany or Spain. As I climbed the track I was soon sweating in the glare of the full sun, and glad of the breeze when I reached the summit of the downs, and gazed out again onto the vivid colours of the harvested wheat fields below me.

I sat down near the trig point in the long dry grass and made myself comfortable before taking out the envelope from my pocket addressed to me by Mary. I had already slit it open with a knife back at the cottage, and knew it contained a letter which I now read slowly with a rising lump in my throat.

266

Dearest Mark,

I thought I would write you this note to say how much I enjoyed your visit the other night. In fact I have thought about you ever since - something I did not feel possible after knowing Michael.

As well as being a wonderful lover, I felt so happy in your company. I only wish that you had stayed the night, but I'm hoping next time you will. Come to dinner next Saturday night, and then we can have a lie in on Sunday morning because I don't have to go to work. (Although perhaps I should go to Mass instead as I'm sure there will be a lot to confess!)

So now you know my secret! But I don't mind! All I hope is that we will get to know one another better. I'm sure there will be so much to talk about - and do!

All my love,
Mary

PS. I've just had a phone call from Tara There has been some sort of problem up at Coldharbour and she wants me to drive up there immediately so instead of posting this I will drop it off at your cottage on my way back to the office. Might even see you!

I felt deeply moved. Only a very brief note, but nevertheless a straightforward expression of love. Quite naive in a way considering Mary was 36 rather than 26. But full of quiet confidence that her affection would be reciprocated. She had taken a risk in expressing her feelings in writing, but even at the last moment she wanted me to know, and it affected me greatly that just before her death she had thrown out her handbag containing the letter for that purpose.

Tears welled up and I just sat and cried my heart out. It didn't matter. I was on my own. This was my own private grief for a woman I really scarcely knew, but everything about her suddenly assumed mythic qualities, and my memories of her will always remain that way.

Of course, I was being sentimental and unrealistic when I thought of the things we might have done together for I was in love with Claire, and would have had to tell Mary at some stage. But if Mary had somehow survived the danger we shared yesterday, I really did not know her well enough to work out how she would have reacted. Our experience would certainly have been a powerful bond,

267

but for Mary it could have made it all the more inexplicable why I preferred Claire.

Only a short while ago, I had been up here for the first time and saw the hunting kestrel and heard the larks. Little in the landscape had changed except the grass was even drier, and the wheat stalks were now stacked like blocks of gold after harvesting.

Just before I got up and started walking downhill all the way to the cottage, the kestrel appeared and hung there in the blue while the larks sang around me and the sky was full of swifts and swallows. All England's magic was mine, yet I wept again for Mary. I cried out for her to the heavens again and again and, of course, there was no answer. In that great silence of the downs, only the larks sang Mary's requiem while the breeze dried my tears and the darting swallows diverted my grief.

Postscript

Shortly after Mary's death, the IRA made a public statement that, 'as of midnight 31 August (1994) there will be a complete cessation of military operations. All our units have been instructed accordingly.'

The British Government responded positively and the Ceasefire seemed to be working for a time, offering hope to so many, both Catholic and Protestant, that life in Northern Ireland could be restored to some semblance of normalcy. It also meant that my life on the run had apparently ceased.

I had a phone connected to Chalk Hill, and was determined to shake off the feelings of being hunted. I settled down to my writing including this account of my experiences during my first three eventful months at the cottage.

It was an immense relief to go about openly, apparently no longer under threat from IRA Active Service Units in England. Yet I remained somewhat dubious about the Provisional IRA's commitment to democracy. They had of necessity lived and died by the gun and high explosive for so long that it seemed unlikely that this philosophy of violence could somehow change overnight.

As subsequent events proved this to be the case, without going into any detail, I have changed all the names of people and some locations in my book, except where they are already known as in the case of the IRA mortar attack on the Channel Tunnel, Mary's death, and the blowing up of Coldharbour, all of which have already been extensively reported in the Press.

Presumably because of the Ceasefire, MI5 did not offer me any form of employment, and apart from a brief intelligence report about the ASU at Coldharbour, which they requested, I had no further contact with them.

However, before I end this account, it is necessary to bring things up to date, but by that I mean only until February 1996. My life after that is another story. A book has to end somewhere and I leave the account as it stands when I completed it. Otherwise one starts to be wise after the event and ones emotions at the time can become diluted with reflection.

In any case, for various reasons, publication proved far more difficult than I anticipated. As explained in my Preface to this book, several years passed since I wrote this account and finally got it published.

Since these events described took place, the Good Friday Agreement of 1998, dramatically increased the chances of peace in Northern Ireland, and my chances of being left alone by the Provos. However, I was only too well aware that the hard core of dissident IRA in South Armagh and across the border remained, and I could do no more than guess at the eventual outcome.

Returning now to the hard winter of 1994/1995, which I spent mainly on my own at Chalk Hill trying once more to regain my mental equilibrium. Claire and I had an uneasy and fraught relationship partly because of my feelings of guilt over Mary. Anyway, by the spring of 1995, Claire and I settled down to a kind of partnership at Chalk Hill while she continued with her post graduate university education at Canterbury. She generally spends the weekends at Chalk Hill with me, while still living at home in the Grange.

There were disadvantages. I could never really wean her away from her family; but the arrangement worked quite well. Her parents gradually became more accustomed to this form of relationship, although they never approved of it. Paradoxically, they also seemed relieved that we were not actually married, so there was still hope for Claire yet!

For Christmas 1995, I drove to Shropshire to spend just over a week with my mother at High Oaks, and Claire joined us on the 27th for a few days, travelling by train to Ludlow, before I drove her back to Kent early in the New Year.

The night after Claire arrived, we were all sitting by a roaring fire in the sitting room. Diana, now married to Howard, and alone at home while he was back at work in London for some reason, had also come over for the evening at my mother's suggestion. (My mother approved of Claire and they got on well, but Diana was still her favourite). Just as I was discovering through some of Diana's remarks how bored she was already becoming with her husband, the phone rang in the hall and I answered it.

270

I knew there was trouble directly the man calling gave my 14 Intelligence Company former codename of Oboe One, and I heard the broad Irish accent and the urgency in his voice. To be brief, it was one of my former agents, the person I have already mentioned earlier in the book who wanted to immigrate to New Zealand. He was living in the Bog country of Co. Monaghan just across the border south west of Crossmaglen, and working as a mechanic in a garage. His codename was Kelly, and he was speaking from a call box probably in Northern Ireland, obviously extremely worried about his personal safety. (I unwisely gave him my home number some years ago only to be used in extreme urgency.)

'Listen carefully - I haven't got much time,' Kelly said. 'There's going to be a very big bomb exploded in London - Docklands area perhaps - by you know who - quite soon, either by the end of January or early February. The vehicle and explosives are just about to leave for the mainland via the Larne - Stanraer ferry. That's all I can tell you and I will not be phoning again. It's too bloody dangerous for me. But this is a big one - do you understand?'

'Yes, Kelly, I do, but keep right out of it. There's nothing that you or I can do about it any longer. The whole intelligence system has changed, and it's not worth risking your life for. No one can help you in any way now.'

'Jesus Christ then! What the fucking hell am I risking my life making this call for?'

'Sorry Kelly - but that's the truth - so keep out of it and survive. I'll inform the authorities, but nothing will happen I'm afraid.'

Kelly rang off before I could say anything more, and I put down the phone and returned to the sitting room deep in thought.

'Who was that?' Claire asked sensing at once I was worried.

I put her off with a non committal reply, but Claire wasn't fooled, and I explained the situation fully once Diana had left and we were alone in my bedroom. Claire was most relieved that I had firmly decided not to become involved, but for Kelly's sake (after all he was risking his life), I phoned Max in MI5 the following morning.

'Hello Max,' I said. 'This is Mark Wynstanley speaking.

'OK. Go ahead. But I'm due at a meeting in five minutes.'

'Right. I'll be very brief. One of my former agents in the Republic phoned me last night to say that he knows there is going to be a very large bomb exploded in London - probably Docklands -

271

sometime late January or early February in the New Year. It will be in a lorry and come to Britain via the Larne- Stranraer ferry very soon.'

There was quite a pause and Max said, 'What the hell are you doing still running agents? You're out of the Army now and anyway this sort of intelligence is our business as you know.'

'I'm not running agents. This man worked for me about three years ago, and still had my home phone number which I unwisely gave him to use in a dire emergency. He wasn't aware I had left the Army or of the new set up and thought he was doing us a favour. We haven't been able to help him at all in the past, but he still lives in hope of us getting him out somewhere I suppose, although I've told him never to contact me again under any circumstances.'

'Good. Well - thanks for the call then. But our assessment and of course that of Special Branch is that there is no threat at all from the Provos at the moment. In fact, I have authorised Special Branch to issue a briefing note to this effect early in the New Year. I think your man was trying to lead you along. As you say he wants out, and may think this sort of info is going to help him. Anyway - thanks for the call - and I'll pass it on without giving you as a source, just in case there's a problem.'

'OK Max. I won't trouble you again.'

'No trouble at all Mark. We'll always be glad to hear from you - although there's nothing much on in your line on at the moment. Happy New Year!'

'Same to you Max,' I said, and put down the phone.

Nothing seems to change, I thought. We Brits always seem to underestimate our enemies. MI5 really think their intelligence is that good, better than anything people like me can provide. I just had a lucky break from years of bloody dangerous work going across the border and Kelly risking his life and now it's probably all wasted. Well just let's hope I'm wrong. But I knew Kelly, and had heard the desperation and disappointment in his voice, so there was no doubt in my mind this information was correct. Anyway, there was not long to wait before we found out. On 9 February 1996, a massive IRA bomb went off in London's Canary Wharf and the Ceasefire dramatically ended. The IRA's England Department had struck again, and we were once more at war.

However, this time, despite pleas from Max, there was absolutely no way I was going to have anything more to do with it. I was no longer prepared to risk my life or my mental well being for my country, although my respect for the SAS remained, tempered unavoidably by the killing of Mary. I intended to get what I could from the State, to pursue gaining all the benefits I was due, including the possibility of compensation from the MOD for what I had been through. My 'Blackthorn Winter' was over, and I settled down with Claire to be as comfortable as we could manage at Chalk Hill. Luckily, the cold weather was followed by another surprisingly long hot summer while I wrote this book and began to earn some kind of a living.

Chalk Hill Cottage, Coppice Lane, Highdene, Kent.

Printed in the United States
65939LVS00005B/123